SULTRY

Even as Rachel spoke, she began to slowly undo the tiny buttons that fastened her frock.

'It is too much risk.' Jess's words came out almost as a groan. Then he felt her naked body move up towards his, her arms entwining his broad back, her white flesh against his black skin.

All Rachel's fears were gone. Her body had assumed a certainty that overwhelmed her. She felt him full inside her now and the rightness and the goodness of it forced everything else from her mind as Jess thrust again and again into her moist, throbbing, eager loins. She arched her body, throwing her head back unawares, her joy erupting in a laugh that surged up from deep within her and escaped her soft wet lips . . .

Also by Rochelle Larkin in Sphere Books

HARVEST OF DESIRE
MISTRESS OF DESIRE

Torches of Desire

ROCHELLE LARKIN

SPHERE

SPHERE BOOKS LIMITED
30/32 Gray's Inn Road, London WC1X 8JL

First published in Great Britain by Sphere Books Ltd 1980

TRADE
MARK
SPHERE

Printed in Canada

For Roslyn Targ
Agent, angel, fan – and friend

TORCHES OF DESIRE

1

Jason kicked at a clod of overturned earth with the toe of his boot. The acrid smell of burned flesh made his nostrils flare and the anger that welled up in him seized his entire being.

He turned his back on the charred remains of what had been the Les Saules slave quarters and looked at the equally despoiled, still-smoldering mass that was once the elegant great house, the mansion he had promised to Emilie as his wedding gift to her. His plan had been so simple: to marry the lovely heiress of Les Chandelles and, by purchasing the adjoining estate of her former in-laws, expand her properties even further. They would jointly manage the great sugar-bearing properties that her great-grandfather and some unknown Creole ancester of her dead husband had hacked and measured and planted from the fetid wilderness that had become Louisiana.

The outlying cane fields, densely cultivated though not so extensive as those of Les Chandelles, had not been put to the torch. Instead the assailants had concentrated their murderous wrath on the slaves and buildings of Les Saules. They knew, Jason thought grimly, what the cane was: a fierce, growing crop that, even if destroyed completely in the field, would quickly reclaim its place. Its destruction would mean the loss of no more than a single growing season, less than a year in time; but lives could never be remade, nor the graceful treasures that had furnished the mansion be readily replaced.

Jason made his way heavily back to where he had left his horse tethered to a sheltering live-oak tree. He glanced up briefly at the overhanging branches. At least that had been spared the ravages of the flames.

He mounted and spurred his horse, turning him in the direction of Les Chandelles. He cared not a whit for the fine furnishings nor even for the great house itself, disturbed by their loss only insofar as they had been promised by him to his beautiful fiancée. It was the sight of the burned and dismembered bodies strewn on the earth of the quarters that had gained his greatest anger and caused him now, remembering, suddenly to sharply rein in his mount and jump from the saddle; he fell to his knees at the side of the road and retched into the short, entangled ravine until his large frame ceased its shuddering and he could right himself again.

Jason stood upright, taking the reins in his hands, walking his horse as his eyes searched the ravine for sight of a fresh, running brook where he might wash the heavy stink of vomit from his mouth.

Curse this damn Louisiana! he thought. In his own Ohio, there would have been clear brooks or creeks aplenty to refresh him. Here in the long-lasting, overwhelming heat that produced such prodigious growth, any water he was likely to find would be the brackishness of a still-water pond or bayou. His comfort would have to wait upon his return to Les Chandelles.

He remounted and spurred again, digging his heels into his animal's flanks with much greater ferocity than usual. He noticed the towering trees overhead and the thick tangles of growth on either side of the narrow road, only to remind himself as he had done before how little it would take for the road to become overgrown and impassable. It would need attending to.

Even more pressing would be the sending of a detail of Les Chandelles people to give as decent a burial as could be managed for the pitiful remains he had just witnessed.

Jason tried to turn his mind from the sight but he could no more control the recurrence of the ghastly visions than he had been able to stem the turbulence in his gut.

He clenched his teeth and tried to keep his eyes wide open, fixed on the endless green on either side of him. But like protesting bolts of light that thrust themselves at him, the ravaged bodies imposed themselves through the tangle of vines and tracery of leaves.

It took no medical examination to tell him what had happened to the almost-intact body of a young female slave he had stumbled upon. She had obviously been thrown atop a mound of earth. Her body lay still now, but with the limbs askew as if she had been stilled forever in a split second of frenzy. Her head had been thrown back and the eyes, which had rolled helplessly about, were now fixed forever in an expression of grotesque unnaturalness. Her body's opening had been thrust wide and savagely used, hot spill still flecking the ashy thighs, but as if that cavity had not sufficed, her assailant or assailants had hacked another open, down the middle of her torso, from the still-forming breasts straight in a line that ended just above her ravaging.

There were charred bones, small, like those one would find about an army campfire after the men had eaten, but these, Jason knew, small though they were, came not from animals slaughtered but from babies. He hadn't stopped to count how many bodies burned, how many broken, but he was sure that none had escaped. The quarters had been set ablaze in the dead of night, when all the hands would have been fast asleep after the long dav in the canebrakes. Anyone who might have been able to flee his burning house would have been shot or butchered by the unknown assailants.

The burying detail the next day would have little enough to do, Jason reflected. There would be no recital of the hundred-odd names of the newly freed slaves who had been killed. The blacks of Les Saules, like those of Les Chandelles, had been kept very isolated from other plantations and Emilie's people would not have known much of their counterparts. Only their master, old Charpentier, might have known them, some of them, by name, but now even the old man was newly dead, having collapsed and expired in the front salon of Les Chandelles right after he and his wife had fled the fire.

The old woman, the mother of Emilie's dead husband, would soon be on her way from Les Chandelles to New Orleans, there to live out the rest of her lonely years. The war had taken both her sons; now its equally if not more savage aftermath had claimed both her estate and her husband.

The Charpentier family would be gone from the parish without a trace, just as the chattel of their estate had been brutally, namelessly returned to that selfsame earth they had worked all of their lives.

Jason thought once again of the familiar landscape of his old home. The crisp autumn foliage of the rich valley where he and his father had their farms was, to his mind, a far cleaner place than this swampy, junglelike southern land ever could be. Yet, he reminded himself sharply, though that land up north had never witnessed the brutality he had found here, filth and violence had overtaken him even in that clean, remembered land.

He spurred his horse again, leaning anxiously forward in the saddle, as if to outrun the suddenly gathering personal pains that came at him, unbidden.

As the dirt road made its last turning Les Chandelles came suddenly into view. It was downcountry from its neighboring estate, and coming from Les Saules, Jason approached the larger plantation from round about, unlike most traffic, which came up through the southern parishes from New Orleans. Jason was struck, as ever, by the foreboding quality of the mansion. The first time he had ever seen it and every time since, it filled him with strange stirrings. Always it seemed to him that there was something here that was more than just a house. Its own fire-broken façade bespoke something negative—perhaps great danger, perhaps great unhappiness. He had known both while quartered there, but overshadowing those feelings was the sweetness of the love he had formed for the mistress of the place. His Emilie was dearer to him than life itself, and his emotion for her far outweighed the singular dislike he felt for her home. Even when Jason turned his thoughts to those aspects of the South he found so loving and congenial, there always stayed in his mind a nebulous dark spot that, for him, was Les Chandelles.

He tossed his head impatiently, trying to flick away the feeling, as one might a troublesome insect. Emilie was there, and that was all that mattered. Indeed, he had to admit to himself, Emilie *was* Les Chandelles. And Les Chandelles was Emilie. To gain the one, he would have to suffer the other.

And gladly enough, he said to himself as he swung himself from his saddle and tossed the reins carelessly to a waiting stableboy, for Emilie I would risk the coast of Hades itself. He smiled at the idea, but the happy turn of mind soon faded as he thought of the scene he had just hastened from. The coast of Hades could hold no deeper horrors than those he had seen bare miles from here.

Emilie stood watching from the veranda as Jason dismounted. She was a small figure, her long black hair billowing about her face and shoulders from the sudden wind that had risen in the twilight. How well he moves, she thought as Jason came walking easily toward her, his steps indeed swift and easy for a man of his height and bulk.

"My dear!" he exclaimed, taking both her hands in his. "Whatever are you doing out of doors on so harsh a day?"

"I wanted to see you the sooner," she murmured, her voice lowering with a sudden embarrassment more like that of a maiden than of a young woman already wed and widowed and ready to be wed again.

Jason's heart softened at the sight of her, as it always did. Now, at least for the moment, the hideous reconnoitering of his afternoon could be banished by her welcome company. Yet, he realized, the situation was as imperative to Emilie as it was to him, and for all the brute ugliness of it, it still had to be told to her.

Emilie looked up into his troubled eyes as she seated herself on a small chaise in the darkened front salon. Jason towered over her, not sitting by her as she had expected him to do. "Is there something very wrong, Jason?" she asked. They had both known of the destruction of Les Saules before he rode out to survey it himself. "Surely it is no worse than Madame had said?"

"Far worse indeed, Emilie," Jason replied. "Whether your mother-in-law was not apprised of the details or sought to shield you from them, I do not know. I hope for her sake it was through ignorance and that I could spare you, my darling, and leave you in the same blissful state."

"Surely you knew the total destruction you would find there, Jason." She searched his face as he remained standing, trying to fathom this dark expression she had never found there before.

"It was far worse than anything we were told," Jason stated bluntly. "It was sheer carnage." His voice was close to breaking.

"But you've been in battle, Jason," Emilie said pleadingly. "You have seen—"

"Nothing like this!" he snapped, interrupting her. "I

haven't seen anything in war, perpetrated by either side, that compared with this!"

Emilie flinched, as she nearly always did when reminded of the fact that she and Jason had been on opposing sides in the war and must even now, in their love, face the disapproval that their own union would bring. That she had taken an officer of the hated Yankees for a lover, soon to be her husband, was sure to bring such disapproval from her neighbors that even her being the richest landowner in the parish would not countenance. Now that the war was over, people would pick up the broken threads of their lives and the rent fabric of society would be rewoven. In the bitterness of the great war and the turbulence already gathering quickly in its wake, there was no telling where each individual would stand. All that she knew was that her alliance with Jason would earn her no love or approval from her neighbors. And what with the ruination of so many plantations, the deaths of the dearest sons, the losing of the war, and the freeing of the slaves, even Emilie, so long sheltered from the great world beyond her domain, knew that the reassembled world must be a far different place from the one that had just gone to destruction.

It would take more than the presence of the hated Union Army, more than the cleverness of her strong and determined Jason, to ensure that Les Chandelles and its people would be secure. That, at least, we must have, Emilie thought, no matter how different things are going to be.

Jason sat down at last. "I'm sorry, darling, for having so upset you with this business." He took her hand again.

"No, no," Emilie insisted. "It was my own thoughts I was lost in just then. You have not told me anything, really."

She looked at him.

"The quarters were destroyed, the people were not

spared. That is all I can say." He looked away, not meeting her gaze.

Emilie slipped from the sofa, dropping to her knees as she covered his with her arms. She looked up imploringly at him, as though trying to will his eyes to meet hers, to softly force him to relinquish that stern, riveted stare that seemed to be looking somewhere far off, ignoring her nearness.

But Jason stayed unmoved. They were two figures in a frozen tableau, seemingly nothing stirring within them except for the rise and fall of Emilie's breathing. What a position for me to be in, she thought finally, the mistress of Les Chandelles at the feet of my Yankee lover and he looking for all the world as though I were not even here. The strangeness of her position suddenly seemed more compelling than the dark disposition of that Yankee lover, and with a sigh, Emilie brought herself to her feet and, rearranging her taffeta skirts, started to walk toward the stairs. "I am going to make myself ready for dinner," she said rather coldly. "I will join you downstairs at the proper time."

Jason leaned back on the sofa that had held them both but now seemed too dainty to encompass his rangy frame. Much as he loved this woman, it was almost a relief to be alone. The burdens that he carried in his mind were too much to share with Emilie and for the first time since they had avowed their love for each other, he felt strangely uncomfortable with her. He got up quickly and cursed this thing that had come between them. So ugly was the brutality that had annihilated the dead that it could not be buried with them but, rather, must remain to haunt the living.

Jason jammed his fists against his eyes. Would he ever be able to rub out those sights from his vision, he wondered, or would those plundered, broken bodies rise up before him forever?

Even through the reddened eyelids that closed out his sight he stood haunted by the ripped and bloodied black flesh of the unknown girl whose grotesque position on the heaped earth seemed to warn him, the bony, distended arm pointing as if to fresh grief ahead.

Emilie's hands were shaking as she stood in her bedroom reaching behind her to undo the small buttons of her long black dress. It was a task newly acquired; only since the slaves had been freed had she decided to make do with only the most necessary ministrations from Missy, who now worked for hire. She faltered, angry at herself for her own ineptness at a simple thing over which the ex-slave's fingers had quickly flown, never leaving Emilie time to think about it. She knew that her own uneasiness was at least partly to blame for the clumsiness. Jason's face flashed before her. It was so unlike him to be afraid of anything, but his haunted expression frightened Emilie. Perhaps, she thought in sudden bewilderment, he now thinks our plans are folly and he wants to disengage himself from me. That unthinkable idea stopped her and she left the task of undressing to press her hands painfully against her bosom.

"He cannot leave me, he cannot!" she whispered half aloud. For the first time Emilie was caught in a quick awareness of how very much Jason meant to her. How completely she had come to lean on him these past swift months. It was he who had steadied her when determination had trembled within; now, if what he had seen at Les Saules had so shaken him that he felt that this land he had seemingly conquered could bend and break him as easily as it had others . . .

Emilie pushed the thought from her mind. It must not be. She and Jason had made their plans, and her whole future and the future of Les Chandelles rested on the foundation he had so skillfully envisioned. The ground must not unsettle beneath her, she must not experience again that shattering uncertainty that she had known on her return to the estate just prior to the war. She had come home to find her father dead, the house half burned, the estate being sold out from under her. She had gathered her strength then, a mere slip of a girl. Now, she resolved, the four years of war and widowhood had made her a woman. No matter what appalling troubles threatened, she would be able to see them through.

For the moment, Emilie reminded herself, she had not only her own gathered reserves from which to draw but, by her side, the strong Yankee captain who had come as enemy and stayed as lover.

Now the minute buttons all but undid themselves as her fingers raced nimbly downward and she threw the afternoon frock to the floor and stepped away from it. She moved quickly to her armoire, reaching for a gown more alluring than the one she had discarded.

As she stood searching among the hanging garments Emilie suddenly laughed. What a sight I must be, she half admonished herself, standing here in only shift and pantaloons, thrusting about as though mad to finish some urgent chore. She stood for a moment, her hands resting on the shoulders of a dress, her dark eyes merry with self-amusement. I should go to him just like this, she thought wickedly; perhaps my unclothed appearance will touch his pity. More likely, she reprimanded herself, my wantonness would arouse far grosser senses.

She took a gown from its wooden hanger and slipped unceremoniously into it, turning around to face herself in the long mirror and smooth the garment into place.

She studied herself for a long moment, searching for the differences between that girl and the woman she was now. Her long black hair, always curling of its own will into tendrils and swirls about her face and shoulders, was the same. She didn't think she had grown taller, yet there was something in the way her back stood slender and firm and her shoulders high that made her feel more substantial than she used to. Her small figure flowed in easy, pleasing lines, but Emilie cast her mind away from such vanity, seeking instead to find in her physical self the strength she felt would be more use to her than her beauty.

A sound outside in the hallway brought her back quickly to the present. She knew it was the snap of Jason's door farther down the corridor, closing behind him. In one of the rooms between them Emilie had set old Madame Charpentier, who had taken to the bed there and not moved. The loss of her husband, coming so suddenly after the destruction of their property, seemed to have tightened her into a near paralysis. Emilie had looked in several times during the day and seen that Madame had neither moved nor seemed to recognize her.

Emilie's brow knit in perplexity. There were so many problems to deal with and all of such urgency. Old Monsieur must be properly laid to rest and his widow sent on to her town house in New Orleans. I must call for the priest tomorrow, Emilie thought wearily, so that it's done as quickly as possible. In the city, surrounded by old acquaintances, Madame Charpentier could perhaps come back to herself; remaining at Les Chandelles, she would be nothing but a burden until time took her as well. Emilie's frown deepened at the thought of a priest coming to the house. Always that bespoke solemnity and unhappiness to her, from the time she had been a little girl and subjected to harsh observance by her mother's zeal. The only time in all her life she had welcomed the coming of a priest was when she'd married Guy, and even that had ended tragically.

But she must do what had to be done. Emilie looked at herself one final time in the mirror, trying to ignore the soreness the thought of her poor dead Guy always brought to her. She thought instead of the man a few doors away who had come somehow to take his place beside her.

The thoughts and images melded and separated in her mind. Suddenly she realized that the priest's coming could be turned to more benefit than just the function of the dreary funeral.

She whirled around and ran to the door of her chamber, gathering her skirts in her hands as she hurried down the corridor and, without stopping to knock, burst into Jason's room.

He looked up, startled. "Emilie," he exclaimed, surprised at the unexpectedness of her entry. "What is it, my dear?"

"Jason, Jason!" Emilie threw herself against him, her arms around his broad back. "We're going to get married!"

His eyes were softer as he gazed down at her. "I know, my darling," he said huskily but with a trace of amusement. "But is that rather old news the cause of this invasion?" He stroked her hair as he smiled down at her.

It's working already, Emilie thought happily. She returned his affectionate smile. "But we're not just *going* to be married, Jason," she said, "we're going to be married tomorrow!" And before he could even articulate his astonishment, she reached up and planted her mouth so firmly on his that he could not have spoken had he wanted to.

Emilie thrilled to the strength of his embrace as his arms enclosed her and she felt herself melting into him in the way she had come to know and love. She let herself sink into the heat and fervor of his embrace until suddenly he moved away from her. Emilie felt something other than affection and exultation from him at her announcement.

She opened her eyes and looked up at him wonderingly.

"Not now, my dearest," he whispered, as if in answer to the question he read in her eyes. "Perhaps later . . ." He left his reply uncompleted.

Emilie felt herself burning from head to foot. Wanton, she reprimanded herself, ashamed at how easily he recognized her needs.

Jason indeed read the emotions that surged through her. "Let us go down to dinner now," he said calmly, taking her arm with the courteousness that had marked his attitude toward her in earlier days. He opened the door with his other hand as he gently guided her toward the staircase but squeezed her fingers tightly within his, as if to assure her there was no diminution of his true feelings about her.

Dinner was brief and fairly quiet. When it was over, they walked into the small front saloon. Emilie went slowly about the room, busying herself with rearranging various objects in the room. Jason toyed slowly with a glass of old Charles Bonfils' finest brandy. Emilie felt as though she walked on a floor as fragile as the crystal that held her lover's drink. The air in the room seemed charged with the same energy she felt barely repressed inside her. It crackled like the southern skies before the thunderclap of a storm.

"Jason, let's go upstairs," she said suddenly.

"Are you tired?" His voice was solicitous.

"No, not that," she admitted, her eyes downcast.

"Emilie."

He set his glass down on a small table and walked over to where she stood. He placed his arm about her waist and kissed her lightly on the temple. "Come, darling," he whispered. They walked slowly up the grand staircase. When they reached Emilie's door, Jason let go of her and bent to kiss her hand. Before he could complete the gesture, she grasped him about the wrist and drew him inside with her.

"Emilie." He said the name in the total darkness of the chamber.

"Now, Jason, now." There was a gentle urgency in her voice he could not resist. He followed her blindly, loving her for wanting him, hating himself for giving in so easily to the passions that controlled them both.

2

Emilie looked at the small gold band on her finger. In the four months since she and Jason had been married there had not been a single night's separation. She rejoiced at the marvel of it, so different from the total separation that had pulled Guy away from her forever. Yet, she had to admit to herself, even with Jason's continual presence, all was not as it should be.

There was a knock at the door. "Come in," she called.

"Good morning, Miss Emilie," Missy murmured, stepping into the room.

Emilie looked keenly at her former slave. Missy, too, had the happiness of a present love. Young Jess had returned from the war, yet Emilie detected the same sort of cloud marring Missy's existence as brought gloom to her own. "Has Jess said anything, Missy?" Emilie asked.

"No, ma'am," Missy replied in a low voice, her head down, eyes staring at the floor. Even though freedom had been granted months earlier, Emilie was disappointed to see how Missy clung to many of the slave habits. She had not taken her new status with the enthusiastic grasp that so many of the others had and she certainly had not been out to seek it, as had her beloved Jess. She was paid weekly wages for performing some of the duties that she had as a bondswoman while Emilie attended to her most personal needs herself, as Jason wished her to. Still, she would have preferred to see the servant girl more attuned to the new order.

Her greatest happiness had shown when Jess returned. Emilie had expected a quick marriage between them, but Jess had not been firm in setting the date. It seemed to Emilie that his situation with Missy was rather taken for granted by everyone while he plunged into other matters, which claimed all of his attention.

Missy's problems made Emilie forget her own for a moment, and as she looked at the girl's unhappy face she felt a twinge of guilt for the doubt she had been feeling about Jason. After all, she had him with her now, secured by the sacred bonds of matrimony. Emilie knew that Missy had set her heart on this very same condition. With the dramatic reappearance of Young Jess it had all seemed assured, and yet nothing had happened.

Even during slavery time, the masters of the parish had been rather circumspect when it came to religious observances for their chattel. Emilie remembered hearing, from time to time, vague stories about the silly, seemingly meaningless procedures through which slaves who wished to marry had been put through in other places. It had seemed to her a cruel joke on the part of the masters who coaxed their slaves to jump hand in hand over a broomstick and recognize this act as sacred and binding. Here, in the upper river parishes, priests performed the nuptials with, if not the same pomp and extravagance that served for the masters, at least the dignity of sacred rite.

Emilie knew how much her servant yearned to be so joined to her beloved Jess. "Missy, what has he said?" she asked gently. "Has he made any mention of marriage to you at all?"

Missy shook her head. "He says there's too much trouble around and too much he has got to do before we can tend to our personal selves." It was about as long a sentence as Emilie had ever heard Missy pronounce, but her voice was low with unhappiness and the words came out in jerking hesitation.

Emilie found herself frowning again. She knew what troubles Missy meant. The matter hung between Jason and herself as well. It had started on the day he had ridden back from Les Saules and its atrocities. He refused to discuss the matter with her except in the most veiled way, yet Emilie knew how heavily it burdened his mind. It was a sickly preoccupation that disturbed all of his other activities. Even, she admitted to herself grimly now, what lies between us as man and wife.

Had the killings at Les Saules been an isolated incident, Emilie knew that Jason would have turned it from his mind by now, but every week seemed to bring word of fresh outrage somewhere. The men talked of it among themselves in hushed tones that Emilie knew were not supposed to reach her ears.

"Jess will get back to himself before long, I'm sure of it," Emilie said, trying to console her servant. But her words echoed back unconvincingly even in her ears.

"Yes, ma'am." It was the same reply in the same muffled tone from Missy that Emilie knew from time immemorial. It saddened her to know that the great new era of freedom, so proudly and happily heralded by Jason at its inception, had done little or nothing to improve things for Missy. She seemed to cling tenaciously to the old ways and old habits as though the security of the old time was preferable to this new, uncertain freedom. Emilie searched her heart, wishing she could find the right words with which to console her, but she did not yet have the easiness with the ex-slaves that seemed to come so naturally to Jason. She had frequently watched as he and Jess sat talking on the wide veranda of the house, and watched them as they walked about the property, lost in deep discussion, man to man, voices and postures never indicating that their condition had ever been anything other than that of free men in a state of equality.

It was a gift of grace that Jason had, Emilie thought, a rare and sensitive thing to be found in a man whose life and ways were as plain and straightforward as Jason's. She felt touched by it, and thought wistfully how good it would be if only he could give some of it to her.

She still felt the rub in the course of almost every day of the changing times in which they all moved. Servants, free servants, could not be ordered about as imperiously as they had been as slaves. Technically they were free to leave her employ and estates and go wherever they pleased. Indeed several had done so, although the bulk of the house servants had agreed to stay on as wage earners. Thus Emilie, from day to day, had to change from the old, familiar bearing she had learned when a babe to a new way of addressing the very same people. It was a problem, but she knew how minor it was compared to the troubles raging everywhere about them.

The two women stood awkwardly silent. Emilie started to extend her hand and say something to Missy when the quiet was suddenly broken by many voices shouting from outside. Emilie gathered her skirts in her hand and ran swiftly down the staircase to the front of the mansion, Missy trailing quickly behind.

Emilie hesitated for a moment at the open doorway, then flew across the veranda and down the steps to where Jason stood, his usually neat bulk spattered with mud, his dark suit torn and ragged, one sleeve nearly pulled from its shoulder.

"My God!" Emilie exclaimed. "What's happened?" Her dark eyes widened as she looked from Jason to the men who stood nearby. She spotted Jess coming toward them. "What's happened?" she demanded again, her words now directed to the black man walking toward her. She glanced up at Jason, who still refused to speak.

Once again her eyes sought Jess as she clung to Jason's arm.

The tall, lean ex-slave, black as his grandfather had been, but with an anger in his eyes that the grizzled old African never dared show, spoke quickly. "It's Higgins," he told Emilie, "they had a run-in just below the fork."

Emilie's glance darted to her husband's face. There was a crescent of freshly dried blood between his cheek and chin and the discoloration of other bruises was starting to show.

Emilie couldn't believe her eyes or ears. "What!" she exclaimed. "That man had the effrontery to strike you? I can't believe it!"

Jason smiled grimly. " 'That man,' as you call him, is as free to strike me as any other man who wishes to," he said.

Emilie was astounded. It was no way for Jason to speak, especially in front of the blacks, who had gathered around. She was so taken aback by this insult to her husband that all thought of how conditions had changed for all of them fled from her mind. "Come, dearest," she coaxed him in an urgent whisper. "Let us go inside so I can tend to you." She took his arm and with the hot flush of shame still burning her cheeks turned back to the house.

"That trash Higgins won't be trying this again," she heard Jess say to the others. "The captain left him probably with his arm broken and maybe a leg."

This pronouncement was greeted with loud guffaws.

"In fact," Jess went on, "if the mean dog hadn't come at Captain Phillips with a dead oak branch, he wouldn't have been able to put a scratch on him."

Emilie closed her eyes tightly as she and Jason went inside. If there was any more to the incident she would hear it from her husband. Just now she wished to shut out all reminders of it.

She knelt before him in her bedroom, soaking a cloth

in a basin of warm water and pressing it gently against his face to cleanse his wounds. Now that she knew his hurts were far less serious than she had first feared, she wanted to know everything.

"Tell me, Jason," she implored, "how did it happen? I can't imagine the nerve of the man thinking he could assault you, of all people, with impunity."

Jason looked at her, one eyebrow raised half mockingly.

"Me, of all people?" He echoed her words. "Do you mean Jason Phillips, Yankee captain, or Jason Phillips, new master of Les Chandelles?"

"As a gentleman, Jason," Emilie retorted. "It's unthinkable that such a man dare raise his hand against you!"

Jason took her by the shoulders. "Emilie, Emilie," he said gently, "it has all changed, dearest. You must remember that, as the slaves are no longer slaves, we are no longer masters. Each man is the equal of any other."

"Is that how it is up north?" Emilie flared. "Is this what your wonderful freedom brings?"

"There will always be excesses, Emilie," Jason replied. "Just as there will always be bad men like Higgins. His attempt to knock me down in the road today was far less harmful than some of the other acts I fear he has perpetrated around here."

Emilie looked at him wide-eyed, her gaze unwavering. Was he going to tell her at last of what she had thus far only guessed at from the whisperings of the men? "What has happened, Jason?" she asked quietly.

He placed his hand on the glossy tangle of curls and then slid his fingers down to hold her chin and tilt it up to face him. "Terrible things are happening that I cannot talk to you about, my dearest," he said. "However, you should know that Jess and I both feel that this Higgins is, if not the sole perpetrator, very close to the heart of the matter."

"But can't anything be done, Jason?" Emilie insisted. "If what he's done is too horrible for you even to repeat, why can't something be done about it?"

Jason smiled sadly. "As I tried to say before," he explained, "I am no longer in the army and so have none of the authority vested in my former rank, nor am I, nor indeed was I ever, master of this estate. So you see, my dear, your husband is still very much a common man, without powerful connections or influence in the parish."

"Les Chandelles is still ours," Emilie insisted.

"Yes, in name and more than that," Jason concurred, "but the feelings of the parish are not with us. Just as I tried to warn you before we contracted this hasty marriage of ours."

Emilie knew that he was teasing her but she could not return his wry smile. "I don't give a care for the neighbors," she retorted. "Les Chandelles was never open to most of the other landowners on a familiar basis, nor did we much care to involve ourselves with their frivolous activities. Therefore I need not concern myself with that." She knew that Jason was referring to the fact that so few members of the local gentry had called at the estate since the end of the hostilities and the announcement of their marriage.

"But it is not the social aspect that concerns me," Jason said. "I know you care nothing for empty society. It is the political stand they are taking that bothers me and the total indifference to the violence and immorality that are raging here."

Emilie touched her hand to his cheek. "You are exhausted from this ordeal, dearest," she said, "and so am I. We can talk about it later. Let us go to bed now."

He looked down with wonder at the appeal that glowed in her heart-shaped face. Even the four months of shared intimacy and the gnawing at his conscience of the atrocities he had seen could not dim the deep love and regard he felt for her.

Yet, he knew, it was growing increasingly difficult for him to translate his emotion for her into the comforting lovemaking of their bed. All the warm arousal he felt on holding her was torn from him when the flashing images of mutilated bodies overwhelmed him. It was as though the same violence that had been enacted on the victims was being perpetrated on his own limbs and sensibilities.

He held Emilie tight, caressing her and stroking her to a blissful unawareness that seemed to fill her completely with contentment as she nestled her head against his shoulder and drew her body and limbs tightly against his. Jason threw his head back on the pillow, his eyes burning and wide open. He hoped that Emilie's sweet quietness meant she had fallen asleep. Such natural respite was no longer easily his.

But the head that snuggled so comfortably against his shoulder was far from serene. Emilie felt her own peace, so sweetly given by him, sundered by the tormenting question in her mind. Jason brought her to easy fulfillment: why did he not mount her body, then, to seek his own? Why had he seemingly no need to take her, with the fervent hugs and infinite kisses and chortled joy that had marked him all those nights, only weeks ago, she knew, yet so long since he had emptied himself into her that it seemed to Emilie more like years?

Trembling, she moved her hand until it rested tentatively on his leg. Jason didn't stir. Emilie bit her lip. She pressed her fingers deeper into the flesh of his thigh. She held her breath. A groan came from deep within him as if against his will. Emilie pressed harder. She moved her hand between his legs, reaching upward. Her fingers touched his sudden hardness. She could feel the throb, the rest of his body stiff. She knew he was holding back.

But fighting her meant that he was alive to her

caresses; it was better, she knew, than the painful indifference she had felt all these weeks.

"Jason!" she breathed. She could hear his own breath, labored and straining. She knew that he was fighting her, but she knew that she could win and that the victory would belong to both of them.

He was rock-hard in her hand now, but still he refused to move, even to take her in his arms.

Emilie bit her lip. Not relinquishing her firm hold on him, she moved until she was atop him. Their faces nearly met but Jason's eyes were tightly shut.

I must do it all, Emilie thought, I must do it all myself. She moved onto her knees until his supine body was between them. Her cheeks burned brightly as she gazed down at him, her body surging with the energy she brought to her task. Once again she nestled her head against his shoulder. Her eyes were closed against the skin of his neck but her mouth was opened and gasping at the hot air she needed. Eyes still closed against the darkness, Emilie forced herself open. She moved her hips against his loins until with a thrusting impact she felt him inside her.

She wound her arms about his neck. She rocked him with her body, keeping him in it and against it with the steady motion of her torso.

Only now did she feel him stirring, the life force collecting itself within him to spill hotly inside her.

She didn't know she was crying until Jason, wildly kissing her cheeks, exclaimed at the salty wetness.

Her only response was to hug him tighter to her. Now she felt nothing of the wanton shame that had gripped her when she started her caresses. Now there was only the unchecked gladness at love's success, her unusual boldness rewarded with equally unusual tears, but these were tears of happiness, mingling with the loud exclamations of joy between husband and wife, the glad discovery of two who had found themselves again.

Jason curled her against him. In a few minutes Emilie had the satisfaction of knowing he was deeply asleep. She had only a moment to wonder whether her bold approaches had solved the problem between them for good when slumber overtook her as well.

3

The flames leaped high in the sultry night. The greedy red fingers seemed to pull the heat from the black air itself. The men seated in the cleared space around the fire stared expectantly into the gloom. One of them half rose suddenly.

"Quiet! I hear something. It must be them," he exclaimed in a harsh whisper.

Two of his companions also got up slowly but the fourth man in the group remained seated, his gaunt figure stretched languidly against a fallen, decaying tree trunk. Only his eyes, narrow black slits, moved in the darkness, darting about in eager anticipation.

A group of men broke through the trees and into the clearing, and Higgins fastened his eyes on them as he rubbed the back of his hand across his stubbly jaw. He watched as the three newcomers edged closer, their progress made arduous by the heavy object they were dragging with them.

It was only when they came closer to the fire that the outline of their burden could be distinguished.

It was a man, bound and trussed, his arms and legs bent back and tied behind him. Even in this state he tried to drag himself away from his captors and slow them down as much as he could.

Higgins roared with anger when he heard the prisoner

begging and pleading to be released. "Shut up, nigger!" he shouted. "No more praying out of you!"

"I didn't do nothing, master, I swear I didn't!" the bound black man pleaded.

"I said shut up!" The harsh voice rang through the clearing.

"Shall I shut him up, boss?" one of the men who held the prisoner asked gleefully.

"Sure, why not?" Higgins replied languidly, with a slow grin.

The man grasped a nearby branch and brought it across the side of the prisoner's face. The man howled with pain as the splintered and rotting wood tore into his flesh, ripping it open and stippling the bark with blood.

"Again?" the man asked in the same gleeful voice.

"Nah, let him be," Higgins decided. "We don't want him done in before the fun's really started now, do we, boys?"

The question was answered with whoops of derision. Higgins smiled to himself. No use giving them their way all the time, even when it came to nigger-beating. He would be able to set himself up as their real leader only if he said no to them once in a while, just to show he was boss and his was the final word. "Let's get him tied to yonder tree." He pointed to a medium-sized thick cypress, whose trunk could not be encompassed by the black's arms, stretched as they were and tied behind his still struggling body.

"What's your name, boy?" Higgins spat out.

The prisoner's eyes bulged with terror, every muscle in his big body, which had been struggling for release only moments before, now quivering with fear. There was no way, he thought wildy, for these men to know what he had done. Charles Bonfils had been a bad master, whipping and working slaves to death. Judd had his chance when the master had come rushing into the quarters alone, and he had done what any man would have.

But how could they know, these crackers? It had been so long ago, before the war, the night of the big fire. He was so certain that no white men had seen him kill old Master Bonfils. Even the overseer had been away that night. Why did these men want him now?

"Your name, nigger!" The words rang out again.

"Judd, from off . . . Les Chandelles." The words came stammering out, barely audible.

Higgins' eyes were gleaming. "We know where you come from, boy," he said. A large smile was curling about his lips. "That's why we brought you from there. All Les Chandelles niggers is a bad lot. Thieves and runaways and God knows what else." He spat on the ground. "Ain't that so, men?"

Affirmative grunts came from the others.

"I ain't done nothing!" Judd shouted hoarsely.

"You ain't said 'master' or 'sir' since you got here, boy!" Higgins rose suddenly and strode over to the bound figure. "That's wrong enough for me!" He reached out swiftly and struck Judd against the unbloodied side of his face.

The ex-slave winced but let out no cry. Higgins' hand was nothing after the splintered branch that the other man, Kane, had struck him with.

The silence enraged Higgins to even more fury. He would not look like a fool or a weakling in front of Kane and Dukes and the other man whom Dukes had brought, whose name he did not know.

His arm flashed out again. This time the fingers clenched into a brute fist. This blow sent Judd reeling, his large head thrown forward on his neck. His legs sagged; only the thick ropes that bound his arms and chest to the tree trunk kept him from collapsing on the earth.

The men watched for a moment. "What will we do with him now, boss?" one of them asked.

Higgins thought for a moment. "Burn him," he said. He spat on the ground at his prisoner's feet.

"Too much timber," the man who wasn't known to Higgins drawled slowly. "Torch the nigger and this whole tract will go up."

Higgins scowled in the darkness. He didn't like anyone, especially a stranger, outthinking him. But the man was right. Higgins cursed himself for a fool. He should have thought before he spoke, but this had been the first black they had been able to catch and secret away. All the other times, they had pounced on small, isolated settlements and destroyed them completely, with no one left to tell the tale. This was to be different. A man spirited away from the large quarters of Les Chandelles would leave the others terrified and quaking in fear. He had wanted a spectacle to mark the success.

He turned his back on the bound black and the waiting men, moving his shoulder contemptuously as though he no longer cared. Best now to do it simple, he thought, use whatever's at hand. "String him up." His words were almost casual.

"Good idea," the stranger said. "Let's get this rope off him, boys."

Higgins whirled around sharply. "You, there," he said, pointing to the stranger, "what's your name?" The question sounded like an accusation.

"Lynch, Jim Lynch," came the reply. "From over by Shreveport. That is, I used to have a place there, before the nigger-loving Yankees came in and burned it to the ground."

"Good man, Lynch," Higgins replied. "Go to it."

He turned and started walking through the swampland back toward his shack. It was going to take them a little bit of time to subdue and hang the nigger. No use being around in the unlikely event that someone should chance by.

"He was a good man. He worked hard. What did he do to deserve—this?" Jess crouched on the ground near the remains of the man who had been missing. He looked up at Jason, as if to find the answer written on his face somehow.

Jason kicked at the scorched earth with his boot. His practiced eye told him that this had been no mere spur-of-the-moment killing. It would have taken the strength of several men to capture and hold as big a man as Judd, let alone hang him. The area was a small clearing made in the thick tangle of trees and brush bordering the swampy bayou. It was evident that it had been cleared and a campfire set, by which the collaborators had performed the ghastly deed. Jason estimated that there had been at least three to four men involved, maybe more. He glanced about. Certainly a greater number would have left more evidence of having been there. Although the cleared site was unmistakable, there were no telltale marks indicating a trail by which the men might have come and left. It had been done by someone who knew what he was about and although this savagery did not follow the same pattern as that of the other acts of terror in the parish, Jason felt sure that it was the work of the same men.

They were nearer the northern limits of Les Chandelles than they were to Higgins' sparse holding, but Jason was sure that Higgins was thoroughly familiar with the terrain. "How far was it from here that Higgins caught you that time you ran away?" he asked Jess.

Jess thought for a moment. "I can't say for sure. I don't know this area well, but it couldn't have been too far from here. It has the same feeling to me. The marshy ground, the trees growing one nearly on top of the other." He looked up at Jason. "You think it was him?"

Jason nodded. "It's only a feeling but the longer it stays with me, the stronger it grows. I've been here long enough now to mark the men of the parish as they've come back from Lee's army. He's the only one who seems to me strong enough to get others to follow him."

"And mean enough, too." Jess spat out the words. "Burning, murdering, killing bastard! He's had it in for me ever since he caught me and brought me back."

Jason had never seen Jess so angry. "He hasn't done this against you," he said gently.

Jess sprang to his feet. "Every murdering act that's committed is against me!" he shouted, pointing a forefinger at Jason as he spoke. "Everything that is done against my people is done against me! Let me remind you of that!" He spun around on his heel, jamming his hands into the pockets of his trousers as if trying to contain himself. Then, just as quickly, he spun around and turned on Jason again. "Where is the law, man? Where is the army that was supposed to protect us? Where is your government that was going to free us from this? We were better off with old Charles Bonfils, Jason. At least when we were property we were taken care of! Now, as free men, we have nothing." His voice lowered with bitterness.

"Everything has changed, Jess, and is still changing." There was a pleading in Jason's voice. "You know that as well as I do, better even. It will take time for a new establishment to get set and to make its authority felt. Surely you don't wish for a return of the old ways."

"I don't?" Jess shot him a look. "When that bastard Higgins dragged me back to the big house on my knees, Charles Bonfils had me untied and sent the cracker packing. Don't you see?" His voice softened as he realized how much anger had overtaken him and come between him and his friend. "Higgins hates not only me but everyone and everything having to do with Les Chandelles! He will get back at us in any way he can as long as there's no law to stop him or authority to uphold that law; the man can do whatever he wants. All we can do is try to stop him before the next outrage."

"We can set up a guard system around the house and around the quarters." Jason was thinking out loud. "What you say is right, Jess—all we can do now is try to stop him. The feelings in the parish, even among the former owners, will be with him and against us. You know that."

"Yes, I know," Jess answered. "We have neither the authorities nor public opinion nor law on our side. All we have is the right—including the right to live. Jason, I can't stand by and see that taken from us!"

"What do you intend to do?" Jason asked, alarmed by the savage tone in his young friend's voice. "You cannot take the law into your own hands, Jess. That can never be right."

"The law kept me down long enough, Jason," Jess said slowly. "Now I'm not a thing to be used anymore. I am going to be the user and not the used anymore. The law is going to learn something about me!"

"What do you mean?" Jason wanted to know.

"There's going to be a new state legislature set up by the federal governor, with supervised elections," Jess said. "I intend to run for office, representing my people in this parish."

"Bravo!" Jason applauded. "We will, of course, support you and help you in any way we can. I think it's an excellent first step, my friend, and I'm proud of you for taking it. You had me worried for a moment." Jason rubbed his cheek as he smiled royally. "For a moment I thought you were intending more direct means."

It was Jess's turn to smile. "That, too," he said quietly. "If I catch Higgins or whoever it is, I'm going to kill him with my bare hands."

4

"I think that Jess might just be undertaking too much." Emilie's brow was puckered in thought. The news that Jason was giving her was causing distress after distress. First the news about Judd, always to the best of her knowledge a hardworking and valued hand, and then, hard on the heels of that tragic note, word of Jess's determination upon a course that would bring untold problems, and perhaps even worse, upon them.

"Yes, poor Judd," Jason said, sympathizing. "He had just earlier in the day gone to draw his share of goods. It was the first pair of shoes he ever would have worn. We found them in his cabin. Poor fellow—he died just as he had lived, barefoot all his life."

"Jess is overseeing the issuing of rations," Emilie went on. "Plus he is involved with getting the school started and Lord knows he'll have more pupils, young and old, than any one person could possibly handle. With so much to do, why must he insist, now of all times, that he stand for office? Surely that would be a difficult enough undertaking even in the best of times, which"—she shot her husband a swift glance—"these most assuredly are not."

"I couldn't agree with you more, Emilie, as far as the burdens that Jess is taking onto himself are concerned," Jason replied. "However, there is no disputing how much there is to be done. No one feels the urgency more than Jess. He insists on throwing himself wholeheartedly into every aspect of improving the people's lot, even if it's to his own detriment."

"Not to mention Missy's!" Emilie retorted. "He has practically ignored her ever since embarking on all these grandiose schemes of his. The poor girl doesn't know where she stands with him and is growing more sullen and miserable by the day. Although," she added quickly, lest Jason think her too harsh on her ex-slave, "he certainly gives her reason enough to feel the way she does."

"Missy must learn, as all women must," Jason said gently, "that when you take on a man, you take on his life's work as well. If Jess wasn't the man he was and doing what he's doing, chances are Missy wouldn't see him for beans."

"Nonsense," Emilie disagreed. "Missy couldn't care less were Jess to do nothing but work the cane and grow a few yams in their front yard. As a matter of fact, I'm quite inclined to think she would prefer him that way."

"All the more pity for her if she does, my dear," Jason mused. "She's misjudged her man and I'm quite afraid that she will pay dearly for it in days to come. Had she wanted a simpler man, merely husband and provider, she should have closen someone else entirely."

"From what I understand, it's far too late for that." Emilie sighed. "She's had her sights set on Jess for as long as she was old enough to think of anyone at all. He just has turned out to be someone far beyond her comprehension, I'm afraid. Alas for Missy, I quite agree with you."

"All the more reason I so appreciate you, my sweet Emilie." Jason knelt to sit down beside her. "What would I have done with a featherbrain who failed to understand what I was about?" He took her hand in both of his and kissed the small, smooth palm. He looked up at her. "I never liked the ways of your forebears or the system by which they lived. Yet when I look at you, I am forced to think it could not have been all bad for it to have produced such a woman as you."

Emilie smiled at him gently. She above all knew the depth of feeling behind his compliment. For Jason, who so hated slavery, to admit that any good at all could come of it was high praise indeed. "We had to be strong in order to rule, my dear," she said simply. "Even if one disagreed with the method and the reason for our ruling."

"Well, all of it is gone now, in any case," Jason said thoughtfully, "and now it is we who are left here and must deal with its consequences." He turned to face her again. "Emilie, I know full well the difficulties this thing might bring upon us, but I cannot, in all conscience, as a man, refuse to support Jess in his determination to seek office."

"But the parish will see it as an effrontery of the cheekiest kind," Emilie contested. "They cannot abide the idea of the blacks voting, let alone holding office. Who knows what might come raining down on us if he persists."

"The parish is more than the old landowners, Emilie." His voice was gentle again in reminding her. "The parish now in law, as well as in reality, holds more black citizens by far than white. They have been freed and given their voices. Nothing can change that, no matter what difficulties and horrors your friends of the old regime might perpetrate."

Emilie shrank back a little. "Surely you don't think that the aristocracy, what little is left of them, is responsible for these horrible burnings and hangings, do you?"

"I don't know," Jason said frankly. "Although I am sure that none of the former masters would dirty their hands with any kind of work, especially the most dastardly kind, they are giving silent consent to the activities of the night riders. Were it not so, all of the disturbances would have ceased by now."

"They are not my friends, yet I can't believe it of them," Emilie said softly.

"It isn't only here," Jason reminded her. "Already the pattern has erupted all over the South and nothing is being done to stop it."

"Then all we have to look forward to is a worsening," said Emilie bitterly. "It is not going to get better."

Higgins rode slowly, not wanting to tire his broken old mare unduly, not in any great hurry to get back to his lonely hovel. The Widow Jarvis was a good woman, he thought as he picked at his teeth with a small, dry twig. The satisfaction of the meal she had just cooked him was full in his belly. She was no great shakes to look at, the widow, but it sure beat having to make his own food. Nor did he much relish eating alone. The widow's cabin, though not much larger than his, was more orderly, he had to admit. It had the woman's touch and the woman's hand, which his own had so long lacked. He spat at the ground, cursing. His own young Kate, his sweet daughter, would have been about the same age as the widow woman's own girl. Higgins pulled himself up sharply in the saddle, remembering the girl who had hovered about the cabin, silently doing her mother's bidding. She was small of stature and lean, so far as he could tell through the heaped-up layers of raggedy skirts she wore. She barely lifted her eyes to look at him, even when he spoke to her, but the little he had seen was enough. Again he spat and cursed the Bonfils, who had robbed him of his Kate. What a comfort she would be now, he thought, my own girl to do for me like she always had; hadn't been more than a slip of a thing, no more than twelve or thirteen, the night that Chaz Bonfils had grabbed her in the fields, pleasured himself on her, and left her there to bleed to death.

She'd be of marrying age before now, had she lived, he mused. That would make her somewhat older than the Jarvis gal. Still, even married, she might find the time to take care of her father like she always had. True, Widow Jarvis had offered today to do his washing if he would but fetch it down to her place. But for the poor few rags he owned it hardly paid to ride old Boss the twelve or so miles even if there was a meal waiting there for him.

The widow had lost her man in the war. She and the girl struggled to bring enough out of their stony bit of land to keep themselves together, with barely enough left over to buy them the other necessities. The hard work showed on them, he had to allow that, but better hard work and no looks in a woman than a lazy one doing nothing but caring for herself all the time. He had made that mistake before.

His mind's eye tried to retrace the outline of the widow's daughter as she bent before him putting his dish on the table. He felt something stirring in his blood and he knew it was not from the warmth of the food in his belly. It might not be worth the while to ride hot, hard miles for wash, but for womaning, that was something else.

He closed his eyes against the glare of the sun and imagined himself, arms outspread, hands cupping and pushing the woman's body against his own. Images of the two of them floated at him in the sun.

He smiled easily. Mother and daughter both, why not? Bring them to his holding, sell off their patch, build a little extra room on the house for the girl. He was no bargain, he knew that, but neither could the Widow Jarvis have much in the way of prospects. There couldn't be too many unattached men left in the parish to begin with, but there were younger and comelier widows and girls everywhere.

Higgins suddenly dug his boots into Boss's sagging underbelly. He had half a mind to reign in and then head back to the widow's but he thought better of it. No need to appear too anxious; her face, sorrow-worn and lined as it was, still showed a shrewish cast. No need to make the woman think she could put demands on him. Better to let his offer come as a boon; waiting out the week till he was due back there wouldn't be so bad. The snatching and killing of the Les Chandelles nigger nights earlier had gone well and he aimed to get a few more done before much longer. That would give him plenty to do, but time enough left over for thinking out what he would say to her and for closing his eyes and collecting for himself the picture he had already conjured of locking all that female flesh around him.

He urged the horse on now, his own hardening need pressing against him and demanding relief. He felt like jumping from the horse and diving into a thicket for the blessedness of undoing his breeches and relieving himself of the fevered images crowding against his eyes.

But he feared discovery. The road was not used that often, but it would be his cursed luck to be seen. He kicked viciously at the horse, pushing her to the outer limits of her endurance. He knew he was not far from his place, and only a few more minutes would permit him to spill his seed behind its walls.

His eyes could barely focus on the road ahead of him, so great was his need. Lucky for him he knew the way so well.

Then it was in front of them. He pulled viciously at the rein to jerk Boss's head toward the small, barely visible path that led off the road into his holding. They were almost there, he told himself.

Just as he came into view of the house he leaped from the saddle without bothering to secure the horse. He ran heavily to the cabin, pushing open the door to the gloom of the single large room.

"Good afternoon, Mr. Higgins," said a pleasant male

voice from the darkness. "We have been waiting for you."

Higgins rubbed his eyes. He could just make out the figures of two men sitting at his table, but the outlines of their fine clothing and the accents of the voice that addressed him told him that these were no ordinary callers. In the dirt and gloom of Jack Higgins' poor house sat two gentlemen, so unexpected they startled him out of the physical passion that had driven him so quickly back to the house, but gentlemen nevertheless.

Higgins felt his knees buckling under him. He could barely stand. He gripped his arms to his sides to keep from lurching forward. He longed to grasp the crude wooden bench that stood alongside the table, but even in his confusion he knew he dared not sit in the presence of his betters.

5

"Sit down, we wish to speak with you," the man said.

Never before had there been members of the gentry under Higgins' roof. Never had he ever been invited by any to sit down with them. Now his fear of being caught was mixed with total confusion. He felt in front of him for the bench, gripping its rough-hewn edge with both hands even as he sat. His shoulders were hunched up, his head thrust forward, trying to recognize his visitors. He cursed inwardly for the wooden plank he had only that morning set against the only window in the room. The darkness was nearly as frightening as the presence of the men themselves. Finally he asked, "Shall I get the lamp, sirs?"

"No, that won't be necessary." The same man was still speaking. "The purpose of our visit here is not one that would be enhanced by light. As you might have guessed, we have secreted our horses around the other side of your house so they might not be seen by any casual passerby. We have come here in complete secrecy."

Fear emboldened Higgins. "What is it you want of me?" he whispered hoarsely. His mind raced with the knowledge that, had they come to arrest him, it would not have been with the hidden means the man described.

"Permit me to introduce myself, sir," the man went on. "I'm afraid that the urgency of our business and our rather long wait for you have made me completely lose my manners. I am Alexandre Romain, and this is my associate, Robert Elmore, Jr., both of New Orleans."

Higgins grunted.

"Yes, of course," Romain said smoothly. "Since we already know your name, it is unnecessary to waste further time."

The other man cleared his throat and spoke. His voice, though cultivated, had a hurried urgency about it. "We know you to be a man of courage, Higgins. We know what you have been about these past months."

His eyes now accustomed to the gloom, Higgins could see that Elmore was leaning across the table toward him, his arms outstretched, his head thrust forward. The visitors, for all their air of mystery and authority, were both younger men than he would have expected, for all their daring.

"We also believe you're a man who believes in the right," Romain said more quietly. "And a man that can be trusted."

"Yes!" Elmore banged his fist on the table. "The right, our *right!*"

Higgins sat waiting, not speaking. He did not know what these men had sought him out for, but, as with an animal confronted in its own lair, every sense came alert, every breath he took was wary of these two strangers. He could not help but be flattered at what they said, yet, his still-racing mind quickly reasoned, how could they know?

"What you have done is admirable." Romain was smiling in the darkness; Higgins could sense it. He's like a cat purring, he thought, but no, more like a panther, stalking and ready to spring. He wondered how much they knew about him and how, indeed, they could know anything at all.

"But what we need is a more planned action." The

purring voice went on. "Not the isolated fires and occasional killings you manage to perpetrate."

Fear opened up again like hackles up and down Higgins' back. If they knew, others must know as well. If two strangers from the city were able to find out so much about him, people in the parish must have told them. Although Romain's voice was soothing and complimentary, Higgins was still afraid. "What is it you want?" he asked.

"We want you to join us!" Elmore exclaimed, leaning even closer across the rough wooden table. "We are organizing everywhere and want you to be our man in this parish!"

Higgins could sense that Romain, the older of the two, was not overpleased with Elmore's outburst. Elmore was more hotheaded, less controlled than the cooler Romain, who was clearly the leader.

"Perhaps we are going a little fast for you, Monsieur," said Romain. Higgins started in panic, knowing that whatever it was that Romain would ask of him, he would be powerless to refuse even if he wanted to. There was something in the man that made Higgins all too aware of his own low birth and grubbing life. Yet at the same time, the man kindled a spark in him that bade him be more than he ever had been. The combination was overwhelming. Higgins knew he would obey Romain as a dog his master.

"You were a soldier in the war for our glorious cause," Romain was saying. "We know you to have done your part in that terrible struggle that has left our land ravaged and despoiled. What we must know now, Higgins, is whether four years in the field have left you strong enough for the battle that is still to come."

"What battle is that?" Higgins asked simply. He was not quite sure what the gentleman meant.

"Bloody as the struggle was, the most important fight is just beginning," Romain replied. "You yourself, in some small way, have already contributed to it. But are you ready to consider yourself a soldier once more? Will you be able to carry out your daring deeds not as a lone pillager but as a soldier once more in the army of the South?"

"The army?" Higgins echoed.

"Not the glorious Army of the Confederacy, to be sure," Romain said. "But an army in the sense of leadership and rank. What we must have is men capable of following orders as completely as if they were those of a commanding officer on the battlefield." He paused for a moment to let the words sink in. "Are you disciplined enough in your love of our land to obey?"

"What must I do?" Higgins asked. He found himself totally caught up in Romain's words.

"You will ride out in the night as you have done before," Romain said quietly. "This is an army not of drums or trumpets, but an army whose banner is fear and whose purpose is to gain back all that has been taken from us. You will kill, you will burn, in the night, but when morning sees the smoke from the ashes, no one left alive will have to wonder from whence the conflagration rose, for we mean to light a fiery light that will crisscross this land until it is ours once again, until it has been scorched of those who would now take it from us and of those who help them." He stared straight at Higgins, fastening his eyes on him, never wavering or blinking for an instant.

"Those hands reaching out for what's ours," Elmore said, breaking in, "you know what hands those are."

"Yes." Higgins' voice was no more than a whisper again.

"Black hands!" Elmore exclaimed. "Filthy, ignorant black devils set free to take what's ours and do away with us."

"Bastards," Higgins agreed.

"They must be stopped! And we are going to stop

them!" Elmore said, stretching out his arm once more and grasping Higgins' hand with his own. "Are you with us, sir?"

"Yes!" No one had ever called him sir or monsieur before and Higgins felt his chest swell and his arms grow as though iron bands were within them. The words of his visitors filled him with an exultation such as he had never felt before, no, never, not even when his general had ridden among the ranks before the big battles, exhorting and cheering the men on to give their lives for the Glorious Cause.

"I knew we could count on you." Romain sounded as if he was smiling again. "Welcome, Higgins, to our ranks."

Now the three men huddled around the table, the visitors explaining to Higgins about the nature of the organization and the initiation he would take in order to join. He was told that he would be the leader in the parish, all of the men he recruited would answer to him, and the secret rites, names, and regalia of the organization would be explained to them in a ceremony, in the dead of a night soon to be agreed upon.

Higgins listened, fascinated. If the niggers had been scared before by their mad night dashes, their flaming torches and piercing warwhoops, what lay before their unsuspecting eyes now would surely cause more terror than anyone could ever have imagined.

When his visitors left after setting the date for the next rendezvous, Higgins felt strangely alone. He had never noticed his solitude so strongly before, but then no day in his life had ever been like this one. He had all but forgotten the morning meal with the Widow Jarvis and her daughter in the greater excitement that had awaited him at home. But for all the sudden loneliness he now felt, there was yet a great exultation buzzing around his head, the excitement not only of recognition by his fine visitors but of the guarantee they had left of greater fury to be spent than ever before. Now it no longer need be just three or four trusty men to do his bidding; now he would be free to range far and wide over the parish, recruiting all of the men who felt as he did. Romain had said that this army was springing up throughout the Confederacy. It was bigger than the parish, bigger than the state. No one would be able to stop them. With enough men beside him, he would be able to burn and kill and destroy until every bad black was gone from the parish, either by his command or on their own feet to carry them in fear.

All this, he thought, looking around, and for once in his life not seeing the scrubby patchiness of his poor holding, all this power come to him. All this, and the Widow Jarvis, too. And the daughter. Both under his knuckle, both to do his bidding. He who had nothing would have power and an army. He who had no one would have two women serving him.

Higgins fell to his knees on the rough earth outside his doorstep. It had been too long, he thought, since he had stopped to thank the Lord, but he absolved himself as he kneeled; it had been too long that the Lord had not brought him such grace as He had today.

6

"They're not going to know it's us by name," Higgins explained to the men sitting around him. "It's a sign so everyone will know it's the organization. No more scattershot killing a nigger here or there, or just stringing one up for the hell of it. We go in with a plan, like I said, and when it's done we set up the cross."

"And then we set the cross to flame!" Dukes broke in excitedly. "The flaming, burning cross, that's us!"

"That's right," Higgins said. He frowned. Now he had to explain to them about the robes that they would wear. He understood the point of it very well himself, but he was uncertain about how the men would take to it. He tried to give a military air to everything that he related to them about the new organization, but he was afraid this part, which he had purposely left for last, would seem like playfulness to them. They were poor men, rugged for the most part, all of them struggling with their small holdings, all of them veterans of long years in the battlefields, wounded by war, scarred by bitter defeat.

He cleared his throat, looking down at the ground, not facing the half-dozen men who squatted beside him. "We want to scare the hell out of them niggers," he said. "We can't shoot down or hang the lot of them, 'cause then there'd be no one left to do the work." He looked up at them then, his eyes scanning each face. "Ain't no white man can stand up to the heat of the canebrakes," he said, chuckling, "and ain't none of us about to try it, neither. What we need, boys, is to give them a good scare. Oh, we'll burn 'em out and string one up every now and then, more than that if they get out of hand, but mostly we just want to make sure they all know who's still boss around here."

"What about the real troublemakers?" one of the other men asked.

"Those we'll either string up as an example to the others or just plain run them out of the parish," Higgins replied.

"Or out of the state and out of the South," the man named Lynch said.

A chorus voiced approval.

"Now let's get back to business," Higgins reprimanded them, angry at Lynch's drawing the men's attention away from him. "Like I said, everybody's going to know the organization was back of the attacks, but who we ourselves are has got to be in strictest secrecy." He looked sharply into each face. "We got to know who we are. We got to know that we can trust one another more than we would trust our own kin, if need be. But everything has got to be kept secret, outside of us. There's still a Yankee government down in New Orleans and still plenty of Yankee spies and sympathizers even here, upriver." His voice was ominous.

"Bastard scalawags." One of the men spat on the ground.

"And worse," Higgins amended. "That's one of the reasons we've got to go in disguise. It's part to hide ourselves and part to scare the niggers even worse."

"What kind of disguise?" Dukes asked.

"We're going to wear white sheets covering us. With just holes cut out so we can see," Higgins explained. "When we come riding in fast, holding up our torches, those sheets will be blowin' around and the niggers'll think we're ghosts comin' down on them!"

"Haunts! They're all afraid of haunts." One of the men cackled with glee. "That'll scare 'em worse than anything!"

"They'll be dropping like flies all around us," another man added. "Won't be nary a need to fire a shot."

"That's it, boys, that's it." Higgins heaved an invisible sigh of relief. They seemed to go for the whole pitch. "Now these two gentlemen will be back at my place two nights from now," he declared. "Ready to give the time and place of the special secret initiation to any man who's going to stand up with us. But I better warn you now"—he looked around the group sternly—"anyone with a drop of coward blood in him had better stay away and forget he ever heard anything about this. The way they tell it, a man has got to be ready to live by the code and to die for it."

The ominous warning was not lost on his listeners. None of the men said anything; most sat with their eyes downcast, their shoulders moving nervously.

Higgins spoke again. "The day of our next meet is set, the place is here, no one says a word about this to no one till then. Now we'll leave like we came, one man at a time, so's not to attract undue notice. You." He gestured with his chin toward one of the men. "You go first."

The man jumped to his feet and the others watched as he disappeared into the tangled growth. Higgins waited until he thought five minutes had passed and then dismissed the next man. He gestured to Lynch this time, figuring he might as well be rid of the one he saw as most dangerous to him. The pattern continued until he was left alone in the small clearing. He got slowly to his feet and stood still, looking around him. There was something about the place that made him loath to leave it. It was not more than seven or eight feet of cleared ground, roughly circular. He had ordered his first three followers to prepare it as a meeting place and the site of their hanging of the Les Chandelles nigger. Burned ends of branches and charred earth marked the place where they set their fire at night meetings. The tree they had used for the hanging stood strong and grim. Beyond this area lay the encroaching tangle that it had been cleared from and that threatened, with its fecundity, to reclaim it at any time. But that, Higgins told himself, he would never allow.

There was a feeling that he had walking about this place or even just standing and looking around it; it was like it was his own, a place where he ruled, more his domain than even the holding he had built and worked on for more than twenty years. There he was alone and struggling; here he was a king whose every word was obeyed by those he summoned. Here, more than any other place he had ever been, he felt himself supreme.

And now, with the coming initiation of him and his men into the secret order and the promised support and growth of their activities, he would become even bigger and more important than he had ever dreamed.

Higgins picked up his dusty, broad-brimmed black hat and jammed it onto his head. It was a good half hour's walk through the brush from here to the homestead, and reluctant as he was to go, he knew he had better get moving.

As they had promised, Romain and Elmore were waiting inside the house when he got in from plowing two nights later. He boarded up the window before setting a thick candle in the middle of the table around which they huddled.

From a large carrying case Elmore drew out a long white sheet; placing it on the table, he showed Higgins where holes had been cut for the wearer's eyes. "Every one of your men has got to wear his own on every raid."

"Sort of like our uniform," Higgins observed.

"Yes, but more than that," Elmore answered while Romain sat silently watching, arms folded, his slender, aristocratic bearing seeming to make him an observer. He was quick with his words but displayed none of the fervor that Elmore could scarcely conceal for the more garish aspects of the enterprise.

"These," Elmore said, indicating the sheets, "the torches and the burning cross which will be left at the site of each raid. These are the signs they'll know us by and the stuff that'll keep them where they belong—or dead."

"How many men will you have with you, Higgins?" Romain asked.

"Not rightly sure," Higgins admitted. "I've got my contacts out with some of my regulars. I know I can count on my men, but I don't know how many others they'll bring along with them."

"Are you sure your meeting place is secure?" Romain asked.

"Sure as you can be about these things," Higgins answered. "We've been using it for a while now to meet. Even strung a nigger up there once."

"I see," Romain said. "Has the evidence been removed?"

"Yes, sir," Higgins said.

"How many days after the hanging was it found?" Romain persisted in his questioning.

"Maybe four, five days, I reckon," Higgins said.

"Do you know how it was discovered, and by whom?" Romain wanted to know.

"Some of the men from Les Chandelles," Higgins said. "They had a party out looking for him."

"Ah, yes, Les Chandelles. The old Bonfils place." Romain was remembering. "The estate has passed on to the daughter now, hasn't it?"

"Yeah, the little bitch and her Yankee husband are running it now, for what it's worth," Higgins said.

"It is probably worth a great deal, man," Romain said

loftily. "It's one of the greatest sugar-raising plantations in the entire state."

"Not anymore," Higgins grunted. "That Yankee bastard Phillips has been carving it up and giving it away to their slaves."

"A rich southern lady, married to a Yankee, and giving away her estate?" Elmore said questioningly. "It doesn't seem possible."

"Possible and done," Higgins replied. "That Miss Emilie was a cool-looking one but she must have been pretty hot under the petticoats to marry up with a Yankee captain."

"Sir!" The reprimand was quick and sharp from Romain. "Regardless of what you claim to be the goings-on at Les Chandelles, I will remind you that you are speaking of a southern lady, and one of your betters. I'll remind you to hold your tongue."

"At least until we ourselves are sure of the situation," Elmore added. "Perhaps we should pay a visit to the place, Alexandre."

"You may be right," Romain murmured. "But let's get on with our business here first. If we do decide to call on the lady it should not be at a time when we might have been sighted coming from here."

Higgins' spine crawled. It was the first time since their unexpected first meeting that the gentlemen had spoken to him in less than courteous, even comradely, tones. To be brought down like this by Romain was humiliating. Once again he had suffered because of someone named Bonfils, even if she knew nothing about it. Once again Higgins promised himself he would get his revenge on all of them.

"We'll tell you how to get word to us when you're sure of your men," Elmore said, breaking into Higgins' thoughts. "When you've got a group that you're completely sure of, we'll set up an initiation rite."

"We will send word back telling you where and when

the ceremony will take place," Romain added. "It will only be necessary for each man to bring his own horse and sheet. Is that understood?"

"Yes, sir," Higgins said. "Am I thinking right that this ceremony is going to take place somewhere else, not around here?"

"Exactly," Romain said softly. "Your men, plus some others we've recruited downriver, will represent this parish. You will be but one contingent among many."

Higgins let out a long, low whistle. "Many," he echoed. "How many are you figuring on?"

"There will be men from all over the state," Romain said proudly. "That night the flower of southern manhood will rise to their feet as one and pledge their lives and honor to our sacred cause."

"The world has never seen anything like it," Elmore added. "Not since the days of the old Roman gladiators have men made such a stand as we are about to."

"Come, Robin," Romain said, rising from the bench. "Our work for the moment is done here. We will let it rest in Monsieur Higgins' capable hands. I know he will not shame this parish when the rolls are called at the initiation. I am sure there will be no laggards there." He bowed slightly toward Higgins, who remained seated in total astonishment. The hurt of the earlier reprimand had vanished from his mind as totally as the two hurrying gentlemen now did across his humble threshold. He walked slowly to the door after they had passed into the open and watched them gallop away in the oncoming darkness. He watched until they disappeared and then he turned and went back inside.

He felt like a man whose belly was full and warm. He would sleep well tonight, he thought. He kicked off his boots and stretched himself out on his bed. He thought of the dazzling prospects his visitors had described and how puffed with pride he would be to be leading the men of the parish. In some ways, since the Yankees were running things and the old plantations were being split up, with this new order of things, it could very well turn out that Jack Higgins would be the most important man in the parish.

Everything had changed so since the war and its bitter aftermath. Why, he reasoned to himself, couldn't some of the changes be for the better? It was about time some good came into his life.

His mind flashed suddenly back to the Widow Jarvis and that daughter of hers. No reason he shouldn't go calling on them the very next morning. Long as he had such a bellyful of this good feeling, he might as well make use of it. Romain had said there was to be no mischief until the men had all been properly initiated. That meant that the only kind of funning for the next few weeks would be the kind that women could provide under the covers.

It was a happy man who made his way in the middle of the next morning to the Jarvis holding. His only regret, as he neared the place, was that he wouldn't be able to tell the widow of the plans that were afoot and the importance that he had right in the middle of it all. That would certainly tell her what kind of man he was, but the gentry had sworn him to secrecy, just as he had his own men, and he was not about to break his word, especially not for the sake of a woman. If she wanted him, she could very well take him on his own merits and come what may.

He reined in at the rock-studded pathway to the house. He spotted the girl just as she spotted him. He smiled broadly as he watched her drop the wash she was hanging on a spindly line, grab her skirt in her hands, and run barefoot to the house. Gone to tell her mama that I'm here, Higgins thought happily. 'And well she might, for all the pleasure I mean to be bringing to the both of them. He licked his lips, wondering how long he was going to have to wait before he made that dream a grasping reality. He liked to think of the two of them, wiggling their bodies around next to him as he pressed and prodded and explored all their femaleness. But he had to put thoughts like that out of his mind, he rebuked himself sternly as he spun himself off his horse, no use getting all hot and nasty over something that needed waiting.

He looped the reins over the post that stood by the side of the house and slapped Boss cheerfully on the flank as he left her to scrape up whatever grass she might find there. He walked into the house, stooping down to accommodate his bulky frame in the low doorway. The Widow Jarvis was cooking something in a heavy black pot. Smoke filled the small room as the daughter hovered nervously in a corner.

She's just like a bird, Higgins thought, feeling almost tender toward the girl, a scared little white bird, afraid to leave the nest and afraid to try her wings. He grinned to himself; we'll take care of that soon enough, he thought.

He addressed himself to the mother. "Morning," he grunted cheerfully.

"Morning, Mr. Higgins," Jen Jarvis replied, wiping her hands on the cloth tied in front of her skirt and coming up to greet him. Although he hadn't yet said anything to make his intentions known, she was sure that it was only a matter of time. A man didn't come visiting regularly unless he had a reason to, another reason entirely, which didn't show. Not everybody could tell, but she knew. There was something about the man when he was ready and she could always tell. She knew his patch of land to be not much more than her own, but she knew that having a man, any man, was better than having none when a woman was in her condition of life. It was impossible for her and the girl between them to do what was man's work on a farm and any help was welcome help, especially if it carried the promise of, if not marriage, then at least an end to the hard workdays and lonely, restless nights.

She had seen enough of life to know that. Hell, what fool wouldn't know it? Jen Jarvis was not pretty; she knew that, had been told it often enough. Her short, coarse black hair lay unruly on her head, just like nigger hair; she'd been teased often enough about that, too. Her teeth jutted out too much behind her upper lip, nor had the years been kind. She had never been one to make the men stand up and take notice, even as a girl; but she could take this man in, cook for him, clean for him, and make things better somehow for both of them. Then, too, she had the girl to think about. Going on sixteen now, she was, and with no more prospects in front of her than her mother had. It was even worse for a poor girl now than it had been before the war, what with so many of the young men of the parish gone off and gotten killed. Her Myrtie was a quiet girl, not given to saying much, but she was hardworking and obedient. If no man came along to claim her she would at least be a help and comfort to her mother.

Higgins sat down at the table. Jen Jarvis filled an earthenware bowl from the pot she was cooking in and motioned to her daughter to set it in front of their visitor.

"Thank you, girl," Higgins muttered. He was suddenly anxious to get on with it. If he asked and got an answer quickly, there would be that much less time to wait. He wondered if she would speak in front of the girl or whether he should send her out of doors. He looked over to where Jen stood watching him, her arms folded in front of her thin body, her small, drawn face an unreadable mask.

He cleared his throat. "I mean to have a word with you," he said. "Would you be wanting to have her"—he gestured toward the daughter with his chin—"be out of the way?"

"Aye, if you've got a mind," Jen answered, indicating the door with a quick gesture. The girl walked out.

Jen walked slowly to the table. She said nothing; she waited for him to continue.

Higgins plunged right in. "It seems no point to me for you to be scratching around this place down here and me doing the same at my holding. We could do better to join up together and work just the one place. We could sell this off, and you and that gal could move in with me." It was a statement but he waited for an answer.

Jen closed her eyes. Neither the idea he presented nor the words he used to say it surprised her. She knew even before he brought up the matter what her answer would be. Now she could be as practical-minded as he was. "Your place bigger than this?" she asked.

Higgins nodded. "More acreage, soil's about the same, but being as it is worked by a man there's more yield."

She nodded. "And the house? Big enough?"

"I aim to build another piece to it," he explained. "Make another room maybe, for the girl."

"That's good," she said quietly.

"Then you'll do it?" The eagerness in his voice surprised her somewhat, but pleasantly.

"Aye." She permitted herself a small smile. "Aye, I'll do it."

Higgins beamed. "When next I see you, it'll be to fetch you and the girl and all of the packings of what you want to bring with you. I ain't got much"—he looked around the sparely furnished room—"but we should do good and someday . . ." He was on the verge of telling her how important he was going to be and how much better off she would find herself, but he remembered the strict warnings of his gentlemen visitors and he held his tongue. He knew it was a test and although he was the only one aware of it, he was not going to fail. He turned the matter instead to the other concern that most occupied his mind. "The girl," he said simply. "How do you call her?"

"Myrtie," she said. "She be called Myrtie."

7

"Jason, what is it?" Emilie's voice was insistent in the dark night air. She felt as though the room were closing in on her, as if Jason, lying beside her, was as hard and immune to her pleading as the very walls of the room and the furniture placed massively inside it. It was only a week before that she had at last broken through to him and felt once again the sweet goodness of their physical love, but her happiness had been almost as short-lived as their embraces of that night. For the very next night, she had found him not the eager lover she thought had returned to her but the same stolid, indifferent stranger who lay unmoving beside her now. And so it had been for all of the week.

Emilie felt a sheen of perspiration clinging to her face and body, curling her hair into damp tendrils around her neck and shoulders. She brushed the mass of dark curls back from her face. She had been gazing down at Jason, her hand cupping her chin for she knew not how long. Now she knew she must have been long indeed in the position, and she felt tiredness aching in her arms. She sighed and lay down completely, her head on her pillow, her body moving in the bed until she was nestled on her side, her back turned to him.

She moved toward the end of the wide bed, leaving a broad space between them. Despite the heat, Emilie unconsciously hugged herself close. She screwed her eyes shut in the darkness and found her thoughts wandering back to Guy and the precious few days she had known with him. The remembrance of his ardor made her flush and grow almost weak with longing; she pressed herself even harder and tried to push his memory from her mind. It was almost as though he were there in the bed with them and Emilie felt overcome with the shame and guilt of disloyalty. She squeezed tightly, trying to force memory from her mind and body.

Jason was a good man; she herself must be wicked indeed to let such thoughts impose themselves on her, she thought.

Yet Guy's lovemaking was as vivid in her memory as Jason's. If her first husband were with her now, she knew she would not be left to fend for herself in the darkness, thinking evil thoughts.

Guy had been torn from her side by orders he could not disobey. Jason had remained with her, for love, he had said, a free man, at his own choosing. Yet for all his presence in their bed, he might as well have been as absent as poor, dead Guy.

Emilie squeezed her limbs tightly together. She wanted Jason and she wanted an heir to Les Chandelles. Both, it would seem, were close enough to touch, but for reasons she could not fathom, neither seemed to be within her reach.

She slipped from the bed and went to the window. The fine white muslin curtains hung almost lifelessly. Even the dark of night in this season could not provide breeze enough for the faintest stirring. The moon hung high in the sky, its sharp outline obscured in the west by a haze of clouds that hung like a soft veil in front of it. The orb's silver gleam illumined the curled edges of the clouds, making them look as meticulously drawn as in an etching. The moonlight touched the top most branches of the tall trees that bordered the far end of the lawn, where the forest area separated the mansion and its grounds from the slave quarters. All that was obscured and the land lay silent and sleeping.

Emilie gazed in the direction of the unseen quarters. There, too, lay something inexplicable to her mind. The newly freed men had for the most part gone enthusiastically about the business of obtaining lumber through Jason and building their own small houses. Jess had been among the first to take advantage of the arrangement whereby freestanding cabins could be built and the cost of the wood and other supplies charged against future yields.

Jess had immediately declared himself unwilling to return to the hut he had shared with his grandfather as a slave. Until his house was finished, he preferred rolling up a blanket and sleeping outdoors in front of it.

But for Missy, Emilie reflected, there was no such choice. Because Jess was unwilling to set a date for marrying her, she was unable to stay with him. It was paradoxical, but the girl who as a favored house servant had always slept in her mistress' chamber was now one of the few blacks to be living in the old, run-down quarters. Most of the others had already completed their simple new residences in the area that Jason, Henrique, the ex-slave overseer, and the surveyor brought up from the city had designated for the new houses.

The irony that Missy, who had always hated and feared the quarters, was now living there was not lost on her former mistress. Emilie wished there was something she could do for her. At least, she reminded herself, I have the comfort of marriage. Jason, save for this wretchedly long and unexplained nightly abstinence, was loving and correct in every other regard, more than fulfilling all of the responsibilities of a good husband. Poor Missy, Emilie commiserated silently, has not even got that. She waited for so long, from the time Jess had run away through all the long hard years of the war. She had never given up her dream of his eventual return to her. Now the dream had been fulfilled but Missy seemed doomed to endless, endless waiting.

There was nothing in the landscape below that Emilie did not know totally in her heart, yet she remained standing barefoot at the window, not wanting to go back to her bed. There was nothing in the scene to keep her, nor anything about the house itself to compel her to leave the bedchamber. Yet she felt seized with a restlessness she could not explain. While all the visible earth and the house itself were silent and unmoving she could not ease herself back into bed and sleep. She was rooted at the window only for want of another place to be.

She had not the management of the estate to worry about; Jason had taken all of those burdens from her. Since his purchase of Les Saules had caused the destruction of its house and the death of the chattel, it was that property that was to be divided among the Les Chandelles people. Because the smaller plantation had lacked its own factory, Les Saules's sugar had always been brought to Les Chandelles for grinding. Now the ex-slaves, growing their own crops on the divided upriver plantation, would be beholden to the Bonfils estate for purchase of their acreage, grinding and shipping the sugar, tools and materials for building the houses and working the fields, and for the starter cane, the cut sections of slender stalk from which all new crops were grown. To pay for all that, the new freedmen would work the Les Chandelles brakes, and Les Chandelles would share in the men's own crops as well. Because of this distribution of land to the former slaves, which provided the means to earn their livelihood, Jason found the idea of sharecropping almost utopian. It would, he had often told her, make the ex-slaves and the South itself prosperous and self-standing. Emilie no longer concerned herself with such things. The management of the land and the people was always meant to be men's work. She had been taught to think of the people who had belonged to her as property and to regard them, and their problems, in that light. She was fond of those whom she had grown to know, but the burden of the fields and the men had almost broken her, and she had been more than happy to relinquish the responsibility for them to Jason. Now only the house itself was her immediate care, that and the problems of the female ex-slaves, who still, out of habit, came to her with their questions and concerns.

Emilie felt suddenly lonely. Les Chandelles had never been, unlike most other estates of its size and grandeur, a social gathering place for the surrounding gentry. She had heard stories, mostly told by the kitchen servants when she was a little girl, about the lavish fetes and glamorous balls that her great-grandfather, the founder, old Raymond Bonfils, had staged in the first years when the estate he had hacked out of the wilderness had become rich and ornate enough to hold such grand entertainments. His son, Étienne, had been, from all she had heard, of much sterner and more businesslike demeanor. Such, she supposed, were the causes of her father, Charles, never holding much for frivolous pursuits. The great exception had been her cotillion debut, and, she supposed, her wedding and that of her dead brother, Chaz, would have been other memorable landmark occasions had they occurred during the old order of things.

But Charles was gone and so was Chaz, both buried beneath the Les Chandelles earth, in a little area set aside and marked by a neat white fence. Emilie often visited the little cemetery to make sure that it was being properly maintained. Sometimes she made her pilgrimage to the site of her father's grave out of loneliness and the great compelling need she had for him. At such times she tried to spill out her heart to him as though somehow he would be able to answer her and tell her in that strong, unquestioning way of his exactly what she should do, but no such answers ever came. Emilie often found herself so choked with loneliness that the visit always ended in her hastening back to the house. It was only on All Saints' Day that, like all the other Louisiana Creoles, she visited each of the family graves in order to decorate them afresh and leave tokens of remembrance—flowers, candles, and sometimes more permanent mementos.

On her last visit to New Orleans, her first sojourn in the city since before the war, she had gone to the French Market and bought two *immortelles*—oval glass plaques set in frames fashioned from wire and set with beads and shipped all the way from France—to decorate each of her parents' graves. The sentiments, inscribed on each in French, were even more somber than they would have been in English, she thought when she selected them.

It seemed to Emilie now that all of visible creation spread out below was as silent and ungiving as the roof-covered cemetery behind the neatly carved little wooden fence. There was nothing, it seemed this night, from which she could draw solace.

Jess started from sleep, the arm cushioning his head on the bare ground suddenly seized with a cramp. He wondered for the hundredth time how long it was going to take for him to finish this house of his and sleep once more, if not on a bed, then at least on a cot. Most of the other houses were completed, or nearly so, wanting only roof or doors to signify them done. In spite of the missing parts, many families had already moved happily into their new homes.

But Jess knew he lacked the single-mindedness for such personal progress. He was more concerned with the building of the schoolhouse, a structure that would sit off to the side of the houses and be bigger and, yes, more important than any of them. He had already started schooling; that was one of the reasons the work on his house was going so slowly. Teaching was taking up many of his daylight hours, yet he could not stop himself. He knew that men, women, and children could sleep on the ground and still be free, but if they could not read and write they would always be slaves, slaves to a destiny no better than that they had just come out of.

The school was only the beginning of what was needed, but, he reasoned, you had to start someplace. Mornings when most of the men and many of the able-bodied women were working in the brakes, he took his mule and rode through the small villages and plantations of the parish telling the people about their rights, exhorting them to go to the polls and vote and that when they did, this last tacked on with a broad smile, they should vote for him. In the afternoons, he came back to Les Chandelles to teach the children and the wives and those of the men who retired early from the fields. Although the lessons were supposed to end at dusk, when nobody would be able to make out the letters and digits he so carefully penned for them, questions would come thick and fast from the people. They longed to know about his experiences in the outside world, what the North was like, and the cities, and the army, and the war that had brought them this sudden freedom. They would keep Jess there for hours sometimes, and in spite of himself, he could not deny them. Work on the house would have to wait for those few odd hours he managed to find each week.

Because the former masters still oversaw the work of the field hands, he was frequently frustrated in his efforts to speak to the men as they labored; thus he had to ride far and wide on Sundays, visiting churches and squalid quarters to deliver his message.

Every little bit of encouragement he received spurred him to work even harder and longer at the teaching. Were he to become successful in his bid for office, that would overtake everything. He would have to leave the plantation and go to New Orleans. He had to teach as much as he could to as many as he could reach, hoping all the while to discover the brightest among them, who could learn enough to fill Jess's place as teacher once the legislature was in session.

Jess wondered, not for the first time, why he was unable to get Missy to come to the classes. She had resisted the idea from the first, and now she didn't even want to discuss it. She seemed resentful of the time he gave over to teaching; that alone should induce her to attend, he reasoned to himself; at least we would be spending more time together. But Missy didn't seem to see it that way, nor did she deem learning to read and write of any great importance to herself. When he asked her what she wanted, trying to understand the horizons of her life, she always gave him the same answer, eyes misting softly and words spoken low: that she wanted to take care of him, and his house and their children. Other than that, the practical side of her argued, she would continue to attend Miss Emilie in order to earn some money. For neither of these outlets did she feel the need to know how to read and write.

Jess would argue gently with her about the importance of education for all of them. He appealed to her strong maternal instinct by describing how good and pleasant it would be for her to teach the children she so much wanted to have, but Missy shook her head. It was the mother's place to feed and clean and care for the children; with such a father as Jess, it would be only natural for him to teach his own.

No amount of persuasive arguing could wrench her from her simply held point of view. It bothered Jess far more than such recalcitrance would, had it come from another slave. He felt a deep affection for Missy, the only emotional bond he had ever formed with any woman. Indeed, if they were to spend their lives as one, her clinging so ferociously to the old ways could not help but be the source of great unhappiness between them. Jess stirred uneasily on the ground, trying to find a more comfortable place for himself. His body was the lean, toughened muscle of the young soldier. Usually he was proud of his strength, but now, he thought wryly, it would have been good to have some padding between his bones and the earth.

Perhaps Missy was right—taking care of your own physical needs and wants should come first. Maybe it was only when a person was truly comfortable that he could give himself to others, but he dismissed that idea immediately. Helping the people, as many of the people as he could, if not all of them at once, was the most important task for any of them. The private comforts would have to be earned; they would come last, not first. Any newly freed man who thought otherwise was a fool and a simpleton. The way was hard and preparation, such as education, was the only way to ease it. If the people were going to allow themselves to be lured by physical ease instead of straining to raise themselves as best they could, it would be a disaster. Already, he thought, there was far too much cheap whiskey and loud gatherings in the quarters, especially on Saturday nights, when the week's work was over and the next day could be spent sleeping it off.

For him Sunday meant yet another continuation of his weekly rounds but Jess was forced to admit to himself that such was not the case for most of his comrades. Even some of the tough field hands who managed to attend his classes, and now, with awkwardly held pencil, could sweat out the making of a few letters, were learning to write in order to get jobs that would mean more money and more leisure. They were ripe to learn—he had to admit that to himself—but he could not help but feel that much of the learning was for the wrong reasons.

Still, they wanted to learn for *something*. Missy didn't want to learn at all. Didn't she see how important it was, how much help she could be to him? Jess shifted his weight again, trying to make himself comfortable. The night was calm and quiet. He knew that there were men standing watch at the road and river borders. There had been no incidents at Les Chandelles since the seizing and killing of Judd and the system of sentries had been decided upon by Jason and himself. Why, then, he wondered, all this uneasiness? On a quiet night like this, his sleep should come quickly and easily. He watched as a blur of clouds blotted out the moon, rendering the landscape about him even darker. But the moon was still there, he reminded himself. Tomorrow the sun would shine, the earth would go right on spinning, and somehow or other, all of the problems would get solved.

There was a sudden stirring in the darkness. Jess sprang up, automatically crouching on all fours as he reached for his gun. "Who's there?" he demanded.

There was no answer, just the rustling noise coming closer to him. He cocked the weapon. Then all was still, the black night air burning and pressing around him. A noise again made him turn swiftly around.

"Jess, it's me, Jess."

He sat back on his heels, relief pouring out. "Missy! What are you doing out here in the dead of night?" he asked.

The reply came low and softly, so softly he had to strain to hear it. "I had to see you, Jess, I had to."

"You see me every day, Missy. You don't have to come to me like this," he argued.

"Yes, I do," she said. Then she was silent. There was no need for words. In the darkness she had joined him as he relaxed once again on the ground. She came to him, stretching her length against his, her arms reaching around him and drawing his body tightly against hers.

"Now, Missy," he started to protest.

"No, Jess, no." Her words sounded against his chest. "Don't send me away. I've—I've got to be with you. Now."

Jess scowled. She was right. What she wanted him for was no daytime errand to be done in front of everyone. The pressing need of her body raised his need in him. During the busy round of days he was able to look past the longing in her eyes. He knew he was hurting her, but he told himself always that what he had to do was more important than their personal desires. But as he lay pressed against her in the darkness, the still heat of the Louisiana night crushing against them, the daytime logic could no longer prevail. He felt himself stiffening against her, not with the resolve that would thrust her away but with his own rising need answering hers. "Missy," he breathed softly, and all the discipline of his demands fell away, as if freeing his flesh from a chafing shackle.

He felt her mouth searching for his and he pressed his lips to hers, startled momentarily by the eager wetness he found there. He held her head in his hand, his strong, splayed fingers grasping the back of her skull so that he could drive his tongue ever deeper, needing her embrace and answering, overwhelming it with the force of his own.

Jess felt Missy trembling against him. The tremor ran through her body with a strength that surprised him. Her small hands made eager fists that pounded against his back as he shifted slightly so that he lay over her.

He felt her legs separate beneath him and he had only to move the tattered remnants of her skirt gently to find her open and ready for him. Even before his guiding hand could show the way, she lifted her legs, accommodating herself to him.

He released his grip on her head and she fell back on the ground. Looking down at her, Jess could see her dark eyes blazing. They burned with an expression familiar enough to him to be understood, yet her passion was softened somehow by the implicit love and trust he saw there also. She was no mere woman come to him in the night solely from animal passion, but a being who knew herself to be his woman and who came to him as such.

Jess bit against his own lip and closed his eyes from the love he saw. He needed her, too, but he knew it was in a way that was different from hers. And he knew, right or wrong, he had to have her. Grateful that she had come to him, he nevertheless felt guilty, knowing that he was giving her less than she was giving him.

But she never felt any lack. Missy drew her limbs back, her fists again busy against him, urging him, drawing him closer and closer to her, longing wetly to feel him inside her and to know that everything was as it should be. It had to feel as good to him as it did to her, she knew, and it would make everything all right between them.

She groaned loudly when she felt him at last inside her and she moved her hips wildly to accommodate him. She breathed in sharply, as if she were finding space inside her for him. Then, with all the fury that her small body possessed, she clenched her legs around his back. She felt his power driving everywhere through her. She was no longer conscious of what she was doing. Her fingers dug into his flesh, her heels spurred him on, digging against his flanks. She was now the driver, now the driven, as the thrusting force whipped them into mindless frenzy. She knew not the gasping sounds that escaped from her mouth, nor the small, bloody crescents her nails were drawing in the smooth ebony flesh of his back. She knew only the fury that compelled her, thrusting her hips tighter against his, forcing the arch in her back that propelled him ever deeper inside her.

She laughed out loud once, her body taken with the delight of his endless caressing, but she was as oblivious of that as she was of everything else she was doing. "Jess! Jess!" Only his name came reeling through her brain, coming in like a breath of air, blowing out again like its release. Her very pulse pounded to his name, unbidden as every other motion of her body, her senses living now a life of their own, her heated distraction now coming closer and closer to its fulfillment.

"Jess! Jess!" It wasn't just the breathing of his name now, but a loud exultation as she felt herself spinning endlessly in the whirlpool of his thrust.

Now her limbs were trembling. Her arms and legs shook as though they lived an independent life. She felt her whole body tremble as she regained her senses and mind, and the flesh sank back, gathering in the delights that had pulsated in her ears, and she closed her eyes. Now, now it all slowed down into quiet little eddies that brought her back to awareness of the night sky glittering above them and the hard, unyielding ground beneath.

"I love you, Jess," she whimpered.

Not Jess nor the ground nor the sky nor anything else answered her.

8

The day dragged on endlessly. Higgins straightened his sweating back from his stooped position in the fields and, with his shielding arm against his forehead, searched the sky for the hundredth time that morning. The hot sun was stubbornly maintaining its position, seeming to him not to be moving at all. This night was to be the most important one of his life, yet the blasted, blasting sun would not inch its way across the searing sky to permit its onset.

Higgins glanced hastily back in the direction of the house before he bent once more over his hoe. He grunted with satisfaction at seeing the thin curl of gray smoke coming from the chimney, which meant she was cooking already and, if he chose to, he could leave the field at midday and go back to the house for a decent meal instead of just the nigger food and jug of lukewarm water that he used to satisfy himself with.

It had been too much trouble and waste of time to leave off farming in the middle of the day, trudge back to the house, and prepare and wait for his own fresh food. But now, since he had brought the two Jarvis females and their muleload of goods to his place, one or the other of them was always fussing about the pots. One or the other, he repeated to himself, grinning—

didn't matter to him which one it was. Not in the kitchen, not anyplace else.

But he didn't want to think of that now. Nothing could occupy his mind this day but the momentous events of the night to come. Men would be riding in, secretly and cautiously, from all over the state. His contingent would be no less important and prominent than any other, when all stood around the cleared field of the rendezvous to take the oaths and light the fires that would make more than brothers all those assembled there. What he was doing with the Widow Jarvis was sinful and what he was planning to do with the daughter even more so. While he usually relished the idea of both and turned them over constantly in his mind, he was determined that no such dirtiness, no matter how much he loved it, would sully the holiness of this day.

Sweat crept between his lids, blurring his vision and stinging his eyes. He leaned one hand on the pole of his hoe and with the other tried to wipe his eyes. The black hat he always wore kept the sun from beating down directly on his head, but it was heavy and seemed to cut like a knife into his brow. Higgins pushed the hoe into the earth at an angle and let it stand. He brushed his hands on his overalls and headed toward the house. At least under the roof he could remove the hat and perhaps find some comfort in the shadowy interior. Anything would be better than this endless sun and its refusal to move more quickly across the sky. The burning orb had not yet reached its zenith; when that happened the day would become oppressively hotter and more unbearable.

He had not planned to work a full day in the fields anyway; the place of rendezvous given to him by Romain on the last visit was several hours away on horse and he had arranged with his men to meet at a spot just outside the parish border so that they would arrive together. Once at the final gathering place, in the dead of night, when the Louisiana men would be assembled, they would be initiated. The grand order of the organization would be explained to them in detail and the various branches for each parish would be established.

This, for Higgins, was the most important part. He was determined that none other but himself should lead.

Inside the cabin he watched silently as Jen, her back to him, leaned over the stewpans. He sniffed appreciatively, then walked inside quietly, coming up behind her and grabbing her about the waist.

The large wooden spoon she held in her hand clattered to the floor as she jumped at his touch. "You—you scared me, she said, almost accusing him, but still with that trace of fear of him in her voice that Higgins had come to recognize and like. She was fearful of displeasing him and very seldom dared to criticize or offer suggestions counter to his own. He liked that trait of obedience in a woman; it made him feel as though he had infinite power over her. He knew it took little on his part for her to do his bidding and that was a source of satisfaction to him.

As for the daughter, she seldom spoke at all, whether yea or nay. She seemed to tremble at his very being and always found silent reasons for being where he was not as soon as he entered the house, but that, he thought, would make it all the more fun when the day came that he would put himself between her and the door. But this was not the day, he reminded himself, to think about that. There was time enough. He could have had them both by now but he rather enjoyed prolonging it. He was tantalizing himself and tormenting the frightened little rabbit of a girl at the same time. All the more would be the pleasure when he broke her at last.

Again he had to remind himself to relinquish such thoughts on this day of days. He had come in from the fields not for fornication or even the thought of it but for the sustenance that would keep him going for the rest of the day. He wanted all his strength and vigor in reserve for the night's activities.

"Who are you expecting that I frightened you?" he asked Jen. "Who else but me would be coming in here in the middle of the day?"

There was almost an accusation in his voice and she grew even more startled. "Nobody, nothing," she muttered. "I just wasn't expecting you, that's all."

He grasped her waist even more tightly, twisting a fold of flesh cruelly until she gasped. Then, smiling, he released it and his hand traveled farther up her bodice, grasping her breast.

She inhaled sharply, completely aghast at his physical approach at such an unlikely time, in the clear light of the day. "Don't," she whimpered as his nails dug harder into the scrawny but yielding flesh. "She–she could come in and see."

"Hell!" Higgins snorted. "She's old enough to more than see. How long you aim on keeping her ignorant, woman?"

"She–she ain't ready." Jen's voice was still a whimper. "Some come to it quicker than others. And this gal, she's slower about it than most."

"Well, maybe we'll just have to see about speeding her up a little bit," Higgins said cruelly, his eyes gleaming, his hand not relinquishing its grip. He was spurred by the fear in Jen's eyes and voice, and his mind was inexorably fastened on the lust he could not put aside.

"I'll take you here and now if I have a mind to," he warned her. "But first I'll have my grub. Go fix it." He let go of her breast and walked over to the table, shoving the bench aside with his boot so he could sit.

She ladled the stew into a big bowl in front of him. Higgins ate in silence as he scraped the last of it. He started to ask Jen where the girl was but then thought better of it, realizing that he didn't particularly care. He had a good full belly and the idea of having to exert himself held no temptation, whether back in the fields or with a female. He arched his back slightly, scratching his ribs, and decided to spend the rest of the day in bed alone. He got up from the table and pushed aside the thin curtain hanging between the two rooms that served for a door. He stretched himself out on the bed, not bothering to take off his boots. After all, he wasn't going to sleep for the night, just resting before meeting the others. No reason to have to tug the boots on again.

In minutes his snoring punctuated the heavy sleep of the weary. It wasn't until he somehow felt darkness coming on that his eyes flew open and he propped himself up on one elbow, trying to shake the sleep from his head. It was almost dusk. Time to be leaving.

He grabbed his hat as he strode out of the house. He unhitched the old mare and got on it. He barely glanced at Jen, standing in the doorway looking up at him wonderingly. He poked the horse and wheeled her around. Higgins rode off without a word to the woman standing in the doorway. He took no notice of Myrtie, standing at the clothesline back of the house, watching him silently as he rode off.

He veered around once he left his property, to take the road that ran alongside the river. This would put him along the boundary of Les Chandelles farthest from the big house and any other activity. He wanted to see as little of them as possible, especially tonight. And wanted them to see nothing at all of him. Since the visit, weeks before, of Romain and Elmore, he had dutifully stopped any activities against the blacks of the area. It chafed him to think of all of the weeks now gone by without incident since the night they had strung up Judd. But soon enough, he thought, gloating, he would be getting instructions and carrying out a more organized program of terror. It would be time enough when the haughty, unheeding folks of the big plantation would get theirs. The destruction of Les Chandelles and its people, black and white, was uppermost in his plans. He knew that once he had the trust of the new leaders he would get their backing as well, and they would be agreeable to listening to his plans and letting him put them in action. When that day came, the people of the plantation would be taken completely by surprise and their anguish and agony would be so much the sweeter to him. He was a patient man; just as he could bide his time with Myrtie, so could he wait to spring his trap on the Bonfils and all who were with them. Someday he would burn Les Chandelles, and as he pictured the licks of flame rising through the cane fields he could see the white body of the girl rising under him. She, too, would burn, Higgins thought, grinning, but in a different way. The girl, the mother, the hated estate—soon they would all know his power and feel the weight of his boot.

He urged the horse into a gallop. He rode without stopping until he came to the agreed-upon meeting place. Four of the men were already there.

"How many more we got to wait for?" he asked Dukes.

"Four more coming," Dukes answered, grinning. Higgins could see his own eagerness for the night's activities reflected in the eyes of his younger cohort. Dukes would make a good second-in-command for him, once the lines had been drawn and everybody set in place. The man had been with him from the first night, the burning down of Les Saules and the butchering of the people. He remembered the reflected light of the fires on Dukes' face and his momentary disappointment when Higgins let the old landowners free. He realized immediately that Dukes would have as soon put a bullet through the old man's head or thrust the two of them into the flames with the ex-slaves. But it had been their first foray and he didn't know how the rest of the gentry would take the murdering of their own, even if they were thought traitors, so he had stayed his hand and let them go on to

Les Chandelles. Dukes would not have and this was important to know, Higgins thought. He would need restraints, but he could be counted on to carry out any orders, no matter how rough.

Within minutes the rest of their cohorts had arrived. Higgins raised his hat in the air with the military gesture to advance. He took the lead and the other men followed fast behind, Dukes riding at his side, not quite even with him but close enough for them to talk and plan as they rode.

A large field had been cleared just above the southern border of the neighboring parish. As they approached they could hear the noise of many men and horses. The road veered through a grove of trees wide enough for them to ride only in single file. Higgins stayed at the head of their small column. Now, beyond the trees, he could see the flare of lights and hear more distinctly the shouts of the men, but it was not enough to prepare him for what greeted him when at last they cleared the trees and were at edge of the field.

There must be a thousand men here, he thought in amazement. Hitching posts had been hastily erected for the quartering of the horses and Higgins slid eagerly out of his saddle and motioned his men to do likewise. When the animals were secured, they walked to the center of the field, where an enormous bonfire was blazing. The perimeters had been marked with uprights thrust into the ground at regular intervals and now these too flared, throwing wildly moving lights and shadows across everything. In the glare Higgins could see men's faces as excited as his own.

As if to a magnet, men were moving from all parts of the clearing to the fire in the center.

"Must be a thousand men here," Dukes said excitedly, echoing Higgins' own thought.

"Not more than two or three hundred, at most." Higgins recognized the always cool, detached voice of

Lynch. Higgins started to argue the number but stopped himself. There was something in the easy knowing of the man's voice that made him grudgingly admit he might be right. Besides, he was more interested in scanning the crowd and looking for the familiar faces of Romain and Elmore than he was in squabbling with someone he had long ago decided was to be nothing more than just another one of the men around him.

Several feet in front of the big blaze, men were piling up lengths of wood plank for a makeshift speaker's platform. The rest of the crowd, merging on the site, stood watching, confident now that the leaders would soon appear and the great business of the evening begin.

Higgins shouldered his way through the crowd, motioning for his men to follow him. They stood waiting, close to the front ranks of the crowd.

Higgins spotted his two mentors. He poked Dukes with his elbow, indicating the two men but not saying anything. Since everything about the organization was supposed to be secret, he felt it was good for him to start learning to hold his tongue. He would confide in Dukes and possibly the others only what was absolutely necessary. He knew that cultivating the same air of secrecy that had so impressed him would work the same way on the men who followed him.

At last the planks were of sufficient height. A man walked gingerly up one side as if he were testing the stability. Higgins was surprised to see Romain and Elmore stay in their places. He had thought that surely they would address the assemblage. He felt a prick of disappointment.

The man who had mounted the platform spread his arms palms down, gesturing for quiet. With the reflex of men only recently out of military life, they all fell silent immediately. The lean and distinguished-looking man smiled his approval. He was dressed in a black frock coat and trousers and his stiff white shirtfront gleamed. His tall black stovepipe hat reminded Higgins of the one worn by the detested Abe Lincoln but he put the thought out of his mind. As soon as the man spoke there was no question but that they were being addressed by the very flower of white southern aristocracy. Higgins glanced over to Romain and Elmore. Their faces reflected the same total admiration.

The man began to speak. "Gentlemen." The word rang out over the crowd like a gift from above. Certainly no one standing in the crowd had ever so titled himself or been addressed that way. They were all, so far as Higgins could tell, poor dirt farmers like himself, wearing the rough, worn breeches and work shirts of the lowly. Only Romain and Elmore, standing close to the platform and somewhat apart from the rest of them, looked or sounded anything like the speaker. The thrill of the greeting seemed to reverberate through the crowd.

"Gentlemen, we are gathered together here this night for a sacred and holy cause. This ground you stand upon is hallowed earth." The man paused, as if to let the importance of his words sink in. "The business we undertake here tonight is the unfinished business of our homeland. Those who fought to defeat us shall themselves know instead its bitterness."

Higgins listened intently as the speaker went on talking about honor and blood and glory.

"That's all right for them dandies," Dukes growled in a low tone to Higgins, indicating Romain and Elmore with a thrust of his stubbled chin, "but what's there in all this for the likes of us?"

Higgins shoved him slightly to quiet him. He didn't understand everything that was being said, but he knew he liked it. He liked the way the man spoke to them, as if they were his equals, as if they weren't coming to this place from different worlds. He wanted to hear what the gentleman had to say, not the disgruntled comments of his own sidekick.

But then it seemed as though the man had somehow heard the complaint. He spoke to the men now about themselves and their condition. "You had little enough before," he told them. "Only what you could get from the sweat of your brow, your breaking backs, the strength of your hands. Then the Yankees came to take that little away from you. They had the guns, they had the factories, they had the ships and the railroads and the rest of the world on their side, and so they were able to bring us down." He paused a moment for effect. "Now that they've come to take it away from us they think they can add insult to injury by giving what little we have left to the niggers. Oh, it's not their land they're giving away. No, sir, you don't see them parceling out sections of Ohio and Pennsylvania, do you?" He made the last a direct question to the crowd. "Do you?" he repeated.

"No!" The answer came rumbling back from them.

"Damn right you don't!" he thundered. "It isn't the food out of their mouths they're giving away, is it?"

"No!"

He stood silent for a moment, towering over them, gesturing again for total silence. He didn't speak until he got it and then his voice rose dramatically. "And it isn't their wives and their sisters and their daughters he's laying helpless in front of those ignorant, murdering, raping nigras, either." His voice was little more than a whisper now but his words carried to the farthest fringes of the crowd, standing spellbound listening to him. "Are we going to stand for it?" he demanded, and got the answer he expected with a roar from the men.

"NO!"

"Repeat this after me," he ordered. "'The South will rise again! The South will rise again! The South will rise again.'" The flames danced higher than ever behind him.

Higgins could hear the hissing and crack of the logs feeding it. Once in a while one fell heavily against another and made a booming noise, but now even that sound was drowned out by the shouting of the men, thundering in unison as they had been instructed. "The South will rise again! The South will rise again!" Higgins shouted until he felt his throat raw and burning and his own words echoing hoarsely in his ears. The shouting continued, the same words over and over again for a full five minutes, while the man stood on the platform, his arms folded, his eyes scanning the crowd ceaselessly, the flickering fire putting his countenance now in shadow, now in bright glow. At last he signaled for quiet and the roar subsided. "Are you ready, men?" he asked. "Are you ready for this great enterprise, ready with your lives to save our country and our women?"

The roar that came back was hoarse, like two-hundred-odd Higginses. It was affirmative as the man, nodding now, knew that it would be.

"We are the Knights of the White Camellia," he said as soon as the crowd was silent again. "We shall ride, we shall burn, we shall kill, until we once again have what is rightfully ours. Are you with me, men?"

It sounded like a thousand voices shouting yes, *yes*, against the flames, against the dark trees, into the sudden wind that had risen in the darkness.

"We shall take the oath," he said, signaling to Romain and Elmore to join him on the platform.

Higgins was elated; even more than by the burning words of the orator was he moved by seeing the two men he considered his friends sharing the prominence of the stage.

"I will recite the pledge," he stated, "and you will, each man, repeat it after me. Then Mr. E. will hold out this holy Bible and will signal each of you up here in turn to kiss the book. That will be your sacred pledge, binding us together for all time. Should there be"—and he looked meaningfully around at the crowd, from side to side, as if scanning each face—"should there be amongst us any coward, he had better leave this company at once. Go now, ye bastards, and speak of what has transpired here tonight only if you want to meet your death."

No one stirred.

"Let us begin. We the Knights . . ."

"We the Knights . . ." the chant came back.

". . . of the White Camellia . . ."

". . . of the White Camellia . . ."

". . . do here pledge our lives . . ."

". . . our lives . . ."

". . . our honor and our fortune . . ."

". . . our honor and our fortune . . ."

". . . to serve our cause, our country . . ."

". . . our cause, our country . . ."

". . . and the sacred honor of Christian white womanhood . . ."

". . . and the sacred honor of Christian white womanhood . . ."

". . . by whatever means necessary," the speaker concluded.

". . . by whatever means necessary," the crowd echoed back.

"Our law is our own law," he thundered. "And the essence of our law is secrecy. Man to man and all of us against the traitors and dogs of the outside world." He put his hand inside his cloak and held aloft a long, gleaming knife that drew a gasp from the crowd. "If any among you is frightened, let him say so now," he warned. "For the oath of the Knights is an oath of blood. Blood we shall give and blood, many times over, we shall take!"

Elmore signaled to a man standing at the edge of the crowd, beckoning to him to be the first to come up to the platform. Higgins watched, fascinated, as the procedure began. The first man ordered was told something—Higgins could not catch the words—to which he mumbled in return, stooping to kiss the thick, black-covered Bible that Elmore held out. Then the man moved on, standing face to face with the speaker, who nodded and grasped the man by the arm. Higgins could see the knife move against the flesh a few inches above the wrist. Romain held a large brass basin in which the blood spurted, then the man rolled his sleeve back down, clenching the wound, walking off the other end of the platform, and disappearing in the anonymity of the crowd.

They were moving quickly now, one man after another, first to reach Elmore and then to receive the sacrificial gash and the rite of bloodletting into the basin.

Higgins found himself growing agitated as he and his men moved closer to the platform. When at last he clambered up, he flashed Romain a wide grin of recognition but the other did not respond. He administered the few words of oath to Higgins and listened for his acquiescence, his hand stiffly holding out the Bible. Higgins stooped over to press his lips against it briefly before moving on, arm exposed, to where the speaker, whose name he was never to know, stood with knife poised.

Higgins clenched his fist, making his forearm muscle bulge. He winced as he felt the knife go in, his eyes shut tightly, not wanting to see it. When he opened them, there was a thin red line in his arm and he held it over the quickly filling basin to contribute his droplets to the others. Elmore showed no sign of recognition, either. This troubled him as he walked off the platform; he would have liked to have established the certainty of his command and the procedure for getting back to the business of subduing the parish. It was with sharp disappointment that he knew all of this would have to wait, wait no doubt until one or the other of the two contacted him. Until then, all would be silence.

He frowned at this, wondering if he would be able to hold the seven men with him for as long as it might take the leaders to make their next move.

He wasn't sure what to do next, whether they were to wait until they were dismissed and told to disburse. But then his attention was caught by two men struggling with a massive crosspiece. It was a thick wooden plank at least eight feet tall, against which a shorter piece of timber had been set about a foot from the top. The men were trying to set the tall cross upright in the soil and Higgins was glad to lend his bulk to help them set it aright. He stood with one of the men holding it in place while the other grabbed a shovel and packed the earth around it so it could stand. This finished, they all gazed up and, with the rest of the crowd that had passed through the initiation, stood waiting. When the last man passed across the stage, the speaker again held his hands out for silence.

"As our cause is holy, so our deeds are holy," he said. Then he signaled to a man who passed a burning torch to Romain.

Romain took it and bent down to the ground, touching it to the bottom of the cross.

It burst into flames instantly and the fire quickly raced up the length of it. Romain straightened and touched the torch to each end of the crosspiece, sending these aflame as well.

The men, hushed now, stood gazing up at the burning cross. The spectacle filled them with awe. Higgins knew he would never forget the sight of it. Although flares continued to burn at the boundaries of the clearing, nowhere was the night so set on fire as where the burning cross stood.

"This is our emblem, gentlemen," the speaker told them. "This is the mark by which all men, friends and enemies alike, will know of our deeds. Go you now, and wait. It won't be long, I promise you. The word will be sent. The deeds will be done. The flames will burn, amen." Then he spoke again, his voice louder than the reverential tone he had formerly taken. "Are you ready?" he roared.

Back came the few hundred voices, sounding like thousands. "Yes! Yes! Yes!"

Then they were sent home.

9

"It's been so peaceful for weeks now," Emilie said. "Perhaps it is over and the worst of it well behind us."

"I wish I could think so, my dear," Jason replied. "But I'm afraid I have not your native confidence in your countrymen."

Emilie looked at him keenly. "Are you forgetting what you have always told me—that we are all once more one country?"

"You're right, of course, Emilie," Jason said, toying with the sweetmeats on his plate. "We are one nation indeed, or will be if the war wounds are allowed to heal peacefully. But if elements in the South insist on reopening them, then I fear we will not see good days for a very long time."

"I don't see why you are so pessimistic about it, Jason," Emilie said. "The parish has been quiet for several weeks now, there have been no killings or burnings here, and from what I have seen of the newspapers the city is quiet as well."

"New Orleans is peaceful only because of the presence of such a large federal military contingent," Jason said. "And once the election is held and the state legislature is reconvened, should power return to the former owners, there may be hell to pay."

Emilie sipped at her Madeira. It was a very old bottle,

dating back, she thought, probably to her grandfather's day. She found it rather musty, although she knew that might be her imagination. No new wines had been brought to the plantation since the outbreak of the war and the reserves of the cellar were satisfying their needs. Even the advent of a large party would make little dent in the vast reserves that had been accumulating since old Raymond Bonfils had first built this house. There was scarcely the likelihood of such an event occurring, Emilie thought sadly. The house, for all its great size and luxury, had never been noted for gaiety. The sole exception, which she thought of repeatedly with great fondness, was her cotillion a year or so before the war. Her first wedding had been conducted with great haste and almost an absence of guests; her marriage to Jason had been sanctified almost in secrecy. Perhaps her parents' wedding or her grandparents' had been celebrated with much festivity, but Emilie could not recollect any conversation of those having been notable events. Now, when she was at last in a marriage that seemed safe and secure, the times were altogether wrong for parties. And the circumstances of her marriage made her something of a pariah among the others of the planter class; she was sure of it. There was very little concourse between Les Chandelles and the other plantations but Emilie knew that they could not look kindly on her marriage to a former Yankee officer.

Les Chandelles seemed somehow fated never to fulfill the role for which it had been built with such great care and expense. Now, five years after the terrible fire, they were just setting about repairing the broken columns of the burned veranda. When, she wondered, would there ever come a time to embellish the property once more, to do more than merely the necessary fixing they were undertaking now? Heaven knew it had taken long enough—all the years of the war—to get even this work done.

All day long the sounds of construction rang out on the plantation, but it was for the building of new houses to replace the old slave quarters. That, and the school that Jess wanted so badly were the reasons for all the activity. Her own house was likely to stand much as it was, maybe even until the end of her days.

"Do houses have roles to play and fates assigned to them as people do?" she asked suddenly.

Jason smiled at her. "Well, I suppose if one believed life to be a series of preordained events, that could hold true," he replied. "What makes you ask such a question, my sweet?"

"It's this gloomy old house," Emilie said with some vehemence in her voice. "It is supposed to be quite the showplace of the parish, if not of the whole state, yet it has anything but the lively history of other places like Belle Hélène or Evergreen. One was forever reading about the fetes and parties held there and the wonderful array of guests who attended."

"And was my lovely young girl among them?" Jason asked gently.

"Once, when I was quite young, perhaps fourteen or so," Emilie recounted dreamily. "I went with my father to visit friends in St. John the Baptist parish and one afternoon we rode over to Evergreen to take tea with the owners. It was quite the loveliest place in the world, I thought then. It had great pillars, like ours, but the veranda was on the second story and two great, wide, curving staircases led there directly from the lawn."

"It does sound lovely," Jason said. He wanted to help her maintain the sweet memory she had found, so unlike the ones that usually haunted her from her past.

"I remembered thinking that if I were lucky enough to live in that house, what great fun I would have just trailing up and down, up and down those round staircases all day." She smiled. "I remember dreaming of what a beautiful sight I would make coming down slowly on the right in a magnificent ball gown to greet the beaux that would be standing at my feet as I descended."

"It makes a very pretty picture even now." Jason smiled.

"Foolish, girlish dreams," Emilie said, "so different from the reality that has come in its stead."

"I know the times must seem bitterly hard to you now," Jason said, leaning across the table and taking her hand, "but perhaps the lovely times can come back again. It needn't be only a dream. If we can build the life I wish to here, then there can be happiness for all of the people and reason enough to open our doors to just such celebrations."

"I hope so, Jason, but somehow I doubt it," Emilie said. "That world seems to me to be completely gone. What little might remain of it, should there be any at all, I fear would be closed to us."

"Does that disturb you very much?" he asked with concern.

Emilie looked up at him and smiled, returning the pressure of his hand on hers. "No, dearest, truly not," she said. "As long as we are happy together, I have no need of extravagant diversion."

"Perhaps your birthday," Jason suggested. "Or our wedding anniversary. Surely we can open the house then and do well by any guest we receive."

"Perhaps," Emilie said. She liked the idea. It gave her something nice to think about, even if it never really would happen. She wondered why she was suddenly plagued by this need for other people. It was hard to admit to herself that the strain of the relations between Jason and herself had opened a gap she had never experienced before. She had been happy enough when she thought the problem had been solved, but when he made no advances to her after the night she had so shamelessly thrown herself on him, the gnawing had begun and now, she had to admit to herself, it had become considerable. Not getting what she wished from Jason, she knew she sought to find something in the company of others.

Not that any amount of company could make up for his lack of passion; she knew sadly that it would be a poor substitute. She counseled patience to herself, knowing he loved her and that she loved him. Perhaps having guests, the diversion of other people around them for a while, would be a tonic for Jason as well. It hit her suddenly that all the while that her old friends from the city, Francine and Gaston Desbrosses, had been with them, evenings downstairs had a ring of gaiety and nights upstairs no lack of that which was so sorely missing now.

"You seem lost in your thoughts, Emilie," Jason said gently.

She looked up at him brightly. "I was just thinking how nice it might be were we to have some company at Les Chandelles again," she said. "When is our agent, Bledsoe, due? Perhaps when he comes up we could invite his wife to accompany him, and Francine and Gaston as well. That should make for lively company, I would think."

"Capital idea!" Jason said. "I think that would suit us eminently. I realize I can't have your pretty face all to myself all the time, it isn't fair."

"Jason, really!" Emilie protested, blushing.

"No rose was ever meant to bloom unseen," he replied, causing his wife to wonder if he was quoting some piece of poetry, for it was so unlike his usual self.

"Then it's resolved," she said. "I'll post a note to Francine tomorrow, inviting them and requesting her to make traveling arrangements with Bledsoe."

Later that night, as she sat before the mirror in their bedroom brushing out her long black hair, she looked up to see him approaching her. He put his hands gently on her shoulders. They looked at each other's reflected image for a moment, Jason squeezing at the pearly flesh that showed above her night robe. "I love you, Emilie," he whispered. "I love you. You do know that, don't you?"

There was a note of desperation in his voice that tore at her heart. Whatever was wrong with Jason, she knew in that instant she was not the cause of it. He was standing there for no other reason than to tell her that. "I know, my darling, I know," she whispered back softly. "Everything is going to be all right."

"They are all coming up on the sixteenth," Emilie said delightedly, scanning the heavy white stationery covered with Francine's familiar, flowing hand. "And she says they are bringing a surprise with them but will not give even the slightest hint of what it will be." She looked up at Jason, her eyes sparkling. "Whatever do you suppose it could be?"

"I haven't the slightest notion," Jason confessed, "but knowing the resources of your lady friend, nothing on earth would surprise me."

The next several days went by in a flurry of activity, leaving Emilie little time to ponder on what Francine's surprise might be. The entire household was shaken out of its usual lethargy. Consultations with cook and housekeeper took up much of Emilie's time. There were important meals to be planned in the greatest detail with Tess, the cook. She, the morose tyrant of the kitchen, seemed to Emilie to be the least changed of all the former slaves by their new condition. Tess had always run the kitchen as a personal fiefdom, her orders to and punishments of the other workers even more demanding and immediate than those the masters themselves gave. She remained solitary, living in a small cabin close behind the big house that, along with several others, domiciled the most important domestic servants. Their little houses near the mansion had always been one of the most important manifestations of their superior status, and though most of the slaves were now building similar houses for themselves and their newly formed families, Tess stubbornly chose to remain where she always had been.

Her two closest peers had not. Robert, since before the time of Charles Bonfils butler and majordomo of Les Chandelles, had married the jubilant, rotund Sully, and, out of his wages, was having a house, large only by the standards of the others, built for them. He had never performed manual labor heavier than that of handling old cases of wine, and freedom was not to make him retrogress from his former status. His wages and Sully's, now paid out monthly by Emilie, permitted him the luxury of hiring labor for his house.

Robert was as correct and detached as ever. But Emilie found her talks with Sully to be rather the highlights of her own day. She was amused at the great change wrought in the little round housekeeper, not so much by freedom as by marriage. Sully preened in being Robert's wife. She strutted about the big house with the appearance almost of a pouter pigeon: breasts held high with pride, bright eyes peering about, always eagerly on the lookout to see if others took notice of her importance. That Robert was having built for her a house of two, *nearly* three rooms was almost enough to make her burst with happiness. Emilie reflected on how wise it was of him to provide himself that extra little private space that the wide-eyed Sully had described to her. His wife's endless, bustling enthusiasm might have overpowered even a more gregarious type than the butler.

It made Emilie feel good to see that things were going so well for these faithful retainers. She knew that others of her own class would have laughed had they known that Robert had insisted that his table at home be laid out with the same meticulous care that was *de rigueur* at the big house. But the idea filled Emilie with delight, not derision.

Now Sully was busied with the preparations for the expected guests. She had once again a flock of housemaids under her wing and she flew about the house all day, issuing orders, ordering supplies, supplying supervision, supervising a round of activity that greatly lightened Emilie's heart. It seemed to her as though the great mansion was once more coming alive. There were only four guests expected but both hostess and staff were determined to make everything perfect.

Emilie especially wanted her table laden with the abundant goodness that the plantation had always been noted for. Even the simplest meals taken *en famille* would have sufficed to feed the most elegant company. All of the plantation's resources and the produce and game of the outlying fields, forests, and stream were chosen by Tess and prepared as only she, so nimble and expert after so many years, could manage.

It was not unusual to have eight or nine courses at an ordinary dinner or for there to be a half dozen or more varieties of meats, fish, and vegetables. Each course was served with its own wine, and the baking ovens were filled from morning to night with the making of breads, pastries, and cakes. It had been a long time, Emilie remembered, since the kitchen was the scene of preparation on such a large scale, but Tess was more than equal to the prodigious task. Quite the reverse, her employer knew, the cook relished the opportunity to make great display of her abilities and seemed to live only for the praise and extra favors that came her way because of it.

Emilie smiled happily at the young maid passing her on the staircase. The girl's face was barely visible over the huge pile of feather-filled blankets she was toting outdoors to be thoroughly aired, beaten, and plumped up before being replaced in the refurbished guest chambers. The house for once seemed not so gloomy to its mistress as the stirring and movement of housekeeping made it come alive. If it was not quite the grand parties she had been thinking of wistfully only a few weeks before, perhaps it was even better. The most lavish fete lasted no more than a night and a day, but the quartet of visitors coming up from the city would stay at least several weeks. The liveliness and sounds of laughter would prevail and keep Emilie's spirits buoyed.

The company arrived just before dusk on the promised day. Emilie, watching from the veranda, was surprised to see that they had made the trip in two carriages. First was the small, familiar, businesslike black coach of the factor Bledsoe, with its baggage and trunks piled high on top. The second carriage was a large, elegantly turned-out brougham, its driver's seat carrying a coachman as well, and Emilie watched as this equally elegantly turned-out personage jumped down to help Francine Desbrosses alight.

Amid the hugs and kisses of greetings, Emilie was barely able to exclaim her admiration for the magnificent carriage when her eye caught a third person being helped down by the coachman. She accepted a kiss on the cheek from Gaston Desbrosses before turning with an expression of wondering to his wife.

Francine caught her hostess' look immediately. "Darling," she declared, "here is my wonderful surprise, in person."

Emilie looked up at the tall, lean young man, startled for a moment by the unexpected handsomeness of his dark-featured face. There was a hint of amusement as well as admiration in his black eyes as he smiled down at her.

Emilie started to greet him, but Francine broke in. "My darling Emilie, allow me to present this handsome devil, my cousin. His name is Robert Camille Gautier Elmore, Jr. Such a mouthful! But we all call him Robin, don't we, darling?" Francine said brightly. "Robin, you may kiss Madame Phillips' hand, but you really don't need me to tell you that, you young rogue."

"Welcome to Les Chandelles, monsieur," Emilie said. "When Francine wrote that she was bringing a surprise, I had no idea what she meant."

"I completely sympathize with you, madam," he answered gallantly. "When my lovely cousin told me of you and your great estate she left me to be equally surprised by the beauty of both."

"I am sorry that my husband is delayed in the fields and was not here with me to greet you," she said smoothly, as though the outrageous compliment had fallen on unhearing ears. "I'm sure he'll be riding up shortly." She turned to the others. "Come inside at once out of the heat, my friends, and take some cool refreshment."

Robert stood silently, holding the great door open as the others followed Emilie inside. The butler motioned to two servants to come forward with silver pitchers of cold tea and fruitades. Then he retired out of hearing, just within sight to receive Emilie's signal when he would be needed again.

"Dear Eurydice." Emilie turned to Madame Bledsoe, whom she had not seen since her marriage to Guy on the eve of the war. "Time cannot touch you, you look exactly the same as when last we met."

"But you, my dear, have grown even lovelier," the big-bosomed and bejeweled Madame Bledsoe replied.

Emilie could not help but be struck by the similarities and differences between the two New Orleans ladies. Both were rather large and blond, commanding presences that seemed to dwarf their respective spouses, but while Eurydice affected much more splendor in her dress and grooming, it was the restrained and sophisticated Francine Desbrosses whose elegance and bearing were the more pronounced. It was as though, Emilie thought, Eurydice was wearing every piece of jewelry she owned all at once, but Francine needed nothing more than the drama of one single gem to set her off. Both women had been good friends to her in times of great need; Eurydice assisting at the hurried wedding preparations that now seemed so long, long ago, and Francine stepping into the breach and coming to Emilie's assistance when Jason had entered Les Chandelles as conqueror and he and she had faced each other as sworn adversaries. It had been Francine who had cooled down both of them and enabled them to see more clearly the irrevocable attraction that was making them fight each other.

Now it seemed like happier times than ever before, and Emilie had all of them here together with her. She followed happily, almost heedlessly, the endless chatter of their conversation, laughing and enjoying herself with a lightness she had not felt in a very long time, her gaiety broken only slightly from time to time as she wondered what was delaying Jason and as she felt the dark, compelling eyes of young Robin Elmore on her.

She tried not to let his obvious attention be noticeable. She glanced at him from time to time as she did at all of the others of the company but kept herself from addressing him individually or singling him out for any special attention.

Anton Bledsoe had always been the business agent for the plantation. Emilie herself had leaned heavily on his advice and instructions over the past five difficult years. The Desbrosses had been family friends for as long as she could remember; they had taken her under their wing even while her parents were still alive. All in all, the two couples were her oldest and dearest friends in the world. She would not allow herself to be discomforted by the presence of the young stranger.

And really, Emilie reasoned with herself as her mind drifted from the eddying conversation about her, he is a distant cousin of Francine's, so there is no reason for me to think of him as a stranger at all. Yet she knew he made her uncomfortable, uncomfortably aware of him as a man and of herself as a woman. Emilie felt faint. I've got to stop thinking like this, she told herself severely. There is no reason for it.

If only Jason were here, she thought wildly, then I'm sure I wouldn't be feeling this way at all. She turned her gaze to Francine, who was describing in great animated detail a recent social gathering down in the city.

"And then, my dear, who do you think he turned out to be," Francine was asking, her voice heightened with drama, coloring the anecdote, "but a Yankee officer?"

"Indeed, and was he someone I might be acquainted with?" Emilie nearly jumped from her seat at the sound of Jason's voice.

For a moment she was terrified that he had come in at absolutely the wrong time and that the point of Francine's story, if indeed there were any, might be taken entirely wrongly by him, but she breathed a sigh of relief when he strode briskly across the room to shake hands with Bledsoe and Desbrosses and smile at the ladies. He stood rather stiffly erect as Robin Elmore was presented to him. Then they, too, shook hands, Jason drew up a chair aside his wife's, and the merriment of the conversation went on unabated.

At last Emilie turned to Jason and said, "I'm sure we are doing our guests no small disservice by allowing them to amuse themselves, Jason, but after the long journey they will be pleased to be able to go upstairs to refresh themselves before dinner."

Almost unbidden, Robert came forward to pull back the chairs and lead the guests upstairs to their respective rooms.

Once behind the closed door of their own chamber, Emilie sat down on the bed with a broad sigh of relief. She looked gratefully at Jason, happy for the bond of love that was so strong between them. She felt protected by his presence, comforted by his strength. It was only at night that he could not fulfill her every need; in every other respect he was a most perfect husband. Emilie sighed again, not in relief this time but with the remembering of his bitter past. As she recalled the unhappiness he had suffered at the hands of his first wife she reminded herself once again that she must not probe too deeply into this problem between them, but must be patient and allow nature to take its course and Jason to work it out in his own good time.

"You are happy having your friends here, aren't you?" he asked tenderly, coming and sitting down next to her on the bed, taking her small hands in his large ones.

"Yes, I am," she answered simply. "Happy that we can open our house to friends and have them here with us." She squeezed his fingers gently.

"What did you think of the surprise?" she asked lightly.

"What surprise?" Jason asked.

"Francine's surprise," Emilie replied. "Don't you remember her letter to me, promising a great surprise? It turns out to be this cousin of hers."

"Oh, yes," Jason said. "Who is he, actually?"

"I really don't know," Emilie said. "Francine has said nothing specific other than that they are distantly related. She seems quite fond of him, though, and I expect we will find out more about him presently."

"I daresay," Jason said. "If those two old war-horses allow him to say anything."

"Oh, Jason, what a thing to say!" Emilie feigned horror. "Those two ladies stand at the highest rank of society!"

"All the more shame to you then, my sweet," he teased her, "for making such an assumption. It was their husbands I was speaking of."

"Oh, Jason!" Emilie kissed him playfully.

"Well, if they don't permit him to declare much about

himself, I'll leave it in your sweet hands to find out whatever there is to know about our surprise guest." He bent his head down to kiss those very hands he was speaking of.

A wave of delight surged through Emilie. Why can't it go on from here? she pleaded silently. Why, oh why must it always stop at this? But she checked herself, ordering her heart to stop its wild beating and rest serene and steady in her trembling breast.

10

Gleaming silver candelabra held flickering tapers that lit the table, and small silver bowls of flowers and fresh fruits graced its length. Everyone was seated, Emilie at the head, wearing her favorite gown, a ruffled pink dress that set off her neck and shoulders most becomingly. From his place opposite her Jason gazed at her with love and pride. Silent uniformed servants carried heaped, ornate platters from the kitchen. Robert himself poured the wine, decanting carefully and waiting for Jason's approval. Then he filled to the brim the tall crystal goblets at each place. Gaston rose to toast Emilie with the first glass; she acknowledged him graciously with a slight nod of her head and blushed. Several rounds were drunk while hot and cold sweetmeats were served. Suddenly Robin Elmore stood, holding his wineglass aloft. "To the Confederacy!" he exclaimed.

Emilie looked sharply at Jason.

Jason lifted his glass and spoke quietly. "To the South," he said. "May she at last know the peace and prosperity due her."

"Hear, hear," Desbrosses and Bledsoe murmured, breaking the tension.

Robin inclined his glass toward Jason, as if in acceptance of his amendment. Then he threw his head back and drank down the contents of the glass in a single gulp.

Emilie felt the breaking of tension at the table. Once more she was grateful to Francine for immediately plunging them all into a merry prattle that required no great effort on anyone's part. She glanced briefly at Robin, who was seated on her right. The fine lines of his face were slightly distorted by his clenched jaw. Emilie could see how angry he was at having been bested by Jason. She wondered if the young man's gesture had been made out of rudeness or was mere bravado. Surely Francine must have told him, probably in the greatest detail, about Jason's background and his having come to Les Chandelles as an officer of the Union Army.

The table gossip soon gave way to conversation on more serious matters. Emilie listened as the men spoke of business affairs. From time to time she asked a question, particularly when something came up that touched upon sugar. She hoped against hope that the conversation would not turn to politics, but she knew that sooner or later it must. It was a subject that had always aroused the strongest passions among the southern aristocracy and now, with their fortunes at such a low ebb and their fate in the hands of others, it was a subject which they could not, and would not, let go.

She wondered afresh at Francine's reason for bringing her cousin to Les Chandelles. She wondered whose idea it had been. Surely if it had originated on Francine's part, it would have been for no purpose other than to enlarge the company and provide additional diversion to the upriver isolated country estate. Emilie's brow puckered. But what reason would the young man have in wanting to make what was likely to be a rather prolonged visit to such a quiet place as Les Chandelles?

"The constitutional convention, I expect, will set everything to rights," Jason was saying, "then Louisiana will have its own duly elected representation."

"The government forthcoming from their supposed convention will not be representative of the Louisiana *we* know, sir!" Robin exclaimed. "They are getting set to disenfranchise us totally, we who have always lived and governed here, while giving the vote to every buck nigger who can hold up his right hand."

Jason looked around the dining room. Robert and several of the other servants stood by, impassive. None of the dark faces revealed any emotion, yet it was inconceivable that they did not hear the angry words.

"Why disenfranchise?" Francine asked. Eurydice wanted to know what the word meant.

"No one of us who served the cause of the Confederacy will be permitted to vote," Robin said, his eyes flashing. "This means at least half of the native white men of this state."

"My dear fellow, we were on the losing side," Anton Bledsoe said calmly, trying to smooth the ruffled feelings of the younger man and restore some tranquil propriety to the table.

"This is still our land," Robin insisted. "Perhaps you think that not being able to vote will have no bearing on you and your fortune, sir!"

Anton was not to be drawn into the fray. "I don't believe it will happen, sir," he said stoutly, "and even if it should, I was in the city, conducting my business all during the fighting. I took care of my own and was careful to give no offense to the authorities. I daresay they will continue to let me go my own way in peace."

"Not so for those of us who fought and risked our lives to make it safe for you!" Robin thundered.

"Easy, easy, my boy," Gaston Desbrosses interjected. "There are still men of affairs and property in this state who will continue to have some influence on her future. Once we have shown that we can exist peacefully, the Union forces will withdraw, and from then on, I can assure you, things will go on very much as they always have."

"Am I to infer from what you are saying, cousin," Robin asked, "that you think that our conquerors want or understand peace? Is this what you think will influence them to be gone from here?"

"I believe I am in the very best position to answer that question," Jason said. "The Union fought solely for its preservation and for the prospects of everlasting peace within our boundaries. Every member state of the former confederacy that has, in convention, sworn loyalty to the United States and to a restoration of the democratic processes has been peacefully readmitted into the Union. Is that not answer enough for you?"

"No," was the resounding reply. "Not until we have restored our—our rights." Robin licked his lips as he faltered over the words. He cursed himself inwardly, realizing that his passion had carried him too far and that he had come close to revealing himself. "Until, that is, there is a recognition of our right to live as we always have, with no outside interference from anyone. Believe me, sir"—and he turned slightly to Jason—"this is all that we are seeking."

" 'We?' " There was a rich hint of irony in Gaston Desbrosses' voice when he echoed the word.

Robin flushed. "All right-thinking Louisianans, sir," he said. "I don't believe I will find any argument on that in this company."

"Well, naturally we would all like to see life go on as pleasantly as possible," Francine said. "We have our own customs and our own ways in Louisiana, far different even from the rest of the South's. Naturally we should be able to enjoy the same degree of civilization we have always known, particularly in New Orleans and on these estates." She turned to Emilie. "My darling, this is easily the best crayfish *étoufée* I have ever experienced. However do you manage to prepare it so well so early in the season?"

Emilie thanked her and gave due credit to Tess. Everyone at the table understood that the comment was more than a compliment; it was punctuation that put an end to the subject being discussed.

Robin was as grateful as anyone else for Francine's tactful interjection. "If the fishing is so good here," he said, once more the Creole gentleman, "then might I assume the game to be superb as well?"

"From what I understand, it is," Jason answered pleasantly. "Although I am sorry to say I have been much too occupied presently to have availed myself of any sport. Do you hunt, sir?"

"Yes, avidly," Robin answered.

"Well, then, perhaps we can arrange a shoot," Jason suggested. "I think that might be an enjoyable diversion during your stay."

"By all means," Eurydice said. "Perhaps you can bring down some quail or wild duck. I'm sure that Emilie's Tess could perform prodigiously with those."

The talk turned once more to entertaining and other amiable matters and Emilie breathed easier. By the time the ramekins of *crème brûlée* were brought around, and the chickory-flavored coffee poured piping hot into her prize Sèvres china, she had quite forgotten the unpleasant exchange earlier. When she and the other ladies withdrew to the front salon, leaving the gentlemen to their brandy and cigars, she walked with a light step, leading her guests down the wide corridor past the curving staircase into the front of the house. She felt quite pleased with the way dinner had gone and in her ability to provide an elegant and plentiful table, one of the surest signs of a great hostess.

She was pleased, too, in recalling that although the equipage had brought an additional, unexpected guest, his appearance had caused no problem or consternation.

There was a room trim and available for him and there had been no unwarranted fuss made. It had all been as smooth as though he had been expected all the while.

Now indeed she could relax and smile with the ladies. If the men remaining in the dining room had slid back to the unpleasant political discussion, it was not her concern and even if passions should rise to the point of heated argument, it would in no way reflect on the house, its hospitality, or its hostess.

As if reading her thoughts, Francine spoke up. "I shouldn't worry about my cousin's fervor, if I were you, Emilie," she said. "That side of the family has always been rather hotheaded and politics is an absolute passion with them. Robin's great-uncle once shot a man dead after dinner."

"My dear!" Eurydice was aghast. "In society? Whatever for?"

"They disagreed on some point or other," Francine said slowly, trying to remember. "I think it had something to do with the current governor. Our uncle considered him a perfect scoundrel and was the sworn enemy of any man who dared to say otherwise."

For all the lightheartedness of her friend's discourse, Emilie was suddenly frightened. "You don't suppose there's going to be any trouble like that, do you?" she asked.

"No, of course not." Francine leaned over and pressed Emilie's hand to reassure her. "I was just relaying a little family history. Besides, I don't imagine Robin has carried a pistol with him to your table, my dear."

They all looked up as the murmur of voices coming from the dining room rose to a loud exchange. Emilie was startled. There was no pistol at the table, to be sure, but suppose Jason was to arrange a hunting party as he had promised. She knew that the two older men were evenly matched in their worldly outlooks and easygoing dispositions. Jason was always in command of himself, but she knew nothing of this Robin except that he was much given to anger, and used his hotheadedness in support of his strongly held views. If there were to be a hunt, all of them would be armed. She hoped that she would be able to dissuade Jason from embarking on any such venture.

The salon conversation drifted aimlessly until the gentlemen rejoined them. Emilie looked expectantly at Jason, but his countenance revealed nothing amiss. Nor, moreover, did that of Robin. He seated himself opposite Emilie, between the other two ladies, and seemed determined to disport himself as nothing other than a dashing young gallant. He tossed compliments extravagantly to his right and left, much to the amusement of the New Orleans ladies. His conversation now concerned itself with nothing more weighty than the new silks just received from France by the city's haberdashers after the long embargo and the more somber cut of cloak being favored by the delta dandies.

Emilie noticed again the slight clenching of his jaw. She knew that he was controlling himself in order to play the role he was now assuming. Once again she could not help but wonder what had brought him to her house. She tried to dismiss from her mind the idea that the sojourn at Les Chandelles was anything but a diversion to please his cousin.

Watching him now, it was easy to imagine him nothing more than a beau calling at the house of an eligible girl whose family he wanted to impress favorably. But there was no such unattached eligible girl at Les Chandelles, Emilie reminded herself. For what purpose, then, was he displaying such captivating graces as he undeniably possessed?

After three quarters of an hour or so, she signaled a hint to Francine that she would be pleased to have the evening at an end. Francine understood immediately and declared to one and all that she was much fatigued with the traveling and events of the day and was quite ready to retire. The gentlemen rose and they all trooped upstairs.

"Whatever was that terrible noise before you came into the salon?" Emilie asked Jason as they prepared for bed.

"I made the mistake of mentioning that Jess intended to run for office once the constitutional convention is finished and the guidelines posted," Jason replied. "I thought your mysterious guest would have apoplexy, young as he is." He seemed to find the incident more amusing than distressful.

"Jason, I don't trust him," Emilie confessed. "I don't like him and I don't trust him."

"Really?" Jason sounded genuinely surprised. "In the salon you seemed to be hanging on his every word, and you found his comments amusing enough."

Emilie looked up at her husband in amazement. "Jason, what are you saying?" she asked. "I am rather frightened by his opinions, and somewhat relieved when he changes his political conversation to one of utter nonsense."

He came and stood in front of her, cupping her face with his hands. "I suppose I am so terribly jealous of you that I can't bear to see your attention on any other man," he said.

"I can't believe you're serious," she said slowly. "On the one hand he frightens me, and on the other I find him a silly, inconsequential bore. As long as he is a guest in my house I suppose I shall have to suffer both those disagreeable aspects of his disposition."

"I don't suppose you'll suffer very much. For all his alarming ways, he's quite a handsome devil, I must admit, and seems to have quite a way with the ladies."

"Perhaps with ladies, but not with me," Emilie said sharply.

"Do you no longer number yourself among the ladies,

my dear?" Jason teased her, running his hand through her hair.

"You know that isn't what I meant at all," she said, smiling up at him impishly. "It's just that I'm not a silly, empty-headed New Orleans Creole madame who has time to listen to his sort of nonsense." Her eyes gleamed as she stared up at her husband. Although there was no reason for it, Jason *was* truly jealous; perhaps it was the spark they needed to reignite the flame that had so happily joined them and was only now cold and forgotten.

She drew herself up on the bed slowly, aware of every movement she was making, her body an overt invitation for him to come to her. But although he kissed her lightly on the forehead before lying down, it was only to hold her close for a moment while he whispered words of love against her ear, then, as he did every other night, he slowly turned his back and fell asleep.

Emilie bit her lip.

The entire company was rejoined at next morning's breakfast. Hot biscuits and cold meats and quantities of eggs—cooked, fried, and baked six different ways—spurred country appetites in all of the visitors.

"I declare I eat more in a day at Les Chandelles than in a week in New Orleans," the plump Eurydice exclaimed.

Emilie smiled at the relish with which she attended her plate.

Jason rose from the table. He leaned over to kiss Emilie and offered his apologies to the other ladies. "I really must be getting to the fields," he explained. "It is already far later than I am used to starting my rounds."

Business being the initial reason for the visit, Bledsoe rose to join him, and Gaston Desbrosses expressed a wish to examine the growing cane as well. Only Robin demurred, saying that he would need only the use of a good saddle mount in order to amuse himself until dinnertime.

"I hope," he said, addressing himself to Emilie, "that I might have permission to wander about your estate at will. I have a great desire to acquaint myself with the countryside."

"By all means," Emilie replied. It was a relief to her not to have to entertain him, but only devote herself to the ladies, whose dual happiness lay in the coolness of the veranda, where they could take their ease and chatter amid the constantly refilled glasses of cold lemonade and plates of sugar-laden sweetmeats.

"Whatever happened to Missy?" Francine asked suddenly. "I thought I recognized her this morning as I was coming downstairs. Has she left the plantation or is she indeed still with you?"

"She still attends me," Emilie said. "Although now, as you know, I pay her wages to do so."

"Is that the biggest difference, Emilie?" Francine asked, her usually placid face now alive with interest.

"Yes," Emilie answered slowly. "I do believe it is. Many of the people, in fact all of them, have chosen to remain here, either working in the fields or in the house as they had formerly. I, myself, see very little change."

"Surely freedom could not have made your cook any more independent," Eurydice said. "She was every inch her own woman, as I remember."

"Take care and don't let my young cousin hear you express such notions," Francine warned playfully. "He is an absolute demon on the subject. Every girl in New Orleans has set her cap for him, but I think he lives only for the day when the old order will be restored. Until then he seems to think of little else."

Once again Emilie was deeply disturbed. There had been no violent outbursts in this parish or the surrounding ones for a few weeks now but the air was one of expectant uneasiness rather than true peace. Fresh outbursts could occur any night if there were many such men as Robin Elmore who believed as strongly as he did and were as willing to set themselves in opposition to the prevailing order. Then peace might never really come.

Emilie was deeply saddened the day she knew the South had lost the war; but she had not allowed herself to dwell on the defeat. She knew that despite what had happened to them all, life must still go on. Even if the Glorious Cause had been trampled and bloodied on a hundred battlefields, one had to set one's sights on the future and not over what was past and could not be brought back. It seemed to her no more possible for the free blacks to once again be enslaved than it would be for Charles Bonfils to spring up and once again walk his land. If men, enough men, set their minds to so doing, it could only bring fresh bloodshed and disaster on them, all over again.

Emilie wished she could question Francine more closely about her cousin, but she did not want to do so in front of Eurydice, especially as the latter seemed to be totally oblivious of his political beliefs or, indeed, any other shortcomings in the young man. She held him to be quite the perfect gentleman of Creole aristocracy and could not quite push from her mind the unbidden and unspoken thought that had he been the man to marry this Bonfils heiress, life would surely have been more comfortable and less complicated for all of them.

Eurydice was used to speaking her mind freely; she felt it an annoyance to have to think beforehand and curb her tongue in front of Captain Phillips whenever she felt herself ready to express an opinion on the Yankees and their doings.

Not that she felt terribly strongly against the Federals; they had made little difference in her life and had, indeed, during the war, managed to fill New Orleans with enough dashing young officers to keep the city's social life quite unwarlike. She believed, as the more sophisticated Francine Desbrosses did, that one must go along with the flow of life's changes if one were to survive to enjoy life to its fullest. But she was a Southerner and found some of the Yankee ways, if not strange, then at least notable for private amusement among her friends. It was only here, in the presence of the former Yankee captain or even that of the woman married to him, that she felt herself somewhat constrained. But alas, she reminded herself with a sigh, as she reached for still another praline, it was a small price indeed for the other pleasures of staying at Les Chandelles.

The other men had not yet returned from their rounds in the canebrakes when Robin dismounted, threw his reins carelessly to a waiting stableboy, and rejoined the ladies in the shade of the veranda.

Emilie was glad that the necessary repair work on the columns had at last been completed the prior week and Les Chandelles no longer was in the state of sad disrepair it had worn all during the long war years.

Robin lounged against one of the white columns, refusing courteously the offer of a chair, saying that after a long day in the saddle, he much preferred standing.

Emilie bade the attending servant to bring the gentleman a brandy cooler. Robin bowed low in her direction in gratitude. Again Emilie found herself blushing when his eyes were fastened on her.

"Speaking of Missy," Francine said, "as we were doing before this young demon broke in upon us, I wonder if I could borrow her this evening to dress my hair."

"Yes, certainly," Emilie replied, forgetting for the moment that Missy was no longer a slave to do any of her mistresses' bidding, but as soon as she remembered, she reminded herself that Missy would present no difficulty. Still, she wondered, suppose Jess did finally agree to marry her and Missy was as much at his beck and call as she was at Emilie's. Could she then be expected to attend to some additional duty, just as Francine had expressed, or would she go on home to prepare her husband's evening meal? A pretty question, Emilie mused, and one that might not be easily resolved. Perhaps there are more changes here than I have yet recognized.

Francine rose to find Missy, and Eurydice offered to accompany her. As the ladies departed, Robin uncrossed his long legs and seated himself in one of the vacated white wicker chairs.

Emilie felt him staring at her. She looked up.

He spoke first. "When I look at you, I see everything that the South has always stood for, everything we went to defend her and die for."

"But you didn't die," Emilie reminded him softly.

He clenched his fist. "No, I didn't," he said. "But now, when I look at you, I almost wish I had!"

Emilie looked at him, startled. She said nothing.

"How can you, you of all people, be such a traitor?"

"Sir, you forget yourself!" Emilie exclaimed. "You call yourself a gentleman, and—"

"And you call yourself, I suppose, a lady," he interrupted her. "No, when I look at you and whom you have married, I almost wish myself fallen in battle so that I might not have seen it!"

"Sir, you go too far!" Emilie exclaimed. "As long as you are a guest in my house, I shall not publicly admonish you, but I must say between us that you have no right to speak to me so!"

He leaned closer to her, his darkened face and lowered voice almost threatening. "I have every right!" he whispered hoarsely. "We went to defend you, not to come back to find you bedded with a Yankee!"

"Sir, I must ask you to quit my company at once," Emilie said coldly, rising to her feet, knowing that the etiquette that had been bred in him would require that he do the same. "I shall not make a disturbance by asking that you leave my property," she said. "But if you persist in this manner, then you will leave me no choice."

"Can't you see how I feel?" he demanded, standing and facing her. "I am the man you should have married,

Emilie! I am the sort of man who should be running Les Chandelles and restoring it as it must be!"

"Sir, your discourse is becoming more and more distasteful to me. I must insist that our conversation cease at once."

"I love you, Emilie. Don't you understand?" he persisted. "Everything you are, I adore. Everything you stand for, I stand for. The lives we should be leading now they have robbed us of. Can't you see what it's doing to me?"

"Indeed I can, sir," Emilie replied, trying to remain calm, her hand touching the base of her throat.

He hung his head. "No, you don't," he said. "You don't understand at all. It is a knife in my chest to know that you share this roof with a Yankee, and you twist it slowly, slowly, by blinding yourself to your traitorous acts."

Emilie turned on her heel and walked quickly inside. She wanted to press her hands to her ears to blot out the ringing of his words. She ran quickly up the great staircase and, closing the door behind her, flung herself on her bed.

He stood on the veranda, watching her retreating figure. Higgins wanted to burn Les Chandelles and destroy it utterly. At first he had acquiesced, but now Higgins would have to be stopped. Robin Elmore himself was going to master Les Chandelles—the plantation and the woman it harbored.

11

Despite the heat of the night, the girl's body was covered with cold sweat. The flimsy curtain that was strung between the kitchen, where she slept, and the room that her mother shared with the man, did nothing to keep their noises out of Myrtie's ears. She knew what they were doing in there. She knew and it terrified her. She wanted to clap her hands against her ears to keep from hearing them, but she knew, from having tried countless times, that it did no good. Besides, he might call her, wanting her to bring something, as he so often did.

Then she would have to scurry outdoors to the pump, fill a bowl with water, stand in their room, watch him drink thirstily from it, trying not to see her mother's face where it loomed beneath him on the bed. Myrtie would have to stand and wait till he finished drinking, then he would thrust the bowl at her and she was free to go, to bring it back to the kitchen and huddle on her own rolled-up blanket in a corner there. She tried not to think of that now; she clenched her fists, digging her nails hard into the soft flesh of her palms, hoping that the pain would save her from being called. She didn't want to see his ample flesh glistening in the night with sweat or her mother's body impaled beneath his massive limbs as he stopped his thrusting just long enough to drink heavily from the bowl.

Maybe this would be a good night, when he didn't call out to her and she didn't have to go crawling in there, covered with the shame that *he* never felt.

Myrtie didn't know how her mother could stand it. Jen looked at her sometimes as though there was something she wanted to tell her, but the only thing that passed between them was that furtive look from which Myrtie turned away as quickly as she dared. There never were any words about it between them, but Myrtie knew there had to be something. There had to be an inexpressible disgust that her mother had to feel for the man and what he was doing to her.

She tried to shut it out but she felt as though she were drowning in their commingled noises. She knew from the way the bedsprings creaked that he was thrusting himself hard and long against her mother's body. Soon there would come the gasping sounds from Jen's throat that made Myrtie feel as though she, too, could not draw in breath enough in her own throat to keep from choking in the hot, dark night.

Sometimes, too, there was the sound of hard slaps, flesh against flesh, as the man's hand stung her mother's cheek or caught her against the side of her head. When that happened, Myrtie could hear him growling, ordering her mother, forcing her to do his unspeakable bidding.

She thought at those times she would die, but she knew she was not lucky enough, neither of them was. They would be better off dead but they would have to live, doomed by the man to do as he said.

"Girl!" His voice was like a roar in her head, shattering against her eardrums and making her want to shout back, but she made no sound, she didn't move.

"Get in here!" he roared again, and this time she knew she had to obey. She got up slowly from the blanket and groped her way along the wall until she felt the thin flutter of the curtain in the doorway. She moved beyond it and stood shrinking in the corner, waiting to know what he wanted.

"Come here," he ordered.

Myrtie walked slowly closer to the two figures on the bed, hugging the wall, trying to stay as far from them as she could, but he reached out and grabbed her thin arm with his hand and yanked her until her shins were scraping against the wood plank of the bed.

"Stand here," he ordered.

Myrtie screwed her eyes tightly shut, but even through the red-rimmed lids she thought she could see her mother lying on the bed, the man towering over her.

"Look here, girl, look here!" His voice jumped with excitement.

"Don't, no, don't," Jen moaned. "Don't make her do it."

Myrtie shrank back trembling as he released his grip on her and swung his open palm against Jen's face. "Shut up!" he shouted. "I want her to see. It's time she knew what it's all about!"

In spite of herself Myrtie opened her eyes. She took in the dim white bulk of his back. She could see how his legs were doubled under, bent at the knees, holding Jen in place. Then he thrust back and forth, the flesh of his buttocks quavering, the sweat glistening, reflecting the flickers of the guttering candle on the bureau nearby. She heard his grunts of satisfaction and the low moans of her mother as she lifted and fell in unison with him, her thin flanks making a small retort whenever they dropped back on the bed.

It was horrible, but Myrtie could not help watching. It was dirty, but she felt something at her own core go all hot and weak as she stood there. Her knees bent and she had to grasp the wall to keep her shaking legs from betraying her.

He reared up, rolling back from his knees. "Good,

huh?" he asked, his voice filled with delight as he tweaked Jen's breast.

Jen started to grimace at the pain, but her expression turned quickly to a weak smile as she saw him raise his hand to strike her again.

"That's better." He grinned. "Now let's show her what you can do." His strength had returned to him, his bulk hovering again above Jen's frail body.

Myrtie watched as his hands thrust her mother's knees apart. It frightened and repelled her but she could not take her eyes off the dark triangle between her mother's legs. She saw the great muscle spring from between Higgins' thighs, pounding like an animal as if it had a life of its own, diving for that selfsame spot that Myrtie could not take her eyes from.

"Now! Now!" Higgins' voice was barely more than a grunt. "Show her, show her what you can do." He stood on his knees, stock-still. Jen thrust her hips upward, her sagging belly jouncing as she brought it up to meet him. Legs still bent, he rested back on his heels, grasping her buttocks, pressing them upward as she worked her loins up and back to meet him.

Jen's head was flung back on the pillow, her hair soaked with sweat, her shoulders hunched as she moved ever up and down, her uncertain strength threatening to desert her at any moment, threatening the cessation of movement that would bring his wrath down on her. She gritted her teeth and forced her thrashing hips to continue their gyrations.

She dared not open her eyes for fear of meeting those of her daughter. Her heart failed within her with the shame of what she was doing, but it was like Higgins said, Myrtie had to know sometime; he was right about that. Her turn would come soon enough to be taken by a man and kept by him in the same endless subjugation that had been her almost nightly torture since the day that she and the girl had left their own place to come up here to his.

She moved, and she thought about the husband who had died in the war. His way with her had not been so different from Higgins', but it seemed to her in memory it had not been so bad and never would he have had the girl as a witness. She was his own flesh; he would not have put them both to shame that this man had.

She thrust again, trying not to think about what she was doing. Better if she gave him all she could at once, then maybe he'd be satisfied the sooner and let her be for the night. Let the girl go back to her place, too.

"Now! Now!" He was screaming in her ear as he fell forward on top of her. She was pinned by his heavy thighs and could not move anymore. But it did not matter; he had taken the momentum from her and now with a few savage thrusts, he would finish and be done with it.

She felt him move against her and she knew he was done. She kept her eyes closed, not wanting to see her daughter's face, knowing by the pressure on her that he was finished.

He grabbed the tattered end of the bedcover and wiped himself on it; then he turned to Myrtie and grinned. "That'll give you something to think about," he taunted her. "Get back in your place now. There'll be plenty of work waiting for you tomorrow."

Myrtie slipped out of the room, past the curtain, and threw herself on her blanket. She drew her knees up to her chest, circling her arms around them and hugging herself close as though to keep out the world. She huddled that way, cocoonlike, until she fell asleep.

In the other room, Jen lay motionless until she heard the heavy snoring that told her Higgins was no longer awake. Then she gave herself over to sleep, too, fearful of how she would face her daughter in the morning after all the shame, grateful that at least he hadn't touched the girl. At least there's that, she thought before she at last fell asleep with him.

Jess looked across the fields at the small group of men on horseback and cursed white people. It had been several days since this horde had descended on Les Chandelles and in all that time he had never been able to get to Jason alone, to speak to him. He didn't know who the men were; it was obvious that they were gentry and guests at the plantation. He wanted urgently to speak with Jason but he knew that he could never dare approach him in front of strangers. Not knowing the men or what they were about made it too dangerous. He would have to bide his time.

The thought rankled him. There was very little he had in life, and one of the things that was most precious that he hadn't much of was time. The school had to be built, the people had to be taught, they had to be explained to about voting, and they had to be confident enough in him to cast their ballots in his name. It all had to be done, and it all had to be done at once. There was not time enough in the day and no one else, except Jason, to whom he could look for any kind of help or understanding.

His disappointment in Missy deepened. Everything he had wanted for them, had run away for, and dreamed about in slave times, he had wanted for both of them, but she seemed to understand nothing of it. He wondered now how he could have been so blind. He remembered when he had first told her of his plan to escape, and how she had clung to him and wept and begged him not to try it. He knew that she had had a much easier opportunity to run away when she was in New York with Emilie and relatively unguarded, but the idea had never been taken seriously by her, not even when he himself had planted the seeds for it.

He couldn't talk to Missy about all the problems

crowding in on him because the only problems that concerned Missy were her own. She still crept to him from the old cabin to the unbuilt house in the dark of the night. He took her, and was glad enough to do it, but all it meant to him was a dark and temporary respite from reality; that was all she meant to him now. The thought stung because he knew that once he had loved her, or at least he thought he had. Now he wasn't sure that it was so. Perhaps in his eagerness to have someone to share his dream he had conjured up a different Missy from the one who had come to tend him every day during his recovery from the whipping Charles Bonfils had had the old overseer lay on him.

He had pictured a partner who would share the new road with him. Instead he had a clinging, frightened woman who wanted nothing more but to hold on to the nothing they had.

Only Jason Phillips, the white warrior who had left the same Ohio to which Jess had escaped, only he understood Jess's dreams. Only he gave sound practical advice on how to implement his plans and strong solid encouragement when the plans seemed unlikely ever to succeed.

Jess liked Jason, liked him freely and openly, man to man, as people were supposed to find each other. But now, as he watched him from the other side of the field, he wondered. Jason was, after all, white; he had chosen to stay in Louisiana rather than go back north. He had married the former mistress, and although the treatment of the people was good and their rule was, if anything, benign, still there was no way of knowing how quickly and easily Jason might succumb to the exhortations of his new friends and neighbors and become just like them.

It would be easier for Jason, Jess had to admit to himself, to take on the style and opinions of the native white planters. Nothing he had done thus far gave any indication of his sliding into those ways, but still Jess knew how easy it would be. Jason was a good man, but he was a white man. If things got really rough, he could turn his back on his black friends and move right into the welcoming arms of the enemy.

Jess knew that it had to be plantation business that had kept Jason so occupied. He could not afford to let his imagination run away with him and think that his one friend was already betraying him. If the planters and their allies were talking politics, he reasoned, they could do it in the shade of the veranda or within the cooler interior of the big house. They needn't be standing around like fools out in the open field in the blazing sun. Jess grinned as he assured himself of that. The cane offered no protection from the sun. No man, not even the most decadent New Orleans aristocrat, could be that dumb. Jason's business was business and he, Jess, knew he was the fool for thinking otherwise.

Still, it was discouraging to have to turn around and head back, another opportunity for talking with Jason foiled by the presence of the, to Jess, unknown white visitors. He turned his back and headed home.

He left the coolness of the wooded area for the hotter but quicker going of the road. He walked along, his tread steady in the heat of the day, but his mind racing quickly as his thoughts darted from one unfinished project to another. He was scarcely aware of the hoofbeats coming up the road behind him. He neither quickened nor slackened his pace, but just moved closer to the edge of the road to let the horseman, whoever he might be, pass him unobstructed.

But such was not the desire of the rider. Coming alongside Jess, he reined in and brought his horse to a near stop.

"What's your name, boy?" the rider wanted to know.

Jess stopped. With his hand he shaded his eyes from the sun and looked up at the man. He was white, although dressed completely in black. He looked and sounded like any of the local gentry, but Jess didn't recognize him.

"I asked what's your name, boy?"

Jess saw his fist tightening on the riding crop he held. "My name is Jess Martin, and—"

"I asked your name, boy, and not anything else," the man interrupted. "When I tell you something else I want to know, then you'll answer me."

Jess knew immediately where he stood with this new adversary, for whoever the man might turn out to be, there was no question but that he was the enemy. The insolent tone, the insulting word "boy," the sneer on the stranger's face, and his ready hand on his crop told Jess everything and more than he had to know. Everything, that is, except the extent of the stranger's interest in him—whether he was just amusing himself by needlessly interrogating a nigger on the road in the middle of a hot afternoon or whether he meant to have real sport with him.

Robin sat straight in the saddle; he, too, knew his man at once. He could tell by the straight back and cultivated voice that this was no ordinary field hand. This, he told himself with a glint of amusement, might even be the Yankee captain's pet nigger, the one he had talked so highly of the other night. "Where did you get your schooling, boy?" he asked.

"I never went to school," Jess answered slowly, trying to erase the northerness from his accent and substitute the soft, slurred tones of the local people.

"I can almost believe that," Robin said sarcastically, "seeing as how no one ever taught you how to say 'sir.' " He looked down sharply at Jess from his position of advantage in the saddle. "But I bet you can read and write, can't you, boy?"

"Yes—yes, sir," Jess replied.

"So you do know how to address a white man after

all." Robin sneered. "Do you say 'Yes, sir' to Captain Phillips?"

"Yes, sir," Jess replied softly. He wanted to reach out his hand—it was so close it would have been easy—to whip the riding crop out of the gloved hand and hit him with it, bringing him down from the saddle and onto his knees in the road. It would have been easy to have laid it across the horse's rump and then send her back down the road while he doubled his fists into the stranger's face and the fancy embroidered waistcoat covering his middle. It would have been easy and he was strong enough to do it, and much as he could taste it in his mouth, he also knew that he would pay for such an act with his life.

It wasn't worth it. Jess knew what lay ahead. There would be hundreds, maybe thousands, of incidents like this peppering his life from now until the day he died, not one of them worth dying over, but the accumulation of all of them would make a life scarcely worth the living. If ever men like this regained control, that's all there would be for black people to look forward to. He had already learned that the end of slavery had also meant the end of the master's protection and the slaves' value as property. Now it was every black man for himself, and unless they got the protection of the law, freedom would be worthless. Freedom without justice was no more than freedom to die.

Robin looked down at Jess with a look of utter contempt. The words he spoke seemed strange coming from someone dressed and dandified as he was, but Jess knew they were no less the truth for all that. He looked away as Robin leaned slightly toward him. "You know, boy, that I'd just as soon spit on you as talk to you and I'd just as soon see you strung up as spat on." He straightened himself in the saddle. "But I am a guest on this damn plantation, so I won't lay a finger on you, but"—his voice rose in warning—"I'll remember you, Jess boy, and I'll remember you on a day when I won't be a guest here; and that day won't be long in coming." He stretched his arm back and flayed the flanks of the mare with the riding crop, galloping off and leaving Jess standing in the dust.

"I'll remember you, too," Jess muttered under his breath at the galloping rider. But he knew in his heart of hearts that if that day of confrontation came, it was scarcely possible that the odds would be in his favor.

He had gained a personal enemy without knowing why. Jess wondered if it was the fate of the road that had thrown him in the stranger's path or whether the man would have behaved the same toward any black he might have met along the way. He realized suddenly that the rider had come from behind him and, after the interrogation, had kept going in the same direction that he himself was walking in. That meant he was heading not away from the plantation but toward the great house. What business had he there? Jess wondered bitterly. What traffic had a man like that with Jason Phillips?

It was not Jason that Robin sought this hour. He galloped quickly, hoping to catch Emilie alone and unawares.

He dug his spurs against the horse's belly, cursing the presence at Les Chandelles of the other ladies, who were constantly in attendance on Emilie. He forgot for the moment that they had been his very entrée to the plantation. Now he saw them only as an obstruction, an unnecessary flutter of laces and ruffles and bonnets that prevented him from being alone with the beautiful heiress.

He paid scant attention to the landscape he was speeding through, having very carefully checked its dominions the first few days of his sojourn there. Now both plantation and mistress were his objectives, and his conquering of them would have to be carefully planned and executed.

He cared not a whit whether he coaxed Emilie to him by playing upon her desires or whether he would have to take her by force. Nor did he care if Les Chandelles had to be burned to the ground in order to be his. It would be more convenient, he knew, to keep it intact, but he also knew the great fecundity of the sugar cane and how easily the crop could be reconstituted. If he had to burn it to own it, then burn it he would.

He thought briefly of Higgins. The man would have to be kept in his place. As a subordinate he could be a very useful tool, but he knew the burning hate Higgins had for everything having to do with Les Chandelles. If he proved himself unruly in his zeal, then he too might have to be destroyed. Nothing, Robin Elmore determined, was going to remain in his way.

Everything he stood for and idolized could be his with the gaining of the plantation. Even if the rest of the world went to rot, Les Chandelles was rich enough and grand enough to sustain life as it had been before the war. Emilie, her head cleansed of Yankee notions, could perfectly typify the southern beauty around whom the whole fallen way of life had been built. Robin smiled to himself as he thought of her. Although he came from a fine old family, the bulk of their fortune had long run out, and the war had left him proud but very nearly impoverished. The plan in his head could change all of that with the quickness of summer lightning. He smiled to himself as he pulled on the reins. I've come here with nothing, he thought, but I'm staying and taking the belle of the ball.

Then the big house loomed just ahead, and he relinquished his tight grip on the reins to dismount gracefully and walk up the stairs to the low, wide veranda. That newly whitewashed structure, it seemed to him, surrounded the big house like a maiden's protective hooped petticoat and the great white marble pillars were like the corset stays that fortified her innocence. Both had to be swept away in order to gain the prize within.

He grinned again as he strode through the open door of the mansion. Would that the rest of it could be so easily gained.

12

The train lurched forward, then regressed jerkily as if falling back on itself. Rachel felt herself thrown ahead and then back with the motion of the clumsy locomotive. She hastily flicked a large black flake of soot from the place it had settled on the skirt of her plain gray traveling suit. The garment was worn enough, she sighed to herself, and had to do her much more service. It would be unfortunate indeed to have any further damage inflicted on it.

Of the damage done to her worn nerves and jostled bones all through this long, lumbering journey across the South, she gave no consideration at all. She was used to being disturbed by all of the problems of an uncaring environment. Life had been hard during the war, it was still hard after the war, but it had never been truly easy for her. Rachel squared her slim shoulders against the seat back and held her head high. Creature comforts had never been among her goals, and the hardships she chose to face were tests of discipline that she was sure helped build strength and good character.

Such welcome attributes, however, would not have been immediately discernible to any observing fellow passenger. More likely she would have been noticed for the pert figure and the air of determination that became, on her pretty features, a softened aura. A few stray wisps of glossy chestnut hair escaped from the tightly pinned bun at the nape of her neck, the rest of her flowing tresses secured by the determined little hat she wore. More than one male passenger had taken note of the attractive young woman traveling alone, but if she was aware of their interest, she made no acknowledgment of it.

The train moved forward again. Rachel tried to concentrate on the landscape that was now passing steadily, if somewhat sluggishly, in front of her window, but it was so like the country through which she had been traveling for the past several days that she could not give it the attention she wanted to. For more than the first time, she found herself wishing that she were a better observer and that she had formed the habit of keeping a diary and making notes on everything she saw on her journeyings. She had never kept a journal. Her mind was always fastened on what she felt to be of far greater moment than the jottings of a simple person like herself, which would be of interest to no one else. Far more important to bring help to those who needed it than to indulge herself in the vanity of fancying she could ever produce writings of note.

From the reticule beside her on the seat she drew out a small paperbound book and began to read. Usually the works of Lord Macaulay held the greatest interest for her and she read his books avidly but this hot morning, for some reason unknown to her, Rachel found herself as unable to set her mind to the pages as she was to the green, flowing landscape that now, as the train at last reached a smooth and steady route, swept past her. She knew that as they traveled southward from Mobile and through Alabama westerly toward Mississippi, the railroad would skirt the shores of the Mexican gulf. Perhaps, she thought, the sight of the vast, open waterway would stimulate her interest.

She remembered her first sight of the Atlantic Ocean

when she had arrived in Virginia in the early months of the war. It had been so long ago, and so much death and fear and suffering had she seen from that time until this, yet even the crowded memories of her nursing duties with the army could not push from her recollections that first great impression she had had of the mighty ocean.

All of her life had been spent in landlocked Ohio, amid the green and growing fields of summer and endless white silent hush of winter. No other landscape was familiar to her, save what she read of in books and tried to conjure with her mind's eye. The ocean then had been a revelation to her, every bit as new and engrossing in its way as had been the tumult and strangeness of that first trip away from the familiar confines of her farmland home.

It had been with her father's blessing that she had left. The old man had worked long and diligently in the dangerous business of helping runaway slaves. Now that his beloved Mr. Lincoln had been elected and the South had seceded from the Union, he could not in all good conscience say nay to his daughter's wanting to continue to serve the same good cause. She was the only living relative he had left in the world. Her mother had died soon after bearing Rachel, and the old man had managed somehow, for all the backbreaking work of farming and nerve-riddling danger of the underground railway, managed to outlive almost everyone else he knew; yet his strong conscience and moral scruples were as much a part of him as his own flesh and blood, and much as it hurt him to see his daughter leave, he was proud nonetheless that the vigorous response to duty he had always taught was so deeply instilled in her.

Rachel didn't recall much of the first train trip that took her from home to the vast and bustling army depot where she would receive her training. So many hours had she spent on trains from that time until this that they were all blurred and dim in her memory, but the swell of the ocean on which the first camp to which she was assigned stood remained clearly before her even four years later. She laid the book, open, in her lap. She could not find the reason for her lethargy this morning and hoped again that the soon-to-be-sighted waters would indeed be a tonic to her spirits, restoring her to her more usual disposition.

The reason for this lassitude was not the only unanswered question in her mind. For so long she had been used to receiving and carrying out orders, first from her father and then from the nursing superiors and doctors among whom she toiled. That had ceased at the end of the war, but she had immediately attached herself to a group of women, newly arrived from the North, embarking on the business of educating the newly freed slaves. Rachel had learned of her father's death in the closing days of the war, and she had no desire to return to the solitary isolation of the farm that was now hers. She had sent instructions for the working and maintenance of the land until such time as she chose to return. She knew she could trust the banker with whom her father had always conducted his business, and who indeed had been the sender of the unhappy news. She had taken her place among the other teachers, accepting whatever assignments she had been given and fulfilling them to the best of her ability.

She found quickly that she loved teaching, especially the young, bright-eyed children who presented themselves to her each morning. After the long years of serving among the dead and dying, it was a pleasurable relief to be greeted by bright eyes and willing young minds. She had taken to the work like a duck to water, feeling herself among the living once more, happy to be able to find pleasure in doing work that her good father would surely have heartily approved of.

But her joy in the enterprise was not shared by the other women. They found the southern heat too arduous, the work too tedious, the open dislike and disparagement of the white southerners too annoying. One or two at a time, they slowly gave up and drifted back up to their homes. Within several months, Rachel found herself the only teacher left in the jurisdiction of the local Freedmen's Bureau. It was with a heavy sadness that the supervisor of the Bureau told her it would no longer be feasible to continue the work she had so eagerly seized upon.

If conditions in the older eastern-seaboard states of the former Confederacy were bad, she knew that the other states could only be worse. She felt that somewhere there had to be a place where she could fulfill what she knew in reality to be a desperate need. At the same time, she was reluctant to return home. There was nothing for her there but the emptiness to be found in a place once inhabited by a giant now gone. Still, there was really no other place for her. She hit upon the plan of not traveling north in the most direct way. Mr. Parish, from the bank, had forwarded her a comfortable enough sum of money to permit her to travel as she pleased and Rachel decided to take the train westward to the Mississippi, as far as New Orleans. From there she could secure riverboat passage up the mighty Mississippi for most of the remainder of the eventual journey. Thus she would be able to see more of the country and perhaps, she barely admitted to herself, find yet the situation that would keep her from going back to the farm. But all of the distance from Virginia through Alabama had yielded nothing. The country, caught in the grip of a defeat it was emotionally unable to accept, seemed to her alien territory, for all of the new laws and treaties that determined to get the southern states back into the Union as it had existed before the war. Everywhere she saw signs of terrible poverty and struggle. Burning and destruction had been rampant throughout the South, yet she knew when she saw still-smoldering remains that these were not the embers of battlefields. Those had long cooled into the earth. Fresh fires were being lit everywhere in the South. Armies no longer fought armies, but aggression against innocents claimed victims every day.

Rachel averted her eyes from such sights as best she could. She wondered how she could remain amid continuous carnage but the worse it was, the more she knew she was needed. She clasped her hands constantly, praying that she would be strong enough to do what she knew, so well, was there to be done.

She knew that by reputation New Orleans was a great city, a truly civilized place. Perhaps there she would find the opportunity she was seeking. New Orleans had had a well-thought-of academy at a time when few colleges and other institutions existed in the South. Perhaps there the government was of a mind to help its newly enfranchised citizens. Perhaps there she would find the place she was looking for. Meanwhile there were more tedious miles of seemingly endless railroad track to traverse than she cared to count. Rachel laid her head back against the high, upholstered seat. She closed her eyes and began silently to count the clickings of the wheels against the rails, hopeful that the metallic rhythm might somehow help her to fall asleep.

She heard movement in the aisle next to her, but she did not open her eyes. She concentrated on numbing her mind to everything around her, but the relaxed serenity she sought was no sooner filling her mind than it was broken by a cultivated masculine voice.

"Excuse me, mademoiselle, but is this seat being occupied?" he asked.

Rachel opened her eyes and looked up at him. She blushed hotly, being totally unused to being so addressed. "I don't believe it is," she answered slowly, turning away quickly to gaze out the window.

"Then I shall be glad to make use of it, that is, if the young lady has no objection."

Rachel shook her head, sorry for the intrusion and not wishing to encourage the man to any further conversation. It was obvious from his accent and dress that he was a southerner. From his mode of speech she knew he was most likely what was considered a gentleman, but in her eyes a monster nonetheless, of the former slaveholding class.

Her wish for silence was not shared. No sooner had the gentleman arranged himself on the seat, and his bags overhead, than he addressed himself to her again. "I hope you are having a pleasant journey," he said. "For myself I had no idea that the tediousness of my trip would be so happily relieved by the presence of a beautiful traveling companion."

"Sir, I . . ." Rachel struggled to find the words that would inform him in a not uncivil way of her unwillingness to enter into conversation with a stranger.

"My dear young lady," he said softly. "I would not dream of intruding myself, a stranger, upon you. Please permit me to introduce myself. My name is Alexandre Romain and since I see you are traveling toward New Orleans, as I am, it might be that we have mutual acquaintances. That would quite change the situation, for we would no longer be strangers to each other."

"I hasten to assure you, sir," Rachel replied quickly, "that I have no acquaintances whatever in that city."

She faced him as she spoke, tilting her determined little chin. She knew that as she spoke her accent would tell him everything he need know about her, that they shared neither acquaintances nor similar opinions. Her dark eyes sparkled slightly; for all her disdain, she could not help but be a tiny bit curious as to how he would receive the information that her words could not fail to impart. She regarded him rather closely, emboldened by the knowledge that she most certainly must have startled him.

But if he was disappointed or upset to find her a

northerner, he gave no indication. He smiled broadly at her, and when he spoke he was as pronouncedly charming as before. "But I see that you are a visitor!" he exclaimed. "All the more reason that I must put myself entirely at your service. We have always been famous for our hospitality and I, for one, will in no way be the cause of its diminution. Please permit me, mademoiselle . . ." His graceful fingers described a sort of circle in the air, clearly indicating that he did not know her name but would like to.

Rachel could not be rude. "My name is Rachel York," she said, her hand moving nervously on her lap.

Whether he correctly understood her feeling ill at ease she would never know. He quickly and gracefully took hold of her fluttering fingers, drawing her hand to his mouth and kissing the back of it. Rachel was startled and quickly tried to withdraw it, but he held it quite firmly in his grip as he raised his head and smiled across at her.

"Enchanted, mademoiselle," he murmured, then he straightened up. "But I must apologize for my clumsiness again. I had forgotten that you are not from New Orleans. Forgive me, I pray you, for speaking in a language that must be strange to you."

But strange or not, there was no mistaking the meaning of his words, and in spite of herself, Rachel found she was indeed enchanted by the softly flowing words. Only once before in her life had she met a man whom she would permit herself, out of the prim strictness of her upbringing, to describe to herself as handsome. The other had been the runaway slave she had helped so many years before. Rachel had willed herself never to think of him, because such memories brought back only the shame of her having flung herself at him, begging him to take her with him to Canada, and the even greater shame of his firm, though kind, refusal. She had taken a long time to learn not to think of Jess and now that this man, so unlike him, had nonetheless put her in mind of him, she felt a pang at her heart that was an old, familiar, not-quite-forgotten wound.

"I do not distress you, mademoiselle," Alexandre Romain asked softly, leaning forward, his face full of concern and quite close to hers now.

"No, sir, you do not," Rachel replied.

"Perhaps you are feeling faint, perhaps it is the warmness of the day," he went on. "I shall endeavor to get a glass of cool water for you from the conductor or as soon as the train stops again."

"No, no, please don't bother," Rachel exclaimed. She wanted nothing from him but to be left alone. Certainly nothing that would obligate her to him in any way. Yet she could not deny that for all her discomfort at his attentions, he was being unbelievably kind and solicitous in a courtly way, which she had never had directed to her before. She felt such a confusion of doubts and emotions all conflicting within her at once that she was sure she was acting quite the fool. This certain knowledge only added to her consternation.

"If Mademoiselle will not think me overbold," he said. "Perhaps this will help you to feel better." He drew a small leather-covered flask from his coat pocket. He smiled encouragingly at her. "I assure you, mademoiselle, that the young ladies of the finest families in New Orleans find themselves somewhat the better for a small sip on many occasions." He held the bottle out to her.

"No, no." Rachel shrank back. She had no idea what it was he was offering her.

He guessed as much. "It is only some very fine old *eau-de-vie*," he said. "A little brandy. It will refresh your spirits and not do you the least harm. I beg you to accept a drop."

Rachel looked down. The bottle was almost level with her nose. She sniffed slightly.

"Ah, that's better," he said, encouraging her. "Only a tiny drop on the tip of the tongue, go ahead."

Rachel took the flask in both hands and allowed a few drops of the amber liquid to fall on her tongue. She swallowed hastily and as quickly thrust the bottle back to him. She let the hot liquid burn its way down her throat. She thought for a moment that she must surely perish from the fire but her anguish lasted no longer than that. She swallowed and found her mouth was full of the pleasantest sensation and only a tiny aftertaste of the sweet, burning liquor. "Thank you," she gasped, and she had to laugh when he did, at the totally unexpected breathlessness in her voice.

Rachel sat back in her seat, feeling somewhat relieved.

Alexandre smiled back at her. "You see, we are not such devils after all," he said.

Then he asked, "Have you been in the South for long, Miss York?" with an air of friendly familiarity that, while completely polite, nevertheless assumed that any misgivings she might have felt toward him had entirely passed, and their conversation could now proceed in the friendliest manner permissible to unattached people of their station. Although he knew that she was no southern lady, there was something about her lovely features and sweet seriousness that told him at once that this was no common girl traveling to a domestic position or to a farm. The very air of mingled innocence and determination intrigued him. He promised himself that by the time they reached their mutual destination she would be a stranger to the city but not to him. Furthermore, being new to the town, she would certainly be in need of his continued guidance and . . . He hesitated, seeking for the right phrase to describe to himself what he expected would be a most interesting and revealing relationship.

He wondered if she were a person of any influence. It would do the cause no harm were he to win a young northerner over to their way of thinking, filling her pretty head with sentiments that could be broadcast once she returned to her home. The idea of combining the business that was closest to his heart with the undeniable pleasure of an unusual relationship with an attractive female seemed the happiest of prospects.

Her clear voice broke into his thoughts. "You were asking how long I've been in the South," Rachel reminded him. "I must tell you that it is more than four years, very nearly five."

He was startled at this piece of information. "Then you were here all during the War Between the States?" he asked.

"Yes," she concurred. "I was a nurse for the Union forces; during the last years I was attached to the army of Ulysses S. Grant."

He was genuinely amazed. "But what a situation for a female," he exclaimed. "Surely your family could not have permitted this. You must have been caught in the vicissitudes of history."

"Not at all, sir," Rachel replied smoothly. "My devotion to the Union cause took me from Ohio and brought me here and my—my poor father," she stammered, "quite concurred with my decision."

"Poor indeed!" he scoffed. "To have permitted such a thing."

"Sir, my father passed on just weeks before Appomattox," Rachel murmured. "His demise is my only reason for using that descriptive word. His life was a richly satisfying one to him. He lived it exactly as he wanted to."

"And you, Miss York?" he asked quietly. "Are you, too, living according to the desires of your heart?"

"Exactly so," Rachel answered somewhat haughtily, with an assuredness that she did not quite feel.

"Is that why you're going to New Orleans?" he asked.

"I am not going to New Orleans for any specific reason," Rachel said. "At the moment it is to me a stopping-off place. I do not know what I will find there."

"Perhaps you will find yourself there," he said slowly. "If that indeed is what you're looking for." He scrutinized her face. "In any event, you will certainly not find yourself closer to home than you were in Virginia."

There was a slight trace of mockery in his voice and Rachel knew he had caught her in a verbal trap. She had been silly to sound so sure of herself when, in reality, she had not the slightest means for backing it up. For not the first time since they had been speaking, she wished that they had never engaged in conversation at all, but it was only a half admission on her part. There was something about the man that was drawing her out; certainly there was no sin in admitting that the journey was progressing far less tediously than it had been when she'd sat alone. Still, he was a city man and obviously far cleverer than she. Even all that she had seen and done during the last years had not sharpened her wits for the kind of encounter she now found herself in. For all that she had seen of life, and death, she was not of a wit for the kind of parrying that was probably child's play for this *boulevardier*.

The conversation had been so engrossing that Rachel had given no mind at all to the movements and lumberings of the train. Now, with a great, winding screech, it came to a sudden halt that threw her forward in her seat and against Alexandre Romain.

Before she could quite recover he had expertly caught her by her upper arms, and rather than press his advantage, he had gently eased her back against her seat, then relinquished his hold on her.

Before she could thank him he spoke. "I see we have come at last to a destination along the line." He stood, reaching for his tall silk hat. "I assume you brought no food with you, mademoiselle."

Rachel nodded.

"Well, then, I shall try to make do for both of us," he said. Before Rachel could protest he put out a hand to stop her. "I will get only the simplest of fare," he promised. "Whatever is freshest and safest to eat." He walked down the aisle and she watched as he swung gracefully down to the railway-station platform.

Within moments he had returned, carrying a small network sackful of round golden oranges. "There we are," he announced proudly, as if having accomplished a major feat. "These beauties should do us nicely until it is time for dinner." He took one of the large fruits from the sack and, with a silver-handled pocketknife deftly peeled away the thick skin. Then he broke the peeled fruit in half, handing Rachel one part.

With his free hand he drew a large lace-edged linen handkerchief from his inner pocket and, without ever quite touching her, managed to lay it across her lap. Rachel was amazed at his grace and courtesy.

"We shall pretend that we are having a lovely picnic instead of being encased in this clumsy, cumbersome vehicle," he declared. "I wish that I had been able to provide more in the way of variety, but I do feel my choice was the safest."

"Oh, it is quite delicious, I assure you," Rachel answered. "It was stupid of me not to have had some food packed and brought with me."

"Not at all, dear Miss York." He smiled. "The fortunes of the road are sometimes the best. Paris' golden apple of the myth would not best these oranges, I'm sure."

His reference clicked dimly somewhere in Rachel's brain. She was not quite sure what he meant but it lifted her to know that he was of a somewhat literary mind, in addition to all of his other, more obvious charms. She found herself smiling at him and felt all warmed by the smile he gave back to her.

"Now that we are quite settled," he said, "you must tell me all about Ohio."

13

"The men who have been disenfranchised are the very men who used to hold all of the power and influence in the state," Jason said. "They will never permit the holding of an election in which they have no part."

"But they can't prevent it, Jason," Jess argued. "It's the law now, and the federal government is in New Orleans, still in force, to make sure that the law is obeyed."

"But what we have seen operating most forcefully here is not the law," Jason countered, "but the outlaws, who have been burning and murdering. *They* are the ones who will most likely determine the outcome of events, at least at present."

"All the more reason I must take my stand," Jess said. "I cannot hide myself here, just teaching school, when the real work to be done is in the capital. That is why I must go and why I need someone to take my place."

"I can understand that part of it," Jason reasoned. "The school has gotten off to a smashing start. It would be shameful to have to give it up now, just when it is beginning to bear the fruits of all your hard work."

"That is exactly why I want to advertise for a real teacher," Jess said. "Once I know that the school will go on, I can give myself over to the election. Jason, don't you see the only way we can really win anything is if we have government and law behind us?"

"I know," Jason said, "I don't disagree with you."

"Then please understand that I must do this my way," Jess said. "I know that it's a dangerous undertaking, but so is everything else that I'm trying to do. I might have guessed that this is the way it would happen. I should have known that the masters would not take their defeat lying down."

"The South was brought to her knees by the war," Jason said. "But she will struggle to stand on her feet no matter what the crimes, no matter what the consequences. I only hope that we here can hold out against this bitter reaction until it has run its course and sensible men once more direct affairs."

"And wouldn't you count me as one of the sensible ones?" Jess parried. "You know you do," he went on without waiting for an answer. "Thus you must support me. At least or until everyone else turns his back on me and I go down in defeat."

"That's not what I'm worried about," Jason said. "I think you'll carry the parish easily. It's your winning, not losing, that will put you in the greatest danger."

Jess grinned. "I know that, but it's too late to turn back now."

The men smiled at each other. "Go ahead, then," Jason said with a wave of his hand. "Find yourself some retired gentleman or schoolmarm who's willing to come up here and apply the ABC's and back of the hand to your precious brats and would-be gentlemen farmers."

Jason reached for his hat, shook hands warmly with Jess, and stooped through the low doorway of the newly finished schoolhouse. While the structure and everything that went on inside it was of Jess's making, the school stood on plantation ground, and Jess never made any important decisions relative to it without consulting with Jason first.

The matter they had just concluded was second only

to his decision to run for the state legislature, the biggest step Jess had taken so far. Until now he had divided himself between the school and electioneering. Now that the date was drawing close for the great event, he knew he had to devote himself to it full time. It was to be the first election ever held in Louisiana or anywhere else in the South in which his people would participate. Not to throw himself fully into such a venture would be unthinkable. It would not be enough for him to stand at the ballot box with the others, hoping that the man they would choose to represent them would truly do so. No, his participation had to be much more than that. He himself had to be the man who would stand in the great hall when the name of the parish was read out. He would be the one who could take the responsibility for the people and deliver to them what he himself, better than anyone else, knew they needed. It was a great new day dawning, full of hope and the promise of freedom that had been so bitterly fought for and, as yet, barely tasted. Jess sometimes felt as though he would explode from the sheer joy and promise of it. The only sorrow he permitted himself to admit to was that his grandfather was not alive to share it with him and that neither his first mentor in the North, Reverend Martin, nor his commanding officer in the army, Colonel Higginson, would be present to see him. But he resolved that as soon as the election was won and things were somewhat settled, he would write to both of them to apprise them of the wonderful news.

Now he sat down at one of the crude desks and with pen and paper painstakingly composed the advertisement that he would place in the New Orleans newspapers. One copy of the advertisement would be carefully posted to No. 64 Camp Street, the office of the *Picayune*. The other he addressed to the *Daily Delta* at No. 76 on the same street. He thought for a moment about penning a third copy for the other important paper but *L'Abeille* was printed in French, and Jess wanted an English-speaking teacher, who could communicate that language to the people. He did not want them learning French or the Creole *patois* of the city. He was determined that they were going to be Americans, good Americans, and as such would use the language of the whole country, not just of the region to which the misfortunes of the slave trade had brought them.

Satisfied with the result of his work, he signaled to one of the small boys playing outside the schoolhouse and bade him go with a companion to the intersection of the Les Chandelles drive with the main road, where the letters could be posted to await the weekly arrival of the mail service.

Jess frowned as he walked back into the schoolhouse. He sat down at one of the makeshift desks, laying his head down in his hands on it. He couldn't help wishing that, for all his pride in the new academy, the meeting he had just had with Jason had been held in the mansion with Emilie present. The former mistress always expressed a great deal of interest in the school and had been quick to donate the parcel of land it stood on and permission to fell trees from the estate for its construction. Jess had long ago put out of his mind the little girl he had played with as a child. As they grew in age so had the distance between them. He was and always would be full of gratitude toward Emilie, for she had been the instrument of his learning to read and write. She had sat quietly, copying the lessons dictated to her by her tutor, and had acted as if the little slave boy sitting a distance behind them did not exist. It was illegal to educate a slave in those days and she, the pampered darling of the plantation, had acted with the cool defiance of an eight-year-old who can break a law she feels herself above.

Jess was sure that whatever instance for kindness was being nurtured and encouraged by Jason, southern-born and -bred Emilie was helping in every way toward making the Les Chandelles community an example for what the new ways could be like.

Again he swore silently at the visitors. It was only the presence of those white strangers in the house that prevented his being there himself, to meet and consult with both Captain and Mrs. Phillips. Once more unwelcome white intrusion had put him back in his place. But at least it was *this* place, Jess thought with satisfaction, sitting bolt upright and slapping his hand against the solid desk top. *This* was no miserable slave hut he was hiding in; it was a *school!* It was more than a beginning, Jess thought. The beginning had been when lessons were held outdoors and he had scratched out the letters of the alphabet with a charred stick on a flattened piece of stone. Now they had a real school, with desks and chairs. Jason had brought paper from the house, and a supply of pencils was expected soon with the next shipment of goods coming upriver to the plantation from New Orleans.

And best of all, now there would be a real teacher. And he, Jess, could go on to his work in the outside world.

Jason rode straightaway to the mansion when he left Jess. His heart was heavy with misgivings, even while his mind was uplifted by the plans he had just discussed with his black friend. As he strode into the house his scowl deepened perceptibly into a frown. Emilie sat on a small velvet settee with Robin, whose presence Jason was finding more and more disagreeable. Only a silent servant hovered in the shadows of the large room. None of the other occupants of the house were visible.

"Jason, darling," Emilie greeted him. "Won't you come and have some tea?"

"Thank you, my darling, but I think not," Jason replied. "I will see you upstairs shortly." Without breaking his stride, he hurried up the big staircase to their chamber.

Emilie was a little taken aback. It was unlike Jason to be so curt with her and so uncharacteristic of him to be issuing what amounted to an order to her. She turned again toward her guest, trying to hide her consternation beneath her cool composure. "These are difficult days for us," she said. "The grinding season has just begun and we are unused to the new conditions of labor that prevail now."

"I cannot tell you how it grieves me to hear a lady such as you discuss those things," Robin said. "If naught else had occurred to press upon one the utter disgrace into which the world has fallen, these words from your lips would suffice."

"I don't quite get your meaning," Emilie said. "I have always taken an interest in the working of my plantation. Ever since the death of my father it has indeed been my prime responsibility."

"But now you have a husband, madam," Robin said in a low voice. "And I assure you that had you chosen to marry a southern gentleman, none of these tiresome, mundane burdens would have been left on your shoulders. I could never have stood such grossness."

"Then you misjudge me entirely, sir," Emilie said loftily. "I am not one of your plantation belles, fit for nothing more than ivory fans and silly flirtations. I have no intention, nor have I ever, of wasting my life on such utter nonsense."

"You are the very essence of southern womanhood," Robin said. "Fearfully, mercilessly hurt and abused by the rank element of this world."

Emilie was startled to see him drop to his knees in front of her. "Sir, get up, I insist," she exclaimed. "I find your behavior extraordinary and unseemly in the extreme!"

He leaned his head against the edge of the settee, close

to her skirts. Emilie tried to move away, but there was no room.

"I love you, Emilie!" he sobbed. "It is living death for me to see you like this!"

"Then I beg you, sir, to get up and quit my house at once," Emilie said coldly. "I find your attentions and behavior most unacceptable. For one who talks of nothing but the proprieties and courtesies of former days, you are so unseemly in your words and actions as to defy the custom of all good society."

"Emilie, I implore you!" he begged. "Understand a heart that is too full of love and anguish to admit reason."

"I am a married woman," Emilie reminded him, "and also much beholden to my friend, your cousin. I do not wish to create a scene or cause a scandal by ordering you from here. But if you persist in this behavior, I tell you now that I must."

He got up quickly and took his seat once again. His face was flushed. The fervor of his passion was undeniable. Emilie was angry, but she could not help noticing the heightened color of his face, the looks of poetic wildness that he cast at her. His gestures and his utterances were too dramatic, but still she could not help feeling flattered at the fervent declarations of love and concern he constantly gave her.

Emilie stiffened. Something in her was longing to put her fingertips to his burning cheek to push back softly the dark lock of hair that had fallen forward on his brow. It needed no more than a look or a gesture from her to encourage him, to let him know that his attentions were welcome, that the words of love could now flow from him to her unchecked. It was a mighty temptation to let him speak and behave as his mind dictated and not as hers forbade. Emilie thought quickly of Jason upstairs and the quiet bed to which she retired each night. How easy it would be, how pleasant, to have an impassioned young gallant to fill her days with romantic notions, to warm her brow before she gave herself up to solitary sleep. How many women in New Orleans, she wondered, would have even hesitated before letting a swain such as Robin express himself?

She rose, standing for a moment on not quite steady feet. "I must go now," she said. "I bid you *adieu* until dinner."

"Emilie!" He leaped to her side and pressed her hand against his brow. She pulled hard, tugging it away. She started to reprimand him but the words died in her throat.

She turned quickly, gathering her skirts in her hands, and fled upstairs to the gloomy reaches of the second story.

14

"I can assure you entirely on the matter of Mrs. Hinsdell's establishment," Alexandre said. "It is one of the few exemplary boardinghouses in the city that will accommodate young ladies who are alone. The proprietor has been there for a very long time and since you are without acquaintances in the city, it is the most appropriate sort of place for you to stay."

"I really don't know how long I'll be remaining here," Rachel said, "and I had thought to take a room in a hotel."

"Quite unseemly, my dear," Alexandre replied. "Even a smart hotel, or I should say especially, is quite an unseemly abode for an unattached female. You are far more prettily situated in a pleasant house such as Mrs. Hinsdell's, where you will be quite *en famille*, with the lady herself clucking over you like a mother hen and quite being a chaperone. I'm afraid a hotel would really be frowned upon."

"But by whom?" Rachel smiled. "I am unknown in society here and, I assure you, perfectly willing to remain so. There is no one who need know or question my morals."

They were standing on the platform of the busy railroad depot in New Orleans. Alexandre had gotten her large carpetbag from the baggage porter and was now refusing to relinquish it until he had seen her properly settled in the city. "I fully intend to call on you," he said firmly, "and to introduce you to some of the finest salons in the city. It will not do at all for you to announce some hotel as your domicile."

Rachel was more amused than annoyed. She had so long been used to making her own way that at first she was a bit resentful of his presumption, but she found her apprehension of him fading and delight in the unaccustomed charms of masculine attention taking its place. Surely what he was proposing now was for her own good, she thought. It was silly to fight him without knowing quite what it was that she was fighting about. Should the accommodations that he recommended prove unsuitable, there was nothing in the world to prevent her from leaving.

She smiled up at him. "Very well," she said, as if giving in. "There is no point in fighting you, I see. Let us go then to your esteemed Mrs. Hinsdell."

"Capital!" he exclaimed. "I'll engage a carriage immediately."

"But I must warn you," Rachel said as he took her arm and hurried her across the platform, "that my taking your suggestion in no way admits a familiarity, sir. I shall be on my guard against that and I shall judge the establishment myself when we arrive there."

"I admire your independence, Miss York," he said, smiling, "but I must warn you as well that I don't intend admiring it from a distance."

Rachel was having second thoughts for more than the second time. "Perhaps it's not such a good idea after all," she said, faltering.

"Nonsense!" he reassured her. "Had I any terrible designs against your person, I assure you I would have carried you instantly to my sister's house, where I am always at home and the door is never closed to me. Instead

I have offered you the protection of a rather formidable lady, as you will soon see."

He helped her into the carriage. Rachel was glad that he dropped the parrying conversation once they were en route. She felt that he could sense her eagerness to see as much as possible of the famed city they were riding through.

New Orleans seemed to her less touched by the war than any of the other large southern cities she had seen. All of the fabled quaintness seemed to come alive in front of her eyes as she watched brightly turbaned mulatto women balancing huge baskets of wash or fruit and other produce on their heads. Other women leaned down from lacy iron balconies to call to the merchant women. The houses were awash in all shades of bright pastel colors. Flowers seemed to bloom everywhere, lilac and bougainvillea and magnolia spreading their bright blossoms amid dark foliage and trailing up the fronts and sides of the houses.

The people selling in the streets hawked their wares in melodious singsong and it seemed to Rachel that the colors of their skins were as various as those of the houses they strolled before. This spectrum of complexions, from black to bronze through beige and cream and white, freely intermingling, was not the case in the other cities she had seen, where people were as separated by color as by any other condition.

Some of the streets were scarcely wide enough to permit a carriage to pass through, yet even the tiniest seemed elegant to her. When they drove along a broad avenue, the bright colors and elaborate fashions displayed under the canopied shop windows made her increasingly aware of the shabbiness and plainness of her own dress. It was vanity to think of such things, Rachel knew, yet something in her longed for the careless ease of the beautifully dressed white ladies she saw walking, arms linked, in groups of two and three, in and out of the shops. Their lives were so different from her own, as different as their dresses, and for a long moment Rachel could not help but wonder what it would be like to live as they did.

The streets were crowded with vehicles of every kind. Rachel especially admired those smart turnouts in which the top was folded back, displaying the grandly dressed ladies who sat proudly behind a liveried driver cracking his whip over a pair of perfectly matched horses. Was this then, she wondered, the fine society that Alexandre Romain had said he wished to introduce her to? Rachel didn't know how she would ever manage to speak a single word in such grand company.

All of a sudden it felt as if the sights of the city were too much for her. She felt overwhelmed by the busyness of it all, the grandeur and the people, those riding in their fine carriages and those walking barefoot on the same streets peddling vegetables and condiments and hardware and laces and merchandise, it seemed to her, of every sort that could ever be imagined. She had passed fleetingly through Atlanta, seeing little more than the charred ruins of that once-great city. Mobile had seemed to her a gray town, harsh and whimpering after defeat. No where had she seen activity to rival the hustle and bustle of the Vieux Carré, as Alexandre explained to her this area of the city was named.

"Is it always like this?" she asked. "Or is the entire city out on parade this particular day?"

"No, it's an ordinary day," Alexandre said, laughing, "but we have arrived at a rather busy time. There is always a great deal of traffic around this hour. The ladies have all arisen from their siestas and the merchants are busy plying their wares."

"How can people live amid so much noise and to-do?" Rachel was amazed.

"The best residences in the city are set away from here," Alexandre explained. "In the Garden District.

That is where the most beautiful homes and gardens of the city proper are. Of course the real wealth and beauty of Louisiana is not concentrated in the town. New Orleans exists for the convenience and amusement of the upriver plantations. Here you will find only merchants and men of business and others who are too lazy to make their fortune from the land. Also I must add"—and she thought she discerned a twinkle in his eyes—"the ladies quite prefer the convenience of having each other's company in town. Many of them reside at the plantations for only a few months of the year and then only in the strictest necessity."

"It sounds like a very indulgent life," Rachel said softly. She did not want to sound critical, but neither could she condone what sounded to her like utterly frivolous and useless existences.

"It was a gracious and very beautiful way of life and those who lived it had earned it," Alexandre said. "But with the war and the change that has been forced upon us, there will never again be such an existence on earth."

"You make it sound very grand," Rachel said softly, "but there was another side to it, too, not half so pretty as the part you describe."

"Ah, I forget," Alexandre rejoined. "That lovely head of yours has been filled with all sorts of Abolitionist propaganda. We will certainly see to the correcting of that."

"I must tell you," Rachel stated, "that my father was a fervent Abolitionist, as I myself am. It is not propaganda, sir, but conviction on this matter that propels my motivations even today."

"Your fervor speaks well for you, mademoiselle." Alexandre made a quick recovery. "However, I would much prefer to see your passions allied to a cause more worthy of you than that one. I am all the more anxious, now that you have told me this, for you to live among us and get to know us and our ways."

"I do not know for how long I will sojourn here," Rachel said slowly, "but this I do know and will tell you, sir. No matter how pleasant this place and its inhabitants, nothing will ever swerve my mind from the course that I know to be God's truth."

"Your strong principles do much to recommend you," Alexandre said. "Yet is it not also very true that where the heart leads, the mind will follow?"

"I have never heard that sentiment expressed before," Rachel said. "Thus I cannot comment on its veracity."

She leaned toward the window, turning her attention once more to the busy street scene outside, hoping to avoid any further conversation with him along those lines. The hired carriage turned in on a narrow street.

"I believe we are almost at our destination," Alexandre remarked. He indicated the house with the tip of his ivory-topped walking stick.

Rachel begged him not to accompany her inside. She had a horror of her prospective landlady's thinking she was being sponsored by a young man of the town. Alexandre acquiesced to her wishes.

"I will call on you tomorrow afternoon at four o'clock," he said, taking her hand and bringing it just to his lips.

"Good-bye then," Rachel murmured. She was relieved when the driver opened the door and helped her to alight. She stood on the pavement while he got down her carpetbag and she peered at the house, whose plaque read No. 5, DIMOND'S ROW. She had not even thought to ask Romain the name of the street, but it did not matter, she reassured herself, here she was. The house looked substantial enough and the street quiet. Should it prove unsuitable, she could arrange for a carriage to take her as quickly as this one had brought her.

She stood on the steps and waited as the driver rang the bell. The door opened and a middle-aged lady entirely in proportion to the house stood in the now-open doorway. Her ample figure was clothed in fabric of a tiny-flowered pattern, and her hair was entirely covered by a cap whose large white ruffle framed her face.

"The young lady is looking for accommodations," the driver said, nodding toward Rachel. "I'll bring in the bag." He entered the foyer, put the carpetbag down on the floor, tipped his hat to Rachel, and left.

She scarcely had time to look about when Mrs. Hinsdell took complete charge of her.

"My dear young lady," the worthy woman began at once, "come right into the parlor and sit you down. I'll have a piping-hot cup of coffee for you in no time."

Before Rachel could protest that the heat of the day would make a hot beverage unbearable, Mrs. Hinsdell bustled out, leaving her new guest alone in a comfortable, if fussily furnished parlor. It seemed to Rachel as though there would be no end of little flowers patterned everywhere. Long swags of cretonne printed with sprigs of violets covered the windows, the round tables scattered about the room, and even provided for tiny curtains on the cabinet shelves. Rachel selected a high-back chair covered in dark purple velvet and sat down primly, hands folded in her lap, waiting for the proprietor of the house to return.

She could make out the faint noises of activity in the kitchen. Other than that, the only sound in the house was the gentle chiming of a tall mahogany grandfather clock standing in front of the wall opposite her. It seemed a pleasant enough place, and Rachel had to admit that Alexandre Romain was a man of judgment.

But for all that, she reminded herself sharply, he was a rebel, a southerner who still stood for everything her father had always denounced. He defended slavery and the right of other people to grow rich from it, never having to put their own hands to toil. Old John York had considered idleness almost as grievous a sin as slavery. Moreover, this new acquaintance not only defended those awful ideas, he advocated a return to them! Rachel shook her head slowly. Everything he proposed was unthinkable.

Mrs. Hinsdell was back with a large tray. She set it down on a table between herself and Rachel and poured two steaming cups of coffee. Then she held out a platter, holding a pile of flat, round confections that Rachel was sure she had never seen before.

"These are pralines, my dear," Mrs. Hinsdell said, as if reading her thoughts. "From your accent, I guess you've never had them before. We consider them a great delicacy, and I'm sure you'll learn to love them."

"Thank you," Rachel said uncertainly, taking one and biting into it gingerly.

"And there's plenty of good chicory coffee to wash it down with," Mrs. Hinsdell went on.

Rachel was amused. The woman was every inch the mother hen that Alexandre Romain had made her out to be, but her flutterings only added to the younger woman's discomfort. She found the pralines overly sweet and the coffee chokingly hot. She didn't know how to forgo disgesting a quantity of each without offending her hostess.

"Will you be staying with us long?" Mrs. Hinsdell asked. "I am sure you will find life here very gay."

"I am rather a quiet person," Rachel admitted.

"Oh, my dear, I didn't mean here in this house," Mrs. Hinsdell said quickly. "I was referring to the many attractions of the city. Some say New Orleans can be compared only with Paris, France."

"Yes, I am sure I have heard that before," Rachel said amiably. "However, my stay here is not predicated upon amusement. If I find a suitable position, then I will stay. If not, I shall quit the city and return to my home in the North."

"What sort of position do you seek?" Mrs. Hinsdell asked.

"I have been a nurse and a teacher as well," Rachel replied. "I daresay I could be of service in either of those occupations or perhaps there is something else I am suited for."

"I take it you have no acquaintanceship in the city," Mrs. Hinsdell said.

"That is correct," Rachel said, "except for the young man whom I met on the train, and who directed me to your house. However, I must hasten to say that he is no more than a chance acquaintance at that."

"Yet he brought you here in a very fine carriage," Mrs. Hinsdell said, "and he took care to direct you to the most proper boardinghouse in the city for an unattached female, if I do say so myself. I have that reputation, you know, and it is quite well deserved and carefully maintained."

"I am sure it is," Rachel said. She was tiring of the conversation and longed for the privacy of a room of her own.

"If the young gentleman is at all well connected, I daresay he will be able to help you find a suitable situation," Mrs. Hinsdell said carefully.

Rachel knew that her landlady was eager for information and in her desire to protect her own reputation, Rachel was obliged to answer. "Mr. Romain is not at all the sort of person who would know of a situation in the areas of interest to me. I believe that the ladies of his acquaintanceship need never trouble themselves about earning a living."

"I daresay not," Mrs. Hinsdell agreed, "if he is of the Romain family, which is so prominent in New Orleans. Still, I think you have made a most fortunate acquaintanceship, my dear."

"I would very much like to be shown my room," Rachel said, rising. "It has been a fearfully long journey and I am rather fatigued."

"Of course you are, my pet." The stout landlady all

but cooed over her new charge. "Let me ring for Adelle, who will take you upstairs at once." She picked up a small glass bell that sat on the table and shook it vigorously until its tinkling sound brought a curtsying maid to the door. "Adelle, you are to show mademoiselle to room No. 4 and attend her if there is anything she needs."

"Yes, ma'am," the maid murmured. Rachel followed her; the beige-skinned girl, she was grateful to see, was clothed in a simple dress of solid mauve with a starched white apron crisscrossed over it; at least there was something in the Hinsdell establishment that was not swathed in tiny flowers.

But the same could not be said for the room that the maid showed her to. It was large and sunny, with a pair of tall windows looking over a garden in back. Rachel was glad it did not face the street, which she feared would be noisy with traffic. The room itself was all of a pattern, the background white with multicolors of minute bouquets on the chintz that flowed everywhere. Walls, windows, bedstead, and canopy were all covered with the ubiquitous pattern.

Rachel sank into a small chair. The room, she supposed, was very pretty. It certainly was different from any other place she had slept before. The furniture at the farm had been made by her father and nothing in their way of life had permitted frills. The tents and cabins she was assigned to as a nurse were no better than the barracks of the soldiers they served. Rachel looked down at her hands, folded in the lap of her gray suit. Although since leaving home she had stopped wearing the strict Quaker dress of her upbringing, her nurse's uniforms and even the few clothes she had chosen herself had differed little from that plain mode. She still chose gray and brown and muted blue to clothe herself in; she had left some of the old ways behind but, she mused now, not all. It seemed to her that any ornamentation of self and surroundings was the needless vanity her father had always described it as.

But everywhere around her, in this house and in the streets outside it, New Orleans was a veritable parade of flowers and feathers and ruffles. Gaily striped awnings fluttered everywhere, over house and shop windows. All of the citizenry, even the barefoot, turbaned women with their fruit baskets on their heads, seemed bent on outdoing one another in the blaze of colors they affected. Were they wrong or was she? All of a sudden it seemed to Rachel that she was wearily out of step with the rest of the world.

She stood up, sighing, and reached back to undo the tiny buttons of her blouse. She slipped out of her long skirt and stood in camisole and petticoat. She walked over to the chest, on which stood a white porcelain ewer and basin. She poured some of the water out, pleasuring herself in grateful coolness as it ran through her hands and splashed on her face. A clean linen towel was neatly folded and she dried herself briskly. She walked over to the bed, thinking how nice it would be to stretch out for a few hours, when there was a light knock on the door.

Rachel was startled. "Who is it?" she called out.

There was an almost imperceptible murmur at the door. Rachel went closer. "Who?" she repeated, then realized it was the maid who had shown her the room. She opened the door, snatching her skirt and covering herself with it. For all her modesty, she did not want to have to get dressed all over again.

Adelle seemed not to notice her state of dishabille. Timidly the girl said, "Here are the day's newspapers, miss. Mistress thought you want to see them." She thrust them into Rachel's hands, dropped a hasty curtsy, and slipped out of the room, closing the door behind her.

Rachel's wondering turned to instant realization when she glanced at the front page of the *Daily Delta*. Between the masthead and the small section at the bottom for news, the largest part of the page had printed on it the unmistakable neat lines and boxes of classified advertisements. Rachel was somewhat amused to find the front page of a newspaper given over to commerce rather than to the important news of the day.

She folded it and resumed the chair instead of the bed and combed through the listings looking for the heading OCCUPATIONS.

She scanned it eagerly; most of the listings were of no interest, asking that the applicants be gentlemen. She picked up the *Picayune*, which had a more conventional front page. She read through it, finding herself caught up in various dispatches and articles. These items of business and financial matters held no interest for her, but she found herself somehow compelled to read all of the various accounts of society doings in the city and its environs. She would not admit to herself that she was hoping to catch a glimpse of the name Romain; instead she told herself that she was silly to be wasting time and effort in the consumption of such nonsense, all of which had nothing to do with her. But still she read compulsively on.

She was totally absorbed in her reading when she was again startled by a knock at the door. This time Adelle was announcing in a clear, singsong voice that "dinner was in fifteen minutes." Rachel put down the paper. She barely had time to wash and dress before presenting herself downstairs. It would not do at all to be late, especially on her very first day.

Her reading gave her the impression that life in the city was an endless round of levees, fetes, parties, and balls, with the arrival and departure of socially prominent citizens the most arresting news of the day. Most of the names were French, with cumbersome spellings, and she was sure she would never be able to master the pronunciation.

What did it matter anyway? she asked herself sharply.

It was not as if she were going to partake of any of the sort of festivities that were recounted in the newspapers. Certainly no mention of the arrival of Mademoiselle or even Miss Rachel York was going to be found in the *Daily Delta* columns. Still, she had to admit to her reflection in the oval mirror above the basin, it was irresistible. Almost like peeping into the front windows of those grand houses Alexandre Romain had hinted at. Or even like the fairy tales she had read at school, so distant were these lives from hers.

She had not advanced far enough in her perusal of the *Picayune* to read the occupations column. She resolved to do so immediately after dinner.

She looked at herself in the mirror again, wondering, hoping that her simple blue dress would not be too plain. A blush rose to her cheeks as she realized the impiety and frivolousness of the thought. Rachel held her head high as she walked slowly down the staircase to the dining room. Was the wickedness of the city so pervasive that merely having breathed its air already made her victim to all its naughty temptations?

15

"See, Emilie, there it is." Jason held the folded newspaper up so she could see it.

Emilie came and stood behind his chair, leaning over his shoulder so that the gas lamp afforded them both illumination. "It's very clear indeed, Jason," she said. "I'm only surprised that there has been no response. Perhaps there will be a letter or a caller later in the week."

"I hope so," Jason said. "Otherwise it will be a delay of more than a week again. The papers run these advertisements only once a week."

"But it can't be!" Rachel protested. "I can't just stay here for another full week without knowing whether or not I have any prospects."

"I am so terribly sorry, miss," Mrs. Hinsdell commiserated. "But when Adelle went to straighten your room after dinner, she was certain that you had already done with the papers."

Once again Rachel admonished herself for having lingered far too long after dinner in the parlor the previous evening. Company at table had proved to be unexpectedly congenial. Aside from the rather chatty spinster lady who was a native of the city but living entirely alone on her dwindling resources, there were also present two gentlemen, in addition to Mrs. Hinsdell herself, presiding over the ample fare. One of the gentlemen, a Mr. Scott, was a merchant from Illinois who had been in New Orleans only a fortnight. Rachel was most eager to talk to him and glean what news she could of the North she had been away from for so long. He had joked, when Mrs. Hinsdell introduced Rachel to the others at dinner, that they were practically neighbors, she being from Ohio and he from a small city in the southern part of his home state.

Dinner then had been a rather more agreeable affair than Rachel had presupposed, and when the other boarders and their hostess entreated her to remain downstairs with them for some mild amusement in the front parlor, she readily agreed.

It was only after she had at last bade the others good night and returned to her room that she found what her innocent dallying had cost her. Adelle had come in to straighten the room and turn down the bed and had taken the newspapers, including the as yet unfinished *Picayune*, and consigned them to the trash basket, the contents of which had already been burned by the time Rachel discovered the loss.

Alexandre, when he came to call as promised, promptly at four that afternoon, was delighted. He could see no cause for Rachel's consternation. "It will take far more than even a fortnight for me to show you the city properly," he declared, "and to give my sister time to organize a fete in your honor."

Rachel received this last piece of information with utter shock. "Why, I would not know a single person there," she said, faltering, "nor would I even have the proper sort of dress!"

"You'll know me," Alexandre said, laughing, "and you'll know Claire. She's invited you for tea tomorrow afternoon."

Rachel sank down slowly on Mrs. Hinsdell's best sofa. "Who . . . who is Claire?" she asked.

"My sister," Alexandre explained.

"Oh, yes, of course, your sister," Rachel murmured. She felt as though she were drowning in a whirlpool of confusion. First the loss of the papers and with it the opportunity she had so been pressing for; next the arrival of Alexandre, with all the novelty of his proposals.

She looked up at him. "I wanted to go for a walk this morning," she declared. "And I realized I don't even know the name of the street I'm living on. It's as if I've been dropped from the sky, and had landed without knowing where I am. And I must say I find all of this quite discomforting."

"There, there," Alexandre said soothingly. "There's nothing at all awry, and all of your misgivings can be easily remedied. You are inhabiting Number five, Dimond's Row, on Tchoupitoulas Street."

"What?" Rachel said. "I have never heard such a word in my life, I declare!"

"Have no fear, I will write it out for you," Alexandre assured her. "To continue. This row is bounded at one end by St. Joseph's Street and at the other by Delord. Should you find yourself anywhere at all in the city, any competent cab will be able to deliver you back here quickly and easily."

Rachel continued to look glum.

"As for the matter of your attire," Alexandre went on, "I would not belittle myself in your esteem by claiming to be a connoisseur of ladies' fashions. However, I must in all modesty admit to having a deep appreciation for beauty, and I assure you, you would look the most splendid lady present in any company. However,"—he smiled at her—"my knowledge of ladies indicates that they all feel themselves quite inadequately displayed without splendiferous garments. I can tell you that my sister will deem it a privilege, nay, a responsibility, to take you under her wing in the best establishment of the city and help you array yourself as you feel necessary."

"I cannot put the burden of myself on an utter stranger," Rachel said, "such as your sister, kind though your offer might be. Nor have I the slightest inclination toward, as you put it, arraying myself. My clothing is adequate and suitable for my station and purposes in life."

"I in no way intended to offend your pride," Alexandre said hastily, jumping into the breach. "But you yourself—"

"Pride!" Rachel interrupted him. "Pride is a sin from which I have always held myself most aloof. I am insulted, sir, by your cheekiness in attaching it to me!"

Alexandre was perplexed. He was enjoying the game most heartily but now he realized that his pretty antagonist was not. It was time to marshal his pieces and withdraw somewhat if she were not to be lost entirely. "Mademoiselle, I beg your forgiveness. You are as without blemish as any maiden I have ever encountered. I deeply apologize if I have spoken too hastily and offended you, but please permit me to point out that what I have said, albeit foolish, was only in response to your own declaration. Please forgive me."

The sentiments were expressed in a voice so strong with feeling that Rachel could only smile and nod. He was trying so hard to be kind to her and she was constantly provoking him and herself as well by reacting so strongly. She chastised herself again and determined to be more amiable with him. "I am sorry for any misunderstanding between us," she said simply. "But please understand that I am being bombarded with so many novel ideas all at once that I scarcely have any time to take breath between considering them." She paused. "I thank you so much for your kindnesses, yet I must tell you frankly that I shall remain in your city only for the next week. If there is nothing presented in the way of opportunity for me then, I shall purchase a steamboat ticket and return north."

"I earnestly hope that we, and I, will not lose you that quickly," Alexandre said. "But if such is your intention I shall do nothing to oppose it. However, I must tell my sister she is to act in all haste in setting an earlier date for your party than we had planned."

Rachel had hoped her declaration of intent would put aside forever the matter of a party, but she realized that she stood little chance of escaping it. Alexandre seemed determined upon it, and if his sister, Claire, was anything like the ladies she had read about the previous day, her life was composed entirely of such organizing. Something told her that the as yet unknown Claire would rise to the occasion of haste rather than be topped by it. In any event, there would be tea with the lady on the morrow, and Rachel would know the worst by then.

She smiled at her visitor and when he offered to take her for a short walk so that she could see something of the neighborhood, she gladly acquiesced.

She ran upstairs to get her bonnet and nodded good day to Mrs. Hinsdell, who opened the front door for the young couple. That lady smiled after them, fortified in the knowledge that she had been right all along, when she had first spotted the substantial carriage and gentleman within delivering her new boarder the previous afternoon. The girl might be new to the city, but she had evidently captured the attentions of a most elegant young gallant.

Mrs. Hinsdell retained her smile all the way back to the kitchen. Should something permanent come out of it, her establishment's reputation would be highly embellished and the influx of other young lady boarders could most certainly be counted on. Such news traveled quickly and widely through the gossip-adoring city and an alliance between one of her boarders and an illustrious family like the Romains bespoke golden returns.

The landlady's spirits soared even higher the next afternoon when an elegantly appointed cabriolet arrived for Miss York. The liveried driver presented himself at the door and gave Mrs. Hinsdell an engraved card bearing the name of his employer. She sent Adelle hurrying upstairs at once to summon Rachel down.

Rachel for all the world could not understand the great fuss that her hostess was making. For herself, she was rather disappointed, having expected Alexandre to call for her in person. She took the gloved hand of the driver to assist her in getting up into the little open carriage. As they drove off she wished she knew whether it would be proper to speak with him. She longed to have the carriage hood raised so that she could sink back in its shadows. With it lowered, she felt herself on display. She might as well have been totally naked for the embarrassment she felt. She resolved to see as much as she could of the city as they drove along and avoid catching the eye of anybody who might be looking at her.

Soon the narrow streets opened onto broader boulevards. The houses that nestled against each other, chockablock, with their ironwork balconies, gave way to high stone walls and thick privet hedges that protected the large houses set well back from the street. From time to time, Rachel could catch a glimpse of an imposing house set between graceful willow and poplar trees. Some houses boasted grounds so large and extensively planted they resembled small parks behind their walls and fences. It was easy to slip into a reverie, imagining the grandeur and elegance that filled such places. She grew more and more curious about the house she was on her way to see. She wondered if it was similar to these dreamlike mansions.

Again she longed to ask questions of the black coachman who sat stiffly in front of her. But she felt tongue-tied, unable to converse because she did not know the proper way to address him or whether any conversation would be considered proper at all. Once again she felt herself filled with loathing for the inhuman system that had produced such situations where human beings could not have free intercourse as they surely were intended to. Slavery was gone but many of its impediments remained, especially for a novice like herself, who had had no part in the earlier system and now was completely at a loss in trying to grapple with the everyday manners of the current situation.

But her immediate question was quickly answered when the equipage turned smartly into a lane that curved to meet the outside of the house she thought surely the equal, if not the better, of any of those they had passed. It was a creamy beige stone in color and the dramatic wrought-iron work that climbed to the second story of the house was more richly designed, Rachel thought, than any such tracery she had seen since she'd arrived in New Orleans. The ironwork took the form of a vine, with delicate leaves and clusters of grapes perfectly captured in the black metal. Creamy yellow roses and thick white waxy magnolias seemed to take on the coloration of the house itself. Rachel looked all around in wonderment as the coachman helped her from the carriage. She took a deep breath as the wide wooden black door swung open silently from inside. Rachel stepped into a high, cool foyer. Huge Chinese vases held fresh, blooming flowers and Rachel could hear the splash of a fountain somewhere in the interior.

"Welcome!" A strong feminine voice floated down at her. She looked up and saw a smiling blond woman in a flowing gown coming down the stairs toward her. "I am Claire Rabineau," she said, extending her hand as she reached ground level, "and you must be the anticipated Miss York."

"I am Rachel York," Rachel said, extending her own hand. "And I want to thank you very much for your kindness in receiving me."

"Not at all!" Claire exclaimed, taking her young guest by the arm and leading her into a pale green drawing room. "It is always a pleasure to have charming visitors and when the visitor is one who has come from a distance, it is even more amusing."

Rachel nodded at a gesture that invited her to sit, and she sank down on a small, comfortable sofa. The room was exquisitely furnished. Even her unpracticed eye could appreciate that. Long drapes of pale green shantung shut out the afternoon sun and the walls were covered in a watered silk of the very same shade. Even the sofas and chairs of velvet upholstery were of the same color. Only the deep carpet beneath her feet was a darker shade of the same verdant hue.

"My brother is completely taken with you, my dear," Claire said, "and tells me that we must open the doors of the city for you, which, I hasten to assure you, it would be my pleasure to do, in any event." She smiled. "However, that rascal has a way of making me outdo even my best intentions. He tells me that you wish to teach."

Rachel was somewhat startled by the quick transition in her hostess's conversation. "Yes," she said. "I have been both a teacher and a nurse and I wish to find a position where I may be so employed again."

"How sad for you that you should need to," Claire said.

"Not at all, madame," Rachel said. "It is quite my own choice. I . . . I have a small holding in the North which provides me with some income but I am unused to a life other than that I have known."

Claire raised her eyebrows. "Surely you could learn to accommodate yourself to such an existence," she said. "It is not in the least bit difficult to cultivate leisure."

Rachel smiled. "I am sure it is not," she said. "But it is not my wish."

"Well, you seem a steady and proper enough person," Claire said. "Do you want to take a position as governess, perhaps in some great house?"

"Oh, no," Rachel answered quickly. "I want to work with people who need me."

Claire's eyebrows remained up. "Such as?" she asked.

"I would like to help teach the newly freed people," Rachel said.

Claire's cup rattled in her saucer. Rachel wondered if she was going to drop it. Her hostess' unease steadied her own reserve somehow and she suddenly felt herself quite comfortable and confident in this elegant house.

"My dear." Claire's voice was scarcely more than a whisper. "It's unheard of!"

Rachel shook her head, smiling. "No, it is not," she said softly. "I have been doing just that in Virginia this last year."

"Does my brother know that?" Claire asked.

"I am quite sure he does," Rachel replied. "I am sure I mentioned it during our conversation on the train."

"And still he thought to bring you here?" Claire spoke out loud but as if to herself. "Fancy that!" She turned her gaze steadily on Rachel, scrutinizing her from the tips of her shoes to the brim of the perky little hat atop her head. It was as though she were searching her person for the reason for Alexandre's attraction. "Well, I daresay you're pretty enough," she decided at last. "But I can't imagine what Alex has in mind. Still," she said, setting her cup and saucer on the edge of a low canewood table, "it really doesn't matter. We shall have our party and our fun. If you are determined to stay in New Orleans. I daresay it is your responsibility to have you see both sides of the life here."

"I am not at all sure that I am remaining in New Orleans," Rachel hastened to explain. "Much depends on my finding a suitable position."

"I don't suppose a position at the Young Ladies' Academy would suffice." Claire made an almost certain answer out of the question.

Rachel smilingly shook her head. She understood what

Alexandre's sister was all about and could not help but admire her for so quickly understanding and absorbing views that were so foreign to her own. Even Rachel's all-but-blasphemous ideals could not swerve Madame Rabineau from fulfilling her social obligations. Obviously these last were of far more moment in her life than politics or ideals.

Claire looked straight at her. "I knew you were a Yankee," she said. "But there are Yankees and there are Yankees. I had no idea a friend of my brother's would turn up an Abolitionist." She leaned across the table to pat Rachel's hand. "But never you mind, dear, how I do run on. It doesn't matter to me in the least. It just adds to the intrigue of that boy. And really, it amuses me to think of an Abolitionist, and pretty as a picture, sitting in the house of Colonel Rabineau."

"Your husband, madame?" Rachel asked.

"My late husband," Claire replied. "The colonel departed this life during the war."

"Oh, I am sorry to hear that," Rachel said quickly. "I can well understand my sentiments being somewhat distasteful to you, especially under such circumstances."

"Tut and nonsense," Claire said. "The colonel died of dysentery, and not a moment too soon, either. He was far older than I, and scarcely a war hero. But he was a gentleman and good to me. It's only that I amuse myself with the thought of what he would have made of *you*."

Rachel realized she must not try to read too much significance into Claire's remarks. Her hostess seemed to flit from topic to topic with the ease and swiftness of a butterfly, contradicting herself at one swoop and finding the most serious matters highly amusing at another. More importantly, she made her young guest feel quite at home and not at all the oddity that her Abolitionist sentiments might have made her in such surroundings. Claire was determined to treat her as another guest, she hoped an amusing one, but in any event one to be entertained royally and made much of.

They chattered away the rest of the afternoon, with Claire doing most of the talking, punctuating their conversation with drafts of sweet herb tea, light *beignets*, and a smaller, less cloying kind of praline than Mrs. Hinsdell had offered. By the time Alexandre joined them twilight was closing in, and the date for the fete had been set for the very next Tuesday.

He offered to see her back to Tchoupitoulas Street, and Rachel accepted. As they made ready to leave, Claire took her hand once more.

"I will come and call for you on Friday morning," she declared. "If your stay with us is to be a short one after all, sweet Rachel, it will be unthinkable for you to have been here and gone without having a silk gown to commemorate your visit. This very Friday we shall go shopping and find something that will be eminently suitable, I'm sure."

Before Rachel could protest, Claire held up her hand. "I am sure that a young lady of your serious demeanor will think shopping a tedious bore. I understand that perfectly, but I assure you, you will find the shops here most amusing."

There was no way to argue with that, and Rachel had to content herself with thanking Claire profusely.

Once in the carriage, she turned to Alexandre. "Your sister is most unusual," was the only way she could think of describing her.

"Most," Alexandre agreed. "Claire could find anything from a shop to a monument to a baby carriage amusing. She could tolerate almost anything in the world, I think, if only it were amusing."

"I must say I liked her very much," Rachel said warmly. "She was kindness itself to me."

"I knew that your politics would not upset her," Alexandre said. "My sister is a survivor. If it's to be the

Yankees who control, then she will make do with the Yankees. If the French should reclaim Louisiana, that, too, would suit her admirably. There is no turn of events, I fear, to which she could not accommodate herself."

"You sound as though you criticize her," Rachel said.

"Not at all, I admire her thoroughly," Alexandre declared. "Although I am seldom in agreement with her. One who loved her less than I do might label her an opportunist, but I see in my sister merely a love of life that propels her ever onward."

"Her husband was much older than she," Rachel said.

"Yes, the colonel was Methuselah to Claire," Alexandre said. "But the match had been made by my parents and, poor girl, she had no say in the matter at all. Still, she made the best of things. Rabineau's mansion, as you can see, was admirably suited for parties and so my sister gave parties." He paused. "And I must say this for her—when the old man was taken, she had grace enough to stop the music for a suitable length of time."

"I could never be like her," said Rachel. "But for all the differences there are between us, I must admit I do admire her greatly."

"I would not want you to be like her or like any other woman in the world," Alexandre said quickly. "I want you to be just the way you are."

"A Yankee Abolitionist?" Rachel asked mockingly, trying quickly to put some gaiety into a conversation that had all at once turned all too serious.

"That, too, shall change, as I told you," he murmured.

Rachel said nothing, but she did not let him take her hand and she sat stiffly and silently apart from him for the rest of the drive. He seemed intent on winning her over, though whether it was her mind or her heart or both he wanted, she was not sure.

She was beginning to trust him a little, but what was so frightening, she was beginning to trust herself not at all.

16

"Les Chandelles is mine!" Higgins' voice, which had always been subservient, now rose to a roar. He slammed his fist against the table. "You promised it to me when I joined up with my men. You said I could do what I wanted with it!"

Robin refused to rise to the challenge, flung at him in the darkened room. He retained the haughty disdain of his class for such as Higgins, and everything in his manner let the man know it. "Things have changed," he said simply, but in a voice that would brook no argument.

"It's going to burn. I swore I would burn it and I'm going to!" Higgins would not let go.

"You will do nothing about Les Chandelles or anything else in the parish until you are given word," Robin said coldly. "If you dare to disobey, you will be stripped of your rank. Your men will no longer be yours to lead, at the very least." He paused for a moment to let the implied threat sink in. Then he decided that bluntness was the quickest way to reach a man like Higgins. "You know the power of our organization. You know what it has done to our enemies. We consider a traitor from within far more dangerous than an enemy from without. Do not force us to turn this power against you."

Higgins hung his head.

"You took a blood oath," Robin reminded him. "You

will keep that oath unless you want to give up every drop of blood that's in you."

"All right." The words came weak and hoarse from Higgins. The fight was gone from him. He knew that he dared not stand alone against the organization. He consoled himself thinking that this beruffled Creole dandy who threatened him now would not always be in a position to command him. Things would change someday and he would be ready. Perhaps Elmore was the real traitor; perhaps he had his own secret reason for protecting the hated plantation.

"In the meantime," Robin went on, to mollify him, "there are other matters to be attended to. Things have been kept quiet in this parish for too long."

Higgins chortled. "That's exactly what I've been saying," he agreed.

"I hope you have been saying it only to yourself," Robin said sharply, reminding him of the disciplined secrecy he was bound by. "We have been deliberately inactive here, to throw them off guard. Now that we are ready to move, we'll catch them unawares." He drew closer to Higgins, trying not to take in too much of the smell that clung to him. He whispered tentative details of the action being planned, action that Higgins would command and execute with his men.

The place selected was a rather small plantation located near the western border of the parish, a three-hour hard ride from where they sat now, in Higgins' house. The former estate had been broken up at the instigation of a deputy from the federal governor and the land parceled out among the former slaves. The master and mistress had taken themselves to their town house in New Orleans, leaving the land forever. Without any white people left in the area, the blacks were growing cane for their own commerce. The crop was reputedly doing well, and thus stood as a thorn in the side of the organization that had sworn to tolerate no such enterprise from the former chattel.

Higgins' eyes gleamed as Robin described the situation. The objective, he said, was total destruction of the crop, the buildings, and the people. How the destruction was to be carried out would be left entirely up to Higgins. Reaching the objective and the burning cross implanting were the only conditions imposed on him.

"Tuesday next?" Higgins repeated the date.

Robin nodded assent. He rose and stretched. Higgins' small property was on the border of Les Chandelles but security demanded that Robin return to the plantation by a roundabout, undetectable way. He had a hard ride in front of him if he was to be back in time for dinner. He nodded a curt good-bye to Higgins and left.

His galloping away was the signal to the women that they could once more come into the house.

Myrtie tried to slip by Higgins in the darkness as she furtively moved along the far wall to her accustomed corner, but he grabbed her by the arm, almost bringing her to her knees. Jen watched as her daughter cowered in fright. She didn't understand what it was about the girl that made Higgins turn so mean. In the early months of their living together, he had been rough with her but not any more so than her first husband had been. It was only since Higgins had taken notice of the girl that his behavior toward both of them had become so violent. Before, he had been content to mount her in the darkness of their room and spill himself quickly, turning to sleep. His demands became ever more forceful, all the more so now that he had insisted that the girl bear witness to the act.

Jen breathed an almost audible sigh of relief when he let go of Myrtie and let her fall to the floor. Had he kept his hold on her, he would have pushed her into the bedroom and made her watch. Jen was grateful that this night, at least, it wouldn't happen that way.

She followed meekly behind him as he made his way into the other room, not daring to acknowledge her daughter or comfort her.

Being let alone was comfort enough for Myrtie. She drew herself up on her blanket, bringing her knees to her chest, dropping her head and hugging herself close with her arms. It had become the position in which she lulled herself from the horrors of the day into grateful sleep.

Before final fatigue overtook her, she always imagined the same short dream she had been nurturing ever since the first night he had forced her to watch them. She imagined herself in the darkness, on a night like this, stealing across the room to get the large knife from its shelf and hide it between her small breasts while she waited breathlessly for him to fall asleep. Then she would tiptoe into their bedroom and, both hands clutching the handle, would hold the knife up and swiftly sink the blade between his ribs. In her vision, she saw him dead from the very first blow, as if she knew that if she had the strength to carry out her plan, she would never succeed in removing the blade and stabbing him again. She saw him lying there with the cold metal deep in his chest, never to be removed from it.

She hugged herself in the darkness, shivering. It was a terrible dream for her to have made up, but it was all she had to go on living for.

In the next room her intended victim was lying awake with excitement. He ignored the presence of Jen, who lay motionless and available next to him. He had no need of her this night. His blood was stirring with anticipation over the raid that Elmore had ordered. It had been too long since the last fires had been lit in the parish. Now he would have six men with him and the authority of the organization behind him. He licked his lips in anticipation. He could already hear the screams of terror as they would come riding down on the unprotected cabins. He could see the destruction beneath the galloping hooves and hear the rising crackle of the fire as they threw the first torches into the cabins. Almost a week to plan and make ready in, to notify the men, to secure the supplies, almost a week in which to relish the fear and fury of which he was to be the perpetrator. He was wide awake with all the details of the raid coming clear to him. It was hours before he could lull his mind into a state of happy rest. It was not Les Chandelles, he reminded himself in his final thought before falling asleep, but it was a mighty good beginning.

It didn't take more than the next two days for all of the men to be notified. They all had ammunition enough, and to Dukes he gave the task of buying the several lengths of rope they would need. Each man would carry a small supply of kerosene and matches. In this dry weather, fire would grow quickly. The buildings would catch one from the other with the least bit of wind. Even the crop in the field was picked and bundled, making it drier and more vulnerable than if it still stood in the ground.

Jen did not know what was preoccupying him but she was grateful for the lack of attention both to her and to Myrtie. He seemed content to have his food ready when he came into the house and asked for little else. Indeed he scarcely spoke for days after the mysterious night visitor had been there. She wondered if that had something to do with the way Higgins was behaving or if maybe it was just in the natural way of things that some of his wildness had been calmed out of him. Whatever it was, she was glad of it. Maybe now things would settle down in this nice, quiet way and she could stop regretting the day she had agreed to give up her own place and follow him here.

The last night before the raid, Higgins was bursting with excitement. He couldn't fall asleep; it was as if the night were never going to end. When at last he fell into a restless slumber, it was near dawn and time for him to be up and about the chores. It was a mighty temptation not to break his back in the fields that day, but it had been strictly ordered that they must follow the natural pattern of things, especially on the days just before and after their midnight enterprises. There was to be no break in patterns that could throw suspicion on any of the participants. This was a law that had to be strictly adhered to. It was as much a part of the operation as the actual raid itself. Even his sending Dukes to buy rope in several different towns was done to allay any suspicions.

It was like being a soldier again, only this time Higgins was sure he was on the side that could not lose. They had everything in their favor—men, organization, ammunition. And the other side had nothing, nothing but their scared and frightened souls. He chortled to himself. Soon enough, this bunch won't have even that to call their own.

He had already decided that this, his first operation for the organization, was going to be a total success. No one, not man, woman, or child, was going to escape. If he had to use all the rope, all the bullets, all the flame there was in creation, he would see every last member of the settlement dead beneath his heels.

He worked his rows under the hot sun until an hour or so before it was time to leave.

He checked his gun, loading it, and packed his sheet and the firemaking supplies in his saddlebag. He patted Boss on the flank, telling himself that if the raid went as he planned, he would get Elmore to provide him with a more suitable mount. The mare could not be depended upon for those bursts of speed that might prove necessary in the course of their activities.

At last it was time to go. He said nothing to Jen, neither where or why he was going nor when he would be back. He didn't even look at her as he swung himself into the saddle and leaned forward as Boss picked her way carefully along the rock-strewn dirt path of the farm that led to the main road.

Once on the main road, he picked up his speed, anxious to get to the place where he was to meet Dukes. When he got there, Dukes was already waiting in the shadows of some overhanging trees. The two men grinned at each other without speaking, then set off at a gallop, side by side, to their next destination.

They had arranged that the others would also travel in pairs, coming together in the vicinity of the attack area. There they would all converge on the quarters.

Some of the other men were already at the rendezvous when Higgins and Dukes joined them. It was a wait of less than five minutes before the remaining pair arrived.

Now was the time to take command. Higgins cleared his throat and spat on the ground. "Mount up," he ordered. "We're going in whooping and hollering and aiming low."

The horses were untethered and the men got quickly into their saddles. They rode quietly toward the edge of the small settlement, Higgins in the lead.

He pointed to the single street slightly below the incline on which they stood. The houses were not in parallel rows, like the usual slave quarters, but stood in clusters of twos and threes, all along the cleared strip to where the canebrakes started.

"Give me a torch, quick," Higgins whispered to Dukes. Dukes swooped low in his saddle, grasping a bundle of long twigs and lighting one end and grinning before handing it to Higgins. Higgins held it aloft, like a beacon to the others.

"Now!" he shouted. "Let's go!" He spurred his horse and dashed forward. Bending low, he tossed the burning wood into the first house. There was a quiet moment and then, before they saw the flame surging through an unpaned window, there came a shout and the noise of quick movement as people rushed out, screaming.

"You two get the next ones," Higgins yelled, signaling to the men. "We'll take care of these!" He drew his pistol out of its holster and with three shots brought down each of the people—man, woman, and child—who had leaped out of the burning house.

"Go get 'em, boys!" he shouted.

Yelling and tossing the burning wood bundles, the men quickly covered the length of the street. Higgins charged forward, firing indiscriminately into the terrified crowd that came running from the burning cabins, only to be greeted by the onslaught of bullets from the well-armed raiders. Higgins looked on gleefully. The weather was dry and the slight wind was more than enough to carry the flames quickly through the little settlement. All of the cabin doors faced onto the cleared strip. There was no other way for the people to get out of the conflagation except to face the rain of bullets.

The street was now flaming with enough light to show clearly the features on each anguished face. Higgins watched as a young woman darted out of her cabin and tried to slip away through the narrow space between her house and the next one.

Dukes had his rifle to his shoulder and was ready to fire when Higgins put his arm out, stopping him.

"Let's have a little fun with this one." He grinned. "She looks just ripe enough."

The flames had shown him the coppery color of her skin and except for the tattered garment she was holding up in front of her, she was completely naked. Higgins got down from Boss and ran easily toward her. He came up behind her, grabbing her around the waist and pulling her up off her feet.

The girl started calling, but the sound could scarcely be heard above the crackling flames and the screams as the bullets reached their marks.

"Eben!" it seemed to Higgins the girl was shouting, but he only grasped the harder, and grinned the more, knowing that whoever this Eben was, he could do precious little to help her; if he wasn't dead already, he soon would be.

He grabbed Boss's reins and threw the girl facedown on his saddle. He looked up and down the street. At the head, the houses were all aflame, illuminating the bodies sprawled in front of them, none of them moving. At the other end the men were still shooting as the helpless victims tried to flee the flames. A man had come out of the last cabin, and as a spray of bullets found their target in him his body lurched slightly into the air, the limbs flailing like a rag doll's, before he fell to the ground. There was a final, convulsive twist and that was all.

Higgins held up his arm. "Hold fire!" he shouted. "No use wasting good ammunition on dead niggers." He signaled the men on the farther end to come back and regroup. He grinned at the happy, sweating faces who clustered around him, their exultation soaring at the ease with which they had completed their mission.

"Good job, boys," he said. "Only thing left to do now is light the cross. But I figure we might as well have a little fun before we do that." He winked and slapped the naked flank of the girl, who lay motionless over the saddle.

"Whoowee," one of the men shouted, while the others whistled and stamped their feet. In all the excitement of the killing and self-congratulations, they hadn't noticed her.

Higgins pulled her off and threw her to the ground. "Dukes, you go first." He conferred first honors on his deputy.

He himself was in no hurry. It would pleasure him to watch the five other men work their ways with her. The watching would incite his own passions till the final release would be as satisfying as watching the entire settlement burn. He leaned against Boss. He was in no great hurry at all.

The girl clung desperately to the little bit of garment she had to cover herself with, but Dukes ripped it away easily, baring her body completely.

"Jesus!" one of the men exclaimed.

Higgins looked closer. The coppery sheen he had noticed was an even glow of color all over her body. She had drawn her knees up in front of her, trying helplessly to hide herself, her arms covering her well-formed breasts. But the slim, terrified girl was no match for Dukes. He grabbed her ankles, yanking her legs straight and forcing himself between them. She screamed out, but his hand quickly shot over her mouth, stilling it. He thrust hard, egged on by the cheering and encouragement of his waiting cohorts. He finished and got to his knees grinning. Then he leaned over the girl, his hand whipping out as he slapped her brutally across the face.

"Don't fight the next time," he taunted her. "Do like you're supposed to. It's all you're good for anyway, nigger bitch."

Her face was bleeding where he had slapped her. Higgins signaled to the next man, who reached down, pressing the girl around on her belly. "Hell," he snorted, "I ain't going in where Duke's stuff went in and I'm damned if I want to look at that bloody mess, either."

This brought a roar of approval from the other men, who slapped their thighs and laughed as they watched and waited their turns.

He placed his hand on her buttocks, spreading them. "Black bitches sure are built high, aren't they?" he said, looking up at his companions with almost a tinge of admiration in his voice.

"That one ain't even black," one of the men said. "She's practically a high yellow."

"I don't care what the hell color she is," the man on top of the girl chortled. "She's got this nice high ass and I'm going in!" His stabbing thrust inside her was accompanied by a wailing scream from the girl that seemed almost inhuman.

The men looked at one another. Lynch strode forward, squatting on the fround near her head and, holding her by the chin, thrust his large red bandanna in her mouth. He got up, brushing his hands on his thighs.

"That'll keep her till I'm ready," one of the men chortled. "I aim to make her do me just there."

"I'm goin' in the way Charlie is," his partner replied. "That is, if Charlie ever gets done with it."

Charlie, still thrusting between the girl's buttocks, grunted. There, too, he could see she was beginning to run red. The scarlet flow against her still-bright skin agitated him, and he unwillingly ejaculated.

"Christ, I thought I'd get more than that," he said, lifting himself from the girl and squatting back on his heels.

"Maybe you can get another shot at it, Charlie," one of the men jeered. "Meanwhile we haven't even gotten our first time."

"Maybe we better speed it up a little bit, boys," Higgins said. He was getting a little nervous about the amount of time the men were taking. "You." He spoke to the man who had just voiced his preference. "Get it in her mouth while he does her." He jerked his thumb toward Lynch, who quietly unbuttoned his breeches with one hand while with the other he turned the girl once more around.

He pushed apart her now motionless legs and grabbed her buttocks from underneath, forcing his ready member easily inside. Lynch started to thrust and looked up. His sidekick was kneeling behind the girl. He had taken her head in both his hands and was forcing her face backward toward him. He pulled Lynch's gag out of her mouth. He stuck his finger inside, feeling her dryness. Then he put his finger into his own mouth, wetting and sucking it. He put it back between her lips, trying to get her mouth wet, never noticing how her eyes stared blankly out of her face.

Satisfied that she could now perform without hurting him, he pulled her jaw open and with his other hand firmly implanted himself. He rocked her head back and forth, causing the momentum she seemed incapable of. At last the rhythm took and the man bounced himself back and forth, still clutching her face and holding himself secured inside her mouth.

Higgins watched breathlessly, the slackened body of the girl now stiffened somewhat by the arched position she was forced into by the ministrations of the two men. He realized that his own mouth had gone dry in the excitement of watching them. He could feel the tenseness in his groin as his member grew and strained against his breeches. He hungered for the two men to finish. Then there would be only one more, the one who wanted to back-door her, before he could get his own pent-up seed rushing through that no longer struggling but still desirable body.

Lynch finished first. The other man kept going, rattling the girl's head and shaking hard to bring himself to quick fulfillment.

At last he was done. He drew himself out, grinning at the other men, letting her head fall back on the ground with a snap.

Once more she was flung over, once more the hapless body sodomized. But the fifth man to take her could find little pleasure. He rose back on his knees, still between her buttocks, and slapped her across the temples. "Move, goddamn you, move, goddamn you!" he demanded. He grabbed her shoulders, pulling her breasts up, arching her toward him. He shook her and then released her. She fell forward in a heap. "No use, damn it!" he swore. "She's dead."

"What!" Higgins exclaimed softly.

"Dead," the man repeated, rolling back on his knees.

"I might as well get done while she's still warm." He gave a few unenthusiastic stabs at the slackened flesh and then stood up in disgust.

"Well, that's the end of that one." He spat. "Tough luck."

"The hell it is," Higgins shouted. He felt cheated and brought down lower than he ever had in his life. He had played the good leader, letting all the other men go before him, waiting for the troops to finish before he took his own pleasure. Now, goddamn it, there was nothing left for him but a hard ride home and the same woman who was always there waiting. "She ain't finished yet," he snarled. "You, Dukes, have you got that stake sharpened yet?" He pointed to the pole that Dukes was cutting for the upright of the cross they would set aflame.

"Just about done," Dukes said, still whittling it with his knife.

Higgins walked closer to the body. He touched it with the toe of his boot, kicking at it until she lay prone and he had her arms and legs stretched out. He turned to Dukes. "I want you to set that cross right there," he said, pointing to the girl's torso. "I want it coming right up out of her."

He turned on his heel and stalked away.

He would get something into that dead bitch, even if it was only the fiery symbol of his having been there that night.

17

"I think you must admit you're enjoying your party very much." Alexandre smiled down at Rachel.

"Yes, I am," she said happily. "And I believe that you are, too."

"Anytime that I have you in my arms, I am the happiest of men and more than enjoying myself," he said, holding her even closer as he spun her around the crowded ballroom.

"You're making me dizzy, Alex," Rachel said, laughing. "You're going far too fast for me." She could scarcely catch her breath as he whirled her again and again.

"It is not I, mademoiselle, the music demands it," he answered loftily, and they both laughed.

Rachel could not believe that such beauty and merriment really existed. And totally, said Alex, who insisted she call him by his nickname, totally in her honor. It seemed a very dream to Rachel, who for the first time in her life was possessed of no other thought save what was happening. If this glorious night must end at last, she would think about tomorrow when tomorrow dawned. Now she was as given to the lights and the music and the charm of the young gallant who held her in his arms as she had ever been to anything else in her life.

"You must promise me one thing." Alex broke into her thoughts suddenly.

"What is that?" Rachel asked brightly, looking up at him.

"That you will never wear anything but pink," he replied. "It becomes you so outrageously that it would not be justice to any other color to have to compete with it."

She blushed.

His ways were still unexpected to her. Whenever she thought he was going to say something serious, he would instead charm her with the most outrageous compliment. Sometimes when she thought him capable of nothing but this gallantry, he would suddenly talk to her of the most serious matters, of politics and patriotism and his constantly expressed yearnings for the world that had passed and that he assured her she would have loved as much as he had.

Listening to him when that mood was upon him, Rachel would have to pull herself back. It would be far too easy to fall into the network of the reverie he was weaving for her. She knew that the old order was evil and stood for wickedness. That he and others like him took his pleasures from it was, if anything, proof. She could not let herself be swayed by him or the glitter he had cast around her. She must stay with the principle she knew to be right. Otherwise it was as though her father had lived in vain and all of her own life, until this very evening, would have no meaning.

But such thoughts were not clouding her mind now. Instead she laughed at his witticisms, blushed at his compliments, and found herself wishing that she could dance every dance with him. The fact that so many of the other young beaux claimed her for dances Rachel ascribed to the extreme politeness and courtesy of the society she had been brought into. She did not seek all this attention, nor did she look to find favor among those who claimed her.

One man like Alexandre Romain was enough; to be inundated by so many others of his sort was really unnecessary. She smiled as she thought it and was glad that he was with her.

"You're the only lady I know who can think while she's dancing," Alex complained, interrupting her thoughts.

"You would not be so upset with me if you knew what I was thinking." Rachel startled herself. She did not know how she had come to say such a thing. Had he challenged it, she would have had to admit that he was the one who was occupying her mind. I'm flirting with him, she thought bitterly, I am actually flirting! She did not know whether to be frightened or amused by her quick assimilation into Alex's circle.

The first guests to leave the party were coming to bid her good night. After they made their farewells, Rachel turned back to Alex. "It's all going to be over very soon, then, isn't it?" she asked. She could not help sounding wistful.

"Nonsense," he retorted, "the evening is still very young. The Belmonts are infamously early sleepers but I assure you, no one else in society pays them the least mind. My sister would be a disgrace to her class, at least in her own eyes, if the dancing did not continue for at least several more hours."

"Speaking of your sister," Rachel said, "I haven't spoken with her since we sat down to supper. Whatever can she be thinking of me?"

"She is notorious for having a better time at her own parties than any of her guests." Alex laughed. "If you had not been the guest of honor she would never have forgiven you for having outshone her this evening."

"I'm sure I did not," Rachel protested. "I don't know

how anyone could possibly look lovelier than she does in her magnificent silver ballgown."

"To say nothing of all the family jewelry," Alex added. "Yes, I must admit she does make quite a sight when she's gotten up in all of those."

He took her arm and they walked to one of the long tables on the side of the room where costumed, white-gloved servants were ladling punch from giant crystal bowls into dainty matching cups. "It isn't her jewelry or her elegance I admire," Rachel said. "It's the friendliness and graciousness with which she has received me. I don't know when anyone has ever been kinder to me."

Alex started to answer, but Rachel's attention was claimed by another young man bowing slightly and claiming the next dance. Rachel hurriedly consulted her dance card. "Ah, yes, Mr. Beaumont, excuse me." And before she could even sip the punch, she was swept away into yet another waltz, while Alex stood watching. He turned back to the table, setting down the crystal cup. "I say, Ben," he said, addressing one of the servingmen, "couldn't you fix me up with something just a bit stronger?"

The barman grinned, a wide, even-toothed smile stretching across his coffee-colored face. "*Pour vous, Monsieur Alex, bien sur.*" In a twinkling, he poured a quantity of amber-colored liquor in a glass. His deft movements were concealed by the table and he handed Alex a glass that might have appeared from nowhere.

Alex winked his thanks and turned around again to watch the dancers, particularly the lady in a pink tulle gown, whose every movement held him fascinated. The marble floor and mirrored walls of the ballroom were long familiar to him, as were the trellised formal gardens outside and all of his sister's house. All of it was as known to him as it was new to Rachel, and he marveled at how this simply bred girl from the North fit so well in this setting.

Alex felt an arm link itself around his. "And what are you doing, thinking such deep thoughts during one of my parties, dear brother?" Claire asked gaily. "Is everything not going just as you wished it to?"

"Precisely, my dear sister," Alex replied. "However, I think I will be leaving very shortly."

"What!" she said mockingly. "Aren't you enjoying my party?"

"Quite as much as I ever do," he said. "Which means that I must take care not to remain to the point where total boredom takes me over."

"This party was your idea, Alex," she reminded him thinly.

"Exactly," he said. "And my chief pleasure in it is the very contribution I made here." He nodded briefly in the direction of Rachel, who was still whirling around the dance floor in the arms of Mr. Beaumont. "Rachel has important business to attend to on the morrow," he said. "And I, of course, have promised to help her. I fear that means an early rising for both of us."

"Surely not together, brother." Claire pretended to be shocked.

"Of course not." Alex smiled his handsomest, most charming smile. "Rachel has very strong ideals, not the least of which, I'm afraid, is propriety. I have business to attend to this night as she does tomorrow and we must each be most happily tucked in." He bowed low over his sister's hand, kissing it. "Permit me, my dearest, to make our *adieux* for both of us."

He made off to claim Rachel just as the music was starting for the next dance. He told her he had already bid his sister good night for her.

"What is this sudden haste?" Rachel laughed. "You who were most anxious of all for this party."

"I have promised to come to see you at an undecently early hour of the morning with your precious newspapers," he reminded her. "And in order to keep that promise, I must make an early night tonight."

The carriage stopped at Mrs. Hinsdell's and he saw her safely inside. Then he instructed his driver to stop at a tavern on the seamy outskirts of the city. Alex jumped from the coach when they arrived at this, for him, most unusual destination and once inside, he tarried but a moment. It was all the time he needed to receive an almost imperceptible nod from a man seated at the first table. Then he leaped back into the coach, ordering the driver to take him home, a smile of deep satisfaction lighting his features in the darkness.

Alex was as good as his word. He arrived promptly at ten the next morning at Mrs. Hinsdell's. The landlady bustled to let him in herself, giving Adelle a good poke in the ribs to send the girl scurrying to bring Rachel downstairs.

Alex spread the skirt of his elegant morning coat as he seated himself on the small sofa in the front salon and watched with quiet amusement as Rachel scanned the newspapers. This time she paid no attention to the gossipy accounts of the coming and goings of the city's luminaries. She went right to the long list of classified ads, holding a pen in her eager fingers with which to mark anything that sounded promising.

She looked up suddenly, catching Alex quite unawares as he sat smiling and scrutinizing her.

Her face was bright with excitement. Her eyes shone. "Do you know of a plantation called Les Chandelles?" she asked him.

18

"Emilie, I insist on your telling me what is wrong," Francine said firmly. The two of them were sitting in the guest room that served as bedchamber for the Desbrosses. She spoke in a low voice, her hand holding that of her young friend.

Emilie hung her head. "No, I cannot," she said. Her voice wasn't much more than a whisper, but it was impossible for Francine not to catch the misery in her tone.

"My dearest girl, what else are friends for?" Francine said. "I am a woman of the world, with much experience, as well as being the one who has come closest to filling your mother's place for you. Please confide in me and let me help you. I can't bear to see you like this."

Emile shook her head, unrelenting. "I know you want to help me, dear Francine, but you cannot," she said. "It is too private a matter for me to discuss with anyone."

"When something is wrong in a marriage, it is usually only someone who stands close to, but outside it who can understand and help," Francine rejoined sympathetically. "Jason is a good man, I like him very much. I know he would not do anything in the world to hurt you. That much, at least, is true, isn't it?"

"Yes, of course," Emilie replied, but there was no enthusiasm in her voice.

"If he is not acting toward you as a husband should,"

Francine said slowly, "then you must discover the reason why." She looked reprovingly at Emilie. "Have you withheld yourself from him?" she asked, taking Emilie's chin firmly enough that the younger woman could not escape her careful scrutiny. "Something is obviously wrong, my darling," Francine stated. "And, if you will forgive me, I have enough knowledge of the ways of the world to guess what it is."

Emilie blushed. She lowered her lids, unable to return her friend's frank stare.

"Is Jason taking you for granted?" Francine asked bluntly.

Emilie shook her head.

"Is he then"—and Francine lowered her voice—"not fulfilling his husbandly—"

"Stop, I beg you!" Emilie interrupted, a flood of tears bursting unbidden from her eyes. "I cannot talk about it, I cannot!" She half sobbed, half choked.

"Emilie, Emilie," Francine said soothingly. "It is not the end of the world, I assure you. Nor need you fear to talk about it. I am afraid that such situations are all too common in the course of many marriages, especially in the early years, when the first blush is over but the comforts of companionship have not yet been firmly established. It is a simple matter and one that can avail itself of an equally simple solution."

Emilie looked up in spite of herself. "And what is that?" she could not help asking.

"You need a diversion, my darling," Francine answered airily and with a knowing smile. "You need something to remind your somewhat forgetful husband that you are a woman, and a woman to be greatly prized."

"And how do I do that?" Emilie asked helplessly. She felt as though she were once more a simple, ignorant girl and that the worldly-wise Francine held all the answers in her knowing hands. Painful as it was to talk about, the promise of help banished the embarrassment in which Emilie had been smothering.

"Perhaps, my darling, Jason has gotten too used to you," Francine suggested.

"Francine!" Emilie protested. "What then is supposed to occur in marriage but that? Husband and wife grow evermore accustomed to and affectionate toward one another."

"All well and good." Francine patted Emilie's knee. "But it frequently happens, even in the best of matches, that a man will begin to take his wife for granted. When a man becomes too sure of a woman, that is a very bad thing."

"I cannot believe you," Emilie said. "What else should Jason know from me but the certainty and security of my love and our situation together? Really, I think that this must be the very foundation of a marriage. I, for one, cannot imagine it any other way." She smiled sadly and then looked up at her friend. "But of course you will say that I am nothing more than a simple country girl, strictly brought up and knowing nothing of the mysterious ways of the world."

"Exactly." Francine smiled her confirmation. "Precious little were you able to learn of the ways of men before all the misfortunes they are capable of providing for women came tumbling down on you. I don't mean," she added, "to suggest any great wickedness on your part. You know that I have always championed Captain Phillips for your favor. I have not seen anything to change that. However, that does not signify that even the best of men and most dutiful of husbands do not need to be shaken up slightly now and then." Emilie started again to protest, but Francine stopped her. "Nor, from the little I gather from you, has Jason been as 'dutiful' of late as he should be."

Emilie hung her head and blushed. The conversation was too personally painful, too embarrassing for her to be able to continue, yet Francine held Emilie's hands firmly encased in hers, and without a dreadful wrenching loose and running away, there was no immediate escape. Emilie knew she was the prisoner of her friend's good intentions and probing questions.

"You needn't be so distressed, Emilie," Francine said softly. "The means for correcting your situation are immediately, and I must say delightfully, at hand."

Emilie raised her head. "Whatever do you mean?" she asked slowly.

"I mean my young cousin," Francine stated, firmly and without hesitation. "He absolutely adores you, and—" She broke off in mid-sentence, halted by the look of utter consternation in Emilie's eyes.

"Francine, I can't believe you are suggesting . . ." Emilie could not find the words with which to complete the thought.

"Yes, my dear, I am," Francine said firmly, tightening her grip on Emilie's hands. "Come, you must not think me so wicked or yourself either, for following a little advice. You know that I desire only your own good."

"I know that," Emilie said. "You have been the best and dearest friend and protectress anyone could wish. But . . . but," Emilie faltered again, trying to find the right words to express her feelings without hurting those of her friend. "I am not as you are," she said, "not having lived in great cities and gay society where such things, I'm sure, are quite everyday occurrences. Perhaps in those circumstances what you are telling me would be acceptable, nay, grasped by young wives eager for such opportunities. But I am not—I cannot—it is not for me to behave so. I am sorry, but I could never do as you suggest."

"I doubt that there will be anything for you to do, dear," Francine said soothingly. "Everything that is necessary will present itself to you. You are not required to seek it or do anything else to make it happen."

"Nothing but acquiesce," Emilie shot back hotly, her sensibilities fired now by the outrageousness of what Francine was suggesting. As much as she longed for a return to the comfort and caresses of Jason's arms, she could never reach that goal by encouraging the attentions of another man along the way.

Nor could she, in all courtesy, tell Francine how much she disliked this dashing young cousin who supposedly had much of New Orleans society at his feet. She could not dishonor herself by admitting to Francine that Robin's attentions had already been thrown at her, nor could she insult her friend by expressing her dislike of him.

"You'd needn't really acquiesce if you don't want to," Francine said quickly, noting Emilie's total consternation. "All that is really necessary, my darling, is that your husband fully understand that you are still attractive to other men. That will be enough, I assure you, to set everything to rights."

Emilie sighed. "I cannot even entertain such an idea," she said. "It is utterly beyond my ken." She leaned over and kissed her friend softly on the cheek. "Please excuse me now," she murmured. "I must go to my room."

But entertain the idea she did, for as she tossed and turned on the big bed, trying fruitlessly to achieve some respite, the conversation and all its implications kept thrusting back and forth in her mind. The whole idea seemed so grotesque to her. It was like an odious growth that had somehow managed to sink its thorns into her flesh and would not let go, no matter how hard she tried to shake it off.

She felt imprisoned suddenly by the conflicting passions that were tearing at her. She had no desire for Robin or, indeed, for any man except her husband, but her want of Jason was not being met, and her need for him was growing. What if she had lost him forever? The question rent her mind. If such a fearful thing was happening, must she not then grasp at any means, no matter how awful to bring him back to her? Emilie scorned that idea. If she knew anything at all about Jason, it was that he was a man of strong and honest principles. To win him back through a pretense would be impossible. Perhaps she did not know the world as Francine and other, more sophisticated, experienced women knew it, but she did know her husband. She felt secure in that knowledge until her mind turned again, asking if she did indeed know him so well, why had she seemingly lost him or at least that aspect of him that had so enriched their marriage and made her so happy?

Emilie got up from the bed and walked to the window, but her torments followed her. The questions were like threatening shadows now, flitting everywhere she turned. It did not matter if she paced about the chamber or stood stock-still staring blankly through the window. Her worries were as perpendicular as she herself; they were not content to stay supine in that very bed that first gave rise to them.

Alex drew on his thin, dark cigar. "If you are determined to go to Les Chandelles, then I am equally determined to take you there," he said, "and to ensure your safe arrival."

He and Rachel were seated opposite each other at a small table in the Bronze Pen on Bourbon Street. It was Alex's habit to take a glass of Madeira or sherry every afternoon at four. He would brook no departure from this ritual, even when accompanying Rachel about the city on her shopping or other small errands. He insisted that the establishment was a completely respectable one and that it would not in any way compromise her reputation if she were to enjoy a glass there with him of an afternoon.

It had taken Rachel several visits to feel the least bit at ease. She had been raised by a totally abstinent father and still looked on the partaking of spirits as evil. But somehow Alex had a way of making the most unusual behavior seem quite harmless. After a full day of activity, after much walking and climbing in and out of carriages, Rachel had to admit to herself that the little afternoon respite was indeed a pleasant comfort.

Nor would Alex permit her to regard his favored light wines in the same category as the liquor she had been taught to despise. He looked upon the product of the grape as one of mankind's finer diversions and spoke about the glass in a way that, while totally charming and light-headed, nonetheless allowed no dissent.

He was so courteous to her and his attentions were given her in such a correct and inoffensive way that she had to agree when he declared himself in no way damaged by his small indulgences. She had even gotten to accept his smoking, although she still wrinkled her nose at the odor of his favored *périque*. Even his choice of tobacco, to hear him explain it, had nothing in common with the rough, coarse stuff that other men smoked or chewed on. The *périque*, he explained to her, was a particular form of the leaf that grew only in Louisiana and, as such, was much finer than what she had been taught to abhor equally with whiskey.

It was as though such substances existed in a finer, more genteel form solely for the use of Alex; or perhaps it was his use of them that provided the distinction. Rachel mused on the matter as she smiled and watched the golden lights reflecting in the yellow liquid in his glass. Somehow he made everything that he touched or that touched him seem of a higher nature. Or, she wondered, did he have her so completely mesmerized that she herself saw no wrong in him that would have been sin in others?

Alex leaned forward suddenly, his face flushed with eagerness, his hand reaching for hers.

Rachel withdrew slightly, avoiding his touch.

Alex seemed not to have noticed. "I cannot have you traveling all over the state alone," he said. "I cannot quite understand your need for going there or their need for such services as you hope to provide. But since you insist on going, I shall go also."

"But you have said that it is such a large and lovely place," Rachel demurred. "What possible harm could come to me there?"

"Les Chandelles is one of the largest plantations in Louisiana," Alex replied. "Or at least it has been. I cannot know precisely what the situation is there now. It is possible that it is being broken up, parcels of it being handed out to the former slaves. I do not know what conditions prevail there or who would be responsible for your safekeeping. Under such circumstances, you realize, it is impossible for me to allow you to travel there alone."

Rachel started to protest, but he interrupted her.

"Additionally, you have no knowledge of river travel or the customs in these parts," Alex went on. "I can foresee all manner of pitfalls and problems for you to inadvertently fall into. If you must persist in this plan, the very least that I can do is to ensure that it is a safe, proper destination for you."

As startled as he had been when she first pronounced Les Chandelles as the place she wished to journey to, Alex had quickly seized upon the unequaled opportunity that had been set before him. He had been casting about for a good excuse to visit the vicinity of the plantation. He wanted to initiate more business with Higgins and he despised the necessity for having to travel upriver under the cloak of secrecy. He had been extremely restless ever since the report of the activity in the neighboring parish the night of his sister's party for Rachel. He was like a stallion now, champing at the bit, anxious to be active and about once more. His hot-bloodedness had been curbed only by his seemingly cool courtship of Rachel.

Her presence alone had provided him with the only activity other than that of the Knights that truly engaged him. Now, through some miraculous stroke of good fortune, the two had dovetailed, enabling him to remain at Rachel's side and once more leap to the forefront of new instigations for the cause.

Lovely as Rachel was, she was almost equally firm-minded, he knew. But he would never allow such an opportunity to slip from his hands. Rachel would be his, and so would the supervision of Higgins, whom Alex knew to be hotheaded and of low birth, therefore not to be trusted to act on his own, as a gentleman could be.

He slipped his gold, wafer-thin watch out of his vest pocket and studied the elegantly curlicued numerals on its face. "It is near five o'clock," he said, snapping the case shut and smiling up at Rachel. "We are just in time for the carriage to take us to the levees. The riverboats all depart around five, and I want you to see the bedlam that you are proposing to set yourself alone and in the midst of." He signaled to the waiter, pressing two fresh bills in his hand. And after pulling Rachel's chair out, he assisted her to the door.

As they settled themselves once more in the elegant coach Rachel found herself admiring yet again how he managed to conduct even the smallest physical acts with a grace and certainty that made the most everyday occurrences suddenly cherishable. She had never known a man like him. On the contrary, she had always known that his breed were despicable beings whom she could consider only with contempt. Now she found herself with a totally different viewpoint, different not only from what she had supposed but from every other feeling she had ever entertained regarding men.

She tried to remind herself that she could be nothing more than a pastime to someone like Alex, a female he somehow felt bound by courtesy and hospitality to assist. She made herself think that there could be no reason for his attaching himself to her, her mind not ready to realize, let alone accept the possibility, that she might indeed be attractive to men—even men like Alexandre Romain.

She tried to despise herself for her weakness in continuing to allow him to wait on her, but whatever arguments she posed alone in the dark at night, in her bed at Mrs. Hinsdell's, were feeble and unconvincing. Her much flaunted former independence seemed hollow and lonely to her now, compared with the warmth and amusement that his company provided. Even on those nights when she determined to put an end to their connection, her resolve melted in the sunshine of the New Orleans morning and his smile.

Now she found herself wondering what indeed it would be like should he suddenly withdraw from her company. Rachel was frightened, not liking the idea at all. Still, she told herself, once she arrived at Les Chandelles, should the place seem suitable, she would have her work and her life's purpose to fill her time and her thoughts. Until then there could be no real harm in permitting herself the small indulgence of his company and the delights of the delta city.

"Whatever are the wondrous thoughts you are occupying yourself with, in lieu of my conversation?" he asked, teasing her suddenly.

Rachel made a quick recovery. "I was wondering about the scarves that all of the street women are wearing. I have not seen them anywhere but in New Orleans. They are so pretty and colorful and seem to be so intricately tied."

"They are called *tignons*," he told her. "And most of the black wenches seem to affect them. Hides their hair, I suppose, or makes carrying the basket on the head easier." He looked at her keenly. "Surely that alone has not had you so deep in thought since we entered the carriage?"

"I was also wondering"—Rachel dimpled—"why, if the levees are as crowded and unpleasant as you say, you are taking me there instead of Lafayette Square. The park is always so cool and lovely at this time of the day."

"Precisely because I want you to see just how difficult it would be for you to make your way alone," Alex replied evenly. He was not going to mince words with her or beg for the privilege of accompanying her, which, he knew, could all too easily be refused. He was determined on his course of action and spoke to her in a way that he felt would ensure her ultimate acquiescence.

The open carriage made its way through the milling streets. The city was fast approaching its busiest hour. Rachel felt herself drawn, as always, into the endless fascination of all that was going on about her. Carriages such as theirs jostled for space over cobblestone streets. They were easily outpaced by gentlemen riding on horseback, unencumbered by such weighty equipage as the various carriages. Rachel looked past them to the throngs of pedestrians on the pavements. These, it seemed to her, provided much of the city's color and interest. At almost any hour of the day while there remained even traces of sunlight, the street vendors and all their various wares were on constant parade. It seemed to Rachel that no fabled bazaar of the East could compete with the sellers of the New Orleans streets. She would not have dared to confess to Alex that she found these scenes of far more interest than the cool, dimly lit establishments of Canal Street that his sister and her friends frequented, for all their elegance. There was a clamor and a life going on here in the streets that was a world apart from the fine homes and fashionable shops she had been introduced to.

"I think you love New Orleans." There was a flicker of amusement in Alex's voice but his face was serious as he studied her.

"Oh, yes," Rachel said. "I have never seen any place

quite like it. Every aspect of it is so different from every other, and all so different from what I knew at home."

"You would find your countryside rather dull after this, I fear," Alex said.

"Yes, everything at home is of a sameness," Rachel agreed. "Although our land is abundant and beautiful and pleasant, it affords no such glimpses of life as you have here. One valley is much the same as another and even our little towns have a similarity about them that would make it difficult for the stranger to differentiate between them."

"Not so New Orleans," Alex said.

"No, not at all," Rachel replied. "The merchants in the streets are so different from those in the stores and the bustle and noise of the town are so forgotten in the hush and quiet of your fine houses. I declare, I find something of novelty everywhere I look. I have been here three weeks already and yet I feel as though I have barely seen it."

"Perhaps you should be thinking of extending your visit," Alex suggested.

She smiled. "No, I'm afraid that is impossible," she said. "There is just so much leisure a body can stand, pleasant though it might be. I know that I am aching for work to set my mind and hands to."

"Then I fear I have not succeeded in my efforts to amuse you," Alex said. "You are longing to return to the arduousness of workaday tasks. I had thought that New Orleans would have turned your head."

"Oh, I did not mean at all to disparage your efforts!" Rachel exclaimed quickly. "I have been so happy in the time I have spent in your company." She blushed and hastened to add, "Yours and your dear sister's. I would not have changed these last few weeks for anything!"

"Glad am I to hear it," Alex said. "I feared that your time with us meant nothing to you."

"Oh, no." Rachel was aghast that he might think her

ungrateful for all his effort and attention. "This has been the loveliest time of my life in many ways. You have shown me things that I would never have seen otherwise and I will be eternally grateful to you for it."

"Only grateful, Rachel?" Alex asked softly. "Couldn't you, in that dear enormous heart of yours, which finds room to accommodate all of the world's suffering, find some sweeter emotion for me as well?"

Rachel stared straight ahead. "I will never be able to thank you enough," she said evenly. "But I have not permitted myself to entertain the notion that your courtesy toward me has been anything but that. We are so different, we come from worlds that are apart and worlds to which we must each, separately, return."

"The war is over, Rachel," he said wryly. "The country is united once more. Your armies have seen to that and we Louisianans have agreed to once more enter its fold. Our worlds are one."

"There is more than geography that comes between us, Alex," Rachel said. "You know that. Even were we to set politics aside, our deeper feelings must keep us separated."

"I have no deeper feelings than those I hold for you, Rachel," Alex declared. "You must listen and believe me."

She shook her head. "Our ways are too different. Perhaps that in itself is the foundation of the feelings you think you have for me." She paused. "For myself, I feel that I must be rather a novelty to you, a female who wishes to spend her time in gainful employment that will be of use to others. I suppose myself a far cry from the fine ladies of your acquaintance. Soon enough, I daresay, you would find me quite commonplace and boring. And we would each be pleased enough to return to our usual niche in life."

"We are near the levee," Alex said, straining forward in his seat and using his hand to shade his eyes. "You are going to see yet another aspect of the city, one that should prove interesting, if not outright dismaying."

Rachel said nothing but leaned forward as well, anticipating the scene that would soon unfold before them. She had learned enough about him to recognize the meaning when he chose to make an abrupt change in their conversation. She held it to be the result of his having been spoiled, a dislike of having things go any other way but his. Rather than answer her gentle rejection of his suit, it was more in keeping with his character to drop the matter and discuss something else entirely. Rachel smiled to herself, at once amused by her own appraisal of this boyishness in him and also glad of her ability to read this man who had come so unexpectedly but emphatically into her life.

Rachel had scant time to occupy her mind with all the ramifications of Alex's behavior. The scene that now stretched out before them was a canvas even more panoramic and engrossing than her first sight of the ocean had been. She thought that never before in her life, even in the overcrowded Union hospital at the height of the war, had she ever seen such a flurry of activity. There was as much traffic on the bank of the river as there was on the water itself. As far as she could see, large paddlewheel steamboats were lined side by side at the wharves. Most of them had two tall black chimneys set towering over the top decks, all of them belching black smoke as the engines were being fed for the imminent departure. On the wharves were a multitude of people even more numerous and busier than those on the city streets. Passengers were hurrying to and fro, making their way to the boats for which they had purchased tickets. Stevedores were everywhere, loading barrels and boxes of merchandise into the cargo holds belowdecks. Rachel watched as a gang of black workmen struggled together to roll an enormous ironclad wooden barrel onto the gangplank of the nearest steamboat.

"I have never seen so many articles of freight in my life!" she exclaimed. "I had thought that the army supply train contained as many things as I would ever see in one place in my life."

"What you see here is far greater than the needs of any army," Alex explained. "What you are watching is the wealth of New Orleans." He pointed to a great quantity of burlap, wrapped around giant blocks and occupying as much space on the levee as a small house would.

"The bales are cotton and the barrels are sugar," he told her. "And New Orleans transports it all to the wide, waiting world."

Horses and wagons thronged the levee, bringing foodstuffs and other produce, both to the holds of the steamboats and to the passengers. Just below them, Rachel saw a woman wearing the now familiar *tignon*, standing in front of a veritable mountain of yellow bananas, plying her trade and extolling her wares to all the hurrying passersby who would stop and listen. The clamor of the steamboats, the engines bellowing, bells ringing, horses going by at an ever-increasing rate, all made it impossible for Rachel to hear the actual words of the banana woman, but she knew, from her experiences in the city streets, very much what the woman must be saying. Rachel wondered fleetingly what the strange fruit might taste like.

But her attention was quickly caught elsewhere. She laughed as the mother of a large brood who had been hurrying along stopped suddenly in her tracks, spun around, and counted her children. It wasn't until she had numbered them three times that she shooed them all onto the gangplank of a waiting steamboat and followed them on.

The noise was very near deafening and the endless momentum of the scene was making her dizzy. She clapped her hands over her ears as the closest steamboat made the levee reverberate with the sound of its foghorns.

"Why must they all leave at the same time?" she shouted to Alex, hoping he could hear her above the din.

He merely shrugged his shoulders in an expansive gesture and smiled.

The last passengers were scurrying onto the boat. The fruit merchants gathered up their wares, knowing that the day's business was at an end. Rachel watched as the banana woman and the young boy helping her drew heavy netting over their high piles of fruit, protecting it, Rachel supposed, from the night air and readying it for the next day's business.

The stevedores drew back, sitting right on the wood plank of the levee or leaning against the hand trucks of their trade. Their day, too, was approaching its end. What cargo had not been placed on the departing vessels would wait for others that would approach the awakening city at its next sunrise.

Idlers stood by watching as friends waved their last farewells to those who had boarded. The momentum was gone from the levee and was now in the river as one after another of the great paddle-wheelers made its way from the slips down to the wide mouth of the gulf and the wider world beyond, or into the broad bend of the Mississippi as it curled itself in the great bend to the north. Rachel marveled at the speed and safety with which the seemingly clumsy craft glided in the water, taking the tide, somehow miraculously managing not to colide with one another. She started counting from the first steamboat, which was now almost lost in the quickly gathering dusk that crept up from the gulf, turning her head until she had counted to the end of the procession of vessels going in the opposite direction. "Twenty-five!" she exclaimed. "However do they manage not to run into one another or the banks!"

Alex laughed. "The steamboats are really very efficient

ships," he said. "And so are the captains who master them. This is quite an average day's sailing."

"All of the people, and the freight!" Rachel was still exclaiming over it as the coachman turned and directed his team of horses back toward the outlying quarter of Faubourg Marigny, where they were to dine at the home of a friend of Alex's.

"Perhaps you can see now why I insisted on accompanying you," Alex began. "What was happening on the levee was scarcely half of what you would have to get through to go upriver."

"Whatever more could there be?" Rachel asked.

"There are all sorts of people, as you may well guess, taking passage on these boats," Alex said. "There are ladies and gentlemen, of course, but there is also a great deal of riffraff and certain elements I could not allow you to be exposed to."

Rachel wondered if he was referring, as he often did in his oblique way, to the newly freed blacks, whom he held in such disdain. She said nothing but let him continue.

"There is a certain class of men who gain their livelihood on the river," Alex said. "Victims, many of them, of our recent tragedy. Many came from fine old families, but the hardship of the war and the aftermath have reduced them to poverty. Having been gentlemen and city-bred, there were no occupations they could turn to that would enable them to live as they had before. Therefore they became gamblers. Many of them are already wealthier than they had been, but such ill-gotten gains cannot support the title of gentleman. And so, having been thrust out of society through no fault of their own, but having taken up a calling that society cannot accept, they have become almost an outlaw class, living a style of life that is peculiar to them and rather odious to those of us who would have expected better."

To Rachel, all gambling was a sin. She could not quite

understand why Alex, who indulged in it frequently, could look down on others who were forced into it in order to earn a living.

"There is a licentiousness in them that would be abhorrent to you," Alex said. "And I'm afraid that a lady traveling alone, no matter how circumspect she might be, could not help but be a target of attention from some of these fellows. That, too, is something I must guard you against."

"Surely you would not think me capable of being enticed into such a life," Rachel parried.

"I deem it unthinkable for you to even be addressed by such men as I am describing," Alex said loftily. "And I must say I find it rather strange that for all your high convictions, you find the prospect rather more amusing than frightening, as I would have expected you to."

Rachel felt constrained. It seemed that no matter what attitude she displayed toward the various aspects of her prospective journey, Alex was not satisfied. Whether she spoke of the project with the seriousness of her convictions or a lightheartedness about what seemed to her the more trivial aspects of the trip, he found cause to complain. She realized there was only one way in which the issue could be settled. And while it was a settlement that was more to his liking than hers, she could not help but feel happy with her decision.

"Very well, Alex," she said softly. "Come with me to Les Chandelles, but I warn you, when we are there, you will find I am my own woman."

"When we are at Les Chandelles," he countered, "you will find yourself with the man you have unknowingly been journeying these past five years to find." The look in his eyes held her. He meant himself; yet, much later, she would remember his remark and wonder what he would have thought if he had known about the other.

19

Rachel could not help but feel excited as Alex assisted her up the gangplank of the steamboat. She lifted her skirts with her free hand as he held her by the other elbow and she stepped up gingerly. The name *Belle Creole* emblazoned in large letters on the stern of the boat, was repeated smaller at the top of the bridge above the top deck and even fluttered in the breeze on a tricolor pennant that waved aloft at the bow.

The open promenade of the upper deck was already filled with fashionably dressed people but the lower deck was so solidly packed with bales of cotton that it looked as if the *Belle Creole* was made of them. Rachel pointed it out to Alex.

"They're loading her to the guard," he said. "That's when there's so much cotton aboard that it reaches from the first deck to the guard rails of the second."

"But why is the cotton going back upriver?" Rachel asked. "I thought that that was where it came from."

"Most Louisiana cotton comes from the western part of the state," Alex said. "That and Texas cotton are most cheaply shipped up north along the river. Then it is taken aboard trains that carry it east to New England, where it is hauled about by ten-year-old children who earn a nickel a day for their labor."

"I see we will discuss politics on our journey after all,"

Rachel murmured as he steered her past the stench of the groaning laborers and onto the staircase that led to the upper decks.

"It is only that when you see the rather sordid luxury of the *Belle Creole*'s accommodations, I want you to remember where the money has come from," Alex said.

The delicacy and refinement she had seen in the great houses of New Orleans did not prepare Rachel for the sight of the ornate main salon of the *Belle Creole.* White-globed chandeliers were suspended from the vaulted arches of a ceiling that seemed to her to stretch the entire length of the boat. Carved wooden columns, made to look like marble, supported the arches and created niches in which were placed red plush and gilt chairs, which were already being occupied by the passengers. There was an enormous pianoforte at the entrance to the salon and there were several small round gaming tables along the length of the ornate carpet. It was lavishness, Rachel decided, laid on with a much heavier hand and less discerning eye than had designed the delicate metal traceries and other elements of New Orleans that she had come to know and admire.

"Well, what do you think of it?" Alex asked. She could hear the amusement in his voice.

"It's rather grand," Rachel said slowly. "But in a much different way from the homes I have seen in the city."

He laughed. "That is because we furnish our houses to please ourselves," he said, "while these floating palaces have been concocted to satisfy Yankee notions of what the Old South was like."

"Does the gambling take place right here, out in the open?" Rachel asked. It seemed to be the purpose for the tables in the center aisle, which surely were not large enough for serving dinner or any other sizable refreshment.

"There might be some friendly cardplaying at times," Alex said. "But the real dens of iniquity are in large gaming rooms off to the side. This salon is primarily for entertainment and the convenience of ladies who do not want to be stuffed up in their cabins for the entire trip."

"It's so huge!" Rachel exclaimed.

"Yes, especially when you remember that there are all of the cabins and dining rooms and gaming rooms besides," Alex said. "It's really rather like a large floating hotel."

"I'm glad you said that," Rachel said. "I have quite forgotten that we actually are on the water. Will we be able to look out and see the countryside along the riverbank?"

"By all means," he replied, taking her arm again. "We can make ourselves comfortable on the outside deck. It will be quite cool and I expect you will rather enjoy the evening breeze. The countryside, I'm afraid, will become rather undifferentiated and boring after a while."

"Oh, I'm sure not!" Rachel rejoined quickly. "I have never been in this area, and I'm sure it will hold much interest for me."

"Cane fields and bayous and prodigious growth that is almost junglelike," Alex said, "miles and miles of it, are what you are going to see. However, if it manages to keep you amused until dinnertime, I will be quite content."

"And after dinner?" Rachel asked, and then blushed quickly. She could have bitten her tongue, so wicked did the unbidden words sound in her ears.

"After dinner"—Alex nodded in the direction of the pianoforte—"there threatens to be an ample-bosomed lady with an unample repertoire of hideously sentimental tunes which she will insist on crooning well into the hours when all gentlefolk take to their beds. If you find that sort of thing amusing, I will perhaps leave you to it in good company while I seek the diversions of the sinful."

"I thought you were accompanying me in order to

guard me," Rachel said, again sounding far more flirtatious than she meant to.

"My dear Miss York, if there is on board an elderly lady of my acquaintance whom I deem a fit chaperone for you, then I shall leave the two of you to enjoy whatever entertainment the *Belle Creole* has seen fit to provide," he said. "In the event that there are among our fellow passengers not the dowagers I seek but the dastards I fear, then I promise I will not leave your side for an instant."

Rachel laughed in spite of herself. She could not resist his charm when he chose to display it so totally. She would suffer the dowager if necessary, but she knew in her heart of hearts, she would much prefer to hear the evening's performance in Alex's company, amused by the whispered comments and asides she was sure his expected *chanteuse* would produce from him. Again she found herself not wanting him to be away from her. She struggled inwardly, trying to dispel the stubborn fact that she preferred being with him to not.

"If you choose to gamble this evening," she said, "perhaps I will retire early to my cabin."

"I won't hear of it." Alex was being the mock disciplinarian now. "This is your first and perhaps only overnight trip on a steamboat. I insist that you experience all the glories that it might provide."

"Even the amply sentimental entertainer?" she said teasing him.

"By all means," he replied in the same playing-at-serious manner. "Her name will be Madame Elga, or Helga or some such, and you'll not find her like throughout all of Ohio. I would not have you miss it for the world."

"Then I shall insist that you stay with me," Rachel said.

"I have seen her a thousand times," he protested.

"Indeed you have not," Rachel said, "you don't even know who is actually performing."

"They're all the same, I assure you," Alex groaned. "But for you to so want me at your side, I must acquiesce and suffer the soprano. And now," he added, "for perhaps our last breath of fresh air before nightfall." He led her out of the salon and onto the wide-open deck of the steamboat.

Wide wooden chairs were provided all around the railed upper deck. Well-dressed ladies sat, their skirts stretched, bonnets secured, fans fluttering needlessly in the coolest and most refreshing breeze that Rachel had yet encountered in Louisiana.

Gentlemen sat with their ladies or lounged against the wooden pilasters or leaned back in chairs, their booted legs on the railing. Nobody looked anxious to Rachel: All aboard, like the few frolicking children among them, seemed to be on holiday. She wondered for what purposes so many people were traveling upriver. Surely none of her fellow passengers had endeavors or ambitions in common with her own.

Rachel felt a flush of guilt as she sat down in a chair that had been hastily brought forward by a white-jacketed attendant as soon as she stepped out on deck. She knew the pleasure she was feeling in the fact that Alex was attentive to her and as elegantly turned out as any of the other men on board.

She was looking forward to the evening's entertainment, no matter what playful scorn Alex heaped on the upcoming performance. He had taken her to the opera in New Orleans, and its opulence had dazzled her. She knew that from where they sat, in a *bombé*-shaped box just above the stage, she was visible to everyone in the hall, those in the parquet as well as the audience seated in the four great galleries above it. It had been the very first public entertainment she had ever been to. Before that, the only singing she had heard had been the small choir in church and the feebly cheerful attempts of the nurses at the army hospital to provide some comfort on occasion for the wounded. It had been one of her most glorious nights in New Orleans, as festive as any of the parties and dinners. And regardless of how Alex might joke, she knew she was looking forward eagerly to whatever entertainment the steamboat presented.

How, then, she demanded of herself, was she any different from the other ladies seated about? Her recent life was as fully frivolous as any of theirs. And, moreover, she could not deny her enjoyment of being amused. Nor could she quite repress the smug feeling that rose irresistibly when she compared her escort with the other gentlemen and could not help noticing the surrounding ladies doing the same. There was no gainsaying the figure that Alex cut and she was the sole recipient of those envious glances from the other females.

Rachel tried to concentrate on the landscape they were steaming past. She set her mind to wondering what wages were being paid the black attendants who served the passengers and whether the poor souls whose backs were bent over in the tasks of loading the vessel were working any less arduously in freedom than they had under the slave driver's whip.

She bit her underlip, trying to force her mind to stay on serious matters and turn away from frivolity. But even if her reserve had been strong enough, Alex would not have permitted it.

It was as though he could read the very conflict that was going on inside her. "You must learn not to forbid yourself the pleasures in life," he said softly, leaning forward in the chair placed slightly behind hers so that he could whisper close to her ear. "You are far too young, too pretty, to take the weight of the world on your shoulders. Look at the people around you. See how they have learned to enjoy life."

"I can never be like that," Rachel said staunchly.

"You should not condemn what you do not know," Alex said earnestly. "Many of these people, even these ladies, have suffered a great deal of deprivation in the past few years. They have suffered the death of sons and husbands, the loss of personal fortune, the sweeping away of much of the life they had held so dear. You cannot, in your high-mindedness, count yourself as having sacrificed more than they. Must you not call them brave, knowing that they are victims of war, yet are strong enough to grasp life and not lose themselves in suffering and self-pity?"

Rachel considered that what he said about the vanquished southerners was true, and yet she could see no sign on their proud and laughing faces of the scourges of war. Not any more than she could discern it in Alex himself, save when he chose to speak of it.

"After all," Alex went on, "you are determined to set yourself an arduous and thankless task. You can certainly permit yourself the enjoyment of this voyage without feeling as though you have thrown your dear principles overboard. It should not be difficult."

"All right," she agreed softly. Certainly it would not be hard. The ruffles of the soft, fine white summer dresses that most of the ladies wore, the ripples of laughter in soft conversation that filled the deck with an agreeable murmur, the smoothly rolling river they seemed to glide on, the green and even landscape stretched along the banks, were certainly all of a piece that took the mind to easy, pleasant avenues.

"The dinner fare on these boats is capital," Alex said. "And tonight you shall dine superbly on Creole cuisine."

"I shall let you choose everything for me," Rachel exclaimed. "I shan't even peek at the menu. It shall all be in your hands."

"I would God that it were!" he murmured softly. "Oh, Rachel, there is so much I want to do for you!"

"You have done so very much already," Rachel said, stiffening slightly and pulling herself forward in her chair and away from him. His breath was warm on her neck and she blushed furiously, wondering if any of the other passengers had seen how close to each other they had been or had heard the declaration he had made to her. She knew that it was only her inner conflicts that made her any different from any of the other women on the deck. A stranger walking among them observing would see no differences. Rachel wore a simple but smart traveling suit that Alex's sister had helped her select at La Maison Blanche on Canal Street. Her head was covered, not by the neat little Quaker bonnet she had always worn, but by a wide-brimmed and beribboned straw hat such as all the New Orleans ladies wore to protect their complexions from the sun. No, she had to admit to herself, no one looking at them would take them for anything other than a New Orleans lady and her preferred beau.

"The lamps will be lit at dusk," Alex said, breaking into her thoughts, "and I will escort you to your cabin, which"—and he cocked his eyebrow playfully at her—"is properly distant from mine, and you can rest and dress for dinner. I will call for you promptly at eight."

"I had completely forgotten about my baggage," Rachel admitted with a startled laugh.

"Everything has been taken care of," Alex assured her, "and you will find it all waiting for you in the cabin."

Everything was just as he promised. When the lowering sun had finally melted behind the horizon, dark had fallen quickly and settled everywhere. Occasionally lights could be seen flickering beyond the shoreline but there was nothing else in the quickly enveloping darkness to hold the eye of the traveler. The passengers dispersed to their respective cabins, and Rachel was glad to have some little bit of time alone to hug to herself.

The comforter on the bed had been turned down and her ball dress and its pair of matching slippers had been laid out by the same unseen hands. She wondered at the effortless efficiency of it all, and it came to her yet again how many women lived lives of such ease. She dropped to her knees in front of her carpetbag, searching inside to make sure that her own, older clothes had been packed by the little maid at Mrs. Hinsdell's. No matter how New Orleansish she was gotten up tonight, Rachel was determined that the morning would find her back in what she thought of as "her" clothes. Lovely as the new garments were, they still seemed to her like costumes she had agreed to wear for the masquerade that had been her life for the past several weeks in the city. But she would reach the plantation dressed as she had always been and as she would continue to dress should she get the position. Then it would be the ruffled and ribboned finery that would be packed away, not quite forgotten, perhaps taken out and looked at from time to time to remind her of the brief splendor she had permitted herself.

But when Alex's light knock came at the cabin door, she was ready, and looking exactly as he wished her to. She wore the gown that had been made for her party at his sister's house and the soft kid dancing slippers made her feel buoyant and almost giddy as she took his arm. She needed that support in the narrow corridor as the sudden shifting of the steamboat reminded her that they were traveling on the water, after all. The slight turbulence of the river was causing the boat to pitch slightly, and she was glad of Alex's seasoned support as they entered the dining room.

Her face was suffused with color and her eyes were bright when she faced him across the table. His eyes fastened on hers, and lest she should blush uncontrollably, Rachel looked about the ornate dining room. It was every bit as elaborate as the long salon they had entered earlier. The gas lamps that were lit everywhere threw deep shadows on the brocades and damasks of the formally furnished room. Black-coated waiters moved briskly and silently among the tables. Palm trees bordered the sides and the room seemed to be planted as well with tall silver-colored wine coolers that stood at each starchly covered table.

Most of these were occupied and couples continued to drift in until the dining room was quite full.

A mustached waiter approached them with two enormous corded and tasseled menus, but Alex waved them away with a small gesture.

"We will have *crevettes en papillote*, and *court-bouillon.* I will order our main course after you have brought the soup."

"Very good, sir," the waiter said. "If I may perhaps suggest, the *daube glacée* is excellent this evening."

"That may be too spicy for mademoiselle," Alex said. "She is not used to our cuisine. I will make another selection for her."

The waiter bowed and hurried away.

The shrimp were served and Rachel pronounced them delicious. Alex explained how they were baked in oiled paper bags according to an eighteenth-century French technique that brought out all of the delicacy. Rachel felt as luxurious having food ordered for her as she had by the laying out of her clothes in the cabin. Indolence was a sin and surely the most tempting one she had ever been exposed to.

She pronounced the soup, of local red snapper, excellent, and Alex ordered a delicate chicken Rochambeau for her and oysters en brochette for himself. "Also *maque choux,*" he instructed the waiter, turning again to Rachel to describe this last as a vegetable dish with tomatoes and corn.

Although she was more than surfeited with the abundance of rich food, Alex insisted that she at least taste one of his oysters, a delicacy she admitted she had never had before.

Nor would he take no for an answer when the table had been cleared, and he insisted on ordering a sweet for her. "*Crème brûlée* is merely a light egg custard with some burned sugar. I know you'll enjoy it," he said.

"And are you having one as well?" she taunted slyly.

"I will have my usual brandy," he replied. The waiter nodded and slipped off again.

Rachel had had nothing intoxicating to drink but the merest sip of wine, yet she found herself once more unaccountably light-headed. She said things to Alex and looked at him more provocatively than she would have done had she been in complete control of herself. She had expressed nothing truly wicked, she knew that, and yet—and yet, once more she felt as though she were playing a role for which she had been suitably costumed but must doff at the earliest opportunity.

Yet she couldn't deny the deliciousness not only of the extravagant meal but of the entire evening and its storybook setting. It was as exciting as the bubbly champagne Alex insisted on ordering once they had been seated in the salon for the evening's performance.

Rachel never knew whether it was the intoxicating drink or the acutely accurate wit of her escort that made everything seem so funny. The evening's entertainment was just what he had promised it would be. Rachel accused him of having seen the posted announcement, but Alex swore up and down that he had not. Madame Rosa Bonsuarte was totally new to him, although she was in every respect exactly what he had anticipated and described to Rachel that afternoon.

An extremely thin gentleman, with sparse hair atop his head but much hanging down between his ears and neck, sat down in his stark black suit at the piano to a mild scattering of applause. He played indifferently for a few moments, or Rachel herself was indifferent as to the quality. Then, with a fanfare, he played a crescendo that served to cue the star of the evening.

Madame strode in, acknowledging the applause, bobbing her head right and left until Rachel was sure that the large red ostrich plume affixed over her chignon must surely break away and fall to the floor.

But no such mishap occurred and Mme. Bonsuarte reached her place alongside the piano all in one piece. She glittered, Rachel thought much like the room itself, her gown of red satin overlaid with black lace echoing the colors of the salon and the many jewels at her thick neck and pudgy fingers flashed in concerted rivalry to the chandeliers overhead. She was a large figure of a woman and they were seated close enough for Rachel to study the heavy applications of kohl that outlined the singer's eyes, and her heavily rouged cheeks and lips.

The pianist started playing again and Madame extended her right hand, lace handkerchief fluttering from between her clenched fingers, and sang in a large, booming voice a song that Rachel could not make heads or tails of, since it was in French.

But from the sobbing catches in the singer's voice and the way she now clutched the lace handkerchief to her bosom, Rachel guessed it must have told a very sad tale indeed, just the sort of sentimentality Alex had also accurately predicted would form the repertoire.

Rachel could not help but smile admiringly at him when she turned her attention from the singer to her escort, who sat smiling quietly as he toyed with his champagne glass.

Rachel looked at him now, his handsome features even more accentuated by being thrown partially in shadow by the flickering gas lamps. She felt more drawn to him than she ever had before, more impelled to open up her heart. There was a quiet interlude between two of Madame's songs. Rachel leaned slightly toward him. She felt almost breathless, carried like a boat herself on a sweet wave of happiness. She looked at him, her heart brimming. "I wish this night would never end," she whispered.

"I wish it would end, but differently from how it

must," he said. His dark eyes fastened on her, pinning her down with a gaze of such intensity that Rachel felt herself immovable, but she could not meet his gaze and quickly lowered her lids. She felt trapped almost, pinned in the web of his being, and her having let herself into it, had entered willingly, made it no less a trap.

His head was close to hers now, she could sense his presence even though she kept her eyes shut tight.

"I will take you to your cabin and see that you are safely inside for the night whenever you wish," he said. "And I will come for you in the morning to continue the journey."

She nodded, still not lifting her head to face him.

The music started again and Rachel turned slightly in her chair, lifting her head at last, watching the performance dumbly, miserably, until at last it was all over and the great chandeliers of the salon were dimmed.

Alex took her back through the narrow corridor of cabins and when she fumbled with the key she took from her tiny reticule, he took it from her, opening the door easily and handing the key back to her.

They stood on opposite sides of the small threshold, not saying anything until Alex murmured, "*Adieu,*" and she closed the door softly, locking it behind her, throwing herself on the narrow bed in a flood of tears she could neither contain nor explain.

20

They breakfasted on the *Belle Creole*, on a very fancy dish called eggs Sardou, which, with all its creamy sauces and unfamiliar vegetables, Rachel could not believe came from the simple, solid objects she used to collect every morning from the hen house.

Alex explained that within two hours they would be at the landing where they would disembark. He would hire a coach and driver to take them on the final step of the trip.

Rachel had gotten used to the swayings and lurchings of the steamboat, and now she looked forward to an hour or so of sitting on its shaded deck. She had spent an uncomfortable night, tossing and turning, more because of the movements of her heart and mind than those of the steamboat. She was glad to find the morning sunny yet a little crisp, not yet heavy with the sultriness that would inevitably come by midday.

Alex seemed to her rather preoccupied, and although he stayed nearby her, not much conversation passed between them. She was glad of this. She needed whatever time she could have to get her thoughts in order. She did not know quite how she would react to anything he might say to her.

He was plunged deep in his own thoughts, wondering if he had perhaps woefully misread his subject. Last night could have been an opportunity that, not grasped, would not quickly present itself again. He thought he had read a wanting and a willingness in her, but he had been afraid that he was wrong and that any advance on his part would have been quickly repelled and all future chances ruined. Now, in the clear light of day, he was not sure but that he should have had better confidence in his own instincts.

There was no telling what they would find once they reached Les Chandelles. The very conditions prevailing at the damn place could quite easily turn Rachel one way or the other, toward him or away from him. A situation of which he had no knowledge gave him little or no control. Such situations he hated to be in, especially when the stakes were so high. Too, he had been disconcerted by Rachel's morning appearance. He had gotten so used to the clothes that she had worn in New Orleans. Her plain gray traveling costume, which he had not seen her in since their first meeting on the train, made her look to him like a closed book. He had more than glimpsed the alluring pages inside but now it looked as if the volume had been snapped shut and returned to a high shelf beyond his grasp.

He cursed himself inwardly for a melancholy fool. Les Chandelles meant other adventures besides his interlude with this lovely Yankee and before too many hours would pass those, at least, would be revealed to him.

Their disembarking was quick and easy, and a suitable equipage was procured. Alex handed Rachel up into the roomy carriage and the driver set off at a smart clip, hoping to spare his passengers the disagreeableness of travel during the hottest part of the day and thereby earning himself a handsome tip.

The thick growth that crowded in on both sides of the road was brilliantly patterned in every conceivable shade of green. But from the ground to the height of the carriage wheels, all of the foliage was thickly coated with the dun-brown dust of the road rising from the tracks made by the horses hooves and the carriage wheels. The dust rose slowly, as Rachel thought everything must, in this heavy, drowsing land. Only the carriage itself moved swiftly, the horses seeming to leap ahead of the whip that flickered mere inches over them and crackled in the heated air.

Conversation, too, languished. They spoke from time to time, Rachel making a comment, Alex merely nodding or posing a question that she answered briefly. Once the driver turned halfway around in his forward seat to tell them it was another hour or so before they would turn onto Les Chandelles' own road.

"You are sure we should go directly to the mansion?" Rachel asked.

"Your letter said to present yourself to Mrs. Phillips. There is where she should properly be," he replied.

"But this isn't a social call," Rachel reminded him. "I am not a guest but a stranger seeking employment."

"Nonetheless, it is the only suitable place on the estate for a white woman to present herself." He said it with a finality that ended any further discussion.

Rachel did not know how she would be received by the great lady she imagined Mrs. Phillips to be and she steeled herself for any possible rebuff that might come as a consequence of Alex's insistence. Should her initial approach to Les Chandelles be made in error, she would be set in her place soon enough but she would not take it as a personal insult, she promised herself.

The fork in the road soon appeared, and the driver directed the carriage onto the narrow path, leading directly along the plantation boundary and up to the great house itself.

The landscape changed now, from the uncultivated, rank growth along the main road to endless fields of cane standing uniformly tall, graceful green leaves moving slightly like draped ribbon bands in the light breeze.

Here and there among the brakes, she could see men and women with hoes and scythes working among the green that towered above their bent backs yet afforded no protective shade against the blazing sun.

She wondered how large the plantation was. The fields seemed to stretch endlessly, one side of the road continuously flanked by them while the other, mainly planted in the crop, was sometimes broken up by acres of grass or vegetable fields.

Then the sun seemed to be blotted out for a few moments as the fields gave way to the forested area, where the arching branches met overhead, affording a short space of cool shade to the road. This was broken by a long stretch of grass, first growing flat, then sloping gently upward to cover the hill on which the great house stood.

On the other side of the road Rachel saw the barns, stables, and other outbuildings that lay to the side and below the imposing mansion.

The driver slowed his horses, and now the barks of many dogs that came rushing out broke the stillness of the air. They climbed steadily toward the wide veranda that fronted the house, each huge white marble column seeming colossus-sized to Rachel. The columns dwarfed the figures of the people she could now see standing on the veranda.

Alex helped her down from the coach while the driver fussed with their baggage. Rachel looked up, smiling uncertainly. The woman standing at the head of the stairs leading to the porch had one hand at the base of her throat, the other held out to one of the tall marble columns. She was dark-haired and slender, tiny as a perfect little doll, Rachel thought. She surely must be Emilie Phillips, in whose name the advertisement had been placed, and the tall, dark-bearded man beside her, her husband.

Alex held her elbow lightly as they walked slowly

toward the stairs. Rachel looked up as a man stepped out of the shadows of the veranda and came forward to meet them. She almost fell back against Alex as she found herself face to face with the never-forgotten features of the runaway slave.

Young Jess!

Rachel kept herself somehow from gasping aloud. She stood stock-still, unable to move. Alex held her arm firmly, but she was unaware of it. Her eyes were locked with those of the young black man standing just above her, his own expression calm, his eyes untelling.

Emilie stepped forward, extending her hand to Rachel. "I am Emilie Phillips," she said. "How do you do? Welcome to Les Chandelles."

Rachel looked at her, grateful for her breaking of the tension.

Emilie's slight smile showed no more than Jess's stolid countenance, yet Emilie knew from the electricity that passed between the former slave and this unknown visitor, somewhere before they had met. She was sure of it. But now was not the time to find out. "This is my husband, Captain Phillips," she went on smoothly. "And this is Jess Martin, the schoolmaster." She looked at Alex, clearly waiting for Rachel to explain the presence of the unexpected stranger.

"How do you do?" Rachel tried to keep her voice as even as possible. "I am Rachel York, come in answer to your advertisement. This"—she turned slightly toward her companion—"is Monsieur Alexandre Romain of New Orleans." She wasn't quite sure whether she had made the proper introduction and she was grateful when Alex took it up easily.

"My dear Mrs. Phillips," he murmured, bending slightly over Emilie's hand. "I am honored to make your acquaintance. I have insisted on accompanying Miss York from the city to your estate, as she is a stranger to our region and I could not permit her the risk of traveling alone."

"Quite right, monsieur," Emilie answered. "And I am grateful to you, as I am sure Miss York must be for your kind courtesy." She smiled at Rachel. "Won't you come inside now? I am sure you must be fatigued after your journey and some cool refreshment should be of help." She made a graceful gesture of entrée and walked behind Rachel through the wide-open doors into the salon. Jason and Alex followed, Jess walking in behind them. When the others sat down, he alone remained standing, his arm clasped behind his back, demurring quietly when Robert, after serving the seated white people, put the tray of tall glasses in front of him.

The sight of Rachel had stunned him, which had not, he hoped, been noticed by the others. He could not imagine by what route she had ended up here. Her letter had been simply signed R. York, and gave no indication of the gender of the writer, although Emilie had been sure it was a female. He had made no connection with that signature, remembering only the girl, having forgotten the name in all that had happened to him since their first meeting.

Now she was telling of her experiences as a nurse during the war.

Emilie listened carefully, trying to find the clue that would link Rachel to Jess.

"Where are you from originally, Miss York?" Jason was asking politely.

"From Ohio," she replied.

"Ohio!" Jason echoed happily. "Why, so am I!"

Emilie looked at her visitor more closely now. The girl had removed her rather prim bonnet, and Emilie could see how pretty she was, with her straight, even features, large warm brown eyes, and the wealth of shiny chestnut hair that had been carefully coiffed and pinned about her head. She felt a strange stirring in her own breast, a more than casual curiosity about this young woman of her own age who now disclosed a possible link not only to Jess but to Jason as well.

Jason was questioning Rachel with an eagerness Emilie had not seen in him in a long time. He wanted to know everything about the section of the state where she had lived. They compared the crops that had been raised on each of their respective homesteads and tried, laughing, to calculate the miles and name the counties that had separated them.

Emilie knew now what name to put on that unfamiliar emotion she could not quell; it was jealousy. The heretofore-devoted husband whose barren bed she shared was now exclaiming over their pretty visitor as though she were his personal discovery. Bad enough, Emilie thought, that there had been something between her and the former slave, hidden though it was. Now there was common ground between Rachel and Jason as well.

And what of this undeniably handsome young dandy from the city who had brought her to them? He hadn't said very much as yet, but was intently and discreetly taking it all in.

Nor had Young Jess made any contribution to the conversation. Emilie glanced up at him now, wondering what thoughts were stirring behind his cool, unreadable ebony mask of a face.

She found herself feeling like an outsider in her own house, a merely performing functionary who did the necessary work of making the introductions and doing the other social necessities. The young Yankee schoolmarm was the center of attention, her connections to the three men in the room still to be sorted out.

Alex turned to Emilie. He had no interest in hearing Rachel's war stories or her reasons for coming to the plantation. He had had enough of both. The mistress of Les Chandelles was another matter. He found her pretty much as he had expected, the beautiful, doll-like heiress to the Bonfils fortune who had taken herself a Yankee husband. He knew something of all this, but only from the rancorous point of view of Higgins and from a few casual words dropped by his friend Robin. He knew that the latter had been visiting the plantation, but they had been out of touch for several weeks, ever since Robin had sent the coded confirmation of the last attack they had planned, not far from here. He was anxious to know if his companion was still about, but he did not wish to tip his hand by asking directly. Perhaps Robin wanted their acquaintanceship kept secret for one reason or another.

Jess found himself in a quandary, as always damnably happened whenever he was forced to deal with white people, even friends. His shock at seeing Rachel had somewhat abated, partly from the memories of how she had helped him run away and even more so from the stories she recounted of her activities with the Union Army during the war. She had grown from the impassioned yet constricted girl he had briefly known to a cool, resourceful young woman, whose heart and mind still cried out with a desire to help his people.

She would be more than commendable for teaching in the new schoolhouse. With her knowledge of the North and her burning abolitionist sentiments, she could be of enormous help to him. He recognized that at once, but stayed the thought quickly as he reminded himself of the circumstances of their parting. It was more than political fervor that Rachel had burned with then, when she had pleaded her love for him and begged him to carry her off to Canada with him. The fire does not only illuminate, he reminded himself, it burns, sometimes so out of control that it destroys everything and everybody it was meant to serve. Rachel's being here could be a great thing, but it could also be the worst danger he had faced since coming home.

Jason was exclaiming over whatever fortuitous stroke

of luck it had been that had brought Rachel here. He could not, he beamingly told Emilie, imagine finding anyone more suitable for their needs. He was even exuberant in his thanks to Alex for having brought her safely to them, although his mind was not quite settled as to what the connection between them was. Still, he was content to gloss over it and take the fellow at his word.

"My dear Miss York, and you, Monsieur Romain, must be tired from your journey," Emilie said. "Let me have you shown to your rooms so that you may rest and refresh yourselves. I assume, monsieur"—she turned slightly to Alex—"that you will give us the pleasure of your company for at least what few days you can spare. We do not receive many guests here, although I must say we are quite blessed with visitors at the moment."

"Yes, we shall be a large and lively company at dinner tonight," Jason put in, echoing his wife's invitation.

Jess knew that no such dinner would include him and he took his leave inconspicuously, pausing only to tell Jason that he would meet with him later in the day. Then he slipped out of the house and back to the school.

The simple new building that had until just now symbolized nothing but hope and promise to him had suddenly been turned into still another problem by the unexpected arrival of Rachel.

Emilie gave Robert instructions for dinner, to be passed on to the cook, then she gaily linked her arm through Rachel's. "Two of my dearest friends from the city are here visiting now," she said as they walked up the grand staircase to the second story and the bedchambers. "With their respective spouses, and another relation. I think it a good idea for you to take a day or so to acquaint yourself with Les Chandelles before you take up your duties here."

Rachel thanked her gratefully. All her fears of being rebuffed by the lady of the great house completely vanished. She did not know how the consequences of her stay at the plantation would develop, but for the moment she was more than content to find herself under Emilie's gracious care.

Emilie, for her part, could not dislike her visitor; that twinge of jealousy she felt toward her was something that she herself would have to exorcise from her being. Until then she owed it to Rachel, and even more so to all of her people, to make the young schoolteacher welcome and happy. They paused in front of a bedchamber door. "I hope you will find this comfortable and to your satisfaction, my dear," Emilie said. "For as long as you remain with us, Les Chandelles shall be your home."

"I . . . I had not quite expected such a welcome," Rachel stammered, finding her eyes suddenly full.

"We have much in common, you and I," Emilie said, her own sentiments stimulated by Rachel's tears. "We are both orphans in the world, women who have seen and suffered much in the war." She blinked the wetness from her eyes and forced a small laugh. "To be quite truthful, I did not know what to expect from your letter, and I was completely up in the air as to what sort of accommodations would be most appropriate for your stay here. But now that I have seen you, all those questions have vanished, and you are to be like one of the family!"

They hugged briefly and Rachel retired to the room given her.

Robert saw to the settling in of the new male guest and Emilie and Jason were at last behind the closed door of their own bedchamber.

"What an admirable young woman," Jason exclaimed. "I think we have found a treasure!"

Emilie smiled. "As well as a charming reminder of home for you," she said quietly.

Jason turned from the chair where he had been placing his jacket and came around to take her in his arms. "I want no links back there, Emilie," he said. "This is my home. Any interest I may have expressed to Miss York in our common birthplace was more to make her feel welcome than from any nostalgia on my part. You of all people should know that."

"She's very pretty, isn't she?" Emilie could not stop herself from asking, although she regretted the words as soon as they were out.

"Is she?" Jason smiled down at her. "I hadn't noticed. But then again"—and he held Emilie's face in both his hands—"when one is used to a beauty, one doesn't really notice the merely pretty, does one?"

"Really, Jason! Your attention to her was undeniable."

"Emilie, Emilie." He heaved a deep sigh. "I think she is perfect for what is needed here. She is of the strength and conviction, as well as the training, to take over admirably and permit Young Jess to get on with his plans."

"Yes, Young Jess," Emilie said slowly, realizing that no one had called the ex-slave that name since the death of his grandfather. Why, she wondered, had Jason suddenly used it? "Did Young Jess serve in the same army that Miss York was attached to?" Emilie asked hesitatingly.

"No, I don't think so," Jason replied. "She was with Grant in the interior, and Jess's division was stationed along the coastal area and the outlying islands. Why do you ask?"

"Because I think they know each other," Emilie admitted.

Jason's brow knitted. "I don't know how that can be," he said. "They surely gave no sign of it."

"I thought they did," Emilie said, smiling slightly. "But then, from where you stood you could not see, or perhaps it was something only a woman could have seen."

"Nonsense, darling," Jason exclaimed. "Why, if they had any prior acquaintanceship surely it would have come out in the conversation." He paused. "I can't imagine any reason they would not openly disclose such knowledge."

"There could be many reasons, Jason," Emilie said. "We know nothing about the young man who brought Miss York here save for his obvious good breeding, and Jess—Jess would surely be most circumspect about revealing his acquaintanceship with a white woman, especially in front of a stranger like her Mr. Romain." She looked down, twisting the gold wedding band on her finger. "There can be any number of reasons for their silence on the matter."

"And the best of those reasons could easily be that it doesn't exist." Jason hugged her tightly. "I think your imagination is playing little tricks with you, my darling. Or perhaps it is the unmistakable influence of our dear Madame Desbrosses, who manages to fill the very air around us with romance and intrigue!"

Emilie joined in his laughter, but she was not convinced. She eyed her husband coolly. "Whoever said anything about a romance?" she asked evenly, studying his expression carefully. "In Louisiana such a thing would be unthinkable, unspeakable, but perhaps in your Ohio . . ." She let the sentence go unfinished as she turned her back to him, reaching for the tiny buttons at the back of the afternoon dress she wanted to slip out of.

Jason watched her as she undressed. He started to say something but stopped himself. He wanted to make love to her, to hold her close to him, to assure her of his unending devotion, but he knew that he could not. It was only words that he could give her now, that and his silent support. Even the sight of her slim white back, curved over as she bent to release herself from the skirts of her dress, could not incite him to the strength he knew he lacked to perform properly. He cursed inwardly at this foul thing that had taken hold of him, this sickness over the sights he had witnessed that clutched at his innards and kept him from being the man he could be. He thought of Robin, who was still hanging around Emilie, and then of this similarly unexpected young man of the same ilk who was now also under their roof. What connection this new young dandy could have with the young Quaker girl he could not imagine. It seemed to Jason he must have used her coming here as his own excuse for being on the plantation. He and Robin would soon find each other, Jason was sure of it, if they did not already prove to be fast acquaintances. They seemed much alike to him, handsome, useless young wastrels who had not accomplished anything before the war but now used it as their excuse for doing even less.

It was all part of this southern sickness, the pride and the indolence that led to idleness on the one hand and atrocity on the other. Between the two extremes he found himself hanging helplessly, suspended between threats to his property, his marriage, and perhaps even his life.

At last he rose, bathed, and dressed for dinner. He kissed Emilie lightly on the temple, telling her he would precede her downstairs in the event that any of their numerous guests were already downstairs and that they would, of course, wait upon her arrival for dinner.

Jason strode into the small salon. "Ah, I see you two are already acquainted," he said.

Robin and Alex straightened themselves quickly, halting the conversation they had been eagerly engrossed in. Jason smiled broadly, his expectations confirmed.

"An aperitif before the rest of the party joins us?" he asked jovially, being the perfect host. There was something conspiratorial in the way their heads had been bent so close together and in the fact that the conversation was held in a whisper although they were quite alone in the room before he had entered. Jason felt not only confirmed in their acquaintanceship but convinced it was something more than mere chance that had brought them together now under his roof. He made no mention of having interrupted their conversation but behaved as though everything was quite usual, joining them in a glass that Robert poured from a filled carafe.

Jason sat down expansively, his large frame dwarfing the small sofa across whose back he had flung his arm. The two young southerners exchanged quick glances but said nothing. Jason smiled, enjoying their apparent discomfort, but he made no effort to start a conversation. The three remained silent until the Desbrosses came into the salon, followed closely by the Bledsoes.

Francine exchanged enthusiastic greetings with Alex, who was apparently an old favorite of hers but unknown to the other couple. She gaily made those introductions, sweeping everyone in the room into her exuberance so that when Emilie at last arrived, arm linked through Rachel's, she found her assembled guests in an apparent state of harmony.

She introduced Rachel to the other couples and then to Robin. Emilie watched intently to see if here, too, there existed a prior connection.

But there was nothing of the sort indicated by the rather perfunctory way in which Robin greeted young Miss York.

Another round of drinks was brought in for the men and after a few moments Emilie led the troop to her greatly enlarged table.

She could not remember the last time there were so many seated for dinner at Les Chandelles. The table was beautifully set with the estate's costliest crystal and heaviest plate. Fresh flowers abounded everywhere. Instead of the gas lamps, which Emilie found convenient enough for the other rooms but rather unsuitable for dinner, there were candelabra with wax tapers set at intervals along the dining table and around the sideboards and other massive wooden furniture that stood along the walls.

For once there was no political discussion from which she had to tactfully divert the company. Indeed, with such a large group and such an effusive lady as Francine Desbrosses present, there was not a great deal that any of the others was called upon to contribute to the conversation. After justice had been done to the cracked crab, little Mirleton pears, and other delicacies, the ladies left the gentlemen to their cigars and brandy and went into the front salon.

Emilie smiled as her two old friends positively pounced on the newcomer, demanding of Rachel all of the latest tidbits from New Orleans. As the young woman related the happenings at the parties and dinners given for her, and the operas and concerts she had attended, Emily saw another side of Rachel. Again she felt that strange pang in her chest, and she had to admit to herself that this time it was jealousy of another sort: the annoying idea that Rachel York, northerner and newcomer to the city, was feted and shown about in a way that she, Emilie, heiress of an old and distinguished Creole family, had never enjoyed. Her father had disliked the ways of New Orleans and had kept her apart from it as much as possible. Her mother, hating to go anywhere, had always preferred dressmakers and merchants coming to the plantation to shopping excursions downriver. In her young years Emilie had never questioned her parents' wisdom or felt their desires for her at cross purposes with her own. It was only now, hearing Rachel describe the house of Alex's sister and the elegance of the party held there solely in her honor, that Emilie realized all she had missed.

Even her two marriages, so hastily celebrated, had not given her that experience of a gala social life that now seemed to give Rachel more in common with Francine and Eurydice than she herself had.

For a girl as plainly and strictly brought up as Rachel had been, for earlier she had described her Quaker background, Emilie thought she had certainly taken quickly enough to the frivolity of New Orleans.

Perhaps her liaison with Alex Romain provided the clue. Emilie liked Rachel, she wanted to like Rachel, she did not enjoy this slight but undeniable bitterness she felt toward her. She was glad when the men rejoined them and the conversation became more general and not so centered on the pretty young northerner.

But now Alex chose to regale the company with an account of their evening on board the *Belle Creole.* They laughed as he described the evening's entertainment he had so accurately anticipated and they ah'd at his and Rachel's description of the sumptuous feast he had ordered for her. Everyone was enjoying their recounting of it, Emilie noticed, except for herself and Robin, who seemed rather to be holding back from it all.

Emilie rose, working her silk-and-ivory fan briskly in front of her, gesturing to all of the men to remain seated. "It has gotten rather warm for me," she said. "Please don't trouble yourselves. I only want to step outside on the veranda for a few moments." They all sat down again except Robin. "If you have no objections," he murmured, and waiting for none, he walked quickly to her side and accompanied her out of doors.

"Your young schoolmarm turns out to be quite the belle," Robin said softly as he stood behind her, sharing the moonlight that beamed down on the lawns and treetops.

"Yes, she is quite lovely," Emilie agreed.

"More than that," Robin said.

Emilie turned to look at him.

He smiled in the darkness. "I think that my old friend Alex is quite smitten with her," he declared.

"Oh, indeed?" Emilie said.

"Well, why else would he have come all the way up here with her?" Robin asked. "She is pretty, but scarcely the type I would have expected him to choose."

"We can never pick for other people," Emilie said airily.

"How true that is," he exclaimed fiercely. "Look at you. Never would I have thought you would choose a Yankee."

"Please," Emilie said. "I have told you many times that I do not care to discuss the subject of my marriage, especially with you."

"I love you, Emilie," he said as if in answer to her argument.

"I have told you that that, too, is not a fit subject for discussion between us," the heiress of Les Chandelles reminded him.

"If I seem to you to talk of nothing else," he pleaded, "it is because I think of nothing else. Emilie, you are in my thoughts both day and night. You do not leave me, any more than I can bear to tear myself away from you."

"You should not have followed me out here," she said coldly.

"I could not help it," he said, defending himself. "I have not been able to speak alone with you for several days now and it has been unbearable for me."

"This is not fitting," she insisted.

Robin was exasperated. "What then is fitting?" he nearly shouted. "Why should I not be out here with you whilst your Yankee captain is inside with your little Yankee visitor?"

Emilie drew herself up sharply. Francine had wanted her to use Robin as her instrument in causing Jason's jealousy, and here, exactly the opposite had happened! And somehow the clever Robin had seized upon it and twisted it around to his own advantage.

"I chose to come out here for a moment's respite, sir." Emilie now sounded even sterner. "My husband could not very well follow me and leave our guests. As far as Miss York is concerned, she has come here seeking employment and I desire to show her every courtesy of my house. If your friend has some other notion in mind in regard to her, then that is his concern and theirs, and neither yours nor mine."

"Emilie, I love you!" He could only whisper it again.

Now she felt truly exasperated. She turned to him quickly, her black eyes flashing. "Then why is it you only seek to anger me?" she demanded.

"Because I love you," he pleaded. "I need you to set me to rights. You have me in torments, you know."

"Robin, there is nothing I can do for you," Emilie said simply. "I'm sorry." She paused a moment. She felt herself drawn to comfort him somehow, to hold her hand out to him, to touch his cheek or his brow, as one would a loved brother or a son. But she could not; she knew that the gesture would be misunderstood by him. That she could not risk. Anything that would encourage him in his advances to her was to be avoided. "Robin," she said as gently as she could, "I am going to return to my guests now. I would prefer it if you did not come back inside with me or even follow me at a short interval. I would prefer we not meet again this evening. Perhaps by tomorrow this conversation can have been forgotten by both of us." She turned to walk inside.

"As you wish," he murmured, low, but his words were lost to her. No matter, he thought, walking sullenly down the steps of the veranda and away from the house. What did she expect of him? he thought angrily as he kicked at a small stone edging the road. Was he to go down into her quarters and pick some black bitch to dally the rest of the night with? His steps were leading him in that direction, although he well knew that the old quarters were practically deserted as the ex-slaves were moving into their own, slightly better new houses. Then, too, their much flaunted new schoolhouse was in that direction. He had no desire to meet that uppity nigger in the dark of night, especially when he was on foot.

He turned around and whirled in the opposite direction. The house stood on its hill up and to the left; on the right were the stables and the other outbuildings. He saddled a horse and continued in the direction past the great house. Several miles of hard riding would bring him to the squalid holding of Higgins. He had seen the man only once since coming to Les Chandelles. Tonight, he thought, would be as good a time as any to make another surprise visit. Then, if he decided on an action after seeing Higgins, his chief subordinate in the area, he could pass the new plan on to Alex in the morning for approval. Although Alex was his superior in the organization, this territory was Robin's. The system demanded that Robin had final word here, although final matters regarding the total organization or its discipline were Alex's province.

Now that they were both at Les Chandelles, Robin knew he had to move carefully around his friend, if plantation and lady were someday to be his.

Sweet Emilie, he thought as he galloped away. Everything you do to me gives me more reason for living.

He reined in at Higgins' place and rather than approach the mean house, he gave the long, low imitation of a birdcall that was the recognized signal between them. He sat straight and still in the saddle for a few moments until Higgins came out.

He walked over quickly, but Robin did not dismount. After the surprises and rebuffs he had gotten that day, he wanted to retain the superiority of the position from which to address his underling on foot.

"Do you have something for us?" Higgins asked eagerly, looking up. He didn't enjoy having to strain himself so in order to talk to Robin, but there was nothing to do but endure it.

"Nothing yet," Robin said disdainfully.

Higgins was angry. They had accomplished much more, attacking on their own, than they did now while under the discipline of the organization he had thought would enable them to do so much. "Why not?" he demanded angrily. The idleness was getting to his men, he explained to Robin, but Robin understood without its being said how much it was getting to Higgins as well. The anger and lack of courtesy in his voice told it all.

"I will give you word when I leave Les Chandelles," he said coldly. "Nothing can happen while I am still in the neighborhood." His own anger at Higgins' demanding ways completely put out of his mind that he had come up there for just that purpose. Insubordination, bordering on insult, had infuriated him to the point where he could not bear to deal with Higgins. He wheeled his horse about sharply.

"Until I send word!" he all but hissed, and digging his spurs into his mount's underbelly, he sped off, leaving Higgins alone in the night to wonder what the point of this hasty and unexpected visit had been.

He walked slowly back toward his house. Waiting for Robin could mean waiting forever. He swore disgustedly and spat on the ground.

I'll give him one week, he said to himself, then we move, word or no word. We move against Les Chandelles.

21

The election was only a week away, and this would be the last chance Jess would have to make the rounds of the parish. He knew that he could make much better time on a horse than on the old mule he was riding, and Jason would surely have lent him one. But the people were used to seeing him on the mule. If now, just before the election that would send him into the legislature for sure, they saw him properly mounted, they might interpret it as his putting on airs, and not vote for him. He had to look as though he was still one of them, no matter how inconvenient it might be and how much harder it made things for him. Jess grinned to himself. He knew he was thinking the thoughts of a politician already. He slapped the mule on her hard gray flank to try to make her move faster.

The bullets ripped the air so close to his head he thought he saw them. He threw himself off the animal, rolling as he did so, throwing himself into the brush that formed a natural trench by the side of the road. Stupidly, he had come out unarmed, and he cursed himself for this oversight. Not that it would do him any good, he realized. He had not been paying attention to his surroundings and had no idea where the bullets had come from. Unless his attacker fired again, he still wouldn't know.

He lay still, stretched out and crouched against the sun-baked earth. All of his soldierly instincts came back to him as he pricked his ear and tried to listen for any telltale sign.

But it took no such concentration to spy out the next round. A barrage of bullets struck down the ambling mule, whose last braying screech of horror told Jess all he needed to know. The shots were coming from the other side of the road. Whether or not they thought he was dead, his means of transportation was, and now they could come and pick him off easily or ride off and allow him to rot.

The number of shots fired so quickly told him that more than one man had lain in wait for him. Jess cocked an eye briefly at the sun. It was almost directly overhead. Les Chandelles was at least a three-hour walk from here, and it was the hottest part of the day.

He felt something wet. He had hit the ground so fast and hard that it wasn't until the impact of the fall had eased somewhat that he realized he had been hit. It wasn't more than a surface wound, but blood was covering his arm and the teeming insect life of the swamp edge was being drawn to it. Already a swarm of tiny flying insects had clustered about the spreading redness. He tried to flick them away without making any undue motion that would attract the attention of his assailants.

He wondered why they were waiting. If they thought he was dead they could have ridden off. If not, they could easily have come and finished him. Maybe they were afraid that he had a weapon.

The sun blazed down on him and the blood kept coming. He could not stop it without moving and revealing his position. The insects were all over him now. He was getting light-headed from the loss of blood and dizzy from the implacable sun.

Soon, he knew, the dead carcass of the mule would start to rot and the stench from it, only a few feet away from him, would be unbearable. Just knowing about it was enough to wrench everything up from his guts.

He had almost passed out when the sudden sound of hoofbeats brought him quickly back to his senses. He lay still, not moving, scarcely believing that the horsemen were headed away from him. They had not come onto the road but were thrashing through the trees and bramble on the other side. But the sound was unmistakable. They were getting farther away from him.

Jess murmured something about his good luck as he waited just a few more cautionary moments and then rose unsteadily to his feet. He managed with his teeth and other hand to tear a strip off his shirt sleeve and somehow bound his arm. He didn't waste any time even glancing at the dead mule but started walking through the thick swamp back in the direction of the plantation.

He felt as though he had been falling and stumbling for days when at last he spotted the intersecting road home. He continued on through the bramble, knowing that he would reach the old quarters first. With any more luck in his pocket, he might even find Missy in the old hut he and his grandfather had shared.

She looked up, startled, when she heard the noise in the brush and ran swiftly to him as soon as she recognized him.

Beneath the dark skin, she went almost pale with fear when she saw the bloodied arm. "Oh, my man, my man," Missy groaned. "What's happened to you?" She pulled him down on the ground beside her, hovering over him, examining the wound.

"It's nothing, Missy," he said. "Just a skin graze."

She got up then and helped him to his feet. She could tell by the way he was allowing her to lead him into the hut how very weak he was. She laid him down on the blankets she used as a bed and carefully peeled away the blood-soaked strip that stuck to the open, uncongealed wound. Then she bathed it carefully, in fresh warm water, and tore strips of clean white linen to bind it afresh.

Jess prodded his arm gingerly around the now covered wound, making sure that the bullets had truly grazed, and not lodged. When he was sure that such was the case, he drank the tumbler of cool water that she pressed to his lips and again let her lead him, this time to a prone position.

It felt good to lay his head down and stretch out fully.

Missy looked worriedly at the wound. It was still bleeding, bright red now seeping through the white linen.

"You need a doctor, Jess," she said slowly.

He found it hard to breathe and form sounds. He nodded at her and gasped for her to go and tell Captain Phillips. Then his head fell to the side, as though his neck had snapped. Missy started to scream, but she caught herself, realizing that he had only passed out and that she must get help as quickly as possible.

She ran through the woods and onto the dirt road to the great house. She slipped inside and luckily found the captain alone in the small main-floor room that served as the plantation office. She spilled the news out quickly, adding only that she did not know how long Jess had been wandering in the woods or how much blood he had lost.

Jason sprang up quickly, sending one of the houseboys to mount and ride quickly for the doctor. He found Emilie and told her what had happened and that he was going to stay with Jess until the doctor came. Emilie looked fearful. "We should move him here if it's at all serious," she said, but the uncertain wavering in her voice revealed to Jason her fear of how her other guests would react to the presence of the black man, wounded though he might be.

Then, as Jason left, her mind reeled back to Rachel. She had not yet discovered what had happened between the two of them. What was unthinkable in Louisiana, she reminded herself, was possible in Ohio. If Jess was in any kind of danger, Rachel, unspoken though her devotion was, had the right to know.

In the few days that she had been at Les Chandelles, Rachel had made the first tentative steps toward familiarizing herself with the schoolhouse and her new charges. There had been little or no time to spend with Jess, Emilie knew, because he had been out, just as he had today, riding the circuit for the upcoming election.

When there was no answer from her bedchamber or sign of Rachel anywhere else in the house, Emilie picked up the trailing skirt of her dress and walked down the road toward the schoolhouse to look for her.

The sight of the mistress, on foot and bareheaded, walking along the dirt road, was not a common one. Wherever they stood working, the ex-slaves paused and inclined their heads to her. Emilie barely responded; her hurried steps took her along at an almost running pace until she flung the door of the schoolhouse open and surprised Rachel, who sat in the near-darkness inside, speaking quietly to three small children sitting at her feet.

"Rachel, come quickly!" Emilie gasped. "Jess has been hurt. We've sent for the doctor and Jason is with him now!"

Rachel turned white. The primer she had been explaining to the children dropped from her hand. She followed Emilie out of the room and together they cut across the green lawns and then through the trees to reach the hut more quickly.

Rachel didn't dare to ask Emilie any questions. She didn't trust herself to speak, nor would she waste words that would keep her from flying, flying to him as swiftly as possible.

It had been many years since Emilie had been down in the quarters, but she remembered that Old Jess had always lived in the hut at the farthest end, and instinct brought her there now. She stopped, looked questioningly up at Jason, who stood just inside the doorway. Rachel rushed inside between them. She threw herself down on the floor in front of Jess, never even seeing Missy standing darkly, quietly against the wall, watching him.

Jess was unconscious, Rachel saw that at once. She deftly examined the binding on the wound, barely touching the linen. Her practiced nurse's eye told her that it had been well bound but not in a way that would staunch the flow of blood.

Looking around quickly, she spied Missy. "Get me more lengths of clean cloth like this," she ordered without stopping to ask or consider who the girl might be. "And hurry." She pressed a gentle hand to his brow. He wasn't feverish, that was good; Rachel inhaled deeply, turning to Emilie and Jason. "I am going to make a tourniquet to stop the bleeding. Other than that, there is little we can do until the doctor gets here."

"Is there a bullet or anything lodged inside?" Jason asked.

"I think not," Rachel replied. "There would be swelling or fever or some other sign if there were." She took Jess's wrist in her hand and turned to Jason again. "Have you a watch, Captain Phillips? I want to take his pulse."

Jason took out his pocket watch and knelt on the floor, next to her.

Emilie studied her face as Rachel counted Jess's pulse beats. The fainthearted girl of a few moments ago had been superseded by the cool, professional nurse who now looked on Jess not as a man but as a patient. Yet, in her initial reaction to the news and the way she had flung herself on the floor beside him, Emilie saw more of what had been between them.

Even now, when Rachel murmured to Jason that the pulse was satisfactory, not alarming, she did not move from her knees.

When Missy handed her the strips of cloth, Rachel worked quietly and deftly, removing the old binding and replacing it with the work of her own fingers.

It was only when she looked from the white face to the black that Emilie realized that whatever the secret between wounded and nurse, Missy was as aware of its existence as she herself was.

Could this be why, Emilie asked herself, Jess had not been forthcoming in asking Missy to marry him? Could he have known of Rachel's impending arrival? But why the use, or was it the *ruse*, of the newspaper advertisement, and the long wait before the first and only reply came from this Rachel York?

Emilie glanced at her husband. It was Jason who had first presented the idea of the advertisement to her. Could he have been part of the scheme that had brought the girl to where she now kneeled motionlessly?

It was too much to contemplate. It had all happened too quickly. Surely this part of it, Jess's wounding, had not been part of any such arrangement. Yet this was what it had come to.

Emilie stared out the unpaned window of the hut, ostensibly to see if the doctor was coming. But the movement was more for herself, to turn her back on the people in the room, to gain a momentary reprieve from the complicated knots she felt all around her. A white man: her husband. A white woman: her guest. A black man: a trusted associate. A black woman: her former slave. Were they all fixed into some strange pattern in which she had no part? Once again Emilie felt herself the outsider, here, here, on her very own property.

Even more bitter was the thought that if Rachel's coming had indeed been prearranged, and Jason privy to it, her husband had acted in an unforgivably deceitful way toward her. He from Ohio, Rachel from Ohio—could it all be just coincidence and the fortunes of war that had brought them all here to this slave hut this terrible afternoon?

She had married a Yankee captain and had agreed to his radical plan for redistributing his lands to the former slaves. She had risked social condemnation and worse, from all of her neighbors, yet she had done it unfalteringly because of her love of him. But if he had brought Rachel here for Young Jess, this was a thing she could not countenance. A white woman and her black lover could find no shelter at Les Chandelles.

Emilie looked pityingly at the stolid mask that was Missy's face. She felt sorry for her, but no sorrier than she felt for herself, thinking of Jason's duplicity in this sorry business.

So wrapped up was she in the intricacies of these crowding thoughts that by the time the doctor galloped down the street of the quarter, she had nearly forgotten the real reason for their being here.

When he had examined Jess and pronounced his condition stable, Emilie turned to Jason. "Take me back to the house now," she said quietly, and, barely turning enough to face Rachel, instructed, "You come, too."

The doctor praised Rachel on the excellence of her ministrations and then turned to Missy, telling her how she was to care for the patient until he rode by again the next day.

The other three walked slowly, quietly back to the great house. Emilie felt a century old by the time she and Jason were alone in their bedchamber.

"Did you know that she was the one who would be coming here?" she asked wearily.

"Of course not. How could I?" Jason replied. "When you first told me that you thought they had known each other, I thought you mistaken, remember? But now—"

"Jason, swear to me that you didn't know anything about this!" Emilie ran to him, grasping his arm with both her hands.

"How could you think I did? I don't understand," he said, looking at her.

"I . . . I just had to know that you did not deceive me in this," Emilie said.

"Of course not, my darling," he said, putting his arm around her shoulder and stroking her hair. "Jess himself didn't know, or he would not have had us place the advertisement. I think it was as great a shock to him to see her as it was for you to realize as you did at once, and as I do now—"

"Has he admitted it to you?" Emilie interrupted.

"No," Jason replied, his voice grim. "But then again he hasn't really had the chance to, Emilie. We never spoke again that first day. I was busy with some matter in the fields. And the next day, you remember, he was gone on his campaigning. Surely, my darling, we must trust Jess. If there was anything at all in this he would have told me, I'm sure of it."

"How can I permit her to stay here, Jason?" Emilie asked. "What will people say, what will they do? It could have the severest consequences for all of us." Emilie walked about the room as though stunned, not knowing which way to turn. "And Missy. Did you see poor Missy!" she demanded.

"Not really," Jason admitted. "I was too concerned about Jess and his condition to really pay close attention."

"This will break her heart," Emilie declared. She sat down on the bed and stared at the floor.

"Darling, wait." Jason's voice was strong, although his words were pleading. "We do not know everything yet. Indeed we know almost nothing. Let's not jump to hasty conclusions until we can safely find out from those concerned exactly what the situation is. You mustn't let it rack you, Emilie. Given Jess's condition at the moment, it may be several days before we can learn all the facts. Until then, dearest, promise me you will not worry yourself overmuch about it. I fear that it is not Jess's greatest problem at the moment."

Emilie looked up. "You think . . . you think he is graver than the doctor told us?" she asked.

"No, not at the moment," Jason said. "But whoever shot him is not going to stop until Jess is dead."

"Jason!" Emilie breathed.

"Unless we find the attacker first," Jason said quietly. "Until Jess is strong enough, he won't even be able to tell me if he knows who did it."

"Every day everything gets more complicated and more frightening." Emilie was close to tears. "It's worse than the war, it's worse than the war!"

He sat down beside her and put his arm around her, drawing her head to rest on his shoulder. "We knew it wouldn't be easy, Emilie," he whispered, reminding her. "We knew that difficulties of all sorts lay in front of us. But we were strong enough to take them on, not even knowing what they would be, and we must be strong enough now."

"Yes, Jason, yes." Emilie felt as though she was promising him her strength as she gave him her tear-choked affirmation, but she wondered how much of that strength she had left.

Was Robin right? Had she taken on too much? she wondered. She had listened to Jason and believed his theories, and believed that the ex-slaves and ex-masters could somehow work out their lives on the same land. Yet the scene just now in the old slave hut showed what could happen when things became too equal between the races. Jess seeking office, Rachel seeking Jess—there was no telling what the outcome of it all might be. Emilie clung to Jason, pressing her lips against his neck where the shirt lay open. "Help me, Jason, help me," she pleaded. She pulled him gently to her as she leaned back on the bed.

He disengaged their arms, looking down at her. For all

the softness and pleading in her voice, there was a bright depth in her eyes, a determination that he had seen shining there before.

"I want you, Jason," she whispered. "I want you now."

He leaned over her, burying his face against her throat and hair. "Yes, my darling, yes," he whispered back hoarsely.

Her body was at once on fire. She didn't even feel him as he quickly took her garments from her. All she knew was that at last his need was as great as hers. She clenched her arms about him, her legs, holding him to her with whatever strength she had, opening herself to the strength he once more possessed. Strength fed on strength again and again as Emilie found herself driven by a vigor that matched his.

All the unanswered needs inside her now rose, demanding fulfillment. Her body throbbed hotly, ceaselessly. Her mind never knew the fury with which she drove herself against him.

Jason never knew it, either. His senses took no realization of the fiercely aroused hunger of his wife. He was too full of his own returned desires, too cognizant of the sweetness and goodness of her, as once more he knew the overwhelming renewed drives of his body. Too long had he lain in the grips of that strange malaise that had kept this honeyed loving out of his reach. Now he knew, and almost laughing inwardly at the fleeting thought, he had all he could do to stop himself from erupting before his time.

His hands were everywhere on her, Emilie realized giddily as she laced her fingers through his thick, dark hair and drew his head down until their lips met. Then it was as though she were being crushed by this irresistible force over her, his large body completely covering her tiny one and forcing her down into the giving softness of the comforter, which in their haste they had not even bothered to throw from the bed.

He looked down at her, his eyes already glazed with lovemaking, staring first at her face, then his eyes traveled down her body, then fastened themselves on the pattern that was formed where their two bodies joined. He seemed forever caught where their limbs touched, totally mesmerized by the commingling of the fluids running between them. He looked up at her face again suddenly, as if drawn by Emilie's quickened breathing, the little gasps that escaped, unbidden, from her.

It was only then that Jason began to move, his long torso primed over her, pinning her beneath him while his groin began the ageless, timeless lifting and release that beckoned the senses, only to drown them.

Emilie felt herself sundered from consciousness. Once again she was plunging into the bottomless eddies of delight, sucked into a swimming fluid of the world that was in her and around her at the same time. She felt as though she were slipping, slipping, but always Jason was there, his hands strong at her back, lifting her and crushing her to him until his was her only support, her body pulled up from the bed. She fought to stay in his arms, her mind suddenly alive and fearful that this, for which she had waited so long, might not yet be consummated.

Her body arched under his hands, her head flung back. Suddenly all of her strength was gone. She clung weakly to him, knowing that her all had been met, but fighting to stay in his grasp until his all had been equally satisfied.

She forced her throbbing limbs to move in accord with his, her mind alert now, her happiness incumbent on Jason's realizing his. Surely they had the right, having so nearly lost it all, to have it all again. She felt a shuddering motion through her and knew that they had both made victory, one with the other.

She hugged him hard now as he flung himself down, all but crushing her with the weight of him.

He lifted his head then and they smiled at each other, almost children with a sudden secret between them.

"Forever, love, forever!" Emilie managed to whisper her determination, her throat seared and dry, making her voice husky.

"Yes!" His answer came in a voice as labored as hers.

Emilie laughed out loud. His single whispered word was a promise and she happily grasped the guarantor to her. Never again would they be apart from each other. Never again would the nights be so long and burning and inconsolable. Now forever she would know his love and know the surge of life within her.

22

Jess looked up quickly. His practiced eye told him that the length of shadow falling across the small hut was too big to be that of his customary visitor, Missy. He struggled to sit up as Jason walked in.

"Don't stir." Jason held out a restraining hand. "I am afraid that the news I bring you is not calculated to help your recovery."

Jess let himself back on the pallet with a groan. He closed his eyes. "Is it very bad, then?" he asked.

"Couldn't be worse." Jason stood, his hands in his pockets, his boot toying with an uneven gnarl in the rough wood floor. "The Confederates have won it all back," he said quietly.

Jess sprang up. "No!" he shouted. "No, it can't be! How can it all be theirs? They lost the war, they lost everything. It's too monstrous."

"But nevertheless it is true," Jason answered in an even voice, trying to calm the wounded man. "Their system of terror has worked. The people stayed away from the polls as they were warned to do."

"Warned!" Jess spat out the echoing word. "Killings and burnings in every single parish! Of course they stayed away. Who could blame them?" His voice was bitter, but tired, as though the overwhelming defeat had robbed him of his slowly resurging strength.

He looked up sharply at his friend. "But the government had foreseen this possibility," he reminded Jason. "All of the Confederate soldiers and sympathizers had been disenfranchised."

"It wasn't enough," Jason said simply.

Jess shook his head as though still disbelieving the news. "They lost the war but they won back the government," he said as though to himself. "We've won our freedom but we've lost the right to everything else, even the right to live."

"I am sure there will be a recall by the government—" Jason said.

"The government!" Jess broke in. "I see now what we can expect from the government." The words were angry and bitter. "I'm sorry, Jason, but I'm afraid I have no more faith left in your government."

"I can't blame you," Jason said gently, "but these things take a long time, Jess. The victory seemed surely ours, I know, and my disappointment is as deep as yours. Still, there is nothing to do but go on working and trying."

"But what odds, Jason," Jess groaned. "But what odds."

Neither of them spoke. The vision of burning and flaming crosses was still strong in their minds.

Rachel waited in the concealing shelter of a clump of trees until she saw Jason stride out of the hut, mount his horse, and gallop off in the direction of the big house. Although as his nurse she had a perfect right and reason to be visiting Young Jess, she blushed at the thought of her real reason for being there, and she could not bring herself to put on a deceitful face for the Yankee captain she knew to be her friend and champion.

She slipped quickly into the hut, glad that there was no one else on the street to witness her entry. The entire plantation was quiet this solitary Sunday; indeed it was the sight of the ex-slaves, Missy among them, heading for the church three miles away that had emboldened Rachel to make this visit. That, she reflected, and her own leisure from the schoolroom tasks she had assumed. She was plagued by the double shame of absenting herself from service, but she brushed that from her mind with the realization that there was no local meeting house to serve the faith she had been brought up in.

She put her basket down and knelt beside it, gazing softly at her patient.

"How does thee feel today?" she asked tenderly, unconsciously slipping into the words of her upbringing.

Jess forced a smile. Jason's news had greatly depressed him. "Not much in need of physical nursing, but I am pleased to see you nonetheless."

Rachel's heart jumped at his words; that burning in her chest that she could not explain to herself burst again and seemed to absorb her whole being. She longed for relief, to quench herself by gazing on that face she held dearer than any other in the world, but she could not bring herself to meet his eyes.

Jess sensed the agitation that had seized her. "What's wrong, Rachel?" he asked gently. Neither of them realized at that moment that it was the first time he had ever addressed her directly by her name. He knew, though, that this was the first instance since she had arrived at Les Chandelles in which they were together, alone, when he was no longer an invalid.

Jess felt strength surge through his still-recumbent body. Rachel sat on the floor, not far from him, but her head was bent and her long dark hair kept him from seeing her face. He wondered what tangle of emotions he might have read there. He felt strong sympathy toward her. Rachel for him was the only reminder of his old life that he could look on without anger and bitterness. He could never forget the part she had played in helping him escape through the northern wilderness, a time that seemed centuries ago. Her nursing him through his wounds had been more than gentle, it was loving. Jess was aware again of the disturbing thought that had pierced his consciousness even through his most enfeebled moments. It was impossible not to realize the strength of Rachel's emotions every time she touched him, even when it was only to change his bloodied dressings.

He knew that she was beautiful, that she was good, and that she loved him. The last realization stabbed at him like a new wound opening. Whatever had brought Rachel to Les Chandelles could bring disaster on all of them, were he not strong enough.

Yet she sat so close to him, unmoving, almost like a statue. But he could smell the fragrance of her skin and sense the turbulence that now shook her usually cool exterior.

They sat silently for a few moments, their positions unchanged. At last Rachel, as if moved by a powerful force outside her, lifted her head timidly and looked at him.

It was as though the silence of the seeming centuries of time was broken. As if all of the teaching and discipline she had been brought up in had suddenly cracked. Rachel felt as though she were seeing clearly for the first time in her life. "I am no different from any other woman," she said slowly. "I knew that when I first saw you and wanted you. I did not know that you were here when I came to this place," she said hastily, almost apologetically, "but you are here and I am and I still want you."

Jess was startled by the sudden transition and the openness of her words. "This is not Canada," he said slowly, feeling his own resolve ebbing away. "What we think is freedom has nothing to do with what you are saying now."

"I know that," she answered. "But it does not change anything for me."

Now his head was bent. "There is too much risk." The words came out almost in a groan.

A sudden realization seized Rachel. "I am a woman, yes, but in name only. It is you who must make me so in fact." She said the words almost slowly, knowing now what had propelled her so shamelessly to Jess this quiet morning. It was the unspoken threat of Alex Romain. Beneath his kindnesses and courtesies, there had lurked for her an unarticulated fear. Now she could name it for what it was. Alex wanted to do for her the very thing she now begged Jess for. It was as though he were still her talisman, the symbol that had brought her through the past five years. It was as if Young Jess's taking of her would ward off Alex.

She began slowly to undo the tiny buttons that fastened her prim frock. "It must be thus," she whispered, almost as if to convince both of them.

Jess reached out for her and took her in his arms. They rolled together slowly for a moment, until Rachel lay back on the pallet and Jess was stretched hovering over her. He carefully finished the task she had begun, unbuttoning her dress until it slipped from her. She pushed all of her other garments away till they, too, fell in a heap beside them. He took her face in his hands, holding her head up from the rough straw, kissing her tenderly everywhere on the fair white skin, covering face and neck and shoulders with thousands of light kisses.

He felt her body move up toward his, her arms entwining his broad back, her movements coupling them together in a rhythm she had never known before but knew now, all at once.

It is no more than breathing, Rachel marveled to herself. All her fears and timidity were quickly gone. Her head was too full of love for him now to worry about whether she would know what to do. Her body had assumed a certainty that delighted and overwhelmed her. Everywhere that Jess touched her, or she could press herself against him, was alive and sparking in a way she had never dared even to imagine.

She felt him full inside her now and the rightness and the goodness of it forced everything else from her mind. She arched her body, throwing her head back unawares, her joy erupting in a laugh that surged up from deep within her and escaped her soft, wet lips. She hugged him to her with a strength that she feared might crush him but that she was nonetheless powerless to stop.

Jess was taken by her movements, thrusting again and again into the live, delighted being he encompassed within his own. Whatever thoughts there were against it would wait another time.

At last she subsided, with an almost physical sigh that shuddered through her body. She released the tight grip of her arms about him, raising her hands till they held his face lightly, at a distance only so far away that she could easily look into his eyes. The brightness of her smile before it was erased by his lips on top of hers amazed Jess. He knew that she had never done this before, yet there was no pain, no awkwardness, no uncertainty. He marveled anew at the strength of the good thing he held close against him.

"Is this what it would have been like in Canada?" she asked happily, her voice almost giggling.

The unexpected question brought Jess quickly back to his senses. "No." He smiled sadly, taking her wrists and drawing her hands off him. "In Canada it would have been like this again and again. Here it must not ever recur."

She started to protest but the words died on her lips.

"No, Rachel, no!" Jess stopped her. "The risk is too great—for both of us."

"But Jess—" she started.

"No," he said. He got up from the pallet and rose unsteadily to his feet. He gripped the back of the room's single chair before sitting down in it. "Some things have changed," he said quietly but firmly. "Others will change more slowly, but some perhaps will never change at all."

Rachel was dressing. She knew what he meant. She felt no shame for what they had done, only an uncontrollable anger at the truth of what he was saying. But she brushed the bitterness from her mind. For now, although she knew she had to flee the cabin as quickly and secretly as she had come, she longed to return to her own room in the mansion. To fling herself on the bed, to recount and relive over and over again the few brief moments of ecstasy that had just passed. Perhaps, she thought, if I hold it close enough to me I can keep it. I can save it and we will be as one again.

"There is my work to do," Jess was saying. "It is and must be the most important thing. I cannot risk our happiness for it, and I certainly cannot risk our lives." He looked over at her, his voice softening. "I do not regret what we have done, sweet Rachel, I only regret that things are as they are. Until it is not so, we have little else but our work. I shall continue mine and I hope you will continue yours. Meanwhile I must wait and see if the government will right this latest grievance of ours."

Rachel smoothed the lines of her dress into place. She nodded, put her hand on his for one brief moment, and ran swiftly from the cabin and back up to the road.

The government in New Orleans did act. The Federals, shocked by the swiftness with which their former adversaries had regained power, quickly called for a constitutional convention to be held on July 30. The governing authorities held this to be the most effective means by which to wrest political control from the ex-Confederates and place it in the hands of those who were friends of the Republic and believers in the democratic processes for which the long bloody war had been fought.

News of the convention cheered Jess considerably. Here was his incentive, all the reason he would need to get back to himself again, instead of lying around on his pallet like a dying man. He had to be strong enough to get down to New Orleans in time to represent the parish as a delegate to this new constitutional convention. It was a way to make his voice heard after that first chance had been so cruelly swept away.

Jason was returning to the house from the fields. He knew how elated Jess was with the idea of the convention that was to be held under the auspices of the federal government. He had misgivings about his own lack of participation. He knew that as a man of substance in the state and a believer in the restoration of the Republic, with a trained legal mind to boot, his place was with the others who would be gathering in solemn conclave. But he felt too vulnerable already, in his position as head of the Les Chandelles estate. He could not put himself wholeheartedly into any action that would jeopardize Emilie or her holdings. Too much had she already suffered from having married him. Jason frowned. The only visitors at Les Chandelles were those friends from the city whom they had invited. The rest of the parish ignored them as though they didn't exist. None of the neighboring gentry had ever acknowledged their marriage, or even his presence there, in a social way. All Jason knew of those people were the cutting looks and turned backs that he met with anytime he encountered any of the other landholders. What he called the southern reign of terror had not reached Les Chandelles. Since the hanging of Judd, there had been no violence on their property. Jess had been shot many miles away, not even within the parish borders. Since Judd, there had been a regular sentry patrol organized among the men of the plantation. So far, it had held. Perhaps it had been enough to keep away the marauders, who Jason knew to be a craven bunch, perpetrating their crimes in the dark of night and in the anomymity of their absurd sheet costumes.

But should he become active politically, their wrath would be doubly incurred. He could not, in all conscience, take a step that might be of great moral satisfaction to him if at the same time he was putting his beloved in danger.

Then, too, there was something else to be considered. Jason visibly relaxed in the saddle, thinking gently of his wife. For so long the raging terror around them had kept him from doing what a man should. Now that the sweetness in the night had been restored between them he could not risk breaking its fragile stay. It was too soon after the rejoining to test the strength of the union. It was no time to absent himself from her.

Whatever obligations lay elsewhere, his primary responsibility was to Emilie. For the present at least, Jason concluded, this must be the sole determining factor.

He nodded briefly at the approaching figure on horseback, touching his fingers briefly to the brim of his hat in the old military way he had not yet broken himself of. But as Robin rode by, Jason's countenance grew heavy and troubled once again. The man seemed in no hurry to leave their domicile and his continued presence prickled like a burr in Jason's side. He wondered for the hundredth time what business the young buck had in the region and what, other than his apparent fascination for Emilie, held him in their midst for so long.

At least he could feel no rancor on that score. Emilie had made her feelings about Robin well enough known to her husband. She disliked her visitor intensely, discouraged any attention, even that of common courtesy, he paid her, and Jason well knew that it was hospitality alone that forced Emilie to endure his continuing presence.

Robin continued riding southward. The recent election, although he was forbidden by Yankee law to partake in it, had left him as elated as his opponents were downcast. It was only a matter of time, he was sure, before the total rule of the state would be in the hands of his friends and his own rising power would be uncapped. To vote himself meant nothing, but free enfranchisement of all of the Confederate veterans would be another important step forward. The only problem that lay in front of them was the damned continual interference by the federal authorities. For months they had grown quiescent; it was only with the election results favoring the ex-Confederates that the Yankees had bestirred themselves again, convening this damn upcoming convention, about which Robin was now hurrying to parlay with his associates.

The terror of the previous months had brought about exactly the results they wanted. Now it was decided that they would lie low, causing no provocation before the holding of the cursed convention. A convention—they grinned among themselves—that would never take place.

Thus Robin had no new instructions for Higgins or, indeed, any other reason to see the man. He assumed that the heavy discipline that had been laid on all of the recruits would hold and that the man would bide his time until called upon.

The next action would be on the day of the convention itself. There were men aplenty in the city to take care of it and there would be no need to bring anyone from upriver, which could possibly alert the suspicions of the authorities in the city. Higgins could very well cultivate his own marshy acres until Robin had need of him.

When Higgins was needed, he would be called upon. There was no way for him to know of Robin's whereabouts and thus no way for him to make an approach to the leaders. This was the way the organization was constituted and Robin was well pleased with it. He wanted as little truck with Higgins and his ilk as possible. Each motion of his horse took him farther south and farther away from the man. And soon, as Robin thought again about the purpose of the meeting he was hastening to, Higgins was far from his thoughts, too.

Little stirred in the baking heat of the summer months. The air was disturbed in its sullen torper only by the occasional crackle of lightning, distantly, at dusk. It was as if the silence stretched over earth and sky. The endlessness of it attacked Higgins, he sometimes felt, right in his gut. The toil in the fields, coupled with the lack of action or even word from his superiors, frustrated him constantly. The political victory of the former Confederates meant nothing to him. He hadn't even bothered to cast his vote. What the hell did the election mean anyway? The important thing was to keep the niggers from the polls and that they had well accomplished.

He wondered if that was enough for the former masters. Now that they were riding high again maybe that satisfied them. It could well be that the current inactivity was not a lull but actually an ending to all the bloodshed that had gone before it. If the masters were satisfied, then the last action could indeed have been the end. Higgins cursed and spat on the dry ground he was tilling. If that was it, then all their rampaging meant nothing. His whole life would be just what it had always been, the backbreaking, thankless work of trying to wrench a living from this poor soil. The masters would be masters again and the poor dirt farmers like himself would be just that—dirt under their fine leather boots, dirt to be ground back into the earth again, no better and no different from the niggers.

Higgins wiped the burning sweat out of his eyes. The

planters always stuck together, he remembered. If they got what they wanted that would be the end of everything. Even Les Chandelles would stand as it was, as it always had. He had no way of knowing how the other gentry acted with the Bonfils bitch and her Yankee captain, but he knew that Emilie was still on her high horse, as exalted and protected as she had ever been.

The knowledge galled him. It ate at him like little rocks rubbing against his insides. The masters had gotten what they wanted and everything was going to stay the same. No rewards for him and his like, the men who had done the dirty work and gotten it all for them. Everything would be as it always had been, hard and relentless as that sun above, the bright sharpness taunting and blinding him.

Blind indeed had he been, Higgins thought grimly. Doing the bidding of the masters, as though they were nothing more than nigger slaves themselves, and getting no more reward for it. He mopped his red, chafed neck with his rough bandanna. Boss stood tethered under the lone tree that gave shade near the house. Higgins dropped his tools on the ground, not caring if they rotted or rusted on the earth. He knew what he had to do. First make a plan, then rouse his men, then burn Les Chandelles to the ground.

He knew that the Yankees had set their convention for the end of the month, July 30. Everyone would be caught up in that event, not paying much mind to anything else. They would be off guard, never expecting any provocation in the upriver region, which had been so damnably quiet for so long. At this Higgins grinned. All of this waiting, which had seemed so useless to him, served a purpose after all. They would not be expecting any trouble.

He had spent many nights on his belly, observing the men standing guard at the plantation. It would not be hard for his men to overpower them quickly. Especially, he realized, if they came not on horses or through the woods but silently downstream, on the lightly guarded river edge of the plantation. Then they would be not only at the fields but at the sugar factory that brought Les Chandelles so much of its wealth. Here in their refinery they processed sugar for much of the rest of the area, in addition to their own. New cane could quickly shoot up even after the preceding crop had been burned in the stalks, but new buildings didn't sprout so quickly. He would get the refineries and the big house. Then it would be the nigger quarters. If the wind was with them and the cane caught flame, so much the better, but even if he didn't reduce the green fields to stubble, the damage he would inflict would be far worse. All he had to do now was study it a little bit and then ride out to tell the men.

23

Jess felt a little shaky at first, but he soon was set comfortably in a saddle on the big roan that Jason had insisted he ride to New Orleans. Both men agreed that traveling the distance on horse, although a longer journey, was preferable to the unpleasantness Jess would be likely to encounter on one of the large passenger steamboats. Once in the city, he would stay overnight with trusted confreres and attend the convention the next morning.

Jess realized with a grin he tried to suppress, that very nearly the entire plantation had gathered to see him off. Aside from the house servants, who stood watching from the darker recesses of the veranda, the usually squabbling kitchen children now stood in the yard quietly attentive, their eyes wide at the sight of him on Captain Phillips' fine horse. Even the stable hands seemed to have stopped working temporarily in observance of the occasion and as Jess rode slowly onto the drive, he waved greetings at the groups of people standing in the cane fields watching him go.

He remembered all too well the burning agony of that work, and much as the unspoken solidarity of the people with him heartened him as he rode, he tried to bring his elation down by reminding himself that any respite from that toil was welcome. They would as soon stop to see a yellow mongrel dog happening along the road as one of their own, mounted and heading for the city, there to make a name for himself and them. His modesty somewhat restored, Jess picked up speed as he approached the intersection from the plantation drive to the main road. He would stay on that road, following it even past the landing where the steamboats docked, until its meandering led him past all the river parishes and onto the paved streets of the city itself.

He galloped on, spurring the roan, wanting to get to the city before nightfall. He would ride until the heat of midday made him stop for some respite, to seek the shelter of a tree beneath which he could rest in shade and eat the prodigious lunch that Missy had packed for him. He would have liked to eat as he rode, munching on the thick cheese and *andouille* sausage she had sent along with crusty chunks of bread and raw vegetables. There were also some hard-cooked eggs in the hamper and Jess could reach back and pry one out without much difficulty. But he knew that the horse would need rest even if he himself didn't, and the midday stop and frequent waterings would help them both, enabling them to go at a steady pace that would bring them to the city as quickly and less fatigued than the racing gallop with which he would like to have covered the entire distance.

Jess patted his pocket, assuring himself again that his pistol was in place. As unpleasant as the steamboat might have been for him, keeping to the road was no insurance against danger, an encounter like the one that had winged him the previous month. But with each thudding hoofbeat, he felt himself safer as he got closer to the city, where the Federals were in strict command and would brook no such outrages as they had seemingly overlooked upriver. Even if some of the forces were secretly in sympathy with the ex-Confederates, as Jess surmised they might be, they could permit no provocation in the city, which they commanded. There, at least, they had to uphold the law that they themselves had instituted but had seemingly forgotten at almost every infraction.

Jess strove to put that bitterness out of his mind. He was going to a meeting now under their auspices, and in the very spirit of the Union that they all believed in. It would not be good for him to be among them with the bitterness that he still felt over their lack of action in the rash of burnings and killings that had pilloried the state.

Those seemed to have abated in the last month or two, since the time of the election, which had put the ex-Confederates back in power. If that had been the purpose of the nighttime terror, it had succeeded, Jess thought. But if this new convention were to supersede that ugly rigged election just past, then the burnings would doubtless break out anew.

But under the power that was sure to be voted at this convention, they would have the men, arms, and authority to deal with any such local uprisings. Then, maybe then, it could all be stopped and the business of life in freedom could go forward as it was meant to.

Jess girded himself with these ideas as he drew near the outskirts of the city. The road was far more crowded now, but happily for him, the entire trip had been accomplished without incident. The road was thronged with nearly as many black travelers as white, and all seemed to be going about their individual affairs without much mind for the others. There did not seem to Jess to be any air of political activity or even awareness of the great event that was to unfold the next morning.

He found his friend's house without any difficulty and spent the most rousing and cheerful evening he had had in a very long time. The soon-to-be-gained victory was in everybody's heart and they talked of nothing but the progress that was going to be made. It was a greatly heartening experience and Jess, a man among peers, savored every moment of it until at last they were reminded that the morrow brought a very important day and they must all prepare for it with a good night's sleep, not the happy carousing that seemed more their wont.

Robin and Alex lingered on the veranda after the rest of the company had bade them good night and gone up the great staircase to their respective chambers. Robin leaned back in his wide wicker chair, tilting it dangerously on its back legs as he put his feet up on the veranda railing. He looked up at the dark sky. "What a marvelously dark night," he remarked. "One can almost count the stars in their places."

"Yes, and what a fortunate configuration that finds both of us here at this time," Alex said.

"Do you believe in that sort of thing?" Robin asked idly, drawing on his cigar.

"Not really," Alex admitted. "However, it is most fortunate that both of us are here and not in the city."

"Yes, I must agree with you," Robin answered. "To be safely ensconced at Les Chandelles for the opening of the constitutional convention is a stroke of luck whether the stars will it or not."

"It wasn't the danger in the city I was thinking of, old man," his companion drawled. "Rather that we are not there to be implicated is what I meant," Alex said. "So much pleasanter to be here with your Miss Emilie."

"And your Miss Rachel," Robin added.

They both grinned. "Would that we had as certain a success up here then as our friends are sure to have in the city tomorrow," Robin said.

"I'd drink to that," Alex said, "if that damned butler or one of his boys would see to these empty glasses." He spoke in a loud voice now, and as if answering the summons, a lightly clad servant darted out and filled both their glasses from his brandy decanter. Then he moved swiftly backward out of the range of their more private conversation, almost melting into the wall, against which he stood for hours waiting on the unhurried young gentlemen.

Higgins stretched out on his bed, his hands locked under his head, his big body as relaxed as it could be in the stifling heat. Everything was set and now he could wait, just repeating the plan over and over to himself, wetting his lips with his tongue unconsciously as he anticipated the glory of the success of his plan.

The excitement in New Orleans would start the next morning. News of it was not likely to reach upriver before dusk. It would be the topic of conversation on everybody's lips that evening. It would leave them all lax and unguarded. Then, in the dead of the night, when all was at last quiet, he and his men would strike. He had no idea of who besides Emilie Phillips and her husband would sleep at Les Chandelles that night. Whoever they were, he reasoned, they had to be friends of the hated owners and deserved to share their fate. He wouldn't waste a breath feeling sorry for any of them. Now there was only this night and the next tedious day to get through before they would strike.

He could hear the stirrings of Jen in the kitchen room. He wondered if the girl was in there, too. It would be nice, he thought, but then all of the weight of the planning and riding he had done to alert the men settled in on him. Best he conserve his strength tonight. But the next night—after the raid on Les Chandelles—would be exactly the right time to indulge himself in all of the fun he had anticipated with the two of them.

His eyes glazed over at the images his mind brought forth and with much tossing about on the corn-husk mattress, he finally fell asleep.

In the morning, Jess rose and washed quickly. He dressed very carefully. This was a far different matter from riding about the parish in his work clothes. Here he was not appealing to the people as one of them, but was acting as a man among his like, doing the important business that so needed doing and had thus far been thwarted. The men he was going among, Radical Republicans all, black and white both, were somber and serious politicians, leaders on whom the burden of caring for the people had been thrust. They had to assemble themselves in solemn conclave, committed to forming and passing the laws that would guarantee the people their rights. No other way that had been tried had worked. All of the gains of the war were quickly being crushed into the dust, as were the people themselves. This gathering was the last hope that they had for stopping the conflagrations and the terror and instituting ethical democratic processes by which people, all people, could live justly.

Jess regarded himself gravely. His mirrored reflection seemed to hold these very thoughts on his features. He resolved to keep his ideals in front of him during the entire session. No matter what infighting or bickering might ensue at the convention, he would not lose sight of the more important reasons for which they were assembling.

At last he was ready. With the others, he left the house and they walked as a body toward the imposing edifice in which the convention was to be held.

They walked several blocks thus, speaking quietly among themselves but for the most part remaining silent. Each of the men was busy with his own thoughts. As they turned a corner Jess heard a loud retort. It sounded like the crackle of thunder at first, but then his practiced ears quickly recognized the gunshot.

The men looked at each other and then, as one, ran to the corner. Jess held his hand out, stopping the others. Slowly he braced himself against the brick wall, his head turned to the street from which the noise had come.

There was a body sprawled out in the middle of the

road. Jess could see blood spreading over the cobblestones, its color a contrast to the starched white shirt and black skin through which it spilled.

He looked around quickly. There didn't seem to be anyone else on the street but the shots might have come from any one of the many windows still concealed by the morning shadows. He knelt quickly to the ground, motioning his companions to do the same.

The street where the corpse lay led directly to the convention site. Jess thought it would be better to approach it from around back. He motioned his companions to the opposite side of the street they had been walking on. They would continue that way instead of turning into the route where the shooting had been. They walked quickly, crossing to the opposite curb and then continuing. Before they reached the middle of the next block, more gunshots had rung out and a larger noise, muffled but thunderous, even more ominous than the shooting, seemed to come from just up ahead.

They walked quickly now, hugging the sides of the buildings, stopping quickly when Jess signaled them to, flattening themselves against the brick façades. As the muffled shouting continued and came closer, Jess edged them slowly forward. At last the open plaza of the convention hall was in front of them.

Jess stood stock-still. Agonizing cries rent the air. There was a tumble of bodies on the street and the increasing shouts came from a huge mob advancing from the opposite side of the plaza. Many of the men in the mob carried sticks, and some of the men, Jess knew, held rifles. His hand reached automatically for his own pistol, but he was stopped by an elderly man who was one of their group.

"Don't fire," he warned. "They outnumber us by at least a hundred to one. They would kill us all quickly. Perhaps we can just walk slowly and reason with them."

"Reason!" Jess scoffed. He started to say something

else, but he stopped. Others were quickly advancing toward where he and his five friends stood. He watched them coming from various avenues leading to the plaza and he realized, in terror, that they would soon be assembled in direct confrontation with the advancing, shouting mob.

"We've got to disperse," he said quickly, looking around at the men he knew and at those who were joining them. "They have guns and ammunition and its clear they mean to keep us from occupying the hall!" He waved his arms about, trying to make them move, but fear and the growing recognition of what was happening impelled them to draw closer to their fellows. "Stop! We've got to go back! Go back to your homes! We will meet again later. Go back! Go back!"

But it was too late. Jess felt himself pressed into the front rank as more and more newcomers arrived, unaware of the immediate danger, crowding impatiently to see what was happening.

Jess raised his arm, his pistol held aloft, as if to warn the encroaching crowd that he, too, was armed.

But they seemed not to notice it as they advanced steadily.

"Break ranks! Run!" Jess shouted, but his voice was drowned in the roaring of the mob that now was only yards away from them.

He heard the command "Fire!" as he felt something smash against his skull. It was only a rock, hurled by someone in the mob. It dazed him for a moment but he shook his head quickly as if to dispel the feeling. The air was full of repeating rifle fire and all around him men were screaming and falling. Pushed along by the momentum of the men around him, Jess was soon engulfed by the still-advancing, firing mob. He beat off a grinning man who held several large rocks in his hands and found himself thrust into the very midst of the shouting and jeering attackers. He looked around quickly, noting that many of his fellows were responding savagely, using their fists and boots to fight back and resist the attack on them. But none of them had firearms and even if they had, they were too close to use them.

Not so with one row of the attackers. Jess saw the savage grins flashing on the faces of a line of men who stood somewhat to the side of the fighting and were firing directly into the ranks of the still-pushing and confused conventioneers.

Men were falling all around him. Jess fought savagely to disentangle himself from the moving wall of bodies that grasped at him. He struggled to get out of their midst so that he could signal as many of the oncoming men as possible to retreat from the fighting area.

The scene was murderous, with men bludgeoned to the ground and others falling amid the corpses trampled to the street. It was far worse than any battle he had participated in during the war. The cobblestones were slippery with blood now. The men newly arriving could see at last what was happening and tried to run from the mob and the riflemen. The area was a tangle of bodies, men attacked and attacking, the cries and agony of the dying and wounded punctuating the roaring shouts of the mob and the repeated *crack crack* of the rifles.

Jess was breathless, his clothes torn from him, his head bloodied from the first rock that had caught him. He looked about in a daze, momentarily stopped in his search for a way out. Then he heard the concentrated roar of more rifles. A sense of panic, animallike, streaked through the mob. Men stopped fighting and began to run.

Jess looked up. The militia had at last arrived. Soldiers were leaping from their horses, trying to round up as many as they could of the now fleeing mob.

The men in his group stood back, obeying the orders of the soldiers, who were trying to make room for the dead and wounded lying in the streets.

"All wounded to be removed to the Marine Hospital." Jess heard the order being crisply given. "All others are to remain as witnesses for questioning." The efficient young lieutenant turned to one of his men, who came quickly forward. "Sergeant, assign a detail for the removal and counting of the dead."

An uneasy silence prevailed over the street. Jess shook his head when a soldier motioned for him to join the other wounded. His was only the grazing of a rock, not a bullet, he tried to explain, but the soldier insisted that he enter one of the horse-drawn hospital wagons quickly approaching.

"I saw everything," Jess said. "I can describe it in detail to your officers."

"There'll be plenty of time for that later," the soldier said in the flattened accent of the Midwest. "Right now, just go along as you're told."

Jess nodded and joined the file of bloodied men stepping up into the ambulance wagon.

Once inside, the men seemed unable to look at one another. They sat, heads hanging, eyes downcast, as though they were guilty of what had happened to them. As though they knew that they, and not those who had attacked them, must take up the burden of what still remained to be done.

The figures were posted at the regiment headquarters when Jess, dismissed from the hospital with a bandaged skull, reported for questioning. Thirty-eight people, almost all black, he was sure, had been killed. The Marine Hospital had treated one hundred forty-seven injured.

Thirty-eight dead, one hundred forty-seven wounded—that was the roll call for the day, Jess thought bitterly. No ayes and nays. No motions passed, no laws enacted. Only a counting up of the dead and the maimed. And, as always, all of the figures were tallied from one side of the house. That house, divided against itself as they had been warned, was falling about them in blood.

The white linen so neatly bound about his head was no badge of honor or courage. It was a sign of despair. Jess gave his account of the riot and then walked numbly into the dazzling white light of the city streets. He stood for a moment, uncertain of which way to turn. He could not bear the thought of bringing his bloodied head back to Les Chandelles. The only thing to do, he concluded, was to return once more to his friends' house, there to commiserate with the others, and try, if possible, to build again from the bloodied bricks of the morning's destruction.

He stumbled through the streets. The militiamen were everywhere, restoring order, although Jess pricked his ear more than once at what he thought was the crack of rifles in the distance. He thought numbly that all he knew was the numbers. None of the names of the dead and wounded had been posted. He did not have the heart to stay around and learn them. He would know soon enough which of his friends who had stood up with him before now would stand no more.

Perhaps, he thought wearily, some good might still come of it. A civil disturbance of such proportions on their very doorstep must force the government to take a sterner stand and deal harshly with the guilty. Perhaps something would rise from this bloodshed after all.

24

All day Higgins had been watching her out of the corner of his eye. All day she had scurried past him furtively like a frightened little animal sensing danger. She always ran when he told her to do anything, as if pushed more by the desire to get away from him than to complete her task quickly. He grinned, looking at her now as she started to walk out of the house to the water pump.

Higgins moved his bulk quickly. With just one step he was able to bring his body to bar the way. Now she was stuck, cowering in front of him, unable to get out of the house, afraid to back away from him without being told to do so. Running, always running, he thought as he grinned down at her frightened face. What if the little rabbit took it in her mind to really run sometime? The thought had occurred to him before; he wondered why she had never tried it. But then the look in her eyes had never been so desperate as it was now that he had stopped her and grabbed her wrist.

He squeezed it hard, hard enough to make her wince, before he released it and let it drop. "Go get the water, girl, and then get back here fast. I've a mind to talk to you."

But what he was thinking of was something else entirely. It would be just his rotten luck to have her try something stupid on the very night he meant to have his way with her, with both of them.

He needed to do something to make sure that when he got back here from Les Chandelles everything would be as he wanted it.

He could not talk to her about running away; putting it into words, even as a warning, might put a thought into her head that had never been there before. No, it would take stronger means than words to make sure he wasn't thwarted in this, the greatest of all the pleasuring he had envisioned for himself.

When she came back into the house, he smiled at her pleasantly. "I don't mean you any harm, girl, you know that, don't you?" he asked.

She nodded, not looking at him.

"And what I do is for your good," he went on. "Yours and your mama's."

Myrtie stood there saying nothing.

"So what I'm going to do before I leave here tonight is for your own protection," Higgins said. "And you and your mama both are going to be grateful to me, aren't you?"

She motioned yes with her head, not speaking, not looking at him.

"Good, that's a good girl," Higgins said. "You and your mama both." He repeated the phrase as though he were savoring it hugely, tasting it in his mouth.

He said nothing to either one of them as they stood watching while he ate his supper, waiting for him to finish so that they might feed themselves from what he had left. When he was full, he turned, grinning, to Jen. "Eat fast and come in there." He indicated their room. "And bring her, too." He got up and stretched himself, the mark of a man fulfilled.

They wasted no time in doing as he ordered. They came into the bedroom, huddled against each other. He could almost read the fright in their eyes, and it pleased him. That they knew his strength and power over them was very important to him.

"I've got to go out tonight," he said, "on some important business. Very, very important business." He said the words over again slowly, as if he were really relishing them. "Get naked," he ordered, his voice crackling with power now, his words etched with urgency.

The girl looked questioningly at her mother. A slight nod from Jen, a brief flicker from her deadened, fearful eyes, and the trembling Myrtie knew she had to obey.

Her face was on fire and her hands icy cold as the trembling fingers undid the few ties that kept her raggedy garments about her. She had been forced to watch the two of them often enough to know exactly what was about to happen to her. She tried to unclothe herself quickly, knowing that if she prolonged her concealment any, his anger could turn on her and earn her swift punishment from his fists.

At last she lay bare under his gaze. She squeezed her eyes as tightly shut as she could, not wanting to see him; even more, she didn't want to witness her mother's nakedness.

But her eyes flew open in terror as she felt his rough hands grasping her breasts, the hard nails tearing into her flesh, causing pain that tore through her whole body. Tears welled up in her eyes; she was as powerless to control them as she was to stop him in his violating of her. He dug harder. A scream escaped her throat.

Higgins roared. "She likes it!" he chortled. "The little bitch has got some heat in her after all!"

Myrtie writhed under the pain and shame. Her body moved back and forth on the corn husk bed as if, rabbit-like, she was trying to flee.

He tightened his grip on one breast and then, as if to stay her, his other hand reached down her body and forced itself against her clenched thighs. She squeezed together with all her might, her knees cracking, as though she could prevent his entering.

He pulled at the dark patch between her legs, pulling hard until the unbearable pain caused her to spread herself on the bed.

"Better," he muttered. He reached inside her, big fingers working at her, drawing wetness from the scratched, now yielding flesh.

She sobbed uncontrollably, but he seemed not to hear her. She was pinned down on the bed, the clawing hand at her breast and the pushing one inside her conspiring to make her immobile.

She gasped, sucking in the sudden onrush of air that seemed to hit her when he at last loosened his grip on her breast. She sighed as he withdrew his other hand from inside her, but the relief was not even momentary. He grabbed her knees, pressing them back toward her as he spread her wide into a position that thrust her hard against her mother's body.

The horror was complete. The fact of Jen's own nakedness could not be lost on Myrtie, pressed as she now was against Jen's rigid frame.

Myrtie screamed. All of the pushing he had done inside her with those two gnarled fingers had not prepared her for the shock of his new entry. Again she clenched her eyes shut but it was not quick enough to escape seeing his darkly triumphant face gloating over her as he pushed against her knees with relentless wrenching, till she felt that the pushing and the hot stream that charged through her body must pull her apart. Let it be now, she prayed inwardly, let it be now. Let him split me open and kill me now. Let me die.

But such was not to be. Higgins had done no more than sate the first part of his dream, with this ravaging of the now bloodied girl. He noted with grim satisfaction the seeping redness on the gray sack sheet and the tiny bubbles of it that flecked her still-quivering thighs.

As if fastidious, he moved carefully from his stance over the girl, placing himself over the mother.

He grasped Jen's hip, turning her over and thrusting her up in one rough motion till her buttocks were raised toward him. He had not satisfied himself in the younger body, ravaging it only to whip his lust and fill him with new strength. Now he would stick that to the other one, he thought gleefully, and when he had done with it, he could lie back and use them to do those things that had till now happened only in his imagination.

He pulled Jen by the ankles, stretching her legs straight out under him, constricting the narrowness of her opening so that its grip, when he entered, brought him to quick emission. Then he pulled himself out and pushed both females away from him so he could lie fully stretched out on his back.

The women hung half on, half off the narrow bed, kept from falling to the floor only by the tight grasp he held on each of them.

Higgins felt like a king in his power. He dug his nails deep into the woman flesh he held, thinking the scars he would make on them would be like medals to him.

The spur of what he had done, the realization of his dreams, was strong enough to bring him quickly back to renewed readiness. Now would be the best part—he smiled to himself—now would come what he had been waiting for. Not the taking of each of them, one after the other, but both of them, together, working on him and doing him.

He pushed until each was thrust against him, bringing them on their sides against his body almost in a posture of protection. He lay this way for only a moment, then he spread his fingers against the back of Myrtie's skull and pushed her down between his legs.

She cowered there until he grasped his member and forced it against her lips. She stayed clenched closed as if to bar him, but a hard smack across the side of her head

had really happened. With his backward movement, he threw her from the bed, and in her shame and her hurt she lay cowering on the bare wooden floor. The force of it overwhelmed her. She was sure she was dead. The room and the world beyond it were silent as graves. The only sound came from Higgins' heavy breathing. From her mother, Myrtie heard nothing. Maybe, she thought, they had got real lucky, maybe they were both dead.

But all too soon the bed moved with Higgins' rousing and stretching himself. He pushed Jen and moved over her and off the bed. A few steps brought him to the other side of the crowded room, where he put his clothes on.

He pushed aside the boxes that concealed his rifle, picked it up, and strode out of the house, closing the door behind him. He made his way westerly, working through the thickets that stretched to the river. There he would meet his men and they would continue stealthily southward till they reached Les Chandelles.

Emilie watched as Missy walked slowly about the room. One did not need a spyglass in order to observe how unhappy the girl was, Emilie thought. Missy moved with even less life, less energy than she had displayed in slave times. It was curious that the new freedom had touched the closest to her of all the former bondpeople seemingly the least. Perhaps, Emilie reflected, it was because it had affected Jess the most and whatever was going on between the two, things were not well between them.

"Missy, do you want to talk to me?" Emilie asked softly.

"Ma'am?" Missy murmured, as if not understanding.

"I know that there is something bothering you terribly," Emilie went on. "Perhaps it would help if you talked about it."

Missy kept on folding the clothes with no change in

her motions. "Nothing to talk about, Miss Emilie," she murmured.

"Has Jess made any plans for you then?" Emilie asked.

Missy shook her head, stubbornly refusing to speak.

"Then something is wrong, Missy," Emilie said. "Why don't you want to talk about it? Perhaps I can help."

"No one can help!" Missy flared up suddenly, the clean laundry falling to the floor as if flying from her of its own volition.

"What is it, Missy?" Emilie pressed.

"It's that—that Miss, Miss . . ." Missy could not bring herself to say the name. "Ever since she's been here . . ." Her voice trailed off.

Emilie knew immediately whom she meant. A shock of fear went through her. "Surely you don't think that there is anything . . ." She could not bring herself to complete the sentence.

"Oh no, Miss Emilie, oh no." Missy's eyes widened with fear, as if begging her employer to thrust the implication from her mind. She could not so hurt her Jess by letting the mistress think there was anything between him and the white woman. Missy cursed herself inwardly; she could have cut her tongue out for even suggesting it. Miss Emilie was kind, but her kindness would not be enough to keep Jess from being killed if such a thing was thought or said about him.

"I believe you're right, Missy," Emilie said quietly. "I don't think there is anything more than interest in a common cause between Jess and, ah, our visitor." She hesitated, unsure of the proper way to refer to Rachel York. "We must put the very idea out of our heads, both of us. Now, then"—and she cleared her throat as if to dismiss the notion entirely—"is it just recently that there has been a reluctance in Jess? Had things been going well before this? I mean, had he spoken to you definitely, Missy?"

"No, ma'am." Missy hung her head, her voice low.

"He was going to, I just know he was going to, but now, now he never will, Miss Emilie." Tears sprang into her eyes and her last words were delivered in a sobbing voice, choked with emotion. Missy hid her face in her hands, sobbing uncontrollably and fearfully embarrassed at having her employer and ex-owner see her so.

Emilie jumped up and walked quickly over to her. She put her arm around Missy's shoulder and squeezed it softly. "There, there," she said soothingly. "You will feel better for releasing all your unhappiness. Let it go, dear, and then you will be free to deal better with your problem."

Missy swallowed back her sobs and tried to face her employer. "I'm sorry, Miss Emilie, I am," she apologized. "It's just it's gotten so I don't know what to do."

"Exactly!" Emilie said triumphantly. "That's exactly what I meant, Missy. I want to help you. The only way I can is if we can talk about it so that I can understand."

Missy nodded. She looked at Emilie imploringly. "What can I do, Miss Emilie?" she asked. "I want him so bad."

Emilie's heart ached for her. "I know, I know," she said soothingly. "You've got to learn to fight, Missy. You've got to fight for everything you want in this world." She realized how patronizing the words might sound, coming from her, who had been born to everything, and falling on the ears of a girl whose bondage had ended so recently. "I had to fight when Monsieur Charpentier was killed," she reminded her softly. "I had to fight every day just to go on living without him. I thought that my life was over and the world was finished. But then, after a while, I met Captain Phillips, and you remember what that was like."

For a moment both women grinned.

"That was a fight, all right." Emilie laughed a little. "I didn't know what I wanted then, but when I found out, it took a great deal of doing. I never would have thought I had the strength for it."

Missy nodded. "You did good, Miss Emilie," she said. "Marrying a fine man like the Captain, not caring what the old people in the parish might be saying." She realized that she was on dangerous ground, criticizing the other landowners to Emilie, but in the brief moments of their conversation an unspoken bond had formed between them. Missy knew that Emilie wanted to help her. She would not hold her to account for anything Missy might say that was true and would help bolster the arguments that both now eagerly sought to hear from each other.

"Exactly," Emilie said. "And exactly what you have got to learn to do. If you want Jess, I'm afraid you're going to have to fight for him. Not fight in the ways that I have, perhaps, but certainly you must find your own way of winning him. I will do everything I can to help you, Missy. You do believe that, don't you?"

"Yes, Miss Emilie, I do," Missy said. "If you only knew what to do and could tell me, I know I'd go and do it."

"Jess waited all his life for freedom," Emilie said. "No, wait is the wrong word." She laughed in spite of the seriousness of the topic. "He ran looking for it, ran away to find it, fought for it, and is now working for it. I would think he expects the same of you. Yet things seem to me to be the same with you as they ever were." She said these last words softly, not wanting to hurt her servant's feelings.

"I can't help that, Miss Emilie," Missy said quietly. "All that freedom really means to me is that it's what Jess wanted all along. I will be happy to know my children will grow up free, but it's them I care about." Her eyes were wide and bright. "It's the children I'll have with him and the living with him that means the most to me. If I can't have that, then freedom is nothing."

"I can understand that, Missy," Emilie answered. "But that isn't enough for Jess. He wants to see you happier than that."

Missy said nothing.

"Don't worry, we'll find a way," Emilie soothed her. Then, without a word being spoken, they went back to their usual roles, both of them busy, as servitor and served, getting the mistress of the house ready for her evening activities. Through it all Emilie pondered the unusual conversation they had just had. She hoped that it had done Missy some good and that the girl would think harder and in new ways about the unhappiness that weighed on her.

Even when she went downstairs and joined Jason and their guests at the table, Emilie's thoughts were primarily with her young servant's problems. It was well for Missy to have Emilie to talk to, but Emilie feared she would not be helped enough. She wished that there was someone she could turn to on Missy's behalf, but there was no one. The ladies of the city could scarcely be expected to concern themselves with the problem of a young black servant girl. The conversation that took place at table swept away the needs and yearnings of the small, inconsequential beings who worked and served and stood silently by while their lives and fates were determined elsewhere.

The lights of the house shown brightly, although it was well past dinner. The events of the day had finally reached them and talk was of little else.

"This is a harsh setback for all of us," Jason said quietly, glancing only briefly at the two young men who were still a mystery to him. "No good can ever come of the sort of mob violence that prevailed in the city today."

"Hear, hear," Anton Bledsoe agreed. "Can't have civil riots going on in New Orleans. We call ourselves a civilized city. News like this can only hurt us."

Emilie listened impatiently to the discussion. The news was very bad, she knew, especially since Jess was there and they had as yet no way of knowing whether he was safe. But her mind was taken by another sort of news, a very private kind to be imparted only to her husband. Terrible as the events of the day had been, she pushed all thought of them aside in her eagerness to dwell on what was good and happy and she yearned for the evening to end so she could share it with her beloved.

But the men seemed bent on making a long night of it. They could talk politics even when nothing had occurred; the spur of such momentous happenings naturally egged them on.

Emilie squirmed fitfully in her watered-silk chair. She hoped that the others would not notice her discomfort. She was helpless, she realized ruefully, a prisoner in her own home, condemned endlessly to the salon, motioning to servants to refill the constantly emptying wineglasses. The men, she thought, had dug their heels in for a long, heated discussion. All the talk would make not a bit of difference or change anyone's mind one iota, but still they could not let go of it. It seemed to be a masculine passion.

But here Emilie smiled tenderly, in spite of herself. She was so filled with the joyful passion that Jason had brought her, she must accept this lesser, less gratifying one, as well. It seemed politics was as much a part of his equipage as any other aspect of the male and to get the one, you had to accept the other. Still, she could wish for a less prolonged debate, this of all nights.

The discussion was reaching the argument level. Voices were raised as viewpoints became more and more hotly contested. Alex glanced at Robin, hoping to catch his eye and silently admonish him to restrain himself from statements whose excessiveness Alex feared would give them away. He motioned to his younger colleague, who flushed and then turned to Emilie.

"Pardon me, madame, but I seem to have forgotten myself." He laughed. "This hot head of mine needs some cooling off perhaps." He rose, bowed hurriedly, and then walked from the salon out onto the veranda.

Alex smiled at Emilie, as if to say that he would set everything right, and walked out after his friend. "Are you completely gone mad?" he demanded in a shrill whisper as the two of them stood outside. "One more word of praise for the flaming crosses and you would have totally declared yourself!"

"I know, I know," Robin admitted, mopping his brow with a fine large linen handkerchief. "It just angers me so to have to sit and behave myself like a gentleman under that man's roof!"

"It isn't any easier for me," Alex reminded him, "but we must be discreet."

"I know." Robin was contrite. "It won't happen again."

Moonlight was filling the vast expanse of lawn, touching the grass and treetops with a tint of silver. Robin gazed into the darkness. On the western horizon he could see a pinkish tinge coloring the dark night sky. "What's that?" he asked, pointing. "It looks like fire."

"I daresay it's the sugar factories," Alex said. "They go night and day."

"But this isn't the grinding season," Robin reminded him quickly. "That isn't until the fall. Surely the fires would have been banked by now for this season's work."

"Let's go and see," Alex suggested. "We can get our horses and ride over." He was not terribly interested in surveying the factories but it would keep Robin out of the salon for a while. Perhaps by the time they rode back the company would have dispersed and gone to bed.

They rode out at a leisurely pace.

Jess spurred the roan to a quicker pace. The landscape

he was riding through, although quite close now to Les Chandelles, seemed bitterly unfamiliar to him, although it was the same passage he had made in going down to the city. He realized grimly it was not the forest that had altered, but his own mood. The ride to the city had been full of bright hope and anticipation, almost making him heady in spite of possible danger, as though he had drunk a little too much wine. Now he was coming back locked in despondency, tasting only the bitter dregs of what he had savored, was it only two days earlier?

So engrossed was he in his thoughts that he would have missed the turnoff for Les Chandelles completely. Luckily the roan knew his way home and headed them both into the junction. Jess grinned in the darkness in spite of himself, telling himself that the animal had more sense than he did. Just for spite, he determined that he would himself settle down for the night before he attended the impertinent mount. He headed back for the old cabin and tethered the horse outside.

There was a fire going in the cabin and Jess was surprised to see Missy stirring a pot over it, but both the sight and smell warmed him. He realized how hungry he was.

"How did you know that I'd be home now?" he asked happily.

"I didn't," Missy said. "I was making this for myself."

"Oh, I thought you had figured out when I'd be back," he said slyly. "I hope there's enough there for two."

"More than enough!" Missy snapped. "And I did figure on when you'd be back, Jess Martin. I knew that, just like I know most everything about you!"

Jess lifted an eyebrow. This didn't sound at all like the usual Missy. He wondered what had gotten her going so.

"I'm sorry if I offended you, Missy," he said slowly. "I just assumed you were cooking for me, since you are in my house—"

"Your house!" She threw the words back at him. "This hasn't been your house since the day you took off from here! This house was your grandfather's house and I took care of him and it, you never knowing or caring what was happening to us. And after he passed, I was the one to stay here, taking care of his things and yours, if the day ever happened that you came back here. The only time this has been your house was when you were too hurt and too sick to be put anyplace else!"

"I didn't mean to take anything for granted, Missy, you least of all," Jess apologized. Then he fell silent. He looked about the little hut, seeing it in a way he never had before. Missy really had taken care of it, he realized; for all its smallness and crudeness, she had somehow managed to make a real home of it. It was scrubbed spotlessly clean, and the few possessions it contained were arranged neatly and carefully about. What with the warm glow of the fire and the good smells of her cooking, there was a coziness in the room that was more than comfort. It was pleasing, Jess realized, a good place to be, to have come home to.

"Missy, I didn't mean to upset you," he said softly. "I really am glad that I stopped here first and that I found you here." There was a weariness in his bones from the hard day's ride and he knew how good it would feel to stretch out on the pallet. He knew that it would feel even better to have her stretched out alongside him.

"There's so much that I've promised you that I haven't given you," he said.

"I know that," Missy said.

"Do you? Do you really?" His voice was suddenly eager, his heart flooded with the feelings he had for her in years past, his nostalgia for the dreams he had nurtured then, dreams that had always included Missy. Something had gone wrong, something had come between them. Perhaps it was not too late.

He had put all of his force and all of his efforts into

his work, preparing for the political career that he had thought would be so important for all of them. Now that dream lay in ashes, colder and deader than those at the bottom of the hearth Missy was cooking in. She had always fought his wanting to raise himself, to go far afield from what they knew and had at the plantation. He had always thought her wrong, and in his heart of hearts, in spite of all the recent tragedy, he still knew that a destiny beyond Les Chandelles was his. Still, for the moment, he could think of nothing more conducive to happiness than the place he was in.

Perhaps he had wanted too much of her. He had asked that she be his equivalent. That her strivings and yearnings shadow and echo his. Perhaps he had been wrong about her, and Missy had been right about both of them. Surely all of the dangers and pitfalls of the world made a man even more needful of the sweet comfort that a home and a woman like this could provide.

"You would be happy if we were always together like this, wouldn't you, Missy?" he asked.

"Is that so wrong?" She asked with a vehemence he hadn't expected. "Do you think it's wrong for me to be happy with just you? This is *all* I've ever wanted. This is *all* that freedom's ever meant to me. I want freedom to be happy. That means freedom to have you." She lowered her head but then raised it quickly, displaying a fire in her eyes he had not seen in years. "And to have our children. I know what this freedom means to you, Jess, and I know what it means to me to see the children I'll have raised strong and proud and not afraid of anything because of what their father's done. *That's* my freedom and my happiness. That's all I've ever wanted."

"I need you," he said quietly.

But she was not finished. "Why do I think I never ran away from Miss Emilie when I was up north with her?" she demanded. "You think that would have been freedom for me? To be alone and cold up there in New

York, not knowing anyone, not knowing I would ever see you again?" She paused. "Maybe I can't read or write so good yet, but at least I know what a word means. At least I know a word is not worth living for or dying for. And if I don't have you, then that's all that freedom is, a cold, empty, old word." She looked at him appealingly. "Only you can make it more than that for me."

He held her in his arms, feeling the warmth of her body alive against him. He felt the undeniable stirrings of the same needs that had let him take Rachel so dangerously, only days before, in this same room. He knew that, given the circumstances, it could happen all over again and that that could have only the most terrible consequences for all of them. He had told Rachel that, and he had sworn to himself that it would never happen again. But what was he, after all, but flesh and blood? What proof was he against the yearnings of that flesh?

He looked down at Missy. "I always loved you, Missy," he reminded her. "Whatever I wanted, I always wanted for both of us."

"I know that, Jess," she murmured, leaning against him, feeling warm and safe and good in his arms. "I love you, too," she said. "I didn't mean to be carrying on at you like that."

"It's all right, it's all right," he soothed her, hugging her even closer. "I think it's just what I need." He kissed her lightly on the forehead. "I think that you are just what I need."

She sighed almost audibly in his arms.

"I'm going to finish building that house, Missy," he promised. "Our house. Will you marry me and make it a real home for me?"

She buried her head against his shoulder, hugging him so hard he could barely hear the answer. Jess smiled; he didn't have to hear it to know what it was. She was almost like a child in so many ways, in spite of the woman she became the moment he led her gently to the pallet. But she was good, good all the way down to her bones. She was the solid strength he would need to draw from if the sordid events of the outside world and the temptations of the closer one were not to bring him down entirely.

The three men on patrol duty were unmounted. Higgins brought the butt of his rifle down on one of their heads and the rest of his men quickly overpowered the other two. He divided them into two groups, sending Dukes with Lynch and two others through the woods in the direction of the new slave cabins. They were at the far end of the plantation and it would take them the better part of an hour to get there, crouching and moving silently as they must. That would give him and his boys plenty of time to set low fires in the refineries. He didn't want them exploding and thus warning the people in the big house before he and his men could throw their flaming torches there.

The others moved off. Higgins kicked idly at the feet of one of the downed sentries and signaled to his men inside the refinery. He didn't care if the bodies on the ground were alive or not; once the fires had been set inside, they would toss them in. They went inside, squatting on the wood floor. He explained that they had to take their time so as not to warn the rest of the plantation. He directed them to different parts of the building, instructing them to find the best places for starting small, low fires.

Outside, one of the men on the ground stirred uneasily. The blow had clipped him, dazing him momentarily but not knocking him out completely. As he had gone down he recognized Higgins towering over him. He lay still, pretending to be dead. He examined both of his comrades quickly, making sure they were still alive and trying to shake them into awareness. They would have to go and warn the others. The man—his name was Leo; the giant, they called him—who with his brother Judd had slain the master that long-ago night, finally roused one of his companions. He whispered hurriedly, sending him in the direction of the big house to warn Captain Phillips. "Don't waste time there," he added. "Get on to the quarters and tell the people. Four of them are inside and the others have already started for the houses."

"What about them inside?" he was asked.

"Never mind them," Leo said. "We can't take on all of them. Let the captain and the others do that. Now run." He hit him smartly on the rump and the man was off.

Let them burn the factory if they want it, Leo reflected. Better to save lives. A life for a life. He knew that it was this same Higgins and his men who had hanged his brother. He knew, too, where Higgins himself lived. Leo got down on all fours. He took a flint and worked it, puffing, feeding it with his breath until he had a small firebrand. He held it in front of him and, wiggling like a serpent, eased himself out of view of the refineries and north, toward Higgins' holding. No matter what the outcome of this night, Higgins would return there, and when he did Leo the giant would be waiting.

In the opposite direction, Linn cut through the canebrakes, heading for the big house. He came out of the brakes and starting running through the grass that bordered the lane from the house to the factories. He stopped when he had to, only to draw breath back into his body. He would have to explain to Captain Phillips how they had been sneaked up on and overpowered. He started running again, stopping suddenly as two horsemen appeared out of the darkness.

"You there, halt," one of them called out to him. Linn stopped, obeying the unknown white horsemen. There had been no sound of horses when they had been set upon and these riders were heading toward the refinery. He had to hope they weren't part of Higgins' band.

"Men at the refinery, master," he said, gesturin wildly. "Going to set the refineries on fire. I'm going t warn the mistress!"

Robin and Alex exchanged quick glances. It was im possible to have such a thing occur while they were o the plantation. "Hurry on, then, and be quick about it! Alex snapped at the frightened black. "We'll go and se what it's all about for ourselves."

"Yes sir," Linn gasped, and started running again.

"You better not be lying, nigger," Alex called out af ter him. Then he spurred his horse to catch up wit Robin, who was galloping ahead.

Robin slowed his pace slightly. "It must be that dam fool Higgins," he said. "Taking matters into his ow hands. I warned him to stay away from this estate."

"We've got to stop him." Alex gritted his teeth.

"By any means necessary," Robin said, drawing hi pistol from its holster and cocking it. Alex nodded an they continued to gallop until they were in sight of th refinery. Alex drew up quickly and grabbed Robin's reins, stopping him. They dismounted, moving cautiously on foot to the refinery, now clearly silhouetted against the pink, glowing sky of the mounting fires.

Higgins whirled around. "Who goes there?" he demanded, drawing his rifle.

"Drop it!" came the order from Robin.

He cocked his pistol and aimed, but Alex put out a restraining hand. "No," he ordered. Then he turned to the remaining three men. "You acted illegally," he informed them coldly. "And according to the law of the society, I would be within my rights to kill you here. But there is more important business to be done. Quick, see to those fires. I want them out, or else you'll answer for it with your lives." He sat back in his saddle, as though he had all the time in the world to wait. The men ran to the river and lugged back empty kegs of water to douse the flames. One of them took a heavy plank and tamped out the just-igniting sparks he had set moments earlier. Robin and Alex sat, watching.

The men came out of the refinery. "It's done," one of them said, dusting his hands on his pants. "All out."

"Good," Alex said tersely, leaning forward across his saddle again. "You men are to return to your homes," he instructed. "There will be no punishment at this time, but we know who you are and what you have done. Disobedience is not lightly looked upon. Discipline is our watchword. You may be sure we will be watching you very closely." He wheeled around on his horse.

Dukes and the others quickly spurred their horses and rode off into the night. Higgins made a few furtive moves, but Robin kept his gun aimed squarely at him. At last the burly figure stood quiet.

Alex sat on his horse, staring down at Higgins, prolonging the moments before he passed sentence in order to make the time as difficult as possible for the recalcitrant farmer. He thought his words out carefully, turning them over in his head, when a shot rang out so close to his ear that he had to grasp the horn of his saddle to keep from falling. As he righted himself he saw the crumpled body of Higgins on the ground.

He turned to Robin in fury. "Damn you! Damn you!" was all his anger permitted him.

"It's done," said Robin evenly, flourishing his pistol for a moment and returning it to his holster.

"I give the orders here, I issue all commands," Alex thundered. "Have you forgotten that, man?"

"He had to be removed," Robin said. "It had to be done." His eyes were fixed on the corpse he had just created. He stared down at the body as if mesmerized by it.

Alex looked at him keenly. He caught the almost crazed expression on Robin's face. As he read it his fury turned slowly into an understanding of what he was witnessing and a calm resolve as to what he had to do. The lean back of his subordinate was toward him. Alex continued to stare at it as he slowly drew his own pistol and in a smooth motion, as graceful as any of his usual actions, aimed it solidly at the spot his gaze was fixed upon.

Robin toppled from his horse, his outstretched body falling on the earth not far from Higgins.

They deserve each other, Alex thought. Now I am well rid of both of them. He dismounted slowly, looking about until he recognized Higgins' old nag tethered to a stile. He bent to the ground, half lifting, half dragging the lifeless body, struggling with the great dead bulk until he somehow managed to straddle it across the nearly spavined back of the horse. Then he gave her a sharp blow on the flank, heading her in the direction of the dead man's holding. Old and decrepit as she was, she would suffer her burden and bring it home.

Alex remounted his own sleek steed, wheeling him about and heading back to the great house. A burial detail could be sent to handle Robin. He did not give his erstwhile companion so much as another contemptuous glance as he quickly rode away from the scene, back to the big mansion.

All was hurry and confusion. The women had been sent upstairs, although Emilie had pleaded with Jason vainly to be permitted to stay and defend her home, but he had insisted and she finally went upstairs with Rachel and the New Orleans ladies.

Jason stood with rifle at the ready. He had ordered Linn on to the stables, telling him to have the men rush to the new quarters and stop the marauders there. He himself stood now on the steps of the veranda close by Bledsoe and Desbrosses with their pistols. He had also given Robert a rifle, much to the chagrin of the other two men, who exchanged glances but nevertheless said nothing.

Jason turned toward the sound of speeding hoofbeats. For the first time since the frightened sentry had burst into the salon, Jason remembered that Robin and Alex were not with them. Now he recognized the mounted figure rapidly drawing up. He wondered where the deuce he had been and where Robin was.

Alex leaped from his saddle as if in answer. "We saw a look of fire toward the west," he announced breathlessly, "and went to investigate. One of your hands was coming here to warn you. He told us that fires were being set in the refinery." He stopped for a moment to draw breath, then he looked directly into Jason's eyes. "We stopped them," he said quietly. "But it has cost us."

"I thank you for that," Jason replied. He would have thought the two dandies to be the ones to have set, not quenched, the fires. "Where is your friend?" he asked quietly.

"He's dead," Alex answered. "Saving this plantation has cost dearly."

"I am sorry to hear it," Jason said. "I am truly sorry. My wife will be distraught at the news." Jason and Alex drew their pistols again. They placed themselves alongside the others, peering with them into the darkness of the lawn, waiting for the approach of the marauders. There was a slight stirring.

Jason inhaled sharply. "Shoot first," he commanded, "ask questions later." For all he knew, Young Jess could be lying dead in the city at the hands of men such as these.

"There they are," Alex whispered, cocking his pistol.

"Fire!" Jason had seen them in the same instant.

Figures lurched forward, leaping momentarily into the air, only to fall as quickly to the ground. The shots rang out until Jason saw no more movement. He held his hand up, and the shooting stopped.

He moved forward quietly. In the years he had commanded here, no blood had ever stained the luxurious green of Les Chandelles. Now, as he moved slowly forward, he had the sudden knowledge that his own might be commingling with that of the corpses he wanted examine. Should the young hothead who had turned help them in this last frantic hour revert to his usual pr clivities, it would not be hard for Jason to get a bullet his back. They would all then join ranks, he suppose like the southern gentlemen they were, still clinging their precious code of honor that permitted the death the outsider while protecting the perpetrator if he we one of their own.

Jason felt a sudden rush of relief when he sense rather than saw Alex standing next to him.

"I wonder who they are," the young man said coolly extending his finely booted foot toward one of th bloody corpses and turning it over. He stared at the nov distended face of death beneath him. "Not that I woul know any of them," he added, "not being from thi neighborhood." They turned and walked slowly back t the house, comrades if only for the moment.

Jason could not shake his feeling of foreboding. Fo all the undoubted help Alex had given them, there wa still something in the young dandy that struck him a dangerous. He seemed to be a man who could chang sides and adversaries as quickly and casually as he did hi fine silken cravats. Under the circumstances, it would b impossible to ask or expect that he leave the property very soon, a condition Jason found himself fervently hoping for. But, at the very least, he thought, it will give me the time to study him closely and find out what, i anything, this man was made of. Should his intentions b against Les Chandelles, after all, it would not be difficult to discern.

Jason threw his rifle down on a damask-covered settee and walked wearily for the staircase, which Emilie was already rushing down to meet him.

Leo the giant stood in front of Higgins' squat cabin. He gripped the small torch he was carrying tightly in his land. He wanted more than anything else to fling it at the shanty belonging to the man he hated more than any other in the world. But his sense of the land warned him against such an action. The night was too hot, the wind too sultry, for the house to contain the fire. It would quickly spread, not only to the fields but also to the thickets of tangled forest growing about the bayou and extending to the borders of Les Chandelles. It would not take much to carry a blaze onto their own land.

Their own land! Leo grinned, almost hugging himself in the dark. It seemed almost a miracle that after all the years of slavery, and in spite of the death and killings, they who survived had a piece of land to call their own. Hard as it was, this new life of theirs, the giant knew there was more to live for than vengeance. He would see Higgins dead, but not at a price that would cost Leo or his friends so much.

He slipped away from the covering tree at his back and inched his way quietly toward the house. He did not know if there would be anyone inside. It seemed as quiet as the stubble land surrounding it.

He pushed the door back on its hinges and walked inside. The room, except for its crude furniture, was bare but as he stood stock-still, senses alerted, Leo could feel the presence of life somewhere inside. He glanced at the curtained opening and walked quietly to it, drawing it back with his hands and gazing inside the second, smaller room.

The fire sputtering in his hand illuminated the two tangled women on the bed. He stopped himself. Here could lie danger more wicked even than the flames he had wanted to raise. He silently thanked himself for not having given in to that rash thought. Had he ever been found responsible for the death of two white women, all he would have to look forward to would be a far more horrible fate than theirs. He started to retreat, not sure of what to do, when a sudden movement caught his eye.

One of the women was rousing herself and now s back, leaning on her elbow and staring up at him. H eyes were wide with fear, her mouth an echoing o forming the scream she dared not make.

They stood staring silently at each other, each froze in place, each fearful to death of the other.

Jen moved uneasily, feeling Myrtie bolt upright ne to her. She shook her head slowly, trying to force he self into consciousness. Then she looked up and saw Le

"Where is he?" she asked hoarsely.

"I don't know," Leo admitted, knowing she mea Higgins.

"Is he dead?" Myrtie asked, and Leo sensed a tone c hopefulness in the younger woman's words.

"He could be, or he could be coming back here."

Myrtie turned to her mother, throwing her arm around her neck. "No, no," she sobbed. "We can't sta here. We can't go through that again."

Jen said nothing, only holding her daughter in a tigh embrace, firmer and more decisive than she had eve been with the girl before.

"Let's go, Mama, please," Myrtie begged. "We can ge away. It could be our only chance."

Jen nudged her slightly, as if to remind her of th presence of the black giant towering over them. Myrti gave Leo a fleeting glance. Somehow she didn't fee afraid of him as she knew she should be. After the ordea of Higgins, no one else seemed truly frightening to her.

Jen groped about in her mind and thought shrewdly "If you help us get away," she said to Leo, "we'll go as far as we can. We'll never come back and we'll never say that we saw you here." She looked at him boldly, her eyes catching his in the small sharp light of his torch. She guessed his purpose in coming there. The situation, so fraught with danger for all of them, had quickly, unexpectedly, made them sudden conspirators instead of fearful adversaries.

Myrtie had none of her mother's shrewdness. "Help us," she begged Leo. "Help us to get away. Please."

The giant nodded. The light was sufficient to show him not only the terror etched deeply on both their faces but the scarred and bloodied bruises on their bodies. His mind could only guess at the bondage in which Higgins held them, a life-in-death servitude whose everyday brutality might, from the looks of them, easily equal or surpass what his own slave days had been.

"Where will you go?" he asked.

"Out of here, farther north," Jen said. "I have a brother in Kentucky. We'll go and find his place."

Leo nodded. There would be nothing for them to come back to here, whether Higgins was dead or alive. He gestured for them to go ahead, urging them to move quickly in gathering their belongings. When they were at last ready, loaded with their bundles and as many of the household articles as they could carry, he walked out of the house, holding the torch.

He broke off a small dead branch and lit one end, handing it to Jen. "This will give you some light," he said. "But be careful with it." Then he led them to the rough path around the far side of the house, which would take them north. He urged them to hurry and he watched after them until his light would not enable him to make out their pitiful, retreating figures. Then he turned his back and moved once more to the large tree facing the house. He leaned against it, resting himself.

He did not know how much time had passed when he found himself suddenly roused by a sound in the night. He recognized hoofbeats coming toward him, but at a slow, almost meandering pace, as though the rider were in no great hurry. Leo pushed his back against the darkness of the tree. He thrust his torch into the ground, deadening the flames. He waited, almost breathless, as the horse trotted into sight.

Now there was only the light of the moon for illumination. Leo could barely make out the shape of the horse and its burden. It was only when the animal came almost abreast of him that he could see the lifeless body thrown across the horse's back.

He knew at once that it was Higgins and he wondered who had done this deed for him. He moved quickly forward, grabbing the horse's reins and stopping her. He reached his other hand to the body she carried, prodding at it as if to make sure that the job had been completely done. He silently thanked his unknown accomplice, not sorry that he had been spared the deed. He let go of the reins. He wanted to feel Higgins' lifeless body with his own hands.

"It's over, Emilie, it's over," Jason whispered gently, drawing her closely into his arms, feeling her sobbing body tightening against him. "You're safe and so is Les Chandelles. Everything will be all right." He started to ease her away from where she had buried her head against his shoulder.

"Oh, Jason, Jason." Her sobs would not abate.

"I must go and see to the others now," he whispered. "You will be safe here. Robert will watch you."

"Jason, I must talk to you," she pleaded. "I must . . . I must tell you something."

"Let it wait, dearest," he said. "I promise I will be back as soon as I know everyone is safe." He kissed her and strode away.

Robert stood at the foot of the staircase, still holding his rifle. The other men, she knew, were out on the veranda and the front grounds of the house. She nodded briefly to Robert and then went upstairs to wait for Jason in their bedchamber.

Already, servants from the house were removing the bodies of the dead invaders, Jason noted as he rode toward the rows of the new cabins. He found himself wishing that the defenders there would prove slightly less successful than his own group had. He had not recognized any of the men and only if one of them was caught alive would they be able to find out who they all were and who had set them against Les Chandelles.

What he found filled him with more horror. The raiders had managed to put two houses to the torch. Luckily the people had been able to douse them quickly, leaving them in charred ruins but, thankfully, with no one hurt. Then they had set upon the four night-riding culprits and killed them. The bodies were not even recognizable as such, Jason thought wearily to himself. They had been killed and then burned, charred masses not even recognizable any longer as once-living flesh. Vengeance had been harsh.

One of them, Jason realized, could even have been Higgins. There might be some sign, some clue, of identification but he had not the stomach to find out. He only nodded briefly to the silent groups of people standing about and staring.

He took the reins of his horse and led the animal back toward the big house. He walked slowly, as though an enormous weight prevented him from mounting or moving swiftly. It had all happened too quickly; barely an hour before, they had been sitting and debating over their brandies and Madeiras. The men had argued. The women sitting, listening, fluttering their silk-and-ivory fans, Francine alone adding her comments from time to time to those of the men; Rachel sitting slightly apart, as though she knew she was not one of them; Eurydice silent, grasping for once that the subject matter under discussion was far above her head, and Emilie, his sweet Emilie, listening intently to all that was being said, her heart and mind as always being torn from one extreme to the other, from the beliefs she had grown up with to those she had learned to accept, with love, from him.

He pushed the ugliness he had just witnessed from his mind and focused all of his being on what lay in front of him; now, at last, he was able to quicken his step, thinking of Emilie, wanting so much to be with her.

It was only the necessity of duty that had propelled him to thrust her gently aside moments before in the front salon. It had been mandatory that he go and see to the condition and security of the people and property. Now that he had done that, and now, sadly, that there was no more that could be done, he could set his mind on her and rejoin her to give her what love and comfort he could.

It would be necessary, he reminded himself, to post a guard around the house and increase the sentries that patrolled the plantation's borders. That the men had been surprised and overcome tonight showed him that the river edge of the plantation was a weak area of defense and that all of the men needed more training at sentry work. That needed to be done, and quickly, and the cabins that had been ruined would have to be swiftly rebuilt, both to accommodate their families and to erase from everybody else's sight the burned ruins. The refineries would have to be inspected in the morning. Alex had assured him that the fires had been put out, but it would take his own eyes and those of the more experienced hands to evaluate what damage, if any, had been done.

The list of things to be done was endless. The people would have to be reassured once more that they would be safe in their homes. And the young new schoolmistress, too, would need reassuring if they expected her to stay and teach the people. There was so much to be done, and along with the ongoing work of the cane, which never ceased. As though the days had not been full enough, of work and worry, of fears and frustrations.

Jason squared his shoulders, as if to adjust himself to the added burdens that this night's misfortunes had brought. It was also the worry for Jess. The clamor of he last hour had put Jess and his fate completely out of Jason's mind. He must find out as quickly as possible what news there was of his great friend.

They were friends, Jason realized, and his heart lifted with the realization. Out of all the fear and terror, the burnings and murders of the past year, some good had grown, after all. If he and Jess could meet as men and walk as friends, then it all was not so totally hopeless as he had felt mere moments ago.

Just as the business of life must go on, he thought, so, too, must life continue and renew itself.

He looked up at the big mansion in front of him. Even after all the time he had lived here, Jason realized he had never explored all of Emilie's house. There was an unknown number of rooms that he had never even entered. Perhaps, long unused, they could be put to some good use now.

He walked heavily up the great staircase, his fingers barely touching the highly polished carved balustrade. He had grown so accustomed to this grandeur, he had taken little note of it of late.

He knocked softly at their door, not wanting to startle Emilie. Then he turned the knob softly, walking to where she sat on the edge of their bed.

She jumped up eagerly, running to meet him even before he could reach her.

"Everything is all right," he said. "No one has been hurt." He was shocked at his own words and added, "None of our people and only minor damage to two houses."

"Thank God!" Emilie breathed. "Oh, Jason, is it always going to be like this?" She pressed herself against him.

"Of course not, darling," he said, comforting her. "I think we have proved tonight that we mean to defend our home," he said. "No one will take what happened here lightly. I don't think any of those who moved against us have survived."

She looked up at him quickly. "Oh, dear God," she exclaimed.

"But we and ours are safe," he said. "That is what matters. Life goes on, as it must."

"As it will," she amended softly. Then she looked up at him, disengaging herself from his hug, holding his hands with both her own at arm's length. "As life will, Jason," she said again softly. She didn't know how to choose the words but then she didn't have to. Her smile betrayed her, telling him all.

"Emilie?" It was a question simply put, but asking everything.

"Yes!" she said, bubbling, unable to contain herself any longer. "Yes, Jason, yes!" She took his hand and placed it lightly on her skirt, just below the gathered waist. "Life goes on." She repeated his words.

"As it must, as it will." He smiled at her. "As we shall."

"It's going to be a boy, I'm quite positive of it." Emilie beamed.

"How can you be so sure?" he chided her, drawing her close to him again and laying her down on the bed. "I'm not sure that I would not prefer a daughter, an absolutely perfect little charmer, a replica of you."

"Someday," Emilie promised. "But for this time, it must be a son." She grew somber and reflective. "This life we have here, this plantation," she said slowly, "it is too much for one man, any man, even you, my dearest. You need a strong young boy by your side. You need a son, my Jason, as I do, as Les Chandelles does. This place has given and taken so much. We must continue to give and to take from it, from this soil, this earth, this land. That is life, Jason, life continuous."

"And life ennobled and rich and worth the living," he said. "This I promise to you, to our love, to our children."

If you love romance, you'll love *Danielle Steel* . . .

Two years ago, she was completely unknown. Today, over five million people worldwide have read and enjoyed the the romance stories of Danielle Steel. Books like *The Promise*, *Now and Forever*, *Golden Moments* and *Season of Passion*. Tender love stories of timeless romance, set against the background of today's modern world.

The glitter and glamour of the top-level international advertising business forms the background to her most recent book to be published in the UK – *Going Home*. A sensitive novel of love's passion, sudden tragedy, and the rebirth of hope that new love can bring, *Going Home* is Danielle Steel at her sensitive but compelling best.

GOING HOME £1.25

THE PROMISE 95p

NOW AND FOREVER £1.10

GOLDEN MOMENTS £1.25

SEASON OF PASSION £1.25